THE EMPIRE'S CORPS

Book One: The Empire's Corps
Book Two: No Worse Enemy
Book Three: When The Bough Breaks
Book Four: Semper Fi
Book Five: The Outcast
Book Six: To The Shores
Book Seven: Reality Check
Book Eight: Retreat Hell
Book Nine: The Thin Blue Line
Book Ten: Never Surrender
Book Eleven: First To Fight
Book Twelve: They Shall Not Pass

THE EMPIRE'S CORPS

CHRISTOPHER G. NUTTALL

The characters and events portrayed in this book are fictitious. Any similarity to real persons, living or dead, is coincidental and not intended by the author.

Text copyright © 2016 Christopher G. Nuttall
All rights reserved.
No part of this book may be reproduced, or stored in a retrieval system, or transmitted in any form or by any means, electronic, mechanical, photocopying, recording, or otherwise, without express written permission of the publisher.

ISBN-13: 9781537024899
ISBN-10: 1537024892

http://www.chrishanger.net
http://chrishanger.wordpress.com/
http://www.facebook.com/ChristopherGNuttall

Recommended Book Picks:
www.nonlinear144.wix.com/bestebookpicks

All Comments Welcome!

CHAPTER ONE

> The Nihilists are a terrorist cult that appeared during the waning years of empire, worshipping death as a political statement – and very little else. Nihilists have no political ambitions or demands; they simply seek to kill as many humans as possible, including themselves, in order to satisfy their lust for destruction. Their attacks are almost always unpredictable and very destructive.
>
> - Professor Leo Caesius, *The Waning Years of Empire* (banned).

The stench of death was in the air.

Captain Edward Stalker walked through what remained of the city-block and shuddered inwardly. It wasn't a pretty sight. Human bodies lay everywhere, some broken and torn, others surprisingly intact, surrounded by the blackened ruins of what had once been their homes. Four days ago, the city-block had played host to four thousand middle-class men and women, bureaucrats who had worked to keep the Empire running. They had lived and worked and played within the confines of their block. Their children had grown up, formed relationships with other children and started families of their own. They might not have had perfect lives, but they had had lives. They'd been happy.

And then the Nihilists had arrived. They'd taken over the block and prevented anyone from leaving, taking everyone in the block hostage against the inevitable response by the Civil Guard. The Guard had failed to dislodge the Nihilists from their positions and, in desperation, had screamed for the Marines.

The Marines had gone into the block and liberated it, at a cost. Over three thousand hostages – and thirty-one Marines – lay dead in the rubble. The Nihilists had never intended to bargain with their lives, or seek a political advantage; the Nihilists had simply intended to blacken the Empire's eye by slaughtering its civilians. They'd somehow shipped in enough weapons and explosives to blast the entire block to dust. It had been sheer luck that they'd failed to blow the complex when the Marines had gone in. Edward knew better than to rely on luck. Marines made their own luck.

He ground his teeth together as he looked towards a billowing cloud of smoke in the distance, towards the other end of the complex. The Civil Guard had sworn blind that there were only a hundred Nihilists within the complex, more than enough to control a city-block full of unarmed sheep, but they'd been wrong.

There had been over four hundred Nihilists within the block and over half of them had attempted a breakout when the Marines went in. They'd hit the Civil Guard and smashed right through them, vanishing into the Undercity before the Marines could get into position to block their escape. Retreating under fire was uncharacteristic for the Nihilists – normally, they fought and died in place, turning their deaths into a political statement – but Edward had to admit that it had worked out for them. Their propaganda machine was already gloating over how they'd escaped the Marines. The hundreds of media reporters now swarming through the remains of the block – after paying a bribe to the Civil Guard Superintendent – wouldn't hesitate to take their propaganda and run it as fact. The Empire would be demoralized, exactly as the Nihilists had intended.

"Captain," Command Sergeant Gwendolyn Patterson said, as Edward entered the small gym. It, like the other rooms in the complex, had been blackened by fire, but the material used to build it could have stood up to a small nuke. The Marines had taken it over and turned it into a prisoner holding facility. "We have seventeen prisoners here and nine others who have been transferred to the Appleton Hospital."

Edward nodded, taking in the sight in front of him. The Nihilists didn't look so threatening now. Stripped of their weapons and combat armour, lying on the hard floor with their hands secured behind their backs, they looked terrified, as if they expected the Marines to start torturing them at any moment. They weren't hardcore Nihilists, Edward knew; hardcore Nihilists would never have been taken alive. They were just young men and women who had been seduced by the Nihilists and recruited into terrorist cells, just for something to do. They might not even have realised that their new masters considered them expendable. It wouldn't matter in the end. They'd be walked in front of a judge, once their brains had been drained dry of everything they knew, and either executed or exiled to one of the frontier worlds as indentured labour. It was one way out of the stifling boredom of the Middle City.

"Good," he said, tiredly. Gwen was short and surprisingly feminine. No one would have taken her for a Marine on first glance, even though she could outfight almost anyone else within the Company. Rumour had it that Gwen had a habit of cruising the bars in the Undercity and beating up rapists, although Edward had carefully refrained from looking into the rumours. He might have had to take official notice of her activities.

"The Civil Guard beat up on a couple of them and raped a third," Gwen added, her face twisting into an expression of distaste. Marines were supposed to be perfectly controlled at all times. The Civil Guard was really a glorified police force. They carried weapons and acted like a military service, yet they were hardly up to Marine standards. "They now want the remaining prisoners turned over to their custody."

Edward scowled, staring down at the prisoners. There was little hope of punishing the Civil Guard for their activities. Their supervisors would hand out meaningless punishments, if they bothered to take notice at all… after all, they'd say, it had only been Nihilists who had suffered. Edward, who'd grown up on Earth, knew just how deeply the Civil Guard were hated by the local population, but their opinions didn't matter. He looked toward the towering spires of Imperial City and the Grand Senate. Only their opinions mattered in the Empire.

"Tell them that we're taking them in for interrogation first," he said, sourly. The nasty part of his mind kept asking why he bothered, but he pushed it aside. "How's Joe?"

"Survived, again," Gwen said, with a wink. Joe Buckley was one of the enlisted men, with a remarkable talent for getting into situations where he should have died…and walking out of them unscathed. This time, a group of Nihilists had jumped him and his platoon as they advanced, blowing the floor and sending both groups plummeting down to the basement. "He was a bit stunned afterwards, but refused to allow me to send him back to the barracks."

Her face darkened. "We lost Lucy, though," she added. "The internal damage was too much for her and she died on the way to the medical centre."

Edward nodded, refusing to let his feelings show. Lucy had been a newcomer to the Company, but she'd fitted in well and become popular with her comrades. He remembered a bright young girl with a promising career ahead of her, now cut short by the Nihilists and their absurd death wish. She had been a Marine in the truest sense of the word, laying down her life to protect others. She had died under his command. Lucy was hardly the first trooper he'd lost, but it always hurt, like a knife in the gut.

His earpiece buzzed before he could say anything else. "Captain, this is Garrison," a new voice said. "The Grand Senate has summoned you to testify before their Emergency Committee."

"Oh, they have, have they?" Edward said, angrily. He needed to pull his men back to the barracks and make the preparations for the farewell ceremonies for the dead, not speak before the political lords and masters of the Empire. "And when do they want me to do this?"

"Now," Garrison said. "They were very insistent. I kept them waiting as long as I could."

"You'd better go," Gwen said, her face reflecting the same distaste for politicians and their manoeuvres as he felt. "I'll see to everything here."

Edward wanted to protest – he was Captain; it was his responsibility – but she was right. "Understood," he said. "*Semper Fi.*"

"*Semper Fi,*" Gwen returned.

Edward walked back out of the complex, barely aware of the two armed Marines escorting him as he headed down towards the landing pad and the handful of aircars waiting there. The press, kept back by a weak line of Civil Guardsmen, shouted questions towards him, but Edward ignored them completely. He knew from experience that anything he said – or any other Marine said – would be mutated into something else before it even hit the broadsheets and reached the public. In the coming days, he knew, the reporters would milk the terrorist attack for all it was worth, interviewing anyone and everyone who might know something about the disaster. They'd probably blame everything on the Marines.

The aircar rose up into the air and headed towards the Grand Senate's building, looming next to the Imperial Palace and the Assembly of Nobles. Edward had always considered the building a monument to grandeur rather than good taste, but he had to admit that it was striking in the dawn, when the light from the rising sun was reflected across the city by the building. Hundreds of other aircars were flying all over the city, most of them heading towards the scene of the terrorist attack. The handful of aircars the Nihilists had shot down hadn't deterred air traffic for long, but really…who would want to walk on the ground? Outside the massive city-blocks, anarchy ruled Earth, no matter what the Grand Senate said. The Civil Guard wasn't up to the task of keeping the streets in order. Earth deported – or executed – hundreds of thousands of criminals each year, yet it barely made a dent in the problem. Edward, who'd grown up on Earth, knew the truth. The undercity dwellers had nothing to live for.

He checked his appearance as the aircar floated down towards the priority landing pad. He still wore the light combat armour he'd donned for the mission, even though he'd removed the helmet as soon as the fighting had ended. The Grand Senators would probably be horrified as soon as they smelled him, the nasty part of his mind whispered, but it was their fault. They should have waited long enough for him to have a shower and change into his dress blues.

The handful of servitors who met him at the pad looked as if they couldn't decide if they wanted to sneer at him, or run screaming. A Marine had no place in their world.

"Come with me," one of the servants said, finally.

Edward smiled tiredly – she was worth smiling at, even though her face and body were probably the result of cosmetic surgery – and allowed her to lead him through the corridors towards the Senate Chamber. The small groups of people they met on their passage leapt aside, stunned by the sight of a man wearing armour and carrying a weapon. The MAG-74 looked fearsome even in the hands of a man who didn't know what he was doing with it. Edward had spent two years at the Slaughterhouse learning how to use it with precision.

They reached the antechamber and Edward stopped, looking up at the massive portrait that hung on one wall. The Emperor's face stared back down at him. Emperor Roland had been crowned Emperor when he had been a child of barely two years. Now, he was sixteen and, if rumour were to be believed, a spoilt brat. It didn't matter. Edward saluted the portrait anyway. Loyalty to the Emperor, he'd been taught, was all that kept the Empire together.

"The Grand Senate will see you now," the servitor said, with a bow that exposed a considerable amount of cleavage. A massive wooden door – real wood, part of Edward's mind noted – swung open. "Please leave your weapon with the security guards and enter the chamber."

Edward unslung the rifle from his shoulder, code-locked the firing trigger, and passed it to a guard. Leaving it with them, he stepped into the chamber, wincing slightly as a spotlight shone down on him from high above. The thirteen Grand Senators, the Grand Old Men of the Empire, stared down at him, their faces expressionless and cold. As long as they worked together, Edward had been told, they could effectively run the Empire to suit themselves. They dominated the Senate and the Assembly of Nobles. The House of Representatives was hopelessly divided.

"Captain," Grand Senator Stephen St. Onge said, his voice echoing through the chamber. "Explain to us what happened."

It was an order. "Three days ago, a Nihilist assault force took control of Joe Rico Block," Edward said, firmly and precisely. He couldn't believe that the Grand Senators didn't already know what had happened, but perhaps they just wanted to hear it from the horse's mouth. "They successfully blocked the exits, subverted the internal security systems – along with the Civil Guardsmen in the block - and asserted their command over the civilian inhabitants. A handful of people with private communicators were able to contact the Civil Guard and inform them of the takeover before the Nihilists destroyed all of their communications systems. The block was sealed off by the Civil Guard, which mounted a rescue mission the following day. The operation failed with very heavy casualties."

He paused, controlling himself with an effort. "The Civil Guard then called in the Marines," he continued. "My Company was deployed to assault the building, an assault plan that had to be launched ahead of time when it became clear that the Nihilists had commenced the second stage of their plan, the mass public execution of the civilians in the block. Owing to inaccurate information from the Civil Guard, we went in and ran into a trap. Luckily, our superior training and equipment prevailed and we were able to rescue the remaining civilians."

"But not in time to save thousands of people," one of the Grand Senators said. There was an angry tone to his voice. "Why did you fail to save the hostages?"

Edward felt his temper rising and controlled it with an effort. "With all due respect, Senator," he said, "you are significantly underestimating the problems involved in a hostage rescue mission, particularly one mounted against a terrorist group that is quite capable of blowing itself up along with the hostages, committing suicide to get at us."

"And you are blaming your failure on the Civil Guard," St. Onge said. "The Civil Guard fought valiantly in both assaults."

Edward stared at the Grand Senator. "Sir," he said, with icy precision, "the Civil Guard provided us with bad intelligence and refused to allow us to deploy our own sensor probes to confirm their intelligence."

"Superintendent Gates has informed us that he refused permission for additional sensor probes because the probes might alert the enemy to the planned assault," St. Onge said, flatly.

Edward's temper snapped. "The Civil Guard got in way over its head," he said. "The Marine Corps requested permission to deploy a Regiment of Marines, not a single Company. The request was turned down because there were only a hundred enemy fighters within the block – only there were actually *four hundred* enemy fighters, all armed to the teeth! We were denied permission to carry out our own intelligence-gathering probes that might have warned us about the enemy trap. To add to the problem, we were ordered to use the Civil Guard in a supporting role and, when the enemy came boiling out in a desperate desire to escape, they smashed into the Civil Guard and the Guardsmen ran. A second Marine Company, deployed to block their escape, would not have broken. They would have held and the Nihilists would have gotten their death wish."

He fought to control himself. "And so we had to take the building back, step by step," he continued. "Only sheer luck saved my entire Company from being wiped out!"

"And you are still making excuses for your failure," St. Onge hissed. "How many civilians were caught in the crossfire and killed?"

"Too many," Edward said, angrily. His career might be at an end, but he no longer cared. "They died because of political pressure to keep the Marine involvement in the siege as low-profile as possible. We could have brought in an entire Regiment, or a Division, and the Nihilists would have been contained and eliminated. Instead, a single Company took on a task that should have been handled by a much larger formation and succeeded, barely. Thirty-one good Marines are dead."

St. Onge's eyes flashed. "It is not your place to question the decisions of this body," he snapped. "Those decisions were made for good reasons…"

"Political expediency," Edward snapped back. "You were terrified of what might happen if you deployed Marines to the streets of Earth. Your decisions gave the Nihilists a chance to carry out their insane agenda and slaughter thousands of people. You sent my men into a death trap. Now, if you will excuse me, I have to see about their funerals!"

He turned and stormed out of the chamber, recovering his weapon from the guards and marching back towards the landing pad so fast that the servitor had to struggle to keep up with him. The hot rage was fading, now that he was away from the political leaders of the Empire, yet he didn't regret what he'd said. The politicians would be furious and would scream for his blood, but the Marines were a world apart. The worst they could do to him was a discharge from the Marine Corps. He'd regret leaving the Marines – they were his real family – but there were hundreds of frontier worlds that would be happy to take him as an immigrant. Perhaps, out on the frontier, he'd be away from the corruption that surrounded the Imperial City.

It was no surprise when, an hour later, he was summoned to the Commandant of the Terran Marine Corps.

Chapter Two

Throughout the Empire, decay and corruption has sunk into every service, with only one exception. The Terran Marine Corps remains the only military service to be pure, free of the stench of self-serving agendas. It is perhaps unsurprising that various prominent figures in the Grand Senate are working to marginalise and/or disband the Corps.

- Professor Leo Caesius, *The Waning Years of Empire* (banned).

The office of the Commandant of the Terran Marine Corps was located in Imperial City, attached to the Admiralty and the other military headquarters, although Edward knew that the Marines were a completely separate service from the Imperial Navy. Unlike the other services, the Marines maintained most of their headquarters on another world – Slaughterhouse, the Marine training world – yet even they had to maintain a presence on Earth. Edward had spent a few months as a Lieutenant on Slaughterhouse, but he'd never visited the Earth-based headquarters before. Marines were only summoned there if they'd screwed up by the numbers.

Major General Jeremy Damiani, the Commandant of the Terran Marine Corps, was a tall man, wearing a Marine dress uniform. He was completely bald – he'd even shaved his eyelashes – and had mismatched eyes, the result of having one of them removed and replaced with a bionic eye, after a disastrous mission against a pirate base on the Rim. Edward had studied his career and had been impressed; he'd held the position of Commandant for fifteen years. Even with rejuvenation therapies, that was a long time to hold such an important position.

"Captain Edward Stalker, reporting as ordered, sir," Edward said, standing to attention. The Marine Corps had fewer formalities than the Imperial Navy or the Imperial Army, but what formalities it did have, it took seriously. The chain of command was vitally important to maintaining discipline, particularly when Marine junior officers and NCOs enjoyed a degree of freedom and initiative alien to the other services.

"You fucked up, son," Damiani said, without preamble. "You will probably not be surprised to hear that I spent the last forty minutes listening to a series of outraged complaints about your conduct. They started by demanding your scalp and moved down to demanding your discharge. What do you have to say for yourself?"

Edward didn't relax. "I told them the truth, sir," he said, flatly. "I told them just what went wrong with the operation and why."

"You did," Damiani agreed, coldly. His voice was very flat. "You grew to manhood among us, son. You didn't realise that speaking truth to power is not appreciated outside the Marine Corps. It may interest you to know that a third of the Grand Senate would like nothing better than to see the Corps disbanded and the Slaughterhouse scorched down to bedrock. Your little outburst today, no matter how accurate or justified it was" – he held up a hand before Edward could say a word – "has not helped our image. I had to call in favours from people I would prefer never to talk to at all in order to maintain the balance of power."

"Sir," Edward said, "why…?"

Damiani fixed him with a gimlet stare. "You're not thinking," he said. "The Terran Marine Corps reports directly to the Emperor. We're one of the weapons in his scabbard. There are…parties within the Grand Senate that would prefer to see the Corps disbanded to prevent the Emperor from using us against them. Our existence is guaranteed by Imperial Statute, yet they can cut funding and interfere with our operations. Your little outburst may provide enough justification to cut more of our budget."

He looked up, as if he'd just realised that Edward was still standing at attention. "At ease, Captain," he ordered, dryly. "I do understand why you told them what you told them. I also understand that we cannot afford another power struggle over our existence and mandate. The vultures are already gathering. The latest round of budget cuts is already underway and we will almost certainly be targeted."

"Yes, sir," Edward said. "If you wish to court-martial me for my outburst…"

"It's not that simple," Damiani admitted. "A court-martial would require an open discussion of just what went down over the last week. The Grand Senate wouldn't be happy with hanging their dirty laundry out for everyone to see. They may think that they control the House of Representatives, but there are factions just waiting for them to show a sign of weakness. Your trial would serve as one such sign, Edward. They would prefer to see you exiled from Earth, along with your men."

"Sir," Edward protested, "with all due respect…"

"Quiet," Damiani ordered. He met Edward's eyes. "You and Stalker's Stalkers will be assigned to Avalon, a world right on the edge of Imperial Space. The Governor has been desperate for reinforcements from the Core Worlds and you and your men should suffice. We'll run you in on a transport ship, along with a final convoy of colonists and indentured settlers. Once you're there, you'll be well away from the politics tearing the Empire apart. We might even manage to bring you back in the next few years."

He hesitated. "Or maybe not," he added. "The Empire is going through a very rough patch right now."

Edward blinked. "Sir?"

"There are things you need to know," Damiani said. "It isn't apparent to the common herd of civilian sheep, but the Empire is in serious trouble. The Grand Senate effectively controls the Empire and, in turn, is effectively controlled by a cabal that owns most of the corporations in the Empire. They wrote the laws that allow them to operate with only minimal supervision and taxation…and, just incidentally, make it hard for anyone to compete with them. In order to keep the civilians happy, they're also operating a massive welfare net that is little more than a black hole for credits.

"The net result of their policies is that the Empire is actually very short of cash" – he smiled bitterly – "and that they have no choice, but to start making massive painful budget cuts."

He nodded towards the holographic starchart. "They're already talking about disbanding several regiments from the Imperial Army and scrapping a number of ships from the Imperial Navy," he said. "They should be cutting welfare payments, but that is politically unacceptable. Cutting welfare will unite the House of Representatives against the Grand Senate and collapse their little house of cards. Worse, they're actually talking about closing several bases along the Rim and pulling out of those sectors entirely."

Edward was genuinely shocked. The Empire's mandate – its main reason for existence – was to unite the human race and prevent a war that might exterminate humanity once and for all. In theory, every human-settled world was part of the Empire, although most enjoyed some degree of internal autonomy and there were some settlements that barely acknowledged the Empire's mere existence. The thought of abandoning hundreds of worlds to pirates and local warlords was unbearable. It should have been unthinkable.

"The problems are bad enough as they are, but they're going to get worse soon," Damiani predicted. "The Grand Senators know that their house of cards isn't going to last forever. When the crash comes, they're going to get hurt. They've been countering this process by building up influence among the Navy and Army, trying to build up a power base that will survive the crash and perhaps put one of them on the Throne. Over the last few decades, they have been quite successful at penetrating both services.

"And, if that wasn't bad enough, the colonies are going to get squeezed harder over the next few years," he added. "They have resources to be taxed and they don't have the representation within the government to avoid it. There are already at least a dozen lunatic fringe movements out there demanding everything from autonomy to complete independence. Marine Intelligence estimates that if taxation levels increase radically, there will be an explosion. The Imperial Navy will have to put it down, hard. The expenditure involved in putting down a rebellion may tip the balance on Earth and cause the crash."

He rubbed his bald head. "The Corps is the only service free of their penetration," he said. "Do you understand, now, why they're scared of us?"

Edward nodded. A Marine always started life as a rifleman; every Marine went through the same training on the Slaughterhouse and spent time as an enlisted man before being considered for promotion. A man with political ambitions – or political masters – would have problems surviving the Slaughterhouse. Marines were loyal to the Emperor and the Empire. Very few Marines went bad and betrayed their comrades. Those who might betray their fellows were weeded out during training.

"Yes, sir," he said. There was nothing else to say. "They're scared we might be turned on them."

"True," Damiani agreed. "We were never created to serve as a Praetorian Guard. It isn't our responsibility to choose who sits on the Throne, or wields power over the Empire."

"Yes, sir," Edward said.

"It could well be that the Grand Senate saved your life by having you exiled to Avalon," Damiani said, with a trace of amusement. "When the crash comes – and I believe that it will come soon – Earth isn't likely to survive. I'm taking some precautions, along with a few others in high places, but…there's no guarantee of anything. We could be staring right down the barrels of a nasty little civil war."

Edward winced. Earth's population had exploded once the Empire's massive welfare state had eliminated the costs of raising a child. Edward's own mother had had five children, feeding them all on the algae-based foodstuffs that had been discovered centuries ago; he'd known mothers who had thirteen children and women who were grandmothers at thirty. The massive expansion of city blocks hadn't been able to keep up with the flow of human beings, nor had the government been able to find work for them. It was no wonder that crime was their occupation of choice, or that almost everyone convicted of a crime, no matter how small, was permanently exiled from Earth to one of the colony worlds. It was still barely a drop in the bucket of Earth's teeming multitudes.

The vast majority of people who were middle or upper class didn't comprehend just how bad life was in the Undercity. They didn't realise how easy it had been for the Nihilists to create an army of young men and women prepared to kill themselves to kill others, or worse. Religious extremism and dangerous cults bred like rabbits in the Undercity, in places where the Civil Guard never ventured. One day, perhaps when the money ran out and the food no longer flowed freely, there would be an explosion.

"Yes, sir," Edward said, finally. "Thank you, sir."

Damiani snorted. "You're getting a…charge as well," he said. "There is a person who is being…exiled from Earth to a frontier world. You are to escort him to Avalon and protect him, at least until he reaches the planet. What happens after that is up to you."

"Sir?"

"Professor Leo Caesius and his family," Damiani explained. "The Professor used to teach at the Imperial Academy, until he wrote a book about the decline and coming fall of the Empire. It didn't go down well with the Grand Senate; the book was officially banned and the Professor lost his job. The Civil Guard kept harassing him and his family until he applied for an emigration permit. I decided to offer him protection within this complex and provide transport from Earth."

"Yes, sir," Edward said. "May I ask why?"

"Not now," Damiani said. "You can talk to the Professor while you're on the voyage to Avalon, if you like. We're keeping the fact that he's under our protection to ourselves."

"Yes, sir," Edward said. "Will there be any problems getting him to the transport ship?"

"There shouldn't be any problems," Damiani assured him. "We'll put him on a Marine shuttle and move him directly to orbit. The Civil Guard won't get a sniff of his presence."

Edward put the issue aside, for the moment. "Yes, sir," he said. "When do we depart?"

"The *Sebastian Cruz* is currently in orbit and I will cut orders for her skipper to take you to Avalon," Damiani said. "The *Cruz* is an entire Marine Transport Vessel, so you can take as many supplies as you can fit into the ship. I suggest you fill the ship up completely. Avalon isn't going to be producing much in the way of Marine-grade equipment and I can't guarantee getting additional supplies out to you. If the Grand Senate decides to close the New Hampshire or Armstrong naval bases, you'll be cut off from Earth."

"Sir," Edward said slowly, "is that likely to happen?"

Damiani sighed. Just for a moment, Edward saw a very tired man staring back at him. "I wish I knew, Captain," he said. "I'd like to believe that the Grand Senate can scrape up the money from somewhere to keep the bases open, if only on a shoestring, but the most optimistic projections we have said that it won't happen. Even if they do, the Imperial Navy is going to be hard-pressed to keep running patrols through the outer sectors and the Rim, which leaves the area vulnerable to pirates and warlords."

"They'll appeal to the Emperor," Edward said.

"Emperor Roland won't care," Damiani said. Edward remembered the portrait of the Childe Roland and shuddered. "The Grand Senate appointed his tutors, after all. The Emperor's practical power is very limited. As long as they keep him happy, he'll give them his blessing to do whatever they want to do. He should never have been crowned Emperor, but he was the person with the strongest claim to the Throne and the youngest. There are lots of years of life in our young Emperor."

He looked up and looked directly at Edward. "I'm not giving you an easy task," he warned, "but it has to be done. Concentrate on securing the planet and maintain some level of civilisation out there. Under the circumstances" – his lips twitched – "we'll give you broad latitude to decide what needs to be done and do it. Do you have any other questions?"

"Yes, sir," Edward said. "My Company is currently understrength. Can I put out a call for replacements?"

"Yes, but you may not get many," Damiani warned. "Your unit isn't the only one with a shortage." He stood up. "Good luck, Captain."

"Thank you, sir," Edward said, saluting. "*Semper Fi!*"

As soon as he climbed into the aircar and programmed the navigational computer to take him back to the Barracks, he keyed his earpiece and linked directly to Gwen.

"We're being shipped off-planet," he said, without preamble. There would be time for fuller explanations later. "We're due to leave in a week, so put out a general muster and explain to the troops that I want to brief them all at the Barracks in four hours. Make sure they all get some downtime first. We're going to be very busy over the next week."

"Yes, sir," Gwen said. If she was curious about why the Company had been suddenly transferred off-world, she didn't ask any questions. Edward was silently grateful for her discretion. He would have to explain to the Riflemen why they had all been banished to the Rim – Marines, unlike the Imperial Navy or the Civil Guard, admitted to their mistakes – and then see if anyone wanted to jump ship to a different Marine unit. The Grand Senate probably wouldn't notice as long as Edward himself went to Avalon, even if Edward went alone. "You get some downtime as well, sir."

"Yes, mother," Edward said, although he took her point. Sergeants were responsible for the health of their superior officers as well as for the Riflemen under their command. As senior Sergeant within the Company, Gwen was partly responsible for supervising Edward himself. They'd worked together long enough to be comfortable with each other. "I'll get a drink in one of the bars and then head back to the barracks and catch a nap."

"At least two drinks," Gwen said, firmly. "Is there anything else, sir?"

"Can you pass the word to Lieutenant Howell," Edward said. Lieutenant Thomas Howell handled the unit's logistics. "Inform him that we have been granted unrestricted access to the storage depots in the system and that he is to go nuts, as long as we can fit it into the transport. I want him to pick up anything we might conceivably require. We may not be in line for resupply for a long time."

"Yes, sir," Gwen said. The aircar banked and came down to land at the Barracks, the massive complex that housed most of the military forces stationed near Imperial City. "I'll let him know."

Edward signed off and stepped out of the aircar, passing through a brief security check before entering the Barracks. Unsurprisingly, the Barracks were surrounded by reporters, each one trying to get a quote from the men and women who were trying to get in and out of the complex. Talking to the media was officially forbidden without prior permission, but he saw a number of Civil Guard officers being interviewed, each one taking the time to put their own views across to the public. They had to have powerful political patrons to risk breaking regulations like that.

Edward would have bet good money that the Civil Guard Superintendent who had supervised the deployment of his Company had *very* powerful political patrons.

He shook his head and walked down the corridor towards the bars. The Barracks provided entertainment for soldiers and marines, saving them the trouble of leaving the military complex to sample the nightlife of Imperial City. Edward, in his younger days, had left the complex with his buddies, but now he had too many responsibilities to leave the place behind.

He was nearly at the bar when he heard the commotion.

CHAPTER THREE

> If there is one issue that can be traced as causing the decline of Empire, it is the lack of civil virtue within the ranks of the government and military. Instead of facing unpleasant truths, government officers and irresponsible bureaucrats – who are never held to account – allow the problems to grow larger. On a smaller scale, given opportunities to enrich themselves, soldiers and policemen have become incredibly corrupt, destroying the trust in Empire that made the Empire work.
> - Professor Leo Caesius, *The Waning Years of Empire* (banned).

Rifleman Jasmine Yamane took a sip of her beer and leaned back in her chair, taking in the surrounding bar as her comrades argued over whose round it was. Being Marines coming off their combat high, the argument sounded as if it were going to explode into violence at any moment, but Jasmine knew better. Besides, she'd bought the last round and knew perfectly well that it wasn't her turn. The other three were still trying to keep track of which rounds they'd bought.

The bar was dark and smoky, inhabited only by a pair of dancers on the stage and the four Marines. It wasn't too surprising, although the Barracks were normally inhabited by thousands of soldiers, spacers and their supporting officers. The Civil Guard and the local regiments of the Imperial Army had been called up to deal with the fallout from the terrorist attack, leaving the Marines of Stalker's Stalkers to their own devices. Jasmine had heard – from rumour central – that someone high up had made the decision to keep the Marines off the streets, after the media started to blame the Marines for the recent disaster.

It had hardly been the fault of the Marines that the Nihilists had decided to slaughter thousands of people to make their point that all existence had to come to an end one day, but people grieving their dead weren't very rational. Jasmine knew – she'd been there – that the Marines had done their best to limit civilian casualties, yet with the Nihilists involved, it was often impossible to prevent them blowing themselves and their hostages sky-high. The bastards turned their own bodies into bombs and blew themselves up in the midst of their victims.

She took another sip of her beer and winced at the taste. For a beverage that cost each Marine four credits, it tasted suspiciously like something that had been poured out of the wrong end of a horse. Her experience with beer was limited – her homeworld was an officially dry world, for religious reasons – but she'd learned to drink since she'd joined the Marines and she was quite sure that it was the worst beer she had ever tasted. It was typical of spaceport bars. Merchant spacers would come off their ships, desperate for some alcohol after spending weeks on their ships, and the locals would quite happily cheat them out of their wages. They saved the good stuff for their regular customers.

"All right, all right," Rifleman Blake Coleman said, pulling out his credit chip. His dark face twisted as he contemplated his empty glass. "I guess it's my round."

"Nice try," Rifleman Koenraad Jurgen said, sticking out his tongue in a surprisingly childish gesture. Or perhaps it wasn't so childish at all. For two Marines who made up one of the best fire teams in the Company, they seemed to spend most of their off-duty time picking fights with each other. Jasmine had long since given up trying to understand the pair of them. "Try and get them to keep the cat's piss out of it this time."

"Nah, she only gives the cat's piss to you," Blake said, as he waved to the waitress. "I think the chances of you scoring tonight are minimal."

"The chances of anyone scoring tonight are non-existent," Jasmine said, shaking her head when the waitress offered to take her beer and replace it. There was no chance of decent beer unless she was prepared to overpay. "We're getting called into a briefing, remember?"

"Fuck," Koenraad said, with feeling. "You want to bet that the Old Man decided to piss us off just for the hell of it?"

"No bet," Jasmine said, before Blake could say anything. "Chances are that they tracked down the death-worshipping masterminds and they want to send us after them before they escape."

"I doubt it," Blake said, as the waitress put a full glass of beer in front of him. Jasmine caught him eying the waitress's breasts and shook her head at him. "If they found the headshrinkers behind the fucking cult, they'll send the Civil Guard jerk-offs after them. They won't let us get into them until the Civil Guard runs into trouble."

"Which will be about ten seconds after they launch their assault," Koenraad said, dryly. "Those assholes couldn't organise a piss-up in a brewery."

"With beer like this, I don't think they would try," Rifleman Joe Buckley said, swallowing half of his glass of beer in one gulp. "Why not organise a gang-bang in a brothel instead?"

"They couldn't get them up," Blake said. He chuckled, rather nastily. "Has no one told you why the Civil Guard wears brown underwear?"

Joe shook his head. "No," he said. "Why…?"

"It's so that the stains won't show when they run away," he said. "They shit themselves when they go up against anyone who might actually put up a fight."

Joe looked down at his battledress and then up again. "Does this explain the brown underwear you gave me on my birthday?"

Blake hesitated. "Well…"

"Of course not," Koenraad said, quickly. "They suited you."

"Asshole," Joe said, without heat. "I'll have you know that I wore my lucky red shirt today and got away with nary a scratch."

"Lucky bastard," Jasmine said, wryly. Joe had a remarkable talent for getting into scrapes that should have killed him, but somehow managing to escape with his life. He had been known to claim that he had nine lives. Jasmine was tempted to believe it. "A pity the same can't be said for the others."

A moment of silence fell as they raised their glasses in silent unison. A Marine Company was a family, no matter how much they bickered and fought when off-duty. The dead would be remembered and entered in the permanent rolls of Marines who had died carrying out their duties, their names and records recited to new Marines who had just joined the Company. They would live on in the thoughts and deeds of their former comrades.

"No," Joe said, softly. "It can't be said for them."

The music in the bar changed and the dancers started to strip off their remaining clothes. Jasmine watched them without particular interest, although both Blake and Koenraad were watching with lustful expressions on their faces. The women in the bars were almost certainly prostitutes as well as dancers, selling their bodies to military personnel for credits. She guessed, from what little she'd heard from the Earth-born in the Company, that they would never be able to aspire to anything higher in life. They had no hopes, no dreams…no future. Her homeworld had been socially conservative and constraining, but even there she'd had opportunities. The lower-class women of Earth had none. They couldn't even find a berth on a colony ship.

"Great lookers," Blake said, swigging down his remaining beer. "I think I'll go try my luck."

"Don't be late home," Koenraad said, as Blake started to get up. "You miss the briefing and the Sergeant will cut off your balls and stuff them down your throat."

Jasmine snickered. "Ah, if men could bend over enough to suck their own cocks, they'd be doing it all the time," she said. Blake gave her a one-fingered gesture. "Have fun; try not to catch anything…"

The door swung open and nine men stepped in, wearing the yellow and black uniform of the Civil Guard. They were unarmed, which suggested that they were off-duty and not coming to try to bust the Marines for some imagined infraction, but looked unpleasant. Jasmine took one look at them and knew how the day was going to end. Their leader glanced around, saw the Marines and the empty glasses in front of them, and scowled at them. The Civil Guard hated the Marine Corps. It was a hatred the Marines didn't bother to return. It would have given the Civil Guard too much credit.

"Ah, assholes," Blake said, as the waitress scurried over to the newcomers. She had to hurry for them. The Civil Guard, unlike the Marines, was permanently attached to the Barracks. A word from the Guard could have the waitress thrown in the stockade or simply sacked and sent back to the Undercity. "They'll insist on dancing and drinking and I won't get a look in."

"They might have done you a favour," Joe pointed out. "You never know whose sloppy seconds you're getting here."

Blake looked as if he were going to say something cutting, when he was interrupted by a scream from the waitress. One of the Civil Guardsmen had grabbed her ass hard enough to hurt, while one of the others had started to grope her breasts in public. Jasmine blinked in disbelief before spotting the telltale signs of drug abuse. A crime that would have a Marine running the Gauntlet before being dishonourably discharged from the Corps meant almost nothing to the Civil Guard. As long as they showed up for duty reasonably sober, no one would give a damn.

"Hey, asshole," Blake shouted, loudly enough to be heard over the din. "You want to pick on someone your own size?"

The Civil Guardsman let go of the waitress, stood up and sauntered over to the Marines. "You want to make a thing of a little bitchy whore?"

Jasmine rolled her eyes as Blake puffed up. He might have looked like a thug, with a very rough and ready demeanour, but deep inside Blake thought of himself as a paladin, a man who protected the weak and helpless from the wolves. It would be a brave man – or a fool – who picked a fight with him, yet she could see the traces of drug abuse in the man's eye and knew that he wouldn't back down. The day was definitely going to end badly.

"Yes," Blake said, standing up. The Civil Guardsman would have been wise to back down at that point – Blake was bigger and stronger than him and it showed – but he was too far gone to care. His pride wouldn't let him back down in the face of the enemy. "She doesn't deserve shit from you."

"And we get too much shit from you," the man returned. His cronies laughed as if it was the funniest thing they'd heard in years. "We just spent the last hour carting out the bodies from your fucking fuck-up!"

Blake's eyes flashed murder. "What did you just say?"

"You killed over five hundred children," the Civil Guardsman snapped. His cronies stood up and advanced behind him, fists balling up into readiness for a fight. "We saw the bodies. Many of them were killed by your fire."

"And your people didn't help," Blake thundered. "Didn't it occur to you to make sure that you got your figures straight before you wet yourselves and screamed for help?"

"Fuck you," the Guardsman replied, bunching up a fist and throwing a punch right into Blake's face. Blake ducked and threw a punch back, smacking his opponent right in the jaw. He howled in pain as he toppled over backwards, just before Blake kicked him in the head and knocked him out. It had probably come as a relief.

"Get them," one of his cronies said, and threw himself at Koenraad. Koenraad stepped aside, allowed the Guardsman to slip past him, and then grabbed him and threw him into a wall. Two more Guardsmen tried to jump Blake, only to be knocked down in seconds as Blake twisted, never quite where they expected him to be. Jasmine sighed inwardly and stood up as another Guardsman came right at her, eyes alight with an eerie lust and fury. There was no point in trying to reason with a stoned idiot. She kicked him neatly between the legs and saw him crumple to the ground.

Joe remained seated until his opponent got within range, and then he picked up his glass and hurled his beer right into his enemy's face. Before the guardsman could respond, he lunged forward and head-butted him in the chest, knocking him down and pouring a second glass of beer over his face. His stunned opponent seemed to think that Joe was pouring acid; he kept trying to cover his face from the liquid. Joe dropped the remaining glass by his side and winked at Jasmine.

"I guess this stuff really is cat's piss," he said, and laughed.

Blake was still fighting with the last two Guardsmen, with Koenraad waiting to see if his services would be needed. It didn't seem likely. Even half-drunk, Blake was a far better fighter than either of the Guardsmen and seemed to find it easy to take them both on. He punched one of them in the chest, knocking him back, and then kicked the other one in the leg. His opponent toppled over and hit the ground with a sickening thud. Jasmine found herself hoping that they weren't seriously injured. The authorities might turn a blind eye to the occasional bout of fighting in the

Barracks, but they'd be far less inclined to smile on actual bodily harm, even if the assholes had deserved it.

"Aw," Koenraad said, when the final Guardsman had hit the ground. "You could have saved one for me."

"Get bent," Blake said, kicking his fallen opponent. The moaning Guardsman didn't look happy at all. "You'd only waste the opportunity."

"Look out," the waitress snapped, her voice somehow echoing over the din. "The Patrol!"

The Marines exchanged glances. No words were needed. They took off as a group and raced down the corridor, heading back to their particular section of the barracks. The Shore Patrol wouldn't hesitate to arrest anyone caught brawling and none of them could afford to spend a night in the stockade. The Sergeants would take a dim view of any of them who missed the briefing.

"Stop," a voice bellowed, as the Patrol gave chase. "You…stop!"

Jasmine braced herself as she ran around a corner, half-expecting to feel a stun blast bursting over her at any second. She almost missed seeing the man wearing Marine uniform, just before her mind caught up and realised that they'd almost run down a Captain. Not just any Captain; their Captain.

"Sir," she said, coming to attention. The others followed her lead. "Marine Rifleman…"

"You," the Patrolman snapped. Four Patrolmen, each one carrying a stunner, stumbled to a halt as they reached the Marines. "You're under arrest…"

Captain Stalker's calm voice somehow overrode his. "Is there a problem…ah, Constable?"

"I'll say there is," the Patrolman said. He was too excited to think clearly, or he would have thought before he opened his mouth. Challenging a Marine Captain in front of his men was not conductive to long life and health. "These criminals assaulted twelve members of the Civil Guard!"

"They did?" Captain Stalker said, lifting a single eyebrow. He didn't sound as if he realised the gravity of the situation. Instead, he sounded as if he were bored. "These Marines in front of you?"

"Yes," the Patrolman snapped. "They're going to spend the night in the stockade and formal charges will be filed against them tomorrow!"

Captain Stalker didn't sound as if he had paid attention. "And what do they have to say for themselves?"

"They started it," Blake said, quickly. "They assaulted a waitress!"

"And they're all still alive," Jasmine added. The Captain's gaze switched to her and she felt her cheeks burn. "They picked a fight and they lost."

"Doubtless," Captain Stalker murmured. "These...miscreants have an important briefing to attend. Their punishment will be handled by the Marines, Constable." His voice was impeccably polite. "Thank you for bringing this to my attention."

"But...they're criminals," the Patrolman protested. "I have to take them in and book them."

"The Sergeant will see to their punishment," Captain Stalker said, with a languid wave towards the Patrolman. The Patrolman looked behind him and jumped when he realised that Master Sergeant Gary Young had somehow appeared behind him. Jasmine wasn't so surprised – the Sergeant was the sneakiest man in the Corps – yet even she was impressed. "You do not have to concern yourself any further."

"I have to take them in," the Patrolman insisted. He broke off as he finally realised that he and his men were outnumbered, even if they were carrying stunners. They were trained for riot control, criminal investigation and little else. The Marines could have overpowered them with ease. "Will you see to their punishment?"

"I assure you that they will regret whatever they have done," Captain Stalker said, a steely note entering his tone. "Now...Sergeant, escort these men back to barracks."

"Yes, sir," the Sergeant said.

The Patrolman admitted defeat and led his men back to the bar. If Jasmine knew the Patrol, they would probably take the Civil Guardsmen in and arrest them instead of the Marines. Someone would have to take the blame for the brief fight, or the Patrol would look bad. It was a relief to know that the Marines didn't place so much stock in appearances.

"You lot, move," Sergeant Young growled. On the other hand, Marines weren't meant to be picking fights in bars, even with Guardsmen. The Marine Sergeants had plenty of ways to punish misbehaving Marines. "Now!"

Jasmine saluted the Captain and then followed the Sergeant back to the barracks. Blake had been right, of course. The Civil Guardsmen had deserved the beating, or so she told herself. The Marines would just have to take the consequences. She looked behind her, just for a second, and caught sight of the Captain.

He was smiling.

CHAPTER FOUR

Among the Marines, there is a culture of personal dedication, personal responsibility and service – service to the Marine Corps and its ideal. A Marine learns to take and shoulder responsibility, or stays out of the chain of command. Outside the Marines, it is harder and harder to find examples where power and responsibility are evenly balanced; power without responsibility is the rule. The results, alas, are predictable. The Empire's rulers possess no loyalty to anything beyond themselves.

- Professor Leo Caesius, *The Waning Years of Empire* (banned).

"Attention!"

Edward was still smiling as he strode into the briefing compartment, although he had to admit that it wasn't really that funny. He'd downloaded the report from the Patrol and had been amused by the various attempts the Civil Guardsmen had made to avoid any kind of responsibility for the brief fight. Their claims that the Marines had attacked them looked increasingly hollow as they kept trying to duck responsibility, leaving Edward firmly convinced that they had deserved their beating. Their CO had lodged an official complaint, but Edward had mollified him by pointing out that the Marines were going to be leaving in a week anyway and there was no point in locking them up. They would be dealt with within the Company.

"At ease," he said, as he took his position at the front of the room. The Marines relaxed with an audible noise. "Sergeant…roll call?"

"All present and accounted for, sir," Gwen said. Her voice echoed in the silent room. "We have seventy-four combat effectives in this Company, sir!"

Edward nodded, allowing his eyes to drift from face to face. A civilian would have been struck by how young they were, yet even the most inobservant civilian could hardly have failed to notice the shared expression in their eyes. The youngest Marine in the compartment was twenty-one years old, yet she had spent two years at the Slaughterhouse before qualifying and being formally enrolled among the Marine Corps. They had all been tested in the harshest of fires. The Imperial Navy might regard the Marines as a luxury and the Imperial Army might regard them as over-paid pretty boys, but Edward knew the truth. The Marines were, man for man, the single most effective fighting force in the Empire.

The Terran Marine Corps had come into existence after the Third World War, yet it could trace its origins far further back, right back to John Paul Jones and the birth of the United States of America, a nation now barely remembered outside the American-ethnic worlds near Earth. The men and women in the compartment were heirs to a tradition that stretched back over a thousand years, one that placed loyalty and competence above all else. It was no wonder, Edward thought, that the Grand Senate was nervous about them. The Marines had far fewer opportunities for graft and corruption than any other service. Every Marine would sooner die than fail his comrades.

And he was their commander. The Company was the largest permanent formation in the Marine Corps; Regiments, Battalions and Divisions were, at best, temporary formations, composed of Companies that could be mixed and matched at will. He'd been told, back when he'd decided to aim for commissioned status, that Captain's rank was the best and worst in the entire Corps. The best because it was the position of ultimate trust; the worst because the lives of one hundred Marines depended upon their commander. His mistakes could get them killed. The Marine tradition of naming units after their commanding officer was not only a reward for good service, but a warning. The Marines were his, in the fullest sense of the word. Their lives were in his hands. He felt the weight of responsibility settling down on his shoulders and he smiled. He would not betray his men.

"Take your seats," he ordered, calmly, and waited until the Marines were seated. A civilian might have been surprised by how informal it was, but there was no need for him to assert his authority by acting like a dickhead. "There has been a development on Earth."

He paused, silently cursing himself under his breath. His mistake, his hasty words, had condemned his Marines to exile. "The Grand Senate wanted my opinion of what happened over the last two days," he continued, finally. Marines learned from their earliest days to confess their mistakes and learn from them. Everyone, Marines included, made mistakes. The trick was to learn from them and not to repeat them. It wasn't quite as easy as it sounded…but then, nothing ever was. "I told them the truth."

"Big mistake there, sir," Blake Coleman said, from the back.

Edward fought down a smile as Sergeant Young glowered at Blake. Like many of the enlisted men, Blake was bored when he wasn't fighting or fucking…and he had no ambitions towards becoming a commissioned officer or an NCO. Smart remarks were the least of his problems, although Edward privately appreciated the humour. It helped to defuse the situation.

"Quite," he agreed, dryly. "The Grand Senate rewarded me for my honesty by exiling me – and you – to Avalon, a planet on the edge of the Rim. Our exile was my fault and I take full responsibility for it."

"Ah, it was getting boring here, sir," Blake said, quickly.

There were some chuckles. "Silence in the ranks," Gwen thundered, with a look that promised trouble for Blake later. Even for Marines, there were limits. "Coleman, I'll see you later."

Edward spoke again before anyone else could interrupt. "If any of you wish to seek a transfer to any other unit, speak to me or the Sergeants about it and we will attempt to honour your request," he said. Marines rarely moved out of their units. It was too hard to fit them into a new unit without heavy intensive training. "Let us know before the end of the day; tomorrow we start preparing for our journey. I'm afraid it will be six months in the tubes for most of us."

This time, the groans were real. The Marines would be placed in stasis tubes once they were onboard the transport and would be taken out of the tubes when they reached Avalon. A handful would remain awake and active, making preparations for the landing, but none of the Marines liked being helpless in the tubes. There were plenty of rumours about colony ships being hijacked and their colonists pressed into slavery on hidden colony worlds. Not that pirate crews would bother keeping the Marines alive, of course. Once they realised what they had on their hands, the Marines would be unceremoniously spaced.

"There isn't an alternative," he snapped, before anyone could make a comment. "If you're fighting already today, what are you going to be like after a month in Phase Drive?"

There was no answer. "Avalon is rated as a Class-Two Colony World, so any of you who wish to invite your wives or sweethearts along should mention it to the Sergeants," Edward continued. Marine Riflemen – the lowest rank – rarely married, but they often formed long-term relationships. "We can obtain permission for emigration from the Colonisation Office, subject to the usual regulations. There are no restrictions on who may enter Avalon."

He saw the implications sinking into their heads, a handful looking more thoughtful than usual. Civilians thought of Marines – and soldiers in general – as dumb beasts; after all, who in their right mind would charge into the teeth of enemy fire? Marines were encouraged to learn as much as possible, particularly history – there were millions of lessons to be learned from history – and that included the early years of human exploration and settlement. A planet with few immigration restrictions would, likely as not, end up with a multiethnic or multi-religious population, a recipe for trouble down the line. The lax regulations – a brief glance at the file had suggested that the development corporation had been desperate for colonists – would come back to haunt them. Or maybe they'd be lucky. There were several worlds that had formed a new culture, or had simply kept the disparate cultures apart.

"We may be there for as little as a year, or much longer," he concluded. "The Grand Senate may see the wisdom in bringing us back sooner than I dare hope. Or maybe we'll be out there forever. I honestly do not know.

"Our mission is threefold. We are to provide some additional muscle for the local government, to train their version of the Civil Guard to acceptable levels and prevent pirate operations in the vicinity. None of that is going to be easy. I know, however, that each and every one of you will give his or her best. *Semper Fi!*"

"*Semper Fi*," the Marines echoed.

"I will see the Sergeants and Lieutenants now," Edward said. "The rest of you…try not to get into any more fights. Dismissed!"

The Marines marched out, leaving Edward alone with his officers and NCOs. There were fifteen of them in all; five Lieutenants and ten Sergeants. It always amazed the Imperial Army how few officers and NCOs actually wore Marine Blues, but the Marines had always believed that every Rifleman had Sergeant's stripes in his backpack. Edward knew of units that had lost almost all of their officers, yet had kept going and won the battle anyway. In the Imperial Army, there were units that could only have been improved if they'd lost all of their senior officers. They were the ones who had bought their commissions, or had been shuttled in to serve as someone's eyes and ears. They were, thankfully, rare in the Marine Corps. It was yet another reason why the Senate distrusted the Corps.

"At ease," he said, when the door had closed behind the last Marine. "Before we start, there is an important issue we have to settle. Do any of you wish to stay behind?"

"Respectfully suggest, sir, that you quit insulting us before I have an attack of brains to the head and realise how far we're going from civilised lands," Master Sergeant Young said, dryly. "Besides, where could we go if we did decide to leave?"

Edward shrugged, although Young had a point. A Rifleman could be transferred to another Company without serious career repercussions, but it was harder for a Sergeant or a Lieutenant. They rarely transferred out without a very good reason, which suggested to the CO of their new unit that there was something deeply wrong with them, forcing them to work harder to prove that they were good officers. It was a silly issue, in Edward's view, but old habits die hard. A really poor officer would have been reduced to the ranks or transferred somewhere where they could do no harm – or discharged, for serious offenders.

"I heard that Melville's Murderers are looking for a replacement Lieutenant," Gwen put in, sharply. "If anyone wants to jump ship, now is the time."

"The Murderers…damn it," Lieutenant Thomas Howell said. "What silly bastard thought that that was a good name for a unit?"

"The Murderers themselves," Young pointed out. "They liked the name and made it stick."

Edward shrugged. A Marine Company was generally named after its CO – hence Stalker's Stalkers – and the enlisted ranks got to vote on the name. The Corps patiently endured names like Burnside's Bastards, Severus' Snakes and Wilkinson's Wankers, although the last one had probably been someone's idea of a joke that had gotten out of hand. Some units ended up with names that no one dared write down. If Melville's Murderers wanted to call themselves murderers, no one had the right to stop them.

"It hardly matters," he said, seriously. "The good news, as I hope Gwen told you, is that we've been given a blank cheque for supplies. Thomas, I want you to go completely nuts and plan on the assumption that we're not going to be re-supplied anytime soon. Look up the data on Avalon, find out what they cannot produce for us, and fit as much as you can on the transport ship. We're going to have a whole transport to ourselves, so have fun."

"Thank you, sir," Howell said. A Marine Transport Ship was intended to transport an entire Marine Division. A single Company would rattle around in its enormous bulk. "We're going to have it completely to ourselves?"

"There may be a few colonists coming along," Edward said, remembering the Professor that the Commandant had told him would be coming along. A Professor…and his family. He hadn't had time to check up on their accommodation, but they could just be put in the tubes along with the Marines. They certainly wouldn't want to spend six months cooped up on a transport ship. "Plan on the assumption that we'll need two hundred tubes and use the rest of the ship's bulk as you see fit."

"Yes, sir," Howell said. Edward smiled. Howell was the current logistics officer for the Company, a task Edward had handled himself when he'd been a Lieutenant, and being told he could get whatever he wanted was a dream come true. The others gathered round, offering suggestions and comments, which he listened to with half an ear. Edward knew that he would have a wish list of supplies the Company desperately needed. "I'll start planning at once."

Edward turned to Young. "I take it that you dealt with our miscreants?"

"They saw the error of their ways," Young said, with equal gravity. "The four of them will be spending their time cleaning toilets with toothbrushes until they're shining at night."

"Have them assigned to assist Thomas with the logistics as well," Edward added. "He's going to need help…"

"If only to hold the irate bureaucrats down as we take everything we want," Howell said, with a grin. There were some chuckles. The Marine Supply Officers were an understanding bunch, but the same couldn't be said for the General Supply Officers, who insisted that any mere logistics officer had to have his requests signed in triplicate before they even considered *considering* granting them. Edward had fought enough battles with the bureaucrats to make him glad that someone else was going to be handling it. It was a shame that shooting bureaucrats was officially Not Allowed. "Or perhaps to help me dig a tunnel into the supply depot to smuggle out the loot."

"I think they'll go to their union about that," Gwen said, sourly. "They're the only ones allowed to loot military supplies."

Edward scowled, wishing that she was joking. In theory, the private possession of guns on Earth was forbidden, with very heavy penalties for anyone who owned a weapon. In practice, there were literally millions of illegal weapons and weapons factories in the Undercity, where violence was common and the Civil Guard never went. And even the more advanced weapons could be found on the black market.

Someone had sold the Nihilists enough weapons to take a bite out of a Marine Company and *that* could never be forgiven. It was probably too much to hope that Marine Intelligence would track them down before the Stalkers left Earth forever, but they would find the culprit and deal with him. The Commandant would probably send a few Marines to assassinate the bastard.

"If they give you any trouble, let me know," Edward said. The bureaucrats would probably not be cowed by a mere Captain, but a call from the Commandant himself – particularly after he pointed out that the Grand

Senate had ordered the Stalkers to leave Earth forever – would probably loosen the purse strings. "I can pull strings for you."

"Yes, sir," Howell said. He glanced around the room. "Is there anything else, sir?"

"We start three days of heavy training in two days," Edward said, firmly. "Gwen, you will supervise that if I'm not present at the time. The Commandant said that we might get a few newcomers to the unit; if so… we'll start working them hard and get them up to standard. After that, we'll start boarding the transport and stocking up on supplies. Keep a close rein on everyone. The last thing we need is another fight at the moment."

"The Civil Guard isn't making that easy," Young said. "The Pacifist League is *really* not making it easy."

"If it was easy, they really wouldn't need us," Edward said. He grinned. "They may whine about us now, but they'll be calling us back soon enough."

"When they need us," Young said. "For its Tommy this an' Tommy that, and 'chuck him out, the brute! But its 'Saviour of The Country' when the guns begin to shoot…"

It was a misquote – Marines were encouraged to study Kipling, even though his poems were unknown to the vast majority of the Empire's population – but Edward didn't mind. "They'll call us back soon enough," he said, firmly. "Until then…keep the faith."

"Yes, sir," Young said.

He watched as the officers filed out, leaving him alone with Gwen. "Tell me something," she said. "Do you think they'll ever call us back?"

"I like to think so," Edward said. He could relax with Gwen. They'd served together for years. She'd forgotten more about being a Marine than most of the enlisted men ever learned. "I don't know, though. I really don't know."

"It could be for the best," Gwen said, frankly. "After what happened today, I doubt that Earth is going to remain stable much longer."

"No," Edward said, grimly. "Forty billion people, most of them fed and watered by processes that might as well be magic as far as they're concerned. Upwards of twenty billion people in city-blocks who have no concept of just how bad the universe can become, or what's waiting for them in the Undercity. If the bomb explodes under them, all hell will break loose. Perhaps you're right."

"Perhaps," Gwen agreed. "Or perhaps they'll call us back to deal with the chaos."

Edward said nothing.

"Cheer up," Gwen said, dryly. "It could be a lot worse."

CHAPTER FIVE

One of the most dangerous signs of decline is the sudden reluctance to tolerate different points of view in political debate. Questions and issues that were discussed freely are suddenly forbidden, limiting the realm of political science. The reluctance to question the fundamental basis of our culture and society is, in itself, crippling free enquiry and freedom of speech.
- Professor Leo Caesius, *The Waning Years of Empire* (banned).

No one would have called the *Sebastian Cruz* beautiful. It was little more than a two kilometre-long block of metal, with a drive section flaring out to the rear. It was ugly, pitted and scarred by the strain of an existence right on the edge, yet to Professor Leo Caesius it – she – was the most wonderful sight in the universe. She represented escape from Earth, escape from the horror that had gripped his family over the last year, and he would have forgiven her anything. He'd accessed recordings of the interior of the Marine Transport – the designers, it seemed, didn't have comfort or luxury in their dictionaries – but even though she was uncomfortable, she was *safe*! He couldn't wait to climb on board her and escape to the Rim.

"We'll be docking in two minutes," the pilot said, from his seat at the front of the tiny shuttle. "When we dock, unbuckle yourselves and climb out the hatch, taking your bags with you. Don't look back."

"Understood," Leo said, nodding towards the young man. He hadn't known if the Marine pilot knew who he was ferrying, not until now. A direct order from the Commandant of the Marine Corps might as well have been an order from God, as far as the very junior pilot was concerned, but he might not have been enthusiastic about it. "We won't delay."

"I hope that there will be some proper accommodation onboard that…thing," Fiona chimed in, from her seat. Her petulant tone made Leo wince. Fiona was the same age as himself – forty-seven – but unlike her husband, Fiona had never been treated with the regeneration therapies that would have restored her lost youth. The first streaks of grey were appearing in her hair, no matter how much she tried to hide them. They reminded Leo of his own guilt. The entire family had been stressed to the limits, because of him. "I could do with a long soak in the bath."

"I'm afraid that there are no bathing facilities onboard the transport," the pilot said, tonelessly. Leo was sure that he was trying to hide a grin. "The bathing compartments are restricted to sonic vibrations and the occasional sponge bath. Water is a luxury in space."

Leo said nothing, watching as the minnow of the shuttle slowly approached the massive whale. Two years ago, he had been a respected academic, teaching the Empire's history to the best and brightest students from all over the Empire. The University of Earth, the most famous university in the Empire, had granted him tenure. A bright future had laid ahead, one where Leo, his wife and his two daughters could make a comfortable life for themselves. They had even been talking about having more children, or buying more comfortable accommodation away from the towering city blocks. The whole universe had seemed to be waiting for them.

And then he'd been struck by the curiosity bug. One of his students, a young girl from the out-worlds, had questioned the very basis of the Empire's mandate. Another Professor would have put her firmly in her place – it was an unquestionable fact that Earth was the political, social and cultural heart of the Empire – but Leo had been curious. He'd started to look into the past, and then into the present, constructing elaborate models of the future of the Empire. It had been an eye-opening experience. He hadn't wanted to admit it, even to himself, but the Empire was starting to enter a pattern of terminal decline. Without a strong man on the Throne – and the Childe Roland was no such man – the Empire was doomed. The competing power bases would tear it apart.

He'd made the mistake of regarding it as an intellectual puzzle. It had simply never occurred to him that his discoveries might have had real-life implications. If the level of social spending was cut, he'd discovered, the Empire would have more resources free to tackle the other problems, such as the upswing in piracy or terrorist operations. If measures were taken to limit Earth's birth rate – expanding constantly, due to the free food and water provided by the Empire – the planet might have a chance to recover from everything humanity had done to it. Born to a safe time and place, he had seen no harm in publicising his results and attempting to draw the Empire's notice to the growing crisis. He should, he knew, have seen it coming. The elite had responded harshly.

Two months after his book had been published, and banned just as quickly, he'd lost his position in the University of Earth. The Dean had been quietly apologetic, but very firm; there was no longer any place for Leo in the hallowed halls of academia. Fiona had been horrified to discover that the family was suddenly without any means of support – apparently, they didn't qualify for welfare – and shocked to realise that no one else would take her husband on.

Shock had turned to fear when gangs of youths, encouraged by someone in the shadows, had started to harass the family, while their name was dragged through the mud by groups so diverse as the Pacifist League and the Crowned Throne. They'd had to move out of their comfy home, down to the very edge of the Middle City, and yet they were still not safe. If the Marines, for a reason known only to their leader, hadn't offered them sanctuary, Leo had no doubt that they would all be dead by now, victims of a violent adult world they had never fully understood. The Empire's masters guarded its secrets well.

He looked back, towards his two daughters. An outsider might mistake them for twins, for Mandy and Mindy were both redheaded girls, wearing the same drab smocks they'd worn since they'd taken up residence in the Marine complex. Mandy, the oldest at sixteen, had been a constant worry; she'd developed crushes on a succession of Marines, although as far as he knew she hadn't found the time to actually court one of the men.

Mindy, thirteen years old, had had to grow up fast. Losing all of her friends and most of her family had hurt her badly, the more so because she couldn't understand why the world had changed and they had to leave their friends behind. There had been no choice, not really. As soon as the word had gotten around, the entire family had found themselves abandoned by their former friends, men and women fearful that the taint would somehow slop over onto them. He should have expected that too. It hadn't been an uncommon pattern in the past.

A dull thump ran through the shuttle as it docked neatly with the massive transport. Leo unbuckled himself and stood up, feeling slightly queasy in the artificial gravity. He had never left Earth before, not even to visit the halo of asteroid stations and industrial nodes surrounding the planet, and the feeling was new and unwelcome. The Marines had assured him that it was perfectly normal, but it only underlined his own weaknesses. He was a husband and a father who couldn't even protect himself, let alone his family. He was dependent upon a military force many of his former colleagues wouldn't have given the time of day to, had they been asked. Leo had never shared their opinion – although, if the truth were to be told, it was because he'd never had to think about it – yet it was humiliating. He helped Mandy to unbuckle, sighing inwardly at her too-tight shirt that showed her breasts to best advantage, and pushed her towards the hatch. Fiona was already there, her face pale and wan. She was no longer the woman he'd married.

"Go," the pilot snapped. "I can't stay here for long!"

The hatch hissed open and Mindy led the way into the Marine transport. Leo felt the gravity field twisting around them as the transport's gravity generator took over, smiling at Mindy's clear delight. Fiona looked as if she were going to be sick. Like him, she had never been off Earth, believing implicitly that barbarians and monsters lurked outside Earth's solar system. She preferred to look down on the colonists and their worlds, even though Leo knew perfectly well that the colonists were just human, as human as his family. A thousand years after the human race had started to expand into space, they had encountered no intelligent alien life forms at all. The highest creature the human race had discovered barely rated higher than a chimpanzee.

"Welcome on board," a man said. Leo looked up and saw a short man wearing a shipsuit and a Marine Rifleman tab on his collar. The entire crew of the transport, he'd been assured, were Marines. The *Sebastian Cruz* was not, technically, part of the Imperial Navy, but part of the Marine Corps. "Professor, the Major would like to speak with you as soon as possible. I have orders to escort you to his cabin and Specialist Nix will escort your family to the stasis tubes."

"Not stasis," Fiona objected, at once. Nix, a tall dark-skinned man with a scarred face and roguish eyes, blinked at her. "I can't stand being frozen."

"You won't feel a thing," Nix assured her, with a generous smile. "I've been in stasis many times and I never feel anything, not even time passing. You'll just blink and you'll be on Avalon before you know it."

Leo winced at his wife's expression. When she'd heard that the family was being moved off-world, she'd tried to bargain for one of the older worlds, the ones settled directly from Earth before the Empire had been formed. The Marines had been quiet, but firm; the family's tormentors would follow them to their new home and keep up the pressure until they were all dead. It was far safer to travel to a world on the edge of the Rim. He suspected that the Commandant had had some other purpose in sending them to Avalon, but he hadn't even been able to guess at it. How could the Marines possibly benefit from his presence?

He saw Mandy eyeing Nix and winced inwardly. Ironically, seeing that seemed to calm Fiona down. She caught hold of her daughter and waved imperiously to Nix to lead them towards the stasis tubes. Leo wanted to follow her, just to make sure that everything was all right, but there was no point. His guide was waiting for him.

"I'm ready," he said, as a hatch clanged shut behind his wife's ass. He caught his own thought and smiled inwardly. Spending time with the Marines had made him crude, clearly. "Please can you escort me to the Major?"

"Of course," his guide said. "Follow me."

Leo had never been onboard a real starship before and, despite the gravity of the situation, found himself intrigued by the Marine Transport. Hundreds of men and women bustled about, performing tasks he couldn't even begin to understand, while small dedicated robots prowled around, carrying out maintenance work on the ship's interior. Senior officers were shouting orders that might as well have been in another language, for all the sense they made to Leo, ignoring his presence. Hatches and bulkheads lay open, exposing incomprehensible circuitry and components to his gaze. It was fascinating. It almost made him wish that he had applied for the Imperial Navy, rather than seeking a career in the academic world. Here, on the ship, men and women were doing things that *mattered*.

"It is not a good idea to wander alone on this ship," his guide said, when Leo asked. "If you want a tour, the Major will have to clear it with the Captain. The Captain has supreme authority on this ship, answerable only to the Commandant."

They reached a hatch marked OFFICER COUNTRY, which opened when the guide touched a key hidden in a bulkhead, revealing drab corridors and better lighting. "Normally, a commanding officer would bunk down with the men, but while on ship they get cabins," the guide explained, misinterpreting Leo's questioning look. "It isn't something the Corps fully approves of, sir."

"Thank you," Leo said. He'd sort it all out later. They reached another hatch marked STALKER. "Where now...?"

The hatch hissed open, revealing a small metal cubicle, barely large enough to hold a desk and a portable terminal. Seeing it, Leo was struck by the disparity between the University and the Marine Transport Ship; the Dean, back on Earth, had had an office large enough to hold a hundred students or lecturers, finely decorated with paintings and small artworks. The only decoration in the Marine's office was a tiny picture of a pretty dark-skinned girl. There was nothing else. A week in the compartment, Leo knew, would have had him begging for mercy.

"Welcome onboard," a man said, rising up from behind the desk. He held out a hand for Leo to shake. "I'm Captain Stalker."

Leo blinked at him. "I was told I was going to meet a Major," he protested. "Why...?"

Captain Stalker laughed. "On board ship, there is only ever one Captain and he's the person in command of the ship," he explained. "Any other Captain who happens to set foot in his realm is automatically given a courtesy promotion to Major or Commodore. There's no extra pay, of course, just the new responsibility of answering to one step above your real pay grade."

"Ah," Leo said. It sounded too complicated for him. "Thank you for clarifying that."

He sat down on the bunk when the Captain waved to it and studied his host. Captain Stalker was tall, with short blond hair and bright blue eyes. He was wearing a Marine standard uniform and wore a Rifleman's tab at his collar, the same as the other Marines he'd seen. He had an air of brisk competence and determination that suggested that anyone in his way was in for trouble. Leo, no great fan of the military until it had saved his life, was privately impressed. Perhaps everything was going to be all right after all.

"My orders are to escort you to your new home and then see to your security, among other things," Captain Stalker said. "I have other orders to carry out and, of course, there may be problems involved in balancing all of those responsibilities. The Commandant was, however, quite keen that you be preserved alive. Why, if I may be blunt, has an academic attracted so much interest from so many different factions?"

Leo paused, gathering himself. Somehow, the direct question cut right to the heart of his problems. "I spoke truth to power," he said, honestly. "They didn't like it."

Stalker laughed. "So did I," he said, seriously. "That's why they sentenced me to exile."

He leaned forward, his eyes meeting Leo's. "I have never read your book, although I'm sure that you have a copy or two in your luggage," he said. "I do know that I will do my best to protect you and your family, subject only to carrying out my other orders. I don't believe that your enemies will chase you as far as Avalon, but if they do, they will regret it."

"Thank you, Captain," Leo said.

"Major," Stalker corrected. He grinned, suddenly. It completely transformed his face. "As a fellow political exile, you can call me Edward. Now, tell me; just what did you tell them to get yourself marked for death?"

"The truth," Leo said, flatly. It still hurt to remember how all of his comforting illusions had been torn away, revealing the naked truth that underpinned the Empire. "I told them that if they continued on their current path, the entire Empire was going to explode like a powder keg underneath them. As for the specifics..." – he shrugged expressively – "where would you like me to start?"

Stalker lifted an eyebrow. "I started looking into the conditions in the more…recently established colonies, the ones established since the Tyrant Emperor was killed," Leo clarified. "Most of them suffer under levels of taxation and debt they can never hope to pay off, not ever. Their children's children will still be paying it off hundreds of years in the future. It made no sense to me so I started tracing the money and realised that most of it was being spent on social welfare to keep the underclass happy. Yet there were limits to how much the Empire could extract from its subjects and there were already small rebellions popping up, all over the Empire…"

"I fought on Han," Stalker said, dispassionately. There was a haunted note in his voice that made Leo shiver. The realities of violence, despite everything he'd been through, were still largely alien to him. "There was no time to think about how, or why, or if they had a cause worth dying for. It was kill or be killed."

"I know," he said. It was scant comfort, but what did one say to a man charged with upholding an edifice that would come toppling down one day and bury them all under the rubble? "There are a thousand more such rebellions just waiting to happen."

"We're going to be talking about this on Avalon," Stalker said, slowly. "I want you to get into your tube now, Professor. We're about to start loading the ship and we don't need you getting in the way."

Leo shook his head. "I'd prefer to stay out of the tubes until we're under way," he said, slowly. He couldn't tell the young Captain why, not yet. "Please…"

Stalker stared at him for a long moment. "We'll assign you a bunk," he said. "It won't be pleasant sailing, but it's the best we can do. Stay out of everyone's way."

"Of course," Leo said. "Thank you for taking care of us."

Chapter Six

It is a curious fact that humans are capable of forming bonds with only a limited number of people; the 'group' becomes more abstract as the group becomes larger. At one end of the scale, with the trillions of humans in the Empire, it is very different to truly put the Empire first. Why not, one might ask, put my own interests first? Is that not for the good of the Empire? The largest number of humans that can be considered a real group, from the point of view of its members, is around one hundred and fifty men. It is for that reason that the Marine Company, generally composed of one hundred men, is the building block of the higher Marine units. Within the Company, loyalty is absolute.
- Professor Leo Caesius, *The Waning Years of Empire* (banned).

Edward smiled to himself as Professor Leo Caesius was escorted down to one of the bunks, a tiny compartment that would give him the same level of privacy as any Marine Rifleman would have, which was very little. Marines practically lived in each others' pockets and shared equipment and private entertainments regularly. The Professor would probably want to jump into his tube after a day or two in orbit, although Edward would be sorry if he did. Based on his brief meeting, Leo would be an interesting conversationalist during transit.

He shook his head, dismissing the thought, and scowled down at the portable datapad. The Marine Corps might have embraced all the possibilities opened up by new technology, but there was still an inordinate amount of paperwork to be carried out by the unit's commanding officer. Edward was responsible for his men and keeping the records in order was one way of ensuring that, if the worst happened, his successor would be able to take over without hassle. It was also a way of ensuring that there was a proper record for posterity. If Stalker's Stalkers went down in the history books, the historians would have a record for each of his men, although God alone knew what they would make of it. He'd been paying more attention to the hundreds of entertainment channels broadcasting to Earth's population recently and he'd been shocked by just how badly the Marines were being slammed. The entire Corps seemed to be taking the blame for the Nihilist attack and its massive death toll.

The Pacifist League had informed the planet that the Marines had gone in hot, shooting at suspected terrorists, and triggered half of the explosives quite deliberately. The League seemed to believe that it was possible to negotiate with the Nihilists and, by listening to their spokesmen and granting their demands, the massive death toll could have been avoided.

Edward knew better than to believe it. The Nihilists wanted death, nothing more, and simply didn't care what their enemies could offer them. They wouldn't have released the hostages for anything. Taking them all down as quickly as possible was the only way to prevent the Nihilists from detonating their explosives and destroying the entire block.

Pure Humanity, a group that had been among Leo's tormentors, had taken the opposite track. Their version of events claimed that the Nihilists had been allowed to get into position because of Marine weakness and that if the Marines had showed strength and determination – and courage, they didn't quite say – the Nihilists would never have been able to take hostages in the first place. It made no sense at all, not to anyone who actually knew what had happened. The Marines hadn't been called in until the Civil Guard had fumbled the ball and, by the time they'd gotten into position and had been briefed, the hostages had already started to die. There had been no choice left but to move.

He stared down at the datapad, not seeing the words displayed on the screen. One of the duties of a Marine Captain was to write to the families of those killed under his command and he'd had to write just under thirty letters in the last few days. They couldn't even use a form letter; tradition demanded a letter handwritten by the Captain personally. It had brought back memories of the dead men and women in happier times. One of the dead men had been up before Edward only a month before he died, charged with being drunk and disorderly on Mars. Edward had thought little of it at the time. The Marine had been visiting his family and, afterwards, had gone out drinking with his mates. And, a month later, he was dead.

It was a relief when his communicator buzzed. "Major" – Gwen used the courtesy promotion as if it were a real rank – "Drill Sergeant Jared Barr has just come onboard and is requesting permission to meet with you."

"Very good," Edward said, after he'd placed the name. Barr was one of the Marines who had requested a transfer to the Stalkers. Edward had learned from his previous CO that it was better to interview such people before approving their transfer. Even among the Marines, there were details that never made it into the personnel files. "Have him brought to my office now, please."

Two minutes later, the hatch hissed open and Drill Sergeant Jared Barr marched in. He stood to attention and saluted as Edward rose to his feet, eyes skimming over Barr's uniform. Everything was perfect; he wore a handful of combat awards, including badges that marked proficiency in over a dozen different specialities. Even for the Marines, Barr was an overachiever. The ribbons on his left arm, marking campaigns he'd served in since graduating from the Slaughterhouse, suggested a long and very active career. His face showed the signs of too many regeneration treatments, a certain lack of movement that suggested plastic surgery.

"Drill Sergeant Jared Barr reporting, sir," Barr barked. Even his salute was perfect. Marines were not sloppy – sloppiness could not be tolerated among the Marines – but perfection was rare.

"At ease," Edward said. He had a good feeling about Barr, right from the start, but he wanted to talk to the man. It wouldn't be easy. "I don't have time to beat around the bush, Sergeant. Why do you want to transfer to my unit?"

Barr didn't relax, much. "I understand that you will be training local Civil Guardsmen and raw recruits," he barked. "If that is the case, I would like to take part."

Edward smiled inwardly. A competent Drill Sergeant – and Barr's record showed that he was very competent indeed – was worth his weight in gold. It took a special kind of man to act like a sadist without actually being a sadist, for a real sadist in a Drill Sergeant's uniform could inflict immeasurable harm on raw recruits. If he'd served a term as a Drill Sergeant on the Slaughterhouse, he would be very well prepared to train new recruits on Avalon.

"I see," he said, and waited.

Barr took the bait. "I was detailed to New Charleston to assist in training their Civil Guard to cope with an insurgency on their planet," he said. "I believe that my experience will be useful to you. My record speaks for itself."

"So it does," Edward said, straightening up. "You are aware, of course, that you will be Junior Sergeant within the Company?"

"Yes, sir," Barr said. Sergeants were always Sergeants, but they often held different titles and responsibilities. Barr might have been entitled to call himself a Drill Sergeant, yet he would not always be serving as a Drill Sergeant. The Slaughterhouse rotated its instructors in and out of line units to keep them up to date on the latest developments…and to keep them thinking of themselves as Marines. "I have been Junior Sergeant before."

"Of course," Edward agreed. "Welcome to the Stalkers, Sergeant. Report to Command Sergeant Patterson for induction, and then we'll drop you in at the deep end. We have a great deal of training to catch up on and very little time."

"Thank you, sir," Barr said. He saluted again. "It will be my honour."

Edward smiled as he marched out of the small compartment. "Gwen," he said, keying his communicator, "I have accepted Sergeant Barr into the Stalkers. Give him the standard welcoming tour and then put him on the duty roster."

"Yes, sir," Gwen said. "Sink or swim."

An hour passed slowly as Edward completed his paperwork. There would be little else to do until he reached Avalon, where at least delay was acceptable. With six months between Avalon and Earth, no one would care if the reports were a week or so late, not when starships could be lost so easily, along with their reports. He filed it in a datachip, pulled it out of the datapad and marked it for transfer by courier to the Marine Headquarters on Earth. The Commandant would take care of it personally. Whatever he'd had in mind – and Edward had a private suspicion that there was more to his operations than just preserving a few people from the mob – he'd deal with the reports. He was about to head down to the training compartment when his communicator buzzed.

"Sir, Rifleman Aaron McDonald is here," Gwen said. It took Edward a moment to place the name. A Rifleman who had requested a transfer to the Stalkers, something unusual for a mere Rifleman. A Drill Sergeant might request a transfer to a combat unit and no one would think much of it. A Rifleman should stay with his parent unit. "He is requesting permission to speak with you."

"Have him escorted up here," Edward said, realising that he probably wasn't going to have a chance to get some exercise before heading back down to the Barracks on Earth. It was just something else to do while they were in transit. "And then send me the training rotas. We don't have much time left to complete matters."

Rifleman Aaron McDonald turned out to be middle-aged, older than the average Rifleman, although that wasn't too uncommon within the Marine Corps. If McDonald hadn't been interested in promotion – his record showed that he'd served as a Corporal at least twice, but that had always been a brevet promotion – he would probably have been allowed to remain as a Rifleman, although he would probably have been quietly encouraged to become an NCO. He'd survived ten years in the Corps, which suggested that there was nothing seriously wrong with him. His file, which Edward had skimmed briefly, hadn't thrown up any red flags.

"All right," Edward said, studying him carefully. McDonald looked to be a combination of ethnic traits, not uncommon among some of the other colony worlds. Despite the name, he looked vaguely Chinese. "Why do you want to become a Stalker?"

McDonald met his eyes levelly, a good sign. "I understand that you are being transferred to Avalon," he said. "Avalon is my homeworld."

Edward silently cursed himself under his breath. That particular titbit would have been in the files, but he'd missed it. Marines, wherever they were born, went through the Slaughterhouse and came out as Marines.

Their pasts didn't matter. Unlike the Imperial Army, which was careful *not* to allow its soldiers to serve on their homeworlds, the Marine Corps didn't care, as long as they were Marines. A career Marine like McDonald shouldn't have been attached to his homeworld. He was half-inclined to refuse the transfer on those grounds alone, but yet…the prospect of having someone who actually knew Avalon attached to his command was tempting. Very tempting. It was tempting enough to suggest that he should overlook the irregularity.

"I…see," he said. "And you want to go back there?"

"I've put eighteen years into the Corps," McDonald said, honestly. "I expect to go on inactive status when I reach twenty years of service. I don't have fond memories of Avalon, sir, but if we build up a proper Civil Guard and deal with those damned Crackers, it might be…livable."

Edward smiled. "You place me in an uncomfortable position," he said, dryly. "You do know that, don't you?"

"Yes, sir," McDonald said. There was no give in him. "I'm sorry, sir."

Edward considered the matter. "Tell me about Avalon," he said. "Who are the Crackers?"

"Long story," McDonald said. He paused, gathering his thoughts. "The short version of the story, sir, is that the Development Corporation that owned the planet – and most of the settlers and their contracts – overextended itself badly and ended up having to squeeze the planet tightly, just to pay their creditors. There were a series of…incidents…that ended with Peter Cracker, one of the original colonists, leading a rebellion against the Development Corporation's puppet planetary government. They didn't have anything left to lose. If they stayed and bowed to the corporation, they'd be in debt for the rest of their lives…and so would their grandchildren. They came far too close to destroying the Corporation once and for all."

Edward nodded. It wasn't an unfamiliar pattern. In order to settle a planet, Development Corporations paid settlers to settle on the planet, giving them land in exchange for their efforts. The settlers would, if all went well, spend around ten-to-twenty years paying off their debts before breaking even and becoming freeholders. The contracts, however, had hidden clauses that actually made the colonists liable for the debts of the overall corporation, forcing them to remain in hock longer if the Corporation needed to keep squeezing them.

Even if they avoided that trap, there were others. The Corporation was often the only source of tools and farming equipment, creating a legal monopoly that forced the colonists to spend their hard-earned credits on newer and better equipment. It didn't take much to unbalance the equation and set off a rebellion, or an outright revolution. It never ended well.

"The Avalon Development Corporation called in the Navy and the Navy smashed the main rebel army from orbit," McDonald continued. "Peter Cracker himself was believed killed in the attack that slaughtered his army. The ADC landed tens of thousands of mercenaries and restored order to much of the planet, but thousands of former Crackers went underground and launched an insurgency against the new Imperial Governor. The survivors were convicted of rebellion and parcelled out as convict gangs, working side by side with the damned indents. It wasn't the planet's finest hour."

Edward scowled. The Empire's solution to Earth's massive overpopulation problem was to deport anyone convicted of even a minor crime. The indentured colonists – slaves in all but name – were deported to new colony worlds and put to work, carrying out the hard labour that was needed to break the ground and turn an Earth-like world into a new colony. They were mistreated and generally regarded with suspicion by the settlers who had paid their way, or even signed contracts with the Development Corporation. They had no stake at all in their new homeworld.

"I see," he said, finally. "And what is the political situation now?"

McDonald laughed, humourlessly. "The Empire put in a Governor after the ADC collapsed, and took direct control of the planet," he said. "There's a planetary council that basically does whatever the Governor tells it to do, although that may have changed. There's a simmering insurgency in the backcountry. Many of the planet's independent farmers pay as little lip service to Camelot as they can get away with. The Civil Guard cannot be trusted to do anything other than fill its pockets with bribes. The planet itself is still in debt and has little hope of ever climbing out of the trap."

Edward frowned. "Why can't they pay the Empire off?"

"The ADC had a grand plan to turn Avalon into a core world for the sector," McDonald explained. "They built a cloud-scoop for the gas giant years ahead of its market. The scoop now has to be maintained, according to Imperial Law, but it doesn't pay for itself. They barely get a handful of ships each year. Oh, it might have changed…"

"It *might* have changed?"

"I left the planet twenty-one years ago," McDonald admitted.

Edward had to admit that he had a point.

"My family…my family are all dead. All of my knowledge is twenty-one years out of date."

Edward stroked his chin, feeling the first hints of stubble. "I see," he said, coming to a decision. "You're welcome to transfer. Report back to Sergeant Patterson and tell her that you're…assigned to Second Platoon, at least until we run through the first training exercises. If you fit in with them, I see no reason why your transfer shouldn't be made permanent."

"Thank you, sir," McDonald said.

"Don't thank me yet," Edward said. He smiled, thinly. "I intend to pick your brains of everything you know about your former homeworld. If we're going to be assigned there, I want to know everything about it before we get there."

"Yes, sir," McDonald said. "Sir…just what does the Commandant expect us to do on Avalon?"

Any other service wouldn't have tolerated such a question, but the Marines were different. "He expects us to do our duty," Edward said, seriously. "We are ordered to deal with pirates, insurgents, and all other threats to the Empire. Who knows where that will take us?"

They shared a long look of perfect understanding. "Report to Sergeant Patterson," Edward ordered. "She will see to your induction."

"Yes, sir," McDonald said. "And thank you."

Edward smiled as the hatch closed behind the Rifleman. Finding McDonald was a stroke of luck. Avalon wouldn't have changed that much since he'd left his homeworld, not a stage-two colony world. They rarely changed quickly, unless something happened to overthrow the balance. And they always had opportunities, if one were quick to seize them. He checked his timepiece and stood up, snatching his jacket and pulling it over his shirt. There was just time for some exercise in the training bay before he returned to Earth.

CHAPTER SEVEN

It is impossible to exaggerate the levels of corruption present at all levels within the Empire. Senators routinely accept bribes from contractors; civil servants frequently steal or 'mislay' vital supplies for their own purposes; military officers cheat their men of their wages, or vital training hours…it is a problem so deeply rooted within the Empire that it may be impossible to even begin to eradicate it. And yet, just by existing, corruption breeds corruption; juniors see their seniors feeding from the trough and wonder…why can't they do the same? The answer is, always, that they can.
- Professor Leo Caesius, *The Waning Years of Empire* (banned).

Jasmine followed Lieutenant Howell out of the aircar and down onto the steps in front of the Supply Corps headquarters. She wasn't particularly surprised to see that the Supply Corps had built themselves a massive and elaborate building, almost a palace among the duller buildings belonging to other sections of the armed forces. The pair of Civil Guardsmen on duty took one look at the two Marines and winced. The Marines, wearing full battle dress and carrying their assault rifles slung over their shoulders, were hellishly intimidating.

She painted a dispassionate expression on her face and smiled inwardly. If the terrorists and rebels the Marines had to actually fight were so easily intimidated, the Empire would have been in a much better state. It still surprised her to realise that some parts of the armed forces were actually scared of loaded weapons, even though everyone who wore the Emperor's uniform was supposed to have at least basic training in using weapons. Perhaps it was a holdover from the Civil Guardsmen, who were routinely cheated of their training by their superiors, who hated doing the paperwork. The Marines and the Imperial Army, by contrast, fired off more rounds in training than they did in combat.

Howell didn't look back at her to check that she was following him; he just marched over to the first guard, who looked as if he would rather be someplace else. Jasmine could understand that impulse; she was meant to be training with the rest of Second Platoon and she would have been, if she hadn't been put on punishment duty. Among the Marines, even punishment duty was meant to educate. She'd need that experience if she ever made Lieutenant or Sergeant herself.

"I am Lieutenant Howell," Howell informed the guard, in a tone that almost broke Jasmine's stony face. The imperious tone made her want to break out into giggles. "I have an appointment with Commander Winslow. You will provide escort to his office."

The guard blinked at him. "Sir, I am under strict instructions to have every visitor to this building passed through security first," he said, owlishly. "I'm afraid I must ask you to wait."

Howell met his eyes, wiping the smile from his face. "And I have strict orders from the Grand Senate itself to ensure that the…irregularities and delays in supplying my unit are cleared up as soon as possible," he said, firmly. "I suggest that you put your concerns aside and escort us to the Commander. What possible harm could we do escorted by your fine self?"

Jasmine didn't, quite, snigger, but the guard looked at her nervously. If she couldn't take him bare naked with one hand tied behind her back, she should be dishonourably discharged from the Marine Corps. A Marine on guard duty would have refused to quail and insisted that they went through a full security check, secure in the knowledge that his superiors would back him up if necessary. The refusal to allow entry would have been backed up with deadly force if it were required. The Civil Guard, on the other hand, would happily hang a mere guard out to dry if the Grand Senate chose to be displeased. Such a low-ranking guard had no protection against his superiors, or their impossible orders.

"I'll have to ask you to check your weapons at the guardhouse," he said, giving in as gracefully as he could. "We don't allow weapons inside the building."

"Yes, I suppose it would be irritating if outraged officers and men attacked the Supply Officers," Howell said, dryly. "We're responsible for the weapons and my superiors would not be happy if I left them in someone else's care."

The guard gave in. "Yes, sir," he said, nodding to his comrade. "I'll escort you to the Commander at once."

Jasmine smirked inwardly as they were escorted into the building. It could have easily passed for a brothel or even a manor house, owned by a rich or well-connected family. The walls were decorated with paintings and artworks, while the carpeting was so lush and warm that she almost wanted to take off her boots and start padding. Hundreds of men and women, wearing the distinctive uniform of the Supply Corps, stared at the two Marines and scattered, like birds suddenly confronted by a hungry cat. It wasn't the normal reaction at all.

The Supply Corps, or so she'd been briefed, had been set up to harmonise the logistics of the different armed forces. Howell had explained that, in theory, the idea had looked good. In practice, the results had been disastrous for all of the armed forces, leaving them desperately scrabbling for supplies. The attempts to improve the logistics system had caused bottlenecks and shortages at the worst possible times, with the bureaucrats in the Supply Corps demanding paperwork in triplicate before granting any requests. The armed forces had responded by setting up duplicate offices and trying to limit what they requested from the official service, but it hampered their operations and created more opportunities for graft and corruption. She had never seen a thin supply officer.

Howell had told her that it was worse out on the frontier, away from Earth. Supply Officers had a habit of selling off military supplies to pad out their wages, often leaving the soldiers and spacers in desperate trouble. The terrorists the Marines fought might well have purchased their weapons from one of the supply officers, or perhaps they'd been passed down a long chain, while the Marines and Civil Guards had to beg for supplies. She had asked why the officers were never arrested and Howell had explained that they often had friends among the Military Police, although it wasn't uncommon for supply officers to suffer accidents. There were dark rumours of how some corrupt officers had met their ends. Exactly how one of them could have committed suicide with his hands tied behind his back was beyond her imagination, suggesting a whitewash. There were limits to what the rest of the armed forces would tolerate.

Commander Winslow's office was just what she had expected. It was twice the size of a Marine Berthing Compartment, decorated in a gaudy style that shocked what remained of her ingrained social conservatism. Pictures of naked women were scattered all over the walls, some of them suggesting perversions that made her feel uncomfortable, others pure vanilla. Commander Winslow himself was short, bald and fishy-looking, eyeing the two Marines as if he expected them to shoot him on sight. No innocent man, even one who believed everything the Pacifist League said about Marines, could have looked so guilty.

"Commander Winslow, sir," the guard said, and made his escape.

"You don't have an appointment," Winslow said. He had a nasal voice that reminded Jasmine of how her little brother had used to whine when he couldn't get something he wanted. "You should have confirmed your appointment with my secretary…"

"I attempted to make an appointment two days ago," Howell said, taking a seat and crossing his legs in a deliberately nonchalant manner. "Your mistress" – Winslow jumped and tried to look as if he hadn't – "was most unhelpful. The earliest appointment she could give me to see you was two weeks from today, which would have been…tricky. We are meant to be leaving this planet in three days. My commanding officer was most upset."

"I can't help you," Winslow protested. "The system has to be respected. I'm sure that your commanding officer will understand."

"He was not very understanding about my failure," Howell said, touching a scar on his cheek. Jasmine, who knew perfectly well that Howell had been scarred two years ago during hand-to-hand fighting with a terrorist, had to fight to hide a smile. The thought of Captain Stalker cutting Howell as punishment was absurd. "My punishment was quite…harsh."

Winslow looked as if he were going to be sick. "I wish I could help you, but I really need the paperwork," he said. He waved a hand at his empty desk. "This is a very busy time and we're working overtime to fill countless requests from hundreds of different units that are about to depart Earth, or start intensive training cycles or…"

Howell slapped the desk, hard enough to sound like a shot. "My commanding officer's next act was to consult with the Grand Senate, who ordered that his unit be deployed to Avalon as soon as possible," he said, as Winslow jumped again. "The Grand Senate was not happy. They want us off the planet yesterday."

"Then go," Winslow said. His voice betrayed his fear. "Half of your requests…they're hardly necessary."

"I'm very much afraid that they are," Howell said, firmly. There was no give in his voice at all. "I would hate to have to go back to the Grand Senate and explain that the reason we couldn't depart on schedule was because the Supply Corps was throwing up barriers. I don't think that even your career would survive their displeasure."

"But…you've requisitioned billions of credits worth of supplies," Winslow protested. "How am I supposed to account for them all?"

Howell smiled. "You're supposed to do your duty and supply them to the officers who need them," he explained, as if he were talking to a child. "I, not you, am responsible for justifying them. You are responsible for supplying them if possible…and I know that you have the items I have requested in storage. I want all of the red tape cut out and the items transferred to the *Sebastian Cruz* today."

"Safety regulations prohibit transferring so many dangerous items within such a short space of time," Winslow said, quickly. "We don't have the manpower on hand…"

"Hire it from the orbital industrial nodes," Howell said, sharply. "Let me worry about the safety. Your job is to make the funds available for their services. Once the pallets are onboard the transport, we can handle the rest."

"But…all these supplies," Winslow said, despairingly. "Fusion generators, portable fabricators, advanced machine tools, databases of colonial production systems and so much else. Why do you even need advanced machine tools?"

"We are going to be operating a long way from any base that can repair our equipment," Howell explained, dryly. "Setting up a local production plant will only improve our logistics and, in the long run, save money. I would have thought that you would be in favour of it."

"With everything you're taking, you could set up a starship manufacturing plant in a few years," Winslow said.

Jasmine blinked in surprise. She hadn't realised that that was even possible. Normally, it was at least three hundred years before a colony world started producing its own starships. Only a handful of new colonies, carefully planned by wealthy and independent foundations, developed an Empire-grade industrial plant within the first fifty years.

"This is going to ruin my budget!"

"It will ruin your career if you don't provide them now," Howell warned. "The Grand Senate will be displeased. My commander will give them me as a scapegoat. I'll give them you. You won't be able to pass the buck to anyone else. It needs your signature, and your signature alone. I suggest that you get on with it."

Winslow looked almost as if he were on the verge of fainting. The sudden menace in Howell's voice was unmistakable. His eyes slipped to Jasmine's face, ran over her uniform and weapons and then fell to the floor. He didn't see her as a woman, but a deadly threat. She was almost insulted. Winslow was probably used to women who would be happy to do whatever he wanted, as long as he saw to their promotions. A woman who could actually look after herself would be alien to him.

"I'll make it happen," he promised, finally. He pulled a datapad out of a drawer and pressed his thumb against the scanner. "You'll have the relevant permissions in an hour."

"Good," Howell said, leaning back in his chair. His voice hardened suddenly. "Because I promise you that I won't be coming back again, Commander. I shall merely allow events to take their course, leaving us stranded here and you with the blame. I would hate to be in your shoes when the Grand Senate catches up with you. You'll spend the rest of your life on a planet where back-breaking labour is the only way to survive."

He stood up and saluted. "Thank you for your time," he said. "We can find our own way out."

Jasmine followed him down the stairs, past the guardhouse and back to the aircar. She didn't dare speak aloud until they were back in the air, heading back to the Barracks. The Supply Corps might have surveillance devices scattered everywhere, just to record everything that was going on in their building. Or perhaps she was just being paranoid. No one in their right mind would want a record of everything that took place in there. It might be used against them at their trial.

"Sir," she said, slowly. Marines were encouraged to ask questions outside of combat, yet she wasn't sure that she knew what question to ask. "Why was he so reluctant to give us anything?"

Howell snorted, staring down at the city below. A mass of protesters were marching along one of the main streets, demanding…something. She couldn't read the banners from high above, but it didn't look pleasant. The Civil Guard were working overtime to move in reinforcements from around the planet. The Marines wouldn't be called in to handle crowd control, thankfully.

"Winslow is a petty little man who thinks his main priority is to build an empire of his own," he said, finally. "He thinks that possessing an item gives him power over it. He's forgotten that the ultimate purpose of the Supply Corps is to make sure that the armed forces get the weapons they need. If he gave them the weapons, he wouldn't have them any longer, would he?"

Jasmine blinked in disbelief. "I don't understand," she admitted. "Why would he care?"

"Think about it," Howell said. "A Marine Company is supposed to have at least two hundred MAG-74 assault rifles, with at least five hundred thousand standard rounds. If those rounds are actually fired off… well, the Company wouldn't have five hundred thousand rounds any more. Winslow and those who think like him believe that the sole purpose of having the inventory is to have the inventory. They are reluctant to use their weapons because that would lower what they have in their inventory."

"Madness," Jasmine said, finally. "They're insane."

"It makes perfect sense, from their point of view," Howell pointed out. "An inspection might show that their inventory wasn't complete, which would mean an investigation, perhaps even career death. In order to protect their careers, they delay as long as they can before sending out anything we might requisition."

"But they could just order a new batch of supplies," Jasmine said. "Or…would that cost them money?"

"Of course," Howell said. "They don't want to look as if they've recklessly spent their department's budget, do they? Think what their political enemies would have made of it. I bet you that by the time we return to Earth, Winslow and his friends will have been purged because they handed over billions of credits worth of equipment to us. The internal auditors will hold them to account for it."

"But we requested the supplies," Jasmine said. "They can't blame Winslow for that."

"You'll be amazed how logical illogical thinking sounds when it's done by a committee," Howell said, lightly. "The more divorced from practical reality any given theory is, the greater its fascination for those who are also divorced from reality."

He smiled as the aircar came down to rest near the Barracks. "Anyway, time to get back to work," he said. "I want you to report to the shuttles in twenty minutes. We need to start supervising the loading before someone manages to mess it all up."

The next four hours passed slowly, but Jasmine barely noticed. A Marine Transport Ship was designed to allow pallets to be slotted in easily, yet they all had to be carefully logged and tracked so that supplies could be pulled out in transit if necessary. It never failed to amaze her just how much could be crammed into a single hull…and how tiny their requirements were compared to the vast stockpile built up in the Sol System. Winslow had had nothing to complain about, really; the Supply Corps had enough supplies stored in the Sol System alone to keep the Imperial Army operating for years. She was tired beyond measure when the loading was finally completed, thinking of her bunk and a long rest before she returned to the training ground. Everyone would be ahead of her.

She walked down to the shuttle hatch and stopped, staring out of a viewport towards Earth. Humanity's homeworld had once been green and blue, but now it was a mixture of blue and a muddle brown colour. The lights of the massive mega-cities could be seen from orbit, lighting up the sky. Humanity's homeworld was dying, killed by the race it had spawned. Jasmine's homeworld, for all of its faults, was kinder than Earth, where there were places no one sane dared venture without a suit of heavy armour.

And yet, somehow, the sight left her with a lump in her throat. No one had said so directly, but everyone in the Company had realized that this wasn't going to be a short posting.

She might never set foot on Earth again.

CHAPTER EIGHT

It may seem paradoxical, but despite having mastered faster-than-light spaceflight, it still takes time to send a message from one end of the Empire to the other. Humanity has spread out so far from Earth that it literally takes six months to send a message from Earth to the Rim, leaving planets on the edge of known space barely represented in the Senate. In the absence of FTL communicators, messages have to be transported on starships, while it can take years to reinforce the Imperial Navy detachments on patrol...
- Professor Leo Caesius, *The Waning Years of Empire* (banned).

Edward stood at one end of the tubing facility on the *Sebastian Cruz* and watched dispassionately as his Marines started to enter the compartment. It could be a daunting sight for civilians, but the Marines took it in their stride; they'd been placed in the tubes before, sometimes hundreds of times over the last few years. The compartment held thousands of tubes for Marines, yet only a handful would be required for his men. They would have plenty of room for supplies.

He glanced at one of the tubes, seeing the young teenage girl frozen in the eerie light. Leo's daughter had been terrified of the stasis field, a common reaction. Time might stop within the confines of such a field, but people feared – irrationally – that thought would go on, leaving them frozen like a fly in amber, yet awake and aware. Edward knew from experience that the universe would just seem to blink and they'd be there. Mandy – or perhaps it was Mindy – wouldn't have to experience the boredom inherent in any long voyage under Phase Drive. Edward had a private bet going with himself that her father would seek to enter stasis himself after he realised just how boring the journey was going to be.

It hadn't always been so simple, he knew. Back in the early days of spaceflight, humans had hibernated like rodents and snakes, their body temperatures lowered to the point where they could be safely frozen and preserved over the years. It hadn't always worked. The early mortality rate had shocked him when he'd researched the period in OCS. It made the Slaughterhouse look like one of the safest worlds in the galaxy. The march of science had, thankfully, removed the need to risk so many of his Marines. If the power failed, as it had on many of the early interstellar colony missions, they would just come out of stasis. They might even be able to survive the aftermath of whatever disaster had cut the power.

He looked back towards the girl, and then looked away. Mandy was too young to be attractive. The confidential reports from the Commandant had warned him that both of the girls had been sulking during their stay in the Marine Headquarters, suggesting that they wouldn't adapt well to Avalon. The Professor's wife had been worse; after all, there was no hope of her ever receiving rejuvenation treatments now. They simply didn't exist outside Earth and the Core Worlds. There were treatments that were offered to colonists who were willing to settle specific worlds, but Fiona was simply too old to take one and live. The Professor wasn't going to have a happy married life.

A line of Marines marched past him, pausing long enough to salute. He was pleased to see that they looked calm and composed, rather than the near-panic that most civilians showed when they came face-to-face with the stasis tubes. A claustrophobe would hate them, even just for the handful of seconds that they'd be in the tube and aware that they were in the tube. But then, a claustrophobe would never have made it through Boot Camp, let alone the Slaughterhouse. Edward remembered crawling through tiny passageways, barely wide enough to admit him, and shivered inwardly. The Slaughterhouse more than lived up to its name.

"All present and accounted for," Gwen informed him. Edward nodded, relieved. Being late for muster was a disciplinary offence, but it happened more often than the Marine Corps liked to admit. Marines would go off on leave, find a girl – or a boy, if their tastes ran that way – and lose track of time, aided by alcohol or recreational drugs. When they returned to awareness, they would be horrified to discover that they had overslept and they were late for muster.

"Good," he said, looking over at the Marines. They looked ready for anything, carrying their weapons and survival equipment with them. There was no need for them to be naked or unarmed within the stasis tubes and so they carried their weapons, just in case of trouble. He raised his voice, hearing it echoing all over the compartment. "You may enter your tubes."

The compartment was nothing, but stasis tubes, each one large enough to hold a good-sized Marine and his or her equipment. Jasmine was reminded, helplessly, of early days at the Slaughterhouse, battling through carefully-designed environments that simulated combat all over the Empire. The tubes still seemed sinister to her, even though she had been through stasis before and never felt anything. She had taken part in an insane charge against rebels in the Han System, something that no one in their right mind would have done, yet it was hard to walk up to her tube and key it open.

She caught sight of a frozen girl, barely entering her teens, and smiled inwardly as she stepped into the tube. If a teenage girl could endure it, so could she. The cold air struck her bare skin and she shivered as she checked her weapon and emergency supplies. The real nightmare was the ship suffering a disaster and losing power, leaving them stumbling their way out of their stasis tubes, completely confused and without the slightest idea what was going on. She'd heard of ships that had lost main drive and yet somehow retained the stasis tubes, allowing their crews to be rescued years later, but few of the stories had any basis in fact. If something happened to the *Sebastian Cruz*, they were all going to die without ever knowing what had hit them.

The tube hissed shut and she braced herself as if she were expecting a physical blow. Back on the Slaughterhouse, she had been hit repeatedly in order to teach her how to take a blow, yet this was different. She felt sick, unsure of her ground, almost as if she were on the verge of panic.

She hadn't fallen to panic since she'd entered her teens. Indeed, her self-control had been remarkable, or so she'd been told. There had been no need to enter a stasis tube on her homeworld and even crawling through tight spaces had still had her in control and aware of her surroundings.

"Stasis field activating in three," a voice said. She could hear a thumping sound in her ears and it took her a moment to realise that it was her own heart. How many other Marines, she wondered, were nervously waiting for the moment of stasis? How many others were on the verge of panic? "Two…one…"

The universe blinked…

"Stasis field activated," a crewman said. He had been a Marine before mustering out and transferring to the auxiliary section, taking up a position on the transport ship. The Corps used it as a way of circumventing the restrictions on the Corps' deployable strength, although it had been too long since the crewman had served as a Marine. "Major?"

"Good," Edward said. It still felt odd to be called by a superior rank, even though he understood the practicalities of the situation. On his first deployment, he'd earned a punishment duty for calling his Captain by his actual rank while on board ship. "Check the power systems and then prepare to seal this deck."

He walked down the compartment, glancing into several of the tubes as he moved. His men hung suspended in eerie light, an unearthly shimmer playing over their faces, frozen in a single instant. They wouldn't endure the boredom of the voyage; they'd come out of the tubes on Avalon, feeling as if no time had passed at all. He would have joined them if it had been permitted, but there was too much work for him to do. There was one final tube in the compartment for the Professor, if he chose to use it.

The massive airlock hissed shut as they stepped out of the compartment, leaving the Marines frozen in darkness. He felt the dull clang running through the ship as the docking clamps were released, allowing the transport to start powering up her drives and begin heading out of the system. A pair of Imperial Navy destroyers had been assigned to escort them, although he knew that they wouldn't be remaining at Avalon once they'd tanked up from the orbiting fuel depot. It was a shame, but there were too many other planets that needed starships and Avalon just didn't rate as important. The entire planet and its population wouldn't even be noticed among the massive sea of the Empire.

His communicator buzzed. "Major, this is Captain Yamato," a voice said. "Would you care to watch the departure from the bridge?"

Edward hesitated, and then realised that it might break him out of his funk. "I'm on my way," he said, hearing a dull thrumming beating through the ship as the drives slowly came up to full power. "Thank you, Captain."

The *Sebastian Cruz's* bridge was massive, large enough to serve as a CIC on a battleship, although only a handful of consoles were operated. Edward had been a Lieutenant during the Han Campaign and he'd seen how a transport had served as the headquarters of the Major-General in command of the operation, allowing him to issue overarching orders from high orbit. He'd been chewing tacks at being unable to go down to the surface, but with the planet in open revolt and enemy-crewed starships in the system, he'd been deemed too vital to be risked. He would probably have been happier as a Captain, even when the rebels had started launching nukes towards the Marines and the Imperial Army regiments backing them up.

"Please, take a seat," Yamato invited. He was a tall Japanese-ethnic man, with a quiet air of competence. Ethnic Japanese were rare among the Marines – the legacy of the Third World War had cast a baleful shadow over the Terran Federation, and the Empire – but those who did pass through the Slaughterhouse were renowned for being among the best. "We're just clearing the high orbital defences now."

Earth floated at the centre of the display, surrounded by enough tactical symbols to almost obscure the planet itself. As humanity's homeworld, Earth was the best-protected world in the Empire, surrounded by over a hundred orbital battle stations and thousands of automated orbital weapons platforms. Hundreds of asteroids, space stations and industrial nodes circled the planet, part of an industrial base that was second to none. The Sol System, with massive orbiting factories around all of its planets, hundreds of cloudscoop facilities and a combined population of over seventy billion humans, was the greatest concentration of industrial might in the Empire. It took five of the oldest colony worlds, settled for over seven hundred years each, to amount to Earth's massive industry. The sight of Earth's halo of industrial stations never failed to fill him with pride.

And yet it was limited. The Terran Federation had had an even greater advantage over its enemies and it had never been able to put down the revolts that threatened its very existence. The Empire, which had replaced the Federation at the height of the Age of Unrest, had made deals with most of its opponents, offering them autonomy within a united human Empire. The remaining ones had been ruthlessly crushed. Yet, still, the Empire couldn't hope to hold down all of its worlds if they all rose against it. Leo had been right. The Empire was more dependent than ever on its population's goodwill…and that was increasingly lacking.

"Thank you, Captain," he said, as they passed the final orbital battle station. Earth's defences were probably rated as overkill. In theory, the entire massed might of the Imperial Navy couldn't break through the defences. In practice…Earth hadn't been attacked since the end of the Age of Unrest, at least not directly. Terrorists and independence movements had attempted to launch covert strikes in the past. "It is a spectacular sight."

"It is," Yamato agreed, seriously. He settled back into his command chair as the two escorting destroyers took fore and aft positions in the tiny convoy. Edward was mildly surprised that they hadn't been asked to escort some freighters as well, but perhaps it was understandable. There was no direct traffic between Earth and Avalon. "It is the safest world in the galaxy."

There was no detectable irony in his voice. Edward had grown up on Earth. Unlike Leo, he'd been aware from a very early age just how thin the veneer of civilisation was over the planet, no matter what the Empire spent on welfare. Millions of people left Earth every year, willingly or unwillingly, yet it was nothing more than a drop in the bucket. He knew how block gangs could hold thousands of people to ransom, or how terrorist cults could pop up, carry out their merry slaughter and vanish again, or how the services could sometimes cut off for hours or days on end. For someone born in the Undercity, Avalon would be paradise itself. Somehow, Edward doubted that they would appreciate it.

"Depends where you live," he said, finally. He'd signed up for the Marines on his eighteenth birthday and never looked back. "How long until we cross the Phase Limit?"

Yamato made a show of checking his timepiece. "Nine hours," he said. "You are welcome to stay and observe, if you wish."

Early human experiments into faster-than-light travel had all failed, without exception. It had taken years of experimenting before the human race realised that it was simply impossible to generate a phase field inside a star's gravity well, no matter how much power was applied by the engineers. The first phase ships had triggered their drives light months from Sol; now, with advanced gravimetric sensors, it was possible to locate the precise moment when it was possible to leap into Phase Space. It had opened up the stars to human settlement.

"Thank you," Edward said, "but I have paperwork to be getting on with. I'll watch it from the observation blister."

Nine hours later, he stepped into the observation blister and was surprised to see Leo standing there, staring out into the darkness of space, lit only by the unblinking glow of a thousand stars. Sol itself, the star that had illuminated Earth since before the human race first crawled out of the sea, was little more than yet another point of light, perhaps slightly brighter than most.

"Major," Leo said, in greeting. "I just wanted to see the transition for the first time."

"It's really something," Edward agreed. Despite himself, he liked the crusty young-old academic. The man didn't deserve what had happened to him. "Take a seat and brace yourself."

The psychologists had insisted that every starship had to have some form of observation blister, even the ones that never went outside their home system. Edward had little time for headshrinkers – it was his experience that no civilian headshrinker really understood the military – but he had to admit that they probably had a point. Having a viewport out into the outside universe was good for morale. On the bigger ships, there was even a strictly regular schedule for spending an hour or so gazing out at the stars. When starships were flying in convoy, it was possible to see them all and even wave to observers in their blisters.

"Here we go," he said. "Brace for impact…"

The stars seemed to leap forward, suddenly becoming agonisingly bright, just before the blister went brilliant white. The light faded – in a sense, it had never been there – revealing a tunnel of light, seemingly speeding away into the distance. It was an optical illusion more than anything else, or so Edward had been told, but it was still spectacular. He peered forward into the shimmering light, trying to make out the shapes of the two destroyers, but they were hidden somewhere in the glare.

"My God," Leo said. He sounded shaken. "We just cracked the light barrier."

"Yep," Edward said, happily. "Next stop; Avalon."

Leo nodded, pulling himself to his feet. "As I understand it, there is no way that we can get a message back to Earth now," he said. "Is that correct?"

Edward blinked, but nodded. "Not until we get to Avalon and send a message back with a starship," he confirmed. "Why do you ask?"

"I was told to wait until we were out of contact before speaking to you," Leo said. He dug through his pockets and produced a golden cross. "The Commandant wanted me to give this to you once you were beyond recall."

Edward took it and stared down at it, puzzled. It was a simple golden Christian cross, nothing else. It meant nothing to him. His religion was the Marine Corps. He'd never been raised to follow any particular religious belief. The cross felt light, almost fragile, in his hand, yet he was perversely sure that it would be very hard to destroy.

"Thank you, I guess," he said. "Did he say why?"

Leo reached for the cross and turned it over, pointing to a tiny indent at the bottom. "See?"

"I see," Edward said. The cross held a cunningly-disguised code key. An encrypted message, coded by a given algorithm would be impossible for anyone else to decrypt. They were illegal outside the government and military and, even for a Marine Captain, possessing one would raise questions. Very uncomfortable questions. "Why…?"

"He said that he might be in touch," Leo said. He keyed the hatch and it hissed open. "Good luck, Major."

CHAPTER NINE

With only a handful of exceptions, the majority of colony worlds established during the Fourth Expansion Period were intended as profit-making enterprises. The founding company (Development Corporation) intended to use its position to permanently milk the colonists for profit, even though this was not always particularly onerous. However, as the Empire's financial problems worsened, the various development corporations have found themselves forced to squeeze their vassals harder, setting off a chain of decline. The results have not been pleasant.

- Professor Leo Caesius, *The Waning Years of Empire* (banned).

The seven helicopters roared out of the morning sunlight, sinking rapidly towards the small township in the distance. Four of them broke off and established a patrol pattern around the town; the other three continued to descend, the crews rapidly lowering lines towards the ground. A number of black-suited figures rapidly rappelled down towards the ground, scrambling down in fear of hostile gunfire. A transport helicopter was never so vulnerable as when it was unloading troops. No incoming fire disturbed the morning and the troops breathed a sigh of relief.

Major George Grosskopf breathed in the morning air as his close-protection detail spread out around him. The small township might look quiet and innocent, but an experienced eye could tell that that was deceptive. Kirkhaven Township had only been established five years ago and the inhabitants had barely succeeded in taming the surrounding area and farming the land. The entire town should have been alive with people

– men going to the farms, children laughing as they headed to school – and their absence was indicative of trouble. The whole area was quiet.

It's too quiet, he thought, as the two companies of Civil Guardsmen spread out further, walking towards the town with weapons raised and ready. The local Police Constable – a fancy name for a man who was effectively a part-time representative of law and order – had missed his daily call and no amount of effort by Camelot had succeeded in raising anyone else from the town. Avalon's planetary communications network was primitive – it would have been a laughing stock on any other stage-two colony world – but the man had been careful to always place his call. The sudden silence suggested that someone had attacked the town. So close to the badlands, it was far too easy to guess just who had attacked – and why.

"I'm getting live feed from the drones now," Captain Yale said. Unlike George, he wasn't former military; he'd spent his entire career in the Civil Guard. It hadn't prepared him for action so far from Camelot and civilisation, such as it was on Avalon. Like far too many of the other recruits, he'd joined up on the promise of three square meals a day. Still, he'd mastered some of the lingo and showed promise. "They're not picking up anyone within the town."

"Send three platoons in to investigate and warn them not to get complacent," George ordered. Avalon's Civil Guard had never been lavishly equipped, even after local production lines had started to produce homebuilt weapons. The drones were third or fourth-generation military surplus, probably originally owned by a third-rate regiment from the Imperial Army. Their sensors were hardly modern mil-grade systems. "The enemy could have left a trap in place to hurt us when we arrived."

The Guardsmen didn't need telling twice. They were all veterans of the simmering war that was being fought out for Avalon's future and, even though they lacked proper training, they had learned from experience. They slipped into the village, keeping well away from anything that could serve as a trap or hide an improvised explosive device. The rebels, bandits and terrorists who hid out in the badlands had set up their own production plants, converting an astonishing variety of civilian produce into weapons and explosives. The Civil Guard could barely keep a lid on the violence. Indeed, although the Governor would never admit it, several provinces were effectively under the control of the enemy.

George followed his men as they checked out the various domiciles, wincing inwardly at the frail shacks many of the town's populace had had to use. There was no shortage of wood or stone near the town, but apart from the early settlers, few of the town's population had proper homes. He saw a wooden barracks block in the distance and scowled. It was a fitting irony that the indents, the town's local work gang of imported criminals from Earth, had better accommodation than most of the free population. The indents themselves had probably not appreciated it. They'd all been minor criminals from Earth and they'd never worked a day of hard labour in their lives until they reached Avalon. Revolts and small mutinies were not uncommon.

But the township had been improving, he told himself, as they finally found a row of new-built homes. They'd been built from stone, suggesting that the locals had finally started to mine for stone and use it to improve their lot. The official policy of the local government was to force the new settlers to become as self-sufficient as possible, even though it meant many of them suffering until they built proper homes and learned to till the fields, a policy that long history encouraged. It didn't make it any easier to watch generations of settlers making the same mistakes time and time again.

He cursed under his breath at the thought. There were times when George wondered if the Crackers had a point; after all, it would be fairly simple to assist the colonists to prevent them from making the same old mistakes. He caught sight of a simple wooden church and smiled inwardly. The influence of the Reformed Church of Christ the Pacifist, which had purchased ten percent of the original ADC stock, had ensured that their priests always had good homes. It was official policy.

George had been on Avalon – and a hundred other worlds before it – long enough to know just how badly life was screwed up on the frontier, courtesy of people back on Earth or the Core Worlds who didn't have the slightest idea of what life was really like. The Cracker Rebellion would never have happened if the ADC had treated the settlers as anything other than human cattle, while the ongoing simmering war could be brought to an end if the Governor had made some basic concessions to the rebels. The vast majority of the Crackers, at least, would be happy if the more idiotic regulations were withdrawn and the planetary government became more accountable to the population. It wasn't going to happen. Over a century of mismanagement, first by the ADC and then by the Empire, had seen to that. It was easy to be cynical.

"Major," Sergeant Evens called. He was one of the few Guardsmen who, like George himself, had some military experience. George kept a sharp eye out for new settlers with military experience and tried to convince them to join the Civil Guard. The locals were either enthusiastic but inexperienced, or corrupt. "You need to come and look at this now."

The warehouse sat on one edge of the town, a testament to the power of political lobbies back at Camelot. Every township was supposed to send a certain level of foodstuffs back to the main cities, yet it would be years before Kirkhaven started to produce enough food to pay the tax. It hadn't mattered. The warehouse had been built – of modern materials, naturally – and left empty until it was time to start filling it with supplies. The town's council had petitioned to be allowed to use it for other affairs, but the planetary government had refused. It was their warehouse and that was the end of it. No one in power cared what a bunch of hicks near the badlands thought. George strode towards it, suddenly aware of an unpleasant smell drifting towards his nostrils, and shuddered. The smell was becoming alarmingly familiar.

"Here," Evens said. He was a short man with an air of calm competence. He'd been in the Imperial Army for just over seven years before being discharged without cause, at least according to his service record. George had kept a sharp eye on him, just in case he'd been discharged for a criminal offence, but over the years he had relaxed his vigil. Evens had given him no grounds for suspicion. "Look what they did, sir."

It was dark inside the warehouse – the lighting elements seemed to have failed – but the Guardsmen had brought torches with them. George unhooked his from his belt and shone it ahead of him, recoiling at the sight. The town's missing population lay in front of him, piled on top of one another, their hands bound tightly behind their backs and their throats slit. Blood had poured down, pooling on the ceramic floor, washing against the waterproof walls. He fought down the urge to vomit – the younger inexperienced Guardsmen were throwing up helplessly – and staggered backwards. Whoever had done that, he vowed, would pay. If – when – they were caught, they would discover the true meaning of hate.

"Organise a work party," he ordered. His voice sounded strange to his ears. "No; organise two work parties. One to get the bodies out and into the light; the other is to start digging graves in the fallow field. Get to it now!"

His men, stung by his tone, started to work. It took nearly an hour to get the bodies out and place them in the open, but it didn't take that long to realise that only half of the town's population had been murdered and abandoned. The township had– officially – a population of over seven hundred souls. There were only three hundred and seventeen bodies in the warehouse. Most of them were male. There were no children and only a handful of women.

"Around three hundred and fifty people completely unaccounted for," Sergeant Evens reported. His terminal contained a complete database of the town's population – at least, a complete database of those who had registered with the government. George knew, as well as anyone else, that there were thousands of people who had simply dropped off the system, or had never been on it in the first place. "Two hundred and seventy of them are young women between the ages of sixteen and forty. Forty of them are male indents. The remainder are young children, born to the townspeople or brought in with their parents. There may well be more children who were never registered."

George scowled bitterly. Avalon had had rare promise when the first settlers started to land, lured by the ADC's promises of cheap land and shares in the growing system economy. If the ADC hadn't run into stormy economic waters, it might even have kept its promises, but instead it had been reduced to trying to extract as much from its settlers as possible. Debts that should have been paid off within ten years had been extended and passed on from father to son. Children had been born, registered with the government and discovered that they were heirs to a growing debt. The unregistered children suffered no such handicap. God alone knew how many free settlements there were out in the badlands, or simply miles from any official settlement. As they grew up, they knew that they would be cheated, that they would be slaves forever...why the hell should they not rebel? The only thing that kept most of the townships and settlers in line was the threat of overwhelming force.

The irony might almost have been amusing, under other circumstances. If the settlers had registered their children, the Civil Guard would have known who to look for, but instead they'd never know if they'd recovered all the children or not. The bandits would probably bring them up as bandits themselves, or sell the children into slavery themselves. The missing indents suggested that the bandits had been former indents too, rather than Crackers. They'd probably attacked the town, freed their fellows and slaughtered the population.

"Start putting them in the grave," he said. The settlers deserved better than a mass grave where they had once placed their hopes and fears, but there was nothing else he could do for them. A more developed world would have summoned a forensic team, but there was no point on Avalon. Cataloguing the full depths of the atrocity was pointless. "I have to make a report to the Governor."

He headed back towards the helicopters, staring towards the mountains rising up in the distance. They might get lucky. The bandit gangs were hated and feared by the civilian population, unlike the Crackers. The Crackers could count upon a friendly reception almost anywhere. The bandits would be shot at on sight. Who knew – perhaps the Crackers would encounter the bandits and dispose of them. Stranger things had happened.

The radio buzzed with static as he keyed it and began to make his report. Like everything else on Avalon, it was either built in an inferior factory on the planet or imported second-hand from the Empire. George was morally certain that the Crackers, at least, had developed the ability to listen in on their communications, but there was no other alternative. The planet-wide datanet – intended to link all the settlements into a coherent whole – was a joke. The Crackers, no doubt, had infiltrated that too.

Two hundred miles to the south, Governor Brent Roeder stood in his office, looking down towards the blue ocean and the harbour that the early colonists had constructed. The ADC's original plans for settling Avalon had placed a high priority on developing a maritime transport network, linking the three continents together without having to import much in the way of heavy lifting craft from outside the system. It hadn't worked out as well as they'd hoped – settlement on the other two continents had barely begun – but he had to admit that sailing was one of the few perks of living on Avalon. Local fishermen had been quick to start building sailing boats and setting off to challenge the waves; Brent himself had even learned to love sailing on a natural boat, so different from a starship or a shuttle. It almost made up for his posting.

Avalon's exact political state was a mess, thanks to his two predecessors. Not a day went by when Brent didn't curse them in seven different languages, for whatever lofty ambitions they had, they had never realised just how fragile the entire planet actually was. The first Governor – appointed after the ADC had lost control of the planet, after the Cracker Rebellion – had tried to crack down hard on the semi-independent settlements, including banning the private ownership of guns.

He had been – quite reasonably – concerned about another rebellion, but the settlers had simply ignored the order. The wild animals that roamed the interior of the continent thought of humanity as just another species of game. No one in their right mind wanted to come face-to-face with a Gnasher armed only with a knife. The Civil Guard had completely failed to carry out his orders. The second Governor had been worse. He'd tried to make political concessions and had managed to create a Planetary Council, without ever considering the implications. The settlers had known all along that the game was rigged. The second Governor had rubbed their noses in it. The results had not been pleasant.

He stared down at Camelot, keeping his expression dispassionate. Camelot would have vanished without trace in one of Earth's teeming mega-cities. The core of the city had been laid down according to a plan drawn up by a soulless machine – it was far too neat and tidy – while the remainder of the city had just grown up around it, like a pearl forming around a grain of sand. The city, though, was hardly a pearl. There were areas that were almost respectable and areas that the Civil Guard wouldn't go without heavy armed backup.

Brent took a final look at the city and turned back to face his Deputy. "George won't be back until tomorrow," he said, with a hint of quiet pleasure. Major Grosskopf took his duties seriously, too seriously. He wanted to wipe out the rebels, yet mounting such a campaign would be far beyond Avalon's limited resources. He'd placed a request at the Sector Capital for additional regiments from the Imperial Army, but nothing had been promised or delivered. "That leaves us with an important question. What do we do about the bandits?"

Deputy Governor Linda MacDonald leaned forward. A tall blonde with impressive breasts, Brent had never really understood why she hadn't been offered the post of Governor, although he could make a few guesses. He'd been given Avalon as a reward for over sixty years of dedicated service in the Imperial Civil Service; Linda, as a native daughter of Avalon, would be unacceptable to the ICS as a Governor, although she could be transferred to another world if she wished to rise higher.

"They're indents, of course," Linda said. Her voice was low and husky. If Brent had been a few years younger, he would have tried to court her. She wouldn't have been interested in a small dumpy bureaucrat, though. "We should send the Civil Guard after them."

"I wish it were that easy," Brent said. "Most of those indents should never have been sent here in the first place."

He scowled. Earth's solution to its population problem was to deport everyone convicted of even a minor crime. Most of the indents who were transported to Avalon found themselves working in the fields in chain gangs, hated and feared by the people they were supposed to be helping. The Crackers made much political capital out of indent gangs and the crimes they committed against innocent settlers. The endless flood of new criminals was yet another factor in the growing civil unrest.

"We cannot let this pass," Linda said, flatly. She was too young for a post like Deputy Governor, Brent decided. She just didn't understand the problems involved in sending the Civil Guard on a wild-goose chase. "We have to act…"

There was a knock at the door. "Governor, I'm sorry to interrupt, but we just received a message from Orbit Station," his secretary said. Abigail had been with him for years and he trusted her judgement and discretion implicitly. "A Marine Transport Ship and two destroyers have just entered the system."

CHAPTER TEN

> Although the Empire likes to claim that planetary development corporations are free to operate without supervision or obligation to the Empire, that is actually very far from the truth. Every settled planet, for example, must build – out of its own pocket – an Orbital Transhipment Station and a spaceport - and maintain a fleet of shuttles for swift and efficient transfer of materials from orbit to ground, or vice versa. More advanced colony worlds – stage-three or higher – are generally encouraged to build a cloudscoop and maintain a stockpile of starship fuel for the Imperial Navy. To put all of this in context, an orbital station alone costs twenty billion credits, a significant chunk of any development corporation's budget. That has to be repaid by the settlers.
> - Professor Leo Caesius, *The Waning Years of Empire* (banned).

The tunnel of light suddenly faded into darkness, a darkness so complete that Edward felt his soul crying out in agony. He stared into the darkened viewport and was unable to withhold a sigh of relief as the stars started to twinkle back into existence. Six months of flight, six months with only a handful of crewmen and Leo for company, were almost over. He couldn't wait to get down to the planet.

"All hands, this is the Captain," Yamato's voice said, echoing over the ship's intercom. "We have returned to normal space. Prepare for heavy acceleration. I say again; prepare for heavy acceleration."

Edward looked over at Leo as the background noise slowly started to rise. Avalon itself lay five light minutes from the local primary, four and a half hours from the Phase Limit. Any system in the Core Worlds would have had a handful of destroyers lurking along the Phase Limit, watching for pirates or starships that had suffered catastrophic drive failure, but Avalon had no ships capable of maintaining its security. It didn't even have powerful sensor arrays that would provide warning of a new arrival. It would be almost laughably easy for any pirate ship to slip up to the planet and open fire.

I guess that's one advantage of being dirt poor, he thought, sourly. Avalon's development corporation had been wealthy, but the planet itself had very little that could be picked up and carried away. Pirates might try to raid the system's deep-space facilities, such as they were, but there was little point in raiding the planet itself. The only thing they could reasonably take from the planet was people. It wasn't unknown, yet the records suggested that no such raid had been mounted against Avalon.

Leo looked up at him, his face pale and wan in the starlight. They'd become friends, of a sort, during the six months of enforced company. Edward had introduced Leo to Kipling – the Marine Corps' favourite poet – and, in exchange, Leo had given Edward a copy of his banned book. Edward had read it over a few nights and had understood just why it had been banned. It was political, social and religious dynamite. The Empire's Grand Senate would not have enjoyed reading about how they were destroying the Empire.

"We're here," Leo said. He sounded rather surprised. The boundaries of his world had shrunk to the confines of the Marine Transport Ship, most of which was off-limits to civilians. "Is there any chance of us being attacked by pirates?"

"I rather doubt it," Edward said, dryly. He smiled. He'd been trying to educate Leo about Marines and the realities of combat, but it had been uphill going. Leo knew details about the Marines without understanding what they really meant. Edward privately likened him to an intellectual who had read a few books and privately considered himself an expert. What did the dreaded March of Death, or the Watery Grave, or even the Crucible itself mean to a man who had never experienced anything like them? He had never walked across a desert, carrying a wounded comrade on his back, let alone fought to hold off rebels from sweeping over a spaceport and destroying all hope of rescue. There was a difference in their perspectives that could never be bridged. "Pretend you're a pirate. Would you dare attack a ship full of armed Marines and escorted by two destroyers?"

"No," Leo said, finally.

"Of course not," Edward said. "Most pirates – who are among the worst kind of scum you'll ever meet – don't want to pick on targets that can fight back. They want helpless little merchant ships they can board, loot and capture, or simply scuttle once they've taken whatever they want from the hull. They go for passenger ships for kidnap victims, transport ships for manufactured components and tools and other civilian ships, but going after a military ship isn't healthy for them. Even if they win the battle, and most pirate ships are poorly maintained and armed, they still have to repair their ship. It's just not cost-effective."

"I see," Leo said. "It's just a business, isn't it?"

"Exactly," Edward said. "They want to maximise their gain and minimise their risk." He shrugged. "There's a good chance that we will encounter pirates in this system, sooner or later. The looted supplies have to be sold and planets along the Rim, ones without any kind of manufacturing capability, are ready markets for stolen goods. You take a bunch of megacity dwellers from Earth and put them in a farming town and they'll be desperate for whatever help they can get. They're not going to ask too many questions about where the modern tools or devices came from, are they?"

He grinned. "You're lucky, in a way," he added. "You're going to be going down to a world where most of the hard work has already been done. The pathfinders, the people who start the first settlements on a new world, are the ones who have the hardest tasks. You'll be able to find a place to live, perhaps a teaching position at their local schools…you won't have to indenture yourself to live."

His communicator buzzed before Leo could answer. "Major, please could you come to the bridge," Yamato's voice said. "We're entering the system now."

"On my way," Edward said. He looked over at Leo. "Enjoy the view from out here. We'll probably start untanking people in the next few hours, trying to get organised before we enter orbit and dock with the

Orbit Station. At least we should be able to land without someone shooting at us."

Leo frowned. "Does that happen often?"

"Often enough that this ship is heavily armoured and is designed to get us down to the surface as quickly as possible," Edward admitted. "A landing on a hostile planet can be the most dangerous operation in history. It's not unknown to lose half of the attacking force in the first ninety seconds."

Leaving Leo with that thought, he made his way back to the bridge. The main display caught his eye as soon as he entered, showing almost no sign of any human activity. Earth's system had been buzzing with starships and in-system spacecraft, but Avalon's system was almost empty. A pair of tactical icons on the display marked the presence of two ships – the sensors suggested that they were light freighters – making their way towards the planet, yet there was nothing else. The entire system looked as dark and cold as the grave.

Edward shivered inwardly. It was an illusion, of course. It was simple to hide a starship's drives from passive sensors. The entire First Fleet could be hiding within the system and the transport would have no idea it was there until it was jumped. A starship was tiny on a cosmic scale. A starship that wasn't burning with energy might as well be a rock as far as hostile sensors were concerned. Edward's old CO had told his junior officers about boarding a pirate cruiser that had taken the risk of stepping down its drives to nothing in hopes of avoiding detection. A few minutes either way and they would have gotten away with it.

"We have reached the Avalon System," Yamato informed him. "I have already transmitted our IFF signal to System Command."

"Such as it is in this system," Edward commented. Yamato nodded flatly. A Core System would have a single unified authority controlling operations and authorising everything, with armed starships on call to back it up if necessary. A colony world along the Rim might not even have someone manning the stations in orbit, watching for incoming ships. It wasn't as if they could do anything about it when they appeared. Avalon's ability to interfere with pirate operations in their system was almost non-existent. "I take it that there has been no response?"

"No," Yamato said. "They should have replied at once, but we have not yet received anything, even a simple acknowledgement."

Edward nodded. Gravity pulses could be used to send FTL signals over very short ranges, allowing a limited degree of FTL communications within any given system. A Core System would have relay stations to pick up and repeat the original transmission, preventing it from fading away and being lost in the background gravity field. Avalon had nothing of the sort and probably wouldn't have for hundreds of years. It was quite possible that their response had simply been lost in the background noise. The Empire had poured literally trillions of credits into developing a method to extend FTL communications range over light years, but so far the experiments had all been complete failures.

"Maybe they think we're pirates," he said, dryly. "They couldn't get a good read on us at this distance, could they?"

"No," Yamato said. "I have reviewed the files on their equipment. They barely have standard civilian-grade gear. They may not even be aware of our presence."

Edward frowned. "I see," he said. "I wonder…"

"Captain," one of the naval ratings said, "we have received a response. They are welcoming us to Avalon and request that we make orbit as soon as possible."

"Good," Yamato said. "Helm; take us in."

Edward smiled. "I'm going down to see to my men, with your permission," he said. "Let me know when we enter standard communications range."

"The Marines?" Brent repeated. He wouldn't have been more astonished if an entire squadron of Imperial Navy starships had shown up in the system, escorting a full Imperial Army Division. "Why are the Marines coming here?"

Linda smiled, her white teeth shining in the sunlight. "Perhaps someone read your messages requesting support and decided to dispatch the Marines," she said. "Or perhaps they're just calling for long enough to tank up and then they'll be on their way out again."

Brent ran his hand through his thinning hair. He'd had the standard rejuvenation treatments when he'd joined the Imperial Civil Service, yet somehow his hair felt as if it was on the verge of falling out completely, or going grey. No one had told him about the stresses involved in running a colony world when he'd been offered the post. They'd talked about the great honour the Empire was doing him by giving him so much trust. It hadn't taken him long to start wondering if the only reason he'd been given the job was because no one else wanted it.

"Abigail," he said. "Didn't they tell you *anything*?"

"It was a standard gravity-pulse transmission," Abigail said. She saw his blank look and hastened to explain. "You cannot actually send much information in a gravity pulse, sir. They pushed it right to the limits just to send us as much as they did. We won't know more until they reach radio range and that won't be for several hours yet."

"They wouldn't want to burn out their transmitter," Linda added. She smiled thinly at him, stroking her long golden locks. "We can wait a few hours to learn what they have in mind."

Brent paused. Another nasty thought had occurred to him. "How do we know that these *are* the Marines?"

"They had the right codes," Abigail said. She looked down at the ground for a long moment, her eyes worried. "They could be pirates pretending to be Marines, sir, but I don't see why they would bother."

"Of course," Linda agreed, dryly. "What could we do to stop them if they decided to attack one of the asteroid mining platforms?"

Brent winced at the caustic tone in her voice, for the asteroid mining program was a sore spot between the two of them. The ADC, under the delusion that Avalon had a chance to jump two colony levels in one bound, had invested in a cloudscoop and a large asteroid mining project, bringing in RockRats from across the Empire to set up one of their mining systems. They'd succeeded, just in time for the economy to take a downturn and leave them lumbered with a massive white elephant…which, according to Imperial Law, they had to maintain in perfect working order. The RockRats, at least, could maintain themselves, but they insisted on being paid in cash. There was no trust in the relationship. There was also little point to it. The planned orbital industrial nodes had never materialised. What industry Avalon had had been built on the ground.

But she was right. In theory, Avalon's Civil Guard had three gunboats and a handful of armed shuttles to stand off any threat. In practice, two of the three gunboats had been cannibalised to keep the third operating, while the armed shuttles couldn't even threaten an armed merchantman. A pirate ship could operate with impunity outside of Avalon's gravity well and all the planet's government could do was watch.

"Nothing," he said, wishing that Major Grosskopf had been in Camelot when the Marines announced their arrival. The former Imperial Army officer would have known the difference between real Marines and posers, or even pirates posing as Marines. His advice would have been useful as well. "All we can do is wait and see what happens."

"Yes, sir," Abigail said. "Do you wish me to advise Orbit Station to prepare berths for the Marines?"

"Yes, please," Brent said. Even if the Marines weren't staying, they could show the flag near the badlands, perhaps scare some of the nastier bandit gangs further away into the mountains. "I'll discuss the other matter later."

He watched her sauntering out and smiled, inwardly. Linda would have been horrified if she'd known what the chair she was sitting on had been used for, only a few days ago. Abigail had been his lover as well as his secretary for years. His wife didn't know, as far as he knew, and wouldn't have cared if she had. She hated him for dragging her to Avalon when she thought that she should have been presented at Court. Poor Hannalore had been born into the wrong class and caste.

"We need to focus on the bandits," Linda said, firmly. She waved a sheaf of paper – there were few datapads on Avalon – under his nose. "I have here reports from seventy different townships. Our...operatives report that many of them have been threatened and coerced into providing support to the bandits. How many more will just...give in after the news of the latest attack gets out?"

"Too many," Brent said. "And how many Civil Guardsmen do you intend to tie up on a fruitless bandit-chasing mission?"

"As many as necessary," Linda said, shaking the papers to underline her words. "Or we start issuing heavy weapons to the townships. God knows, they need them."

Brent snorted. "And how many of them will end up being pointed at us?"

"If the bandit gangs, to say nothing of the Crackers, keep pushing at us like this, we'll see their weapons aimed at us within five years," Linda said, sharply. "Fuck the Council, Governor; just do it."

"I think you know better than that," Brent said, coldly. Linda met his eyes and he had to look away. "We cannot just tell the Council that their views don't matter to us."

"Then perhaps we should hold proper elections," Linda retorted. "Who knows? You could hardly end up with a worse problem."

Brent looked down at his hands, and then up at the political map of Avalon. Linda was right, in a sense; his predecessor's stroke of insanity had come home to roost with a vengeance. He'd created the Planetary Council – a development normally held back until a world reached stage three or four – in hopes of preventing another rebellion. Unfortunately for him, the Council was dominated by the conservatives, the wealthy – insofar as that term meant anything on Avalon – and those who owned the debt. They had no interest in changing the planet and every reason to oppose easing the restrictions on arms sales. They knew, beyond a shadow of a doubt, that they were on the Cracker death lists.

"The Council would have to approve that," he reminded her. "I cannot put the Council aside, not now. They'll complain to the Sector Capital and they'll remove me and put someone more pliable in my place. That will be the end of any hope of reform."

Linda sniffed, loudly enough to be clearly audible. "And what hopes would those be?"

Brent scowled at her. The subtext had been easy to read. "Maybe the Marines will stay for a few months," he said, although he knew better than to believe it. Avalon barely rated a mention on the Sector Capital. Who on Earth, outside the Indenture Program, knew about Avalon's existence? "Perhaps we can make progress without the Council."

Linda sniffed again. "Don't count on it," she said. "The bandits aren't going to be scared of a few Marines. The Marines will be gone soon enough and what will happen then?"

She stood up, placed the papers on his desk, and marched out of the room, leaving Brent alone with his thoughts. Slowly, almost against his will, he looked down at the images taken by the Civil Guard, just before they'd buried the dead. Linda was right, he knew; there was no other defence against the bandits. They had to burn them out…but how?

CHAPTER ELEVEN

> It is a – generally – sensible policy on the part of the Empire to ensure that a colony world becomes self-sufficient, at least in foodstuffs, as soon as possible. As a world progresses from stage-zero to stage-one, the first priority is to develop farmland and start growing a healthy crop. The intent is to grow a surplus that can cope with any unexpected demands. The rising population must be fed. This takes priority over everything else, including paying off the massive costs incurred by the development corporation. It is therefore obvious that the local system authorities will seek to cut costs wherever possible.
> - Professor Leo Caesius, *The Waning Years of Empire* (banned).

…And opened its eyes.

Jasmine caught herself, blinking in surprise as the tube started to hiss open. Surely they hadn't been in stasis? She felt absurdly ridiculous as she stepped forward, wondering at why they were being brought out of the tubes again. Her mind caught up a second later and her head swam. Six months had passed in an eyeblink. There had been no sense at all of time passing. The universe had just blinked. A wave of dizziness overcame her and she concentrated on the disciplines, banishing it from her mind and finding her centre. It was just another wonder of the modern galaxy, just something else to take in her stride.

"All right," Gwen bellowed, marching past the tubes. "Everyone out; fall in!"

Jasmine stepped out of the tube, feeling a dull thrumming running through the ship as she stepped onto the deck. The starship was still in transit, but unless she missed her guess, they'd reached their destination and were proceeding toward Avalon at sublight speeds. It was fairly customary to bring the Marines out of the tubes, just in case a pirate decided to be stupid enough to attack them. Jasmine grinned, taking in the expressions of her fellow Marines. They'd be delighted if a pirate ship decided to attack them. Marines, who were often the first people into a ship pirates had wrecked, loathed the bastards on a visceral level. Taking them alive required immense discipline.

The line was forming in front of the tubes and she hastened to find her platoon. Her fellows were rapidly recovering from their own disorientation, snapping into position and saluting the flag hanging listlessly from one corner of the massive compartment. Gwen strode up and down in front of them, her eyes darting over their uniforms and occasionally prompting one of the Marines to fix a tiny problem. Jasmine braced herself as the Command Sergeant's gaze swept over her body and relaxed, just slightly, as Gwen moved on to the next Marine in line. She'd passed inspection.

"Attention on deck," Gwen said, once she'd finished her inspection. "Listen up; we are on approach to Avalon now and will be docking at the orbiting station within two hours. As soon as we dock, we will move to secure the station and ensure that there are no unpleasant surprises waiting for us before we start moving down to the surface. First and Second Platoons will take the lead; the remainder will hang back and be prepared to move in support if necessary. Questions?"

"Yes, Sergeant," Blake said, from his position two Marines down from Jasmine. "Can we not take the shuttles to board the station before the *Cruz* docks?"

Gwen shook her head. "The Captain wants to get us on board the station as soon as possible," she said. Jasmine winced inwardly. There was no reason to suspect that trouble was waiting for them, but she'd been in far too many ambushes when there had been no warning at all before the enemy had opened fire. "He is keen to begin unloading his ship."

"I guess he can't wait to get rid of us," Blake muttered, just loudly enough for a handful of Marines to hear. "You wouldn't see this happening on a perfectly-run ship."

"Doubtless," Gwen said. Jasmine privately suspected that she agreed with Blake. "However…form up in platoons and draw your armour. We dock at the station in two hours."

Jasmine glanced down at her timepiece as it bleeped, updating itself from the starship's master computer. The Imperial Standard date had jumped forward six months, as she had expected, while the time had moved forward three hours. Local time, displayed alongside EST, suggested that Avalon's day was slightly longer than Earth's. She scowled inwardly, bracing herself for the onset of starship lag, before moving forward to join her platoon. There was no time to waste. Combat armour had to be donned, weapons had to be checked and plans of the station had to be studied rapidly.

"Rules of engagement are Beta-Three," Gwen said, when asked. Jasmine nodded in understanding. Beta-Three had been designed to allow the Marines to secure the station without making additional enemies. If the station had been in enemy hands, Jasmine and her fellows would have stunned everyone and sorted out the guilty from the innocent afterwards, but stunning harmless civilians would not endear them to the civilians after they awoke with banging headaches. "Try not to hurt anyone unless you have no other choice."

A commotion disturbed her and she glanced down towards the handful of tubes at the bottom of the compartment. A youngish-looking man – with the attitude of an older man, suggesting that he had had rejuvenation treatments at some point in his life – was hugging a teenage girl, who wasn't enjoying the experience. Jasmine remembered when it had suddenly become embarrassing to be hugged by her own father and felt a silent moment of sympathy, although she wasn't sure who she was feeling sorry for.

The girl's older sister was openly eying some of the Marines, while her mother looked torn between disapproval and fear. She'd probably watched hundreds of reports that had made the Marines out as trained killers, rapists and looters, rather than the most highly-professional military force in the Empire. It had to be galling to be dependent on men she feared would ravish her poor innocent daughter – although, judging from the girl's lustful expression, innocent was not a word that could be fairly applied to her.

"Nice piece of ass," Blake muttered, as he squatted down beside Jasmine. "I could ride on her all day."

"And then the Sergeant cuts off your nuts and wears them as a trophy," Jasmine muttered back. The briefing they'd been given on their civilian guests had been scanty, but Gwen had left them in no doubt as to what would happen if any of them were molested. Jasmine had found that rather insulting herself – none of the men in her Company would molest a girl – but she understood the Sergeant's attitude. A court martial would disgrace the entire Marine Corps - and generate entire *realms* of paperwork. "Besides, looking at her, I bet you she's been had by hundreds of men already."

"So have the whores who gather around the barracks and we don't complain," Blake countered. "What's wrong with a girl who shares her charms with everyone, as long as she shares them with me?"

Jasmine pretended to consider it. "This might be why we got our asses royally fucked back on training last year," she said. Blake had been squad leader at the time. "You were unable to risk the temptation to stick it in a convenient orifice and got us all buggered."

"That's not what you said at the time," Blake protested, dryly. "You were telling me what a genius I was before the first grenades started to detonate."

"It might have been tolerable if they hadn't gloated about it afterwards," Jasmine said, with a wink. "They kept telling us that they were *sure* that we wouldn't walk into that trap."

She pulled out the armour pieces and placed them in front of her, then started to strip down to her underwear, removing anything that couldn't be worn under the armour. Blake followed her example, looking away to grant her what privacy he could. Fraternisation was forbidden within the same Company, although the rule was sometimes ignored and Jasmine was used to stripping down in front of the men. No one said anything. They all depended on each other to stay alive when the shit hit the fan.

Jasmine looked up and saw the girl staring at Blake's torso as he pulled off his tunic. She had to admit that it was a nice torso, although the scars were a reminder of everything they'd been through together. She looked over at the girl and saw her blush and look away, her face as bright as a red stop sign. Jasmine smiled as Blake blinked at her, puzzled. He had completely missed the byplay.

"Never mind," she said, as she started to pull on her armour. "Just remember the Sergeant's motto and you'll be fine."

It felt good to be back in the light armour again, although she knew that some Marines had been roasted like chestnuts when their enemies had deployed weapons capable of punching through their armour. Heavy combat armour, by contrast, was almost indestructible, but those suits had to be custom made and cost as much as a frigate. It was hard enough to convince the Grand Senate to fund a few hundred suits a year. One day, she was sure, the technology would advance to the point where every Marine could have a heavy combat suit, but not for a very long time. And, by that time, heavy armour would be considered light armour. Some things never changed.

She pulled the helmet down over her head and blinked as the suit came online, transmitting a series of signals right into her eyes. The armour's sensors provided a complete image of what was outside, an image that could be rotated at will, while hundreds of tiny windows popped up to mark out points the suit's onboard computers considered interesting. Blake's armour was marked as FRIENDLY; the civilians, staring at the armoured Marines in astonishment, were marked as UNKNOWN. Blake's armour powered up beside her and he chuckled, a noise picked up by the intercom and transmitted to her.

"Armed and armoured," he said. The civilians thought of powered combat armour as something that clunked around the battlefield, but the truth was very different. "We're hot and free."

"Keep your weapons on safe until I give the order," Gwen said. The armoured Marines were starting to form up now, allowing the civilians to walk past and out of the stasis chamber. "We just have time for some training before we board the station."

Two hours later, the station – imaginatively named Orbit Station – came into view. Jasmine had been briefed that many early colony worlds used the same names and terminology to prevent misunderstanding, but in her considered opinion it was an excuse for bureaucratic lack of imagination. The station looked like a giant starfish; it could easily have been named Starfish Station, or even something more exotic. She'd seen a sex toy that looked rather like a station, although she was fairly certain that no colonial government would accept such a name. They'd be the laughing stock of the sector.

Orbit Station had been constructed out of prefabricated parts and should, according to the files, have been either expanded or replaced as local production came online, allowing the settlers to build their own facilities. Avalon's Government hadn't invested in the station, however, doing only the bare minimum to keep the station running and meet their obligations to the Empire. A dozen habitat nodes had been attached to the original station, while an old tramp freighter lay in dock, affixed to one of the docking tubes. There were eight in all and only one of them was in use. Earth had thousands of starships docking and undocking every day.

"All hands, this is the Captain," a voice said in her ear. "Prepare for docking. I say again; prepare for docking."

Jasmine followed Blake and four other Marines through the ship's corridors and down to the main docking section. The great advantage of the powered combat armour was that it could also serve as a spacesuit if required, allowing them to operate even if the enemy managed to depressurise the section and blast them all out into space. Captain Stalker met them there, wearing his own armour; Jasmine's armour reported that he was exchanging encrypted messages with Gwen. She could guess at the content of the messages. He wanted to lead his Marines into the station and Gwen, quite rightly, was saying no. Captain Stalker was the senior Marine in the system and, as such, couldn't be risked unless the shit had really hit the fan.

A dull thump ran through the ship as it docked. Jasmine stepped forward as the hatch slowly swung open, carefully checking that her suit was armed and ready to go. It was a habit that had been drilled into her at the Slaughterhouse, where she'd been warned that equipment, no matter how advanced, could fail at any moment and leave her in the lurch. The Drill Sergeants had sometimes caused equipment to fail at bad times, just to ram the message home. Anyone whose suit failed had to drop out of line at once and report themselves as unfit for combat.

She smiled inwardly as the Marines advanced. The Marine Corps had hundreds of legends and one of them involved a Marine whose equipment was always going wrong. He hadn't been a coward – he hadn't lacked moral fibre, as the reports put it – yet nothing had ever gone quite right for him. One day, he'd done four parachute drops and in all cases, the main parachute had failed to open. His instructor had, angrily, taken him for a final jump, carefully supervising every moment of preparation. *Both* of the instructor's parachutes had failed, sending him tumbling to his death. The Marine, understandably shaken by the experience, had resigned from the Corps.

The long tube yawned open in front of her, sending chills down her spine. An enclosed area was dangerous. She checked her weapons again, making sure that the stunner was ready to fire if necessary, before the second hatch opened and they stepped into the station. A young girl, barely more than nine years old if that, stepped forward and stopped, gaping at them.

"She looks a bit young for this," Blake muttered, on the platoon's channel. "What's she doing here?"

"It's run by a family," Joe muttered. The girl had shrunk back. If she'd never seen a Marine before, God alone knew what she thought they were. "She's one of their children."

Jasmine nodded in understanding. The space-born, the men and women who had spent all of their lives in asteroid settlements, had a habit of pressing children into work from an early age. A young child could certainly carry out most tasks in an asteroid, even if it was something as minor as minding the algae farms or repairing mining equipment. Some of them, later, joined the Imperial Navy and were among the most highly-decorated combat commanders. They knew, instinctively, the realities of space combat.

"Hello," she said, unhooking her helmet and disconnecting from the tactical *gestalt*. "My name is Jasmine. What's yours?"

"Flora," the girl said, her eyes going wide as Jasmine emerged from the armour. "Who are you?"

"My name is Jasmine," Jasmine said. Nothing in her training had prepared her for dealing with young children, but she'd helped raise nieces and nephews. "We're the Marines. Can you take us to your parents?"

"Her father is here," a heavily-accented voice said. Jasmine recognised the accent; an ex-asteroid miner from one of the Scottish-ethnic systems. "Why have you boarded my station?"

"We have to secure it before we start unloading," Gwen explained. Her voice echoed from her suit's armour. Jasmine caught the undertone of annoyance. There was no threat here, just a frightened child. "We're not going to damage anything."

"I hope not," the man said. "I'm Douglas Campbell, manager of this station for my sins. Would you like me to call out my family?"

"That would make life easier," Gwen said. She changed to the Marine-only channel. "Start searching the station. Do not damage anything if possible."

Jasmine smiled inwardly as she pulled her helmet back on and sank into the electronic universe surrounding her. Campbell's family – seven men and women – nineteen children – came at his call, waiting in one of the massive – and empty – loading bays while the Marines checked out the station. Jasmine guessed that it was an open family, with mixed relationships rather than a single mother and father, a not uncommon pattern among RockRats. Who cared who fathered a child, or who gave birth to her, as long as the children were loved and cherished? The conservatives on her homeworld would have been horrified, of course, but Jasmine didn't care. Besides, she and every other Marine in existence were married to the Corps. She only took lovers occasionally.

The interior of the station was in surprisingly good shape, although some of the maintenance looked jury-rigged and dangerous. That wasn't too surprising. The technology in most of the station was primitive, dating from the early days of spaceflight, just to make it easy to repair. It was something that had struck her as odd when she had started reviewing the histories of settled worlds, but serving in the Marines had taught her the wisdom of the practice. A piece of technology that was impossible to repair when broken was effectively useless.

"It's clear," Blake reported, finally. "No weapons apart from a handful of low-power laser cannon and railguns. There's nothing here that can threaten us."

"Good," Gwen said, briskly. "Blake, Jasmine, Joe; report to the shuttle-bay for close-protection duty. The rest of you report back to the ship and prepare to start unloading the *Sebastian Cruz*. The Captain wants to be rid of us and we might as well oblige."

Jasmine smiled, delighted. Close-protection duty meant that she would be going down to the planet first. There was nothing, absolutely nothing, like stepping onto a new world. It made everything else worthwhile.

CHAPTER TWELVE

> The Empire's system of planetary government is intended to evolve as the planet itself evolves. In theory, within the first fifty-hundred years, the planet should have evolved a local council that eventually becomes a planetary government. In practice, with development corporations striving to extract every last credit from their investment, the planetary government becomes a corrupt sham. The game is rigged against the children of settlers, who never signed a contract and were never in hock to the Development Corporation.
> - Professor Leo Caesius, *The Waning Years of Empire* (banned).

From orbit, Avalon looked as green and blue as Earth had looked, before the human race had come alarmingly close to killing its own homeworld. Edward watched as the shuttle started to head down towards the largest continent, admiring the green blur that hid the human settlements. Earth glowed in the night, illuminated by the lights of a thousand megacities; Avalon looked pristine and unspoiled. There were religions that worshipped untainted worlds and pressed for an end to colony flights, although they had never had a chance of convincing the Grand Senate to abandon their main source of wealth. Besides, the more distance between the different human sects, the better. It kept the bloodshed down.

He pressed his face to the viewport as the main continent took on shape and form. Avalon had three main continents – named Arthur, Lancelot and Galahad by the Captain of the survey vessel that had discovered the world – each one about the size of Africa and spread out across the planet. Hundreds of islands, ranging from the size of Cuba to the size of Nantucket, were scattered across the remainder of the oceans. Some of them, according to the briefings, played host to human settlements established in defiance of the planetary government. It was hardly an uncommon development on a planetary surface, but in the long run, such tiny colonies were eventually absorbed into the mainstream. The human race had learned a harsh lesson about allowing too much ethnic or religious diversity on a planetary surface.

Like almost all colony worlds developed by a corporation out for profit, development had focused on one of the continents and concentrated on building up a local farming infrastructure as quickly as possible. The survey team that had spent a year on the surface, catching and studying the wild crops and animals, had calculated that Earth's crops could be added to the soil without risking ecological collapse. The native animals were generally edible – although there was one specific kind of animal that preferred to eat humans rather than be eaten – and fish and other creatures had been released into the sea.

The blue seas below him teemed with life, including a creature that the original team had named the Jonah Whale, a monstrous creature that was the undisputed king of the food chain. They had taken to eating dolphins and lesser fish with enthusiasm. The briefing paper had warned that hunting Jonah Whales was asking for trouble. Luckily, there weren't many of them and they tended to stay away from humanity's ships.

The same couldn't be said for the Gnasher. The photographs included in the briefing notes had suggested nothing more than a large black dog, one that a young boy might enjoy romping through the woods with, chasing rabbits and catching sticks. It was an illusion. The creature had a gland within its heart that somehow supercharged it and allowed it to literally rocket towards its victims, savaging them with teeth that bit though flesh and bone with equal abandon. The briefing notes had warned that the safest thing to do with confronted with one of the monsters was to shoot it at once with explosive bullets. When supercharged, they had an astonishing ability to absorb damage and somehow keep going.

He pushed the thought aside as the shuttle descended towards one edge of the largest continent. The city of Camelot lay below him, the largest settlement on Avalon, although that didn't mean very much. It was tiny to his eyes, barely holding a few hundred thousand people at most. The handful of other settlements weren't any more impressive, although the briefing papers had suggested that some of them had been built from scratch and were generally more orderly than the capital city. He pushed that thought aside too. Avalon was six months from Earth and it was astonishing how much nonsense, or downright falsehoods, could creep into the files. He'd just have to wait and see what happened when they landed.

"We're coming down towards the spaceport now," the pilot said. He sounded astonished. "They built it twenty kilometres from Camelot."

Edward nodded. "A very droll way of saying 'fuck you' to the Empire," he said, dryly. "If they have to maintain the damn thing, they can at least make it inconvenient for nosey bastards from Earth."

He snorted. By law, every planet had to maintain at least one spaceport, even the planets inhabited by agricultural communities that had settled their worlds to get away from technology and all of its evils. Most worlds, particularly the ones that were intent on building up their own technological and industrial base, didn't regard it as a burden. It was, however, a serious expense for a stage-one colony world and not something that would pay for itself quickly. It took decades for a spaceport to break even.

Camelot looked untidy from the air, although he knew from experience that such impressions were deceptive. Massive prefabricated buildings dominated one corner of the city – the homes of the planet's industry, such as it was – while other buildings were constructed out of bricks or stone. People thronged the streets, some gazing up at the shuttle and wondering what it portended, while others just ambled about, looking for trouble. Camelot just didn't look dynamic at all. It looked more like a city that had never quite found itself.

The spaceport came into view as the shuttle banked towards it, heading down towards a landing pad that had been clearly marked by a beacon. A handful of other pads were dominated by aggressive-looking helicopters and aircraft, either shipped in from the Empire or built on Avalon itself. He hoped it was the latter. Shipping almost anything across interstellar distances was expensive as hell. A number of prefabricated buildings dominated one side of the spaceport, covered in grass and lichen. It looked as if the planetary government barely bothered to maintain the place at all. Given how few starships visited the system, it was easy to see why they thought it wasn't worth their while.

He glanced down at his datapad, showing the latest download from Orbit Station. Gwen had copied the station's logs into the Marine databases and they told a depressing story. Avalon was visited only once every two months, at best, by a freighter and they never stayed long. Avalon just didn't have much to offer beyond cheap fuel and foodstuffs. The four freighters in-system had all lost their drives and would vanish in a heartbeat if they were repaired. Their owners simply didn't have the money to hire a repair ship, or tow their freighter to a spaceport. They worked for the planetary government because it was the only game in town.

"There are no fences," he commented, sourly. The spaceport was supposed to be secure, but it looked as if anyone could just walk down the line of helicopters and casually toss a grenade into each one. It suggested that the Civil Guard were either firmly on their toes and ran regular patrols of the surrounding area, or they were criminally incompetent. "I want one of you to stay with the shuttle at all times."

"That's you, Joe," Rifleman Blake Coleman said. Edward had been impressed with Coleman's record, although he had been less impressed with the string of demerits for smart remarks at the wrong time. Blake would not see a permanent promotion for years at this rate. "Jasmine and I will escort you, sir."

The shuttle paused over the spaceport and lowered itself down towards the hard ground. Edward felt the bump as the shuttle touched down, smiling inwardly at the thought of how an Imperial Navy Admiral would have thrown a fit at even the slightest bump. They had no sense of proportion at all. Any landing you could walk away from, or so he had been told, was a good landing.

"Thank you," he said, as Jasmine moved ahead of him to climb out first. "It was an excellent flight down to the ground."

The scent of Avalon hit him as Jasmine opened the hatch, a curious mixture of greenery and of the smell of petroleum-based engines spooling over in the distance. He could hear the sound of birds chirping – it was rare to see a wild bird on Earth, outside the reserves – and the sounds of mechanics working on some of the helicopters. Now that he was on the ground, he could pick out the sight of a handful of guards patrolling the field, watching for trouble. The spaceport might not be sealed up tighter than a virgin's ass, but it was fairly secure. It would take a determined attack to destroy the facility.

"Captain," Blake said, quickly. "We have one vehicle incoming."

A jeep was making its way towards them. It was an old-tech vehicle, something that would have been horrendously out of place on Earth, yet it made sense on Avalon. The plans might have been shipped out in a database, but the jeep itself would have been produced on Avalon, giving the Civil Guard unrivalled mobility and, just incidentally, encouraging local industry. A jeep could be repaired easily. A Mark-VIII Hover Tank would have to be shipped off-world once the spare parts ran out.

"No trace of any heavy weapons," Jasmine added. "They're just carrying assault rifles and pistols."

Edward shrugged, keeping his expression calm and composed. There was no such thing as a dangerous weapon. There were just dangerous men. A Marine Rifleman was a qualified weapons-master, capable of using almost any weapon in the Empire with neither hesitation nor delay. A man holding a weapon who didn't know what he was doing – or what the weapon could do, or what limitations it had – was no problem, at least not to anyone on the opposite side. Back when he'd been a mere Rifleman himself, his platoon had penetrated an Imperial Army base wearing nothing, but underpants. They hadn't even been armed and they'd managed to shut down the entire base for hours.

The jeep came to a halt and an older man jumped out, wearing a Civil Guard uniform. Like the Marines and the Imperial Army, the uniform was fairly standard, but where Marines wore their Rifleman's Tab, the newcomer wore a stylised golden image of Avalon. The Civil Guard, unlike the senior services, owed their loyalty to their homeworld, not the Empire as a whole. There were some quite senior figures who questioned the wisdom of giving so much firepower to people who might not be entirely trustworthy.

"Welcome to Avalon," he said. He looked rather suspicious, for which Edward could hardly blame him. No one would have informed him, or anyone on Avalon, that the Marines were on their way. No message could have reached them unless it had been carried on the *Sebastian Cruz*. "I am Major George Grosskopf, the commanding officer of the Avalon Civil Guard."

"Captain Edward Stalker, Terran Marine Corps," Edward said, saluting. Technically, he – not George – was the senior officer present, but there was no point in splitting hairs. A bad rapport with the local Civil Guard officer would not make their operations any easier. "I know that all of this was sprung on you at short notice."

"No one told us that the Governor's pleas for help had reached Earth," George said. "The last help we received from the Empire was no help at all."

Edward studied him, noted the way he held himself, and nodded inwardly. "As a former Imperial Army officer, you have to know that there are too many brushfires for us to put out," he said, grimly. "My Company is here to help you."

George surprised him by laughing. "And be content with what we get?" He asked. "That sounds quite like the Empire we all know and love. You'll be pleased to hear that the Governor wishes to speak with you at once. He doesn't quite believe that you're here to stay."

"Believe it," Edward said. He'd spent part of the six months in transit studying reports that would not normally have been made available to him. It was hard to think of serving in the Marines as living a sheltered existence – the very idea was absurd – but it was alarmingly clear that the Commandant had, if anything, understated the scale of the Empire's problems. The entire system seemed to be on the verge of breaking down. Crime was on the rise, trade was falling rapidly and corruption was spreading everywhere. The official news reports were often censored to hide the true scale of the problem, leaving the general public unaware of the growing stresses tearing the Empire apart. Terrorists were mounting isolated attacks against the Core Worlds while, out on the frontier, the

Secessionist League was moving from strength to strength. "We may be here to stay for a very long time."

George was no fool. "They're going to close the bases then?"

"It looks like it," Edward confirmed. "If that happens, they'll abandon a dozen sectors to their fate, including this one. We could be here permanently."

"I won't lie and say that I'm not happy to see you," George admitted. "How many men do you have?"

"Eighty-one, not counting the auxiliaries," Edward said. He was tempted to mention the supplies they'd brought with them, but he didn't dare discuss them until he knew if George could be trusted or not. A former Imperial Army officer would have a file in the database back on the *Sebastian Cruz*. "I suppose we'd better not keep the Governor waiting."

"Eighty-one men," George repeated. He looked shaken. "We need far more than that, Captain. We need an entire army."

"We have eighty-one Marines," Edward said. Pressing auxiliaries into front-line service was frowned upon, but they were thousands of light years from the Slaughterhouse. There was no other choice. "I think that should be enough to make an impression."

"We'll see," George said. He hopped back into the jeep. "Climb aboard, Captain. The Governor won't wait for us forever."

Edward allowed Blake and Jasmine to go first, and then followed them into the rear seat. They were all crammed together, but they could all fit, luckily. The jeep's engine roared to life and the driver turned around, taking them right across another landing pad. Old warnings surfaced in Edward's mind and he winced – no one on Earth would dare drive across a landing pad – but it was perfectly safe. The Marines would probably break Avalon's record for shuttle arrivals in a single day.

"We had the indents building the road network from the start," George explained, as they roared out of the spaceport and down a surprisingly well-maintained road. "There are roads running all around the coastline now, linking the cities together, and others reaching up into the hinterlands and towards the badlands. I hoped to have them completed this year, but the bandits or the Crackers keep shooting up the work crews. We also had to start cutting the foliage back from it after they started using it for cover, letting them get a few shots in at our vehicles. It's a war of nerves and they're winning it."

The jeep raced over a bridge, showing Edward a river heading down towards the sea. "We used to have people canoeing on that river, racing up against the current or diving down towards the sea," George continued. "We still do, sometimes, but mostly people don't dare in the wake of a few shootings. The damned Crackers are very good at slipping through our defences and spoiling one of the few things that make living on this planet worthwhile."

Edward said nothing, thinking hard. Clearly, the reports had understated the scale of the trouble on Avalon's surface. There was no time to pick George's brains, but he made a mental note to look into it as soon as possible, perhaps detailing Rifleman McDonald to investigate and catch up on what had happened since he'd left his homeworld.

Jasmine asked the obvious question. "Sir," she said, "is there a chance that we could be shot at, now?"

"I had teams out beating the bushes, so I hope not," George admitted. He didn't sound certain of anything, Edward realised. Marine battledress was surprisingly good at absorbing bullet impacts, but his head was uncovered and unprotected. "No one is supposed to know that you arrived in the system, but I doubt that secrecy held. The only thing that moves faster than rumour here is bad news."

Edward sat back in his seat and tried to relax. The driver was taking them into Camelot now and he concentrated on studying the city, taking in the sights. Parts of it were surprisingly respectable, other parts were little more than slums. It made no sense to him.

"They're former indents who served their term and were released, or people who lost their farms to their creditors," George explained, bitterly. "Put a set of ex-indents out on a farm and they'll be dead in a couple of weeks. Either that, or they'll make a run for the badlands and we'll lose them. Some of them get temporary work as labourers; others go into prostitution or fall even further into debt. It's never a pretty sight."

The jeep was pulling up outside Government House. It was easily the most imposing building in Camelot, although it would have been laughable on Earth. Edward studied it and rolled his eyes. There was a certain mindset that demanded luxury, whatever the cost, and that mindset had designed this building. It was far too elaborate for its value.

"Doubtless," he said, wishing that he was back on a nice honest battlefield. "Come on. Let's go meet the Governor."

Chapter Thirteen

> The standard form of colonial government – at least in stage one and two colonies – is rule by the Development Corporation. The Corporation appoints a Governor and a law enforcement force, who can be counted upon to enforce the law the 'right' way. As time passes, democracy is introduced into the system, with the eventual replacement of the Corporation's law with a democratic state. If only it worked out so well!
>
> - Professor Leo Caesius, *The Waning Years of Empire* (banned).

"So," Linda said. "Those are the famous Marines."

Governor Brent Roeder didn't take his eyes off the screen as the Marines stepped into Government House. Two of them looked to be nothing more than soldiers, even though they seemed more lethal than the Civil Guardsmen who were trying to convince them to leave their weapons behind, but the third looked…interesting. He couldn't say how he knew, yet he was convinced that he was looking at their leader. The other two seemed intent on protecting him at all costs.

"Don't underestimate him," George had warned. "He survived the Slaughterhouse and he's served as a Captain of Marines for over two years. That means that he has earned the respect of some very dangerous men and women."

Brent settled back in his chair, feeling his bones ache. The Council had wanted to be included in the first meeting – unsurprisingly, the news about the Marines had leaked out to them within minutes of their arrival – but Brent had dissuaded them as best as he could. He, Linda and

George would be the first official representatives of Avalon to meet their new ally. He hoped, despite himself, that the Marine walked away with a good impression of them. It was vitally important that they learned to work together.

His intercom – a locally produced piece of shit, in his considered opinion – buzzed. "Governor, this is Bill from Security," a voice said. "The Marines are refusing to leave their weapons at the front desk."

Brent rubbed his forehead, feeling one of his headaches coming on already. He'd banned weapons from Government House after two Councillors had fought a duel in the Council Chamber, over a political argument that had made no sense to anyone else. Government House was the most heavily defended building on Avalon. They should not have been in any danger at all – or so he told himself. It was only a matter of time before the bandits started attacking within the city itself.

"Allow them to keep their weapons," he said, finally. If he couldn't trust the Marines, who could he trust? The list of people he trusted completely was depressingly small. "Have them escorted up here as quickly as possible."

He settled back in his chair and waited. It took four minutes before there was a knock on the door and George stepped in, followed by a tall blond man wearing a Marine uniform. Brent stood up to greet him, holding out a hand for him to shake, taking the time to study the Marine carefully. Captain Stalker's bright blue eyes seemed to miss nothing. Brent had the uncomfortable sense that the Captain was used to such reactions and was giving Brent time to study him as much as he wanted.

The Marine looked surprisingly average, but there was no weakness in his handshake and his eyes were steady. He might have been sent far from the Core Worlds, far from the centre of power, but there was nothing wrong with him. Or perhaps he was completely wrong. Brent's life as a civil servant hadn't prepared him to run a military campaign, let alone judge military officers. It had never been included in the training courses he'd taken as a junior assistant civil servant.

"Captain Edward Stalker reporting, sir," the Marine said. He had the same kind of briskly formal voice George had, although in his case it was more clipped, more precise. His accent was definitely Old Earth, yet that could mean nothing. Earth was the centre of the Empire's culture. Everyone who was anyone tried to cultivate an Earth-style accent.

"Ah, thank you for coming," Brent said, trying to remember what little military protocol he knew. Nothing seemed quite appropriate to this situation. "Please, take a seat. I'm delighted to see you." He nodded to Linda. "This is my Deputy, Linda."

"Pleased to meet you," Captain Stalker said. He shook Linda's hand. Oddly, he didn't look at her as a pretty girl, but as just another person. Brent found himself wondering if it was a sign of homosexuality, before realising that Stalker would have been trained to think of everyone as a possible threat first. Or perhaps he was just being polite. Brent sat back down behind his desk and tried to think of something to say. It wasn't easy.

"We weren't expecting you," he said, finally. "Is there some reason why you were sent to us without any notification?"

Captain Stalker smiled. It was an expression that didn't quite touch his eyes. "I believe that there are few lines of communications between Earth and Avalon," he said. "It was decided to dispatch my unit only six months ago. There was simply no time to send you any advance notice of our coming."

"Well, I'm still glad to see you," Brent said. "How many Marines do you have on your ship? I believe that it can carry a Division?"

"We have eighty-one Marines," Captain Stalker said. Brent stared at him, almost not catching his next words. "Part of our remit is to train your Civil Guard to a level where it can cope with open insurgency and warfare."

"Eighty-one Marines," Brent repeated, dazed. "How much do you intend to do with just eighty-one Marines?"

"Quite a bit, actually," Captain Stalker said. There was absolute confidence in his tone. Brent found himself hoping that it was not misplaced. "The Company is the single most powerful military unit in the system. Man for man, my Marines are better than any other armed force in the Empire. I think we can make an impression on the enemy."

Brent studied him carefully, trying to divine the underlying meaning in his words. It seemed almost as if Captain Stalker was dissembling… and then he realised that dissembling wasn't something that would come easily to the Marine. It was ignorance. Captain Stalker didn't realise how bad things were becoming and how soon it would be before the planet became ungovernable. He opened his mouth and closed it again. How could he find the words to explain exactly what was going on to the young man in front of him? And he was young; Captain Stalker showed none of the signs of being rejuvenated in the past. He couldn't be much older than thirty, if that.

"Captain," he said, slowly. "Do you have any idea how bad things are here?"

"I haven't had a complete briefing yet," Captain Stalker replied, calmly. "I do know, however, that we are effectively stuck out here for a very long time. We may be here for as long as five years. We could spend our time bemoaning how bad things are becoming, or we can start trying to deal with the situation. I prefer to be optimistic."

Brent smiled, almost despite himself. He could have liked Captain Stalker under other circumstances. "Let's see," he said. "We have three different insurgency movements operating against us. We have a political logjam that simply won't break. We have a Civil Guard that is weak and not particularly effective" – George snorted angrily at that – "and our local industry can barely produce what it needs to keep us going. And, if that wasn't enough, we have pirate ships using the system as a base. Can you deal with that, Captain?"

"Give us time and we can deal with anything," Captain Stalker said seriously. He pulled a datachip out of his uniform pocket and placed it down on Brent's desk. "My orders from the Empire."

Brent picked up the chip and opened one of his drawers, pulling out his datapad and slotting the chip into it. The datapad was irreplaceable. There was only a handful on the planet – when they would be dirt cheap in the Core Worlds – and Avalon's industry couldn't even begin to produce them, not yet. The investment required to boost the local industry to a higher level simply didn't exist. He studied the short brisk prose and blinked. The orders were vague in the extreme.

"I see," he said, finally. It was something he would have to discuss with George and Linda, at least before they brought the rest of the Council in on it. "Do you have any immediate requirements, Captain?"

Captain Stalker didn't even blink at his tone. "I need to use the spaceport for unloading the *Sebastian Cruz*," he said, flatly. "We have a mountain of supplies that we brought from Earth. We also need an isolated location near Camelot that can serve as a base of operations *and* a full and accurate briefing on the current political situation. Once we get everything down on the planet and organised, we can start training up the local Civil Guard."

Brent exchanged a quick glance with George. "I recommend Castle Rock as your base of operations," George said. "It's actually a mid-sized island off the coast of Arthur – this continent – and it already has a landing strip built on it. There are a handful of indebted families down on the ground, but they'd be happy to move if the Governor bought out their contracts. If you have plenty of supplies, you really need an island. Your supplies are going to attract every thief in the city."

"The Wilhelm Family owns Castle Rock," Linda pointed out. "You may have to negotiate with them over rent or purchase."

"Maybe not," Brent said. For once, he could put a finger in their eye and it would be perfectly legal. "If we buy out the settlers, the island reverts back to the government and we can hand it over to the Marines if we want. The owners can go to hell."

"Thank you," Captain Stalker said. "With your permission, then, I will start moving my men down to the spaceport. The sooner we get started, the sooner Captain Yamato and his ship can leave the system."

"I will have dispatches for them to take back to Earth," Brent said quickly. "I'll have them sent up this evening."

"Of course," Captain Stalker said. He looked out of the window, towards the mountains in the distance. He didn't know that rebels were lurking there. "You have a beautiful planet."

"We like to think so," George said, dryly. "My driver will take you back to the spaceport."

Captain Stalker saluted and left the room.

"So," Brent said, once the door had closed behind him. "What do you make of our new ally?"

"Handsome, determined, and ignorant of the local realities," Linda said. Brent looked at her in surprise. Was Linda attracted to the Marine? "It was clear that he didn't have any real idea of what is going on here."

"That isn't actually surprising," George said, flatly. "Earth simply doesn't care about tiny issues on faraway planets. They wouldn't have had access to any real briefing papers, certainly nothing up to date. They'll learn, of course. Marines have the highest rating of all when it comes to adapting to new situations."

Linda smiled. "Are they even better than your old regiment?"

"Only by a tiny margin," George said, quickly. They shared a laugh. "Of course, my old regiment was commanded by an idiot who got his post through political connections and didn't have the slightest idea which end of a gun fired the bullet. The Marine officers have to work their way up through the ranks. It gives them a major advantage over us poor mortals in the Imperial Army."

He paused. "Which does make you wonder," he added. "Just what did Captain Stalker do to be exiled out here?"

Linda smiled. "Let's see," she said. "I was left here for refusing the advances of a superior officer. You were sent here because you won a battle by disobeying every order you were given. Half of the staff in Government House were sent here because it was cheaper than firing them. What do you think Captain Stalker did?"

"It wouldn't have been anything that rated a dishonourable, or he would have been discharged from the Marine Corps," George said. He chuckled. "For all we know, he was caught in bed with a Senator's daughter and her outraged father insisted on him being exiled to Avalon, along with his Company."

"Or," Brent said quietly, "they're all the reinforcements we're going to get."

The room seemed to grow colder. Brent had been appealing to the Sector Capital for help for years, but nothing had ever materialised, not even an Imperial Navy destroyer. Trade was falling all over the sector. The flood of new colonists – even the involuntary settlers from Earth – had become a trickle. Captain Stalker's men were the single largest group to land on Avalon all year. Brent didn't want to think about it – he had been a loyal servant of the Empire and had served it faithfully – but what if the Empire was on the verge of abandoning Avalon completely?

He knew the local sector fairly well, for he'd been based there for his entire career. Avalon's sector was right on the Rim, the border of space controlled by the Empire. Beyond the Rim, there were hidden pirate bases, black colonies and strange eerie rumours about encounters with aliens, told in spaceport bars by drunken spacers. If the Empire abandoned Avalon completely, what might come out of the darkness to threaten his adopted world?

And yet, even that wasn't the real worry. The Crackers had been smashed once before by the Imperial Navy. What would happen if they realised that the Imperial Navy would never return to Avalon? They'd push forward as quickly as they could and the Civil Guard wouldn't be able to stand in their way. How long would it be before they took Camelot and put her inhabitants to the sword? The Crackers had no reason to love the Council or respect its authority. His never-to-be-sufficiently-damned predecessor had made sure of that.

"George," he said slowly. "How much of an impact can they make on the enemy?"

George hesitated. "In the short term, quite a bit," he said. "In the long term, perhaps nothing, unless they succeed in turning out new recruits for the Civil Guard. Even so, the Council will probably try to hobble it, if only because a stronger army is a danger to them as well."

They shared a long look. George and a handful of other professional military officers did what they could, but the Avalon Civil Guard was an unwieldy creature. Officially, it had five thousand soldiers, yet realistically it was far fewer. Many of the senior officers were political appointees, men and women trusted by various Councillors to respect their interests. Others were deeply corrupt and – perhaps – working for the enemy. Launching any sort of military campaign against the bandits, let alone the Crackers, was impossible.

"I see," Brent said. "I'm going to give him complete control over Castle Rock. Legally, the Council won't be able to do anything about it, not without compromising their own positions." He snorted at the thought. Half of the Councillors were in it for the money, what little of it there was on Avalon. The other half were in it for the power. "At least that should keep their influence off the island."

"Maybe," George said. He stood up. "With your permission, I have to get back out to my men. I want to do a sweep through the countryside. We might just catch a few bandits to hang."

"Good luck," Brent said. They both knew that the operation wasn't likely to succeed. "And good hunting."

One of the little secrets the Marine Corps had somehow never got around to sharing with anyone who hadn't passed through the Slaughterhouse was that each Marine was issued a subcutaneous communicator. It was low-powered, meaning that it had very short range, but it was effectively completely undetectable outside of the Core Worlds. Marines trained endlessly to be able to speak privately to each other, without anyone on the outside having any idea of what was going on. It had been used, more than once, to give the Marines a tactical advantage.

"So," Blake said. Anyone looking at him would have just seen him standing there, as unmoving as a rock. His jaw didn't even twitch. The two Civil Guardsmen eying the Marines warily heard nothing. "What do you make of our posting?"

"There's more trouble than they told us about," Jasmine said, in reply. One of the Civil Guardsmen was staring at her as if she was a creature from another world. The thought made her smile. In a sense, it was perfectly true. "They took a risk when they drove the Old Man from the spaceport to here."

She glanced at the wooden doorway leading to the Governor's office. A wooden door would have been unthinkable on Earth, outside of the Imperial Palace itself. What few forests remained on Earth were under heavy protection, with guards authorised to shoot on sight. On Avalon, it was commonplace and a single hard kick would bring the door down in splinters.

"Or perhaps they were exaggerating the threat," Blake said. "It wouldn't be the first time that someone has tried to convince us that matters were worse than they seemed."

Jasmine nodded, remembering deployments where the Marines had been sucked into the maelstrom of local politics, where one side had attempted to use them to forward their own political agenda. Avalon might be barely developed, but it certainly had a political maelstrom brewing. She sighed inwardly. Wonderful; another campaign where no one knew who was the good guy.

The door opened before she could reply. "Come on," Captain Stalker said. He looked as calm and composed as ever, but Jasmine could just see something else beneath his face. "We have to go back to the spaceport."

CHAPTER FOURTEEN

> One of the many symptoms of decline is the sudden profusion of intelligence agencies. Where once Imperial Intelligence (the dreaded Double Eyes) handled all of the Empire's intelligence requirements, there are now dozens of different intelligence agencies. Some work for specific branches of the armed forces – Naval Intelligence, Marine Intelligence – while others work for individual Senators and even for the media. The results have not been good.
> - Professor Leo Caesius, *The Waning Years of Empire* (banned).

Four hours after Edward returned to the spaceport, fifty Marines had landed and conducted a thorough sweep of the surrounding area. They'd found nothing incriminating apart from a few caches of locally-produced drugs, but it hadn't been hard to convince the Civil Guard to move their helicopters to a nearby airstrip and leave the spaceport to the Marines. There was simply nowhere else on Avalon that could be used to land so much gear so quickly.

Lieutenant Howell had set up a command post in one section of the spaceport and was conducting operations quickly and smoothly, while Lieutenant Young had been dispatched to Castle Rock to carry out a quick survey. Edward wasn't entirely happy at being based on an island – even if they were Marines – but it would provide a barrier between the Marines and the local political struggles. It would also be easy to secure.

He'd had orbital images downloaded to his terminal on the trip back to the spaceport and he'd studied them carefully. Castle Rock – and he had no idea how it had picked up that name – was a medium-sized island about twice the size of Nantucket on Old Earth. It had some good farmland and fishing opportunities and he hadn't understood why it wasn't more heavily settled, but a quick look at the survey report had informed him that there was simply much better farming on the continent itself. The settlers who had started to try to farm on the island hadn't been very successful, something that puzzled him. They should certainly have been able to feed themselves by now.

"The remainder of the Company is assisting Captain Yamato to unlock the pods and start loading them onboard the shuttles," Lieutenant Howell explained. "I think we're going to have to run our own security until we get everything set up on Castle Rock. I didn't realise just how dirt poor this planet actually is until I had a good look at their local records. We might as well have landed entire mountains of gold, sir."

"Keep two platoons back at all times to maintain guard on the spaceport," Edward ordered. It was a dangerously thin security blanket. Marines or not, it really required at least a full Company to hold and secure a spaceport. Twenty-one Marines wouldn't be enough to stand off a determined assault. "Once we get the drones and assault vehicles unloaded and set up, we can start deploying them to the island and on random patrols."

"Yeah," Howell said. He didn't sound happy, but then, few logistics officers ever were. The Marines rotated such posts around the Lieutenants to ensure that they all understood how to handle logistics, yet Howell had been unlucky. Stalker's Stalkers had never had to operate at the end of such a long supply chain before. Offhand, Edward couldn't remember any Marine unit in recent history that had. "I bet you ten credits that we'll have locals out here soon enough offering to assist us in exchange for vital supplies. A single fusion reactor would completely change the balance of power here and we have ten of them."

Edward nodded. "I didn't discuss what we'd brought with the Governor," he said. "We'll have to see who we can bring in locally to assist us. God knows, we can't handle everything ourselves."

"No," Howell said. "In fact…"

Edward's communicator buzzed before he could finish speaking. "Captain, this is Rifleman Lin on the front gate," a voice said. "You have a visitor. She says she's from Naval Intelligence."

Edward exchanged a brief glance with Howell. "Naval Intelligence?"

"Yes, sir," Lin said. "She wants to talk to you as soon as possible."

"How unusually polite," Edward murmured. Naval Intelligence, in his experience, tended to issue demands and threats instead of polite requests. They considered themselves the senior military intelligence service, second only to Imperial Intelligence. "Check her, and then have her escorted into the main building. I'll see her in the spaceport manager's office."

He'd inspected the office earlier. It was surprisingly simple for such a post, decorated only by a handful of posters of movie stars who had been out of fashion long before word that they were in fashion reached Avalon. The manager, he'd been told by the Civil Guard, only worked part time, unsurprising when starships only visited the system every few months. She had offered to come in and assist the Marines, but Howell had turned her down, warning her that it could be dangerous. The real reason was far darker. Spaceport managers on the frontier had a habit of assisting smugglers and thieves to supplement their limited income. It was something he felt the Company could do without. He took one of the seats – the manager hadn't believed in comfort, evidently – and waited.

"Captain, this is Colonel Kitty Stevenson of Naval Intelligence," Lin said, knocking on the open door. "She's clean."

"Thank you," Edward said, standing up and holding out a hand for Kitty to shake. "Please close the door behind you."

Kitty Stevenson was a tall redheaded woman, wearing a simple Imperial Navy tunic without rank insignia. She actually reminded Edward of Mandy and Mindy, apart from the air of quiet desperation that seemed to hang around the older woman. Her tunic was unbuttoned, showing off a certain amount of cleavage, but her gaze was sharp and direct. Edward let go of her hand and waved her to a chair, holding out a datapad to her.

"I'm afraid I'm going to have to ask you for your prints," he said. "I wasn't briefed that you were going to be here."

Kitty nodded and pressed her fingers against the pad's sensor. A moment later, the pad bleeped up a file; Colonel Kitty Stevenson, Naval Intelligence, assigned to the local sector fleet and then to Avalon, for reasons unknown. Edward skimmed through the highlights and nodded inwardly. Kitty was who she claimed to be.

"I wasn't told that the Marines were going to be coming," Kitty said. "I was just promised that Avalon would receive some support sooner or later."

Edward felt his eyes narrow. "Who promised you that?"

"One of my superiors on Earth," Kitty said. Her face revealed nothing. "He just told me that some form of military support would be coming soon."

Edward frowned inwardly, thinking hard. He hadn't known that he would be heading to Avalon until just after he'd told the Grand Senate exactly what was wrong with them and their ideas, yet the Commandant had organised the transfer remarkably quickly. Had he intended to send a Marine Company out to Avalon, or had it simply been a matter of slotting a round peg into a round hole? And then there was the encryption key he'd been given. Just what, he asked himself angrily, was the Commandant up to on Old Earth?

"I see," he said, finally. It wasn't something he could ask her. Chances were that she was just as ignorant as him. "And, now you're here, why are you here?"

Kitty showed no offence at his brusque manner. "Officially, I am in charge of the Imperial Navy recruiting station on Avalon," she said. "Practically speaking, the station is moribund and has been so for years. I have thousands of kids on my lists who want to enlist, but without transport to a training centre they get nowhere. By the way, I'd like to send them back on your transport."

She shrugged. "Unofficially, my task is to monitor the situation on this planet and report to higher authority."

"Sneaky," Edward said, dryly. "What's on Avalon that makes it so important?"

"It's not on Avalon," Kitty countered. "It's the cloudscoop. If the system was to be…lost, the cloudscoop might fall into pirate hands, allowing them to become more aggressive. If it fell into Secessionist hands, the results might be far less pleasing." She snorted. "And, Captain, this world is within six months of falling into enemy hands."

Edward jerked upright. "Hellfire," he said, sharply. "Are you sure?"

"I've been on this godforsaken planet for the last ten years," Kitty snapped. "Of course I'm sure!"

"Six months," Edward repeated. He looked up at a frayed map hanging on the wall. "What the hell is going on here?"

Kitty assumed a pose Edward recognised, the pose of an intelligence officer on the verge of imparting information to the ignorant – everyone else. "Just under a hundred years ago, there was a brutal rebellion on this planet, which the Imperial Navy terminated by striking from orbit," she said. "The original rebellion was broken, but seeds of a new movement survived and prospered. The first two Governors didn't help…"

She took a breath. "The first Governor put heavy restrictions on the planet's inhabitants," she explained. "He tried to ban guns, issue ID cards…everything seemingly calculated to annoy people who might otherwise have been loyal. The local wildlife wouldn't be impressed by unarmed humans; the farmers didn't dare disarm, not when their children could be attacked and eaten by one of the local monstrosities. There was no second rebellion, but there was a great deal of discontent, passive resistance, and brief outbursts of violence. Eventually, some kindly soul put a bullet through his head and he was killed.

"The second Governor wasn't much better," she continued. "He relaxed the restrictions, but he firmly believed that the only way to heal the planet would be to allow the inhabitants to have some say in their future, so he created the planetary council. On paper, it was an excellent idea, but in practice it was a dreadful error. By law, the only people who could vote in elections were people who had paid off their debts, and barely ten percent of the planet's population – if that – could legally vote. The results weren't pleasant. The Council is effectively dominated by interests who don't want to extend the franchise, cancel debts, make vast new investments…or anything else that might actually help fix the world's problems. Worse, seeing the Council has been legally formed, the third Governor cannot simply dissolve it. He has to listen to them."

"Fuck," Edward said, mildly. He'd seen screwed up planets before, but this was something new. "And the rebels are trying to tear all of this down?"

"Yes," Kitty said. She paused for a moment to gather her thoughts. "One group is effectively bandits, without any political agenda. They're largely composed of escaped indents who have nowhere else to go. They're responsible for some of the worst attacks, but have absolutely no hope of surviving if the Civil Guard had the firepower and numbers to go after them. They have no support whatsoever from the locals unless they take it at gunpoint. A few hours before you arrived, one of their groups attacked a township, wiped out the men and took the women as slaves. Or worse.

"The other two groups are both descended from the original Cracker movement," she said. "They want to get rid of the planetary government, scrap all debt and establish a new representative government. They differ in their aims slightly. One group basically wants autonomy within the Empire; the other wants complete independence. They may have links to outside forces."

"The Secessionists," Edward said. "Or it could be pirates."

"Could be," Kitty agreed. "I have no proof either way. This planet's satellite network is barely functional and no one has bothered to put aside the funds to repair it."

She shook her head, sending ripples running down her red hair. "You'll get a full military briefing from the Major, no doubt, but the short version of it is that the government is losing control over the outer settlements and may well be on the verge of losing complete control. There is almost no support whatsoever for the government outside the main cities, because the government is seen as the enemy, the tool of the loan sharks who keep the locals in debt. The Crackers don't have to intimidate the population, Captain; they have more friends and allies than they could possibly require. I suspect that their aim is to force the Civil Guard to come out and fight on even terms, whereupon they will crush it and march on Camelot."

Edward considered it. "Do they have heavy weapons?"

"Not very many," Kitty said. "A few weapons disappeared from Civil Guard storage depots and more may be coming in from off-planet, but mostly they have only what they can produce for themselves. Unfortunately, they are quite ingenious. Their industrialists show far more energy and application than the government's, which isn't entirely surprising. The Council has the whole system tied up, preventing any honest competition. The whole planet, Captain, is the Empire in microcosm."

Edward let that pass. "Tell me about the Council," he said. "Who and what are they?"

"You'll meet them all later," Kitty assured him. "The Governor was already talking about a formal ball to welcome you and your men to Avalon." She shrugged expressively. "There are twenty-one councillors in all, each one representing a specific district, at least in theory. Seven of them basically bought thousands of miles of land from the ADC when it was trying to sell off its assets. Seven more own ninety percent of the planet's industry between them. Two of them – the Wilhelm Family – are debt sharks. They bought the debt contracts of thousands of people and used it as leverage to turn them into serfs. Markus and Carola Wilhelm have a fair claim to being the most hated couple on the planet. The remaining five were elected by the middle class, insofar as this planet *has* a middle class. They're reasonably honest, but they're not above taking bribes if they're offered.

"The Council's exact position relative to the Governor isn't clear. The Governor is the Empire-appointed Head of State and Government, but the Council can interfere with his programs if they don't like them. Governor Roeder isn't a bad man – he's certainly not as bad as either of the last two Governors – yet he doesn't have the strength of will to go up against the massed opposition of the Council. He controls the Civil Guard, at least on paper, but many of the Guard's senior officers were appointed by the Councillors. The possibility of a civil war within the Guard's ranks cannot be completely discounted. Major Grosskopf is a good man, but only five hundred of the Guardsmen can be ranked as good soldiers. The remainder go from average down to bad. He wanted to go after the bandit gang that hit the township, but the Guard is simply not equipped or trained to take on the bandits, let alone the rebel Crackers."

She gave him a charming smile. "Sorry you came yet?"

Edward smiled back. It would require some investigation, but he was already beginning to see possibilities in the situation. And, besides, his orders from the Commandant had been delightfully vague. The Grand Old Man of the Corps might not know everything about Avalon, but he'd granted Edward vast latitude to act as he saw fit. Perhaps the planet could be saved after all.

"Not yet," he said, with a wink. One more question had to be asked. "Where do the indents fit into all of this?"

"They're right at the bottom of the social scale," Kitty said, coldly. "They're criminals, sentenced to spending at least ten to twenty years working as slave labour before being freed and granted a small patch of land. Most of them should never have been sent here. Others complete their sentences, only to discover that they're still at the bottom of the social scale. They don't get their land; they're lucky not to be lynched on sight. They gravitate to the shanty towns surrounding Camelot and just… stay there. They don't have any hope at all. If the Crackers took over, they'd all be killed out of hand. They kill indent gangs on sight."

Perfect, Edward thought calmly.

"Above them are the indebted, the ones who will never pay off their debt," Kitty added. "And then we have ones who might succeed, if the screws don't get tightened any further. And then we have the ones who are free, yet burdened by taxes intended to help pay off the planet's overall debt. The whole planet is a mess. It is no wonder, Captain, that the Crackers are being so successful. Why should anyone outside the upper crust – and the indent gangs – try to resist them?"

She stood up. "My orders from my superiors are to make myself of use to you, Captain," she concluded. Edward smiled inwardly at how much pride she – and her superiors – had had to swallow to issue such orders, let alone follow them. "What are your orders?"

Edward considered the matter. "I want you to prepare a briefing for my senior officers and NCOs," he said. The briefing would be recorded and shown to the enlisted men as well. "And then I want you to sit down with some of my people and start going over maps and planning operations. I don't intend to sit on my ass at Castle Rock doing nothing."

Kitty stared at him. "Captain," she said slowly, "how do you intend to send a hundred Marines against an enemy you can't even track?"

"You might be surprised," Edward said, seriously. An idea was already forming in his mind. He'd have to study the maps before he came up with a final plan, but he was fairly sure it would work. "I think the bandit gang that hit the township would make a suitable first target for our wrath, don't you?"

CHAPTER FIFTEEN

> There are two vital elements of any colonisation project that must succeed if the world is to develop properly; the farming, to provide food, and the industry. If those two elements fail, the colony world will either stagnate or collapse. It should be evident that it is vitally important to encourage those elements at all costs, yet far too many planets are concentrating merely on the short-term and neglecting the long-term health of their colony.
>
> - Professor Leo Caesius, *The Waning Years of Empire* (banned).

Leo stepped out of the shuttle and took a deep breath. The smell struck him at once. There was a hint of jet fuel and the ionisation caused by shuttle drives, but all of that was minor compared to the fresh wind blowing across the landing strip. Earth's atmosphere had stunk…and he hadn't even been aware of it until he'd set foot on a starship. The pollution had been terrible. He knew, from his own private studies, that it caused massive death rates among the Undercity dwellers, but there were always more where they came from. The stink of hydrocarbons and far too many human beings pressed together had been ever-present. He had just never been aware of it until he'd smelled cleaner air.

He turned slowly, stepping away from the shuttle, and caught sight of the mountains in the distance. They were like nothing he had ever seen before. They seemed to reach up endlessly into the clouds, dominating the surrounding countryside for miles around, with green flecks of trees and grass covering their lower levels. He'd seen pictures of Earth's mountain ranges, of course, but he'd never been able to afford a family holiday to the few remaining preserved areas of Earth. Those had been the playground of the rich and famous.

"Dad," Mandy said. It was almost a whine. "Help me down, please."

Leo turned and held out a hand to his daughter. She was shaking, overwhelmed by her new surroundings, for she had definitely never set foot outside her home city on Earth. Avalon was vast and unspoilt by the human race, a paradise for the tired and weary, yet Mandy seemed daunted by the sight. The young were supposed to be more adaptable than the old, or so he had learned in his studies, but Mandy looked doubtful. Mindy didn't seem to have so many doubts. She ran down the shuttle's ramp and down onto the ground, staring around in awe.

"It's so green," she said. "Daddy…what is that?"

Leo followed her pointing finger and saw a strange animal moving around the edge of the spaceport's new fence. A chill ran down his spine as it sank in that he was truly on an alien world. The animal looked like a weird combination of a dog, a horse and a donkey. It gave them a disdainful glance with fish-like eyes and wandered off, grazing as it moved. He wondered, absently, what it was called or if anyone had bothered to try to tame it and its kin. Was it even good eating?

"So," Fiona said. "This is Avalon."

The scorn in her voice made him wince. "Yes," he said, silently wishing that she would shut up long enough for him to work out what to do next. They had to go into Camelot and find somewhere to live, and then start seeing about jobs. He'd checked Avalon's local net – such as it was – and found no mention of a university. The schools seemed to be mainly technical ones, designed to turn out the next generation of industrial workers. "Welcome to our new home."

Fiona snorted again, but mercifully kept her peace. She'd been complaining all the time since the shuttle had undocked from the massive transport, demanding that the pilot take it easy as they descended down towards the planet. Leo remembered what she'd been like when they had first married and wondered, not for the first time, what had happened to the woman he'd married. It was far too easy to understand. She'd had peace, security and wealth – at least for their class – and his actions had torn it away from her. The whole family had been exiled thousands of light years from the core of the Empire.

Mandy realised that she was clutching her father's hand and let go of it, her eyes flickering around the spaceport. Leo watched her with some concern, but she seemed to be recovering; her eyes were following a group of Marines as they unloaded another shuttle. Leo winced inwardly again. Mandy had grown up in a world where she had had no responsibility for her actions and it showed. He had a feeling that life was going to be much more serious on Avalon than it had ever been on Earth. Mindy didn't seem to have any problems at all. She looked as if she wanted to start running all over the spaceport. Only the possible danger kept her firmly in her place.

"Welcome to Avalon," a voice said. Fiona jumped. Leo turned slowly to see Captain Stalker and another Marine standing behind them. He hadn't even heard them coming up to the shuttle! "What do you make of your new home?"

"It smells strange," Mandy said, sullenly. For once, she wasn't eying the Marine. "I don't want to be here."

Leo gave the Captain a glance, silently willing him to understand. "What a remarkable coincidence," Captain Stalker said. His voice was exaggeratedly cheerful. "I don't want to be here either. Orders are orders."

"Yes, but that's different," Mandy protested. "You have to obey orders and go where they send you. I…" Her voice trailed off.

"I cannot prove this to you, not now, but you are far better off here than in the Undercity back on Earth, or dead," Captain Stalker said bluntly. He looked up at Leo. "I understand that you intend to head into Camelot as soon as possible?"

"Yes," Leo said. He recognised the brisk businesslike tone. "We can't presume on your hospitality forever."

"True enough," Captain Stalker agreed. "I have taken the liberty of asking Rifleman Jasmine Yamane to accompany you until you get your bearings. I hope you won't find her too much of an imposition."

Leo, who recognised an order when he heard one, however expressed, nodded slowly. "I'm sure that we won't," he said, ignoring Fiona's angry look. She couldn't wait to be away from the Marines, if only to keep Mandy out of trouble. Leo silently wished her good luck with that. His daughter seemed determined to sleep with each and every male Marine in the Company. "How do we get into town?"

"Jasmine has a locally-produced car for your service," Captain Stalker said. "Let me know how you get on."

He nodded briskly to his subordinate and walked away, leaving Jasmine with Leo and his family. "If you'll come this way," she said, politely. If she was aware of how both of Leo's daughters were staring at her, she didn't show it. "I can drive you into town and help you find lodgings."

The locally-produced car turned out to be a copy of a design that had been old when the Empire was young, large enough to carry Leo's entire family in some degree of comfort. It was a new and strange sight to both girls and they stared in awe as Jasmine steered them out of the spaceport and onto the highway leading down towards the sea. None of the family could drive. On Earth, they had been restricted to using either the transport tubes or aircars, and the aircars had been controlled by their onboard processors. Privately-owned vehicles weren't legally banned, but they were very rare outside the wealthy. The expense was just too much.

Avalon, on the other hand, seemed to have hundreds of privately-owned vehicles. The closer they got to the city, the more vehicles they saw on the road, ranging from cars to buses and trucks. He saw a van drive past carrying live horses – Mindy stared in astonishment, clearly planning to find out where she could get riding lessons – and another carrying newly-picked fruit. Some people rode animals instead, from horses to creatures that had to be native to Avalon itself. The standard colonisation program, he'd learned while he'd been carrying out his research, always included thousands of young animals, cloned and decanted on the new world. Horses, pigs, sheep and cattle reproduced naturally. It was another measure to prevent the complete collapse of a new colony world. Offhand, he couldn't recall a colony world, one established after the rise of the Empire, that had actually failed. They were regarded as very solid investments.

The thought made him study Camelot with a new eye. Parts of the city looked strong and prosperous, other parts looked poor and downcast. He saw men and women who strode purposefully around the city, as if they had places to go, and others who loitered on street corners, without any purpose to their existence. He spotted a line of women who had to be prostitutes, selling themselves for the best that they could get, and a line of men looking for labouring positions. Camelot looked as if it was spending its seed capital, rather than investing in the future. A chill ran down his spine. He had studied how colony worlds could go bad, but seeing it in person was different. The piles of litter in some parts of the city were a very telling sign.

"This is the finest hotel in Camelot," Jasmine said, as she pulled up in front of a blocky stone building. It looked reasonably clean, at least. "The Governor suggested that you stay here for a week while you look for somewhere more permanent."

"Thank you," Leo said, as they stepped out of the car. Apart from a few bags of clothing they'd brought from Earth, they had almost nothing with them. Fiona had mourned the loss of her jewels and fashionable clothes ever since the Marines had taken them in. A mob had looted their house and burned what was left of it to the ground. He looked down at his wife and scowled at her expression. "Coming?"

Jasmine followed them as they stepped into the lobby. If it was the finest hotel on Avalon, Leo would have dreaded walking into a less-prestigious hotel. The lobby was barely clean, with paint coming off the walls and carpets that had never been washed or even vacuumed. He was sure he saw something move on the table as he walked up to the single desk, operated by a girl who looked bored. Her mouth chewed incessantly on a piece of gum.

"Welcome to the Hotel Avalon," she said. Her voice somehow suggested that their presence was an imposition. "One room for the five of you?"

"Two rooms would be fine," Leo said. Mandy looked as if she wanted to protest, but Fiona shot her a glance that made her shut her mouth. He looked over at Jasmine. "Ah…?"

"I'll be returning to the spaceport tonight," Jasmine said, dryly. "I won't have to stay here."

The receptionist stared at Jasmine, and then looked back at Leo. "Two rooms," she said. She quoted a price that made Leo splutter, all in credits. Avalon's local currency clearly wasn't very strong. He named a counteroffer and she nodded, leading him to suspect that he was still overpaying them for the rooms. "If you'll follow me…"

The rooms weren't actually as bad as he'd feared, although the chambermaid didn't look very competent at all. Fiona spent an hour inspecting them minutely, complaining about everything, before finally admitting that they were acceptable, for the moment. Mandy had thrown herself down on her bed while Mindy bombarded Jasmine with questions about the Marine Corps and how one joined up. Jasmine answered as patiently as she could, even when Mandy started firing off questions about what it was like to serve with so many handsome men and which one was best in bed. Fiona slapped her and sent her back to her bed in a rage.

A knock on the door revealed a messenger wearing the closest thing to a formal uniform they'd seen on the planet. "Professor, Chief Councillor Ron Friedman would like the pleasure of your family's company at Afternoon Tea," he said, once Jasmine had checked his identity. "He wishes to welcome you to the planet personally."

"Excellent," Fiona said, before Leo could say anything. "Please tell the Chief Councillor that we would be happy to attend his little meeting. We'll be along as soon as possible."

Leo opened his mouth to object, saw his wife's face, and knew that it would be futile. There was no stopping Fiona when she got into one of those moods. Besides, a new social life might just help her adapt to their new home.

"Very well," he said, seriously. "When does it start?"

He'd half-expected Jasmine to object to them going to the meeting – or get-together, or whatever it was – but the Marine Rifleman said nothing. He wasn't quite sure why Captain Stalker had assigned her to look after them anyway. The town might not be as nice as the briefings from the ADC had made it sound, but they hadn't run into any actual danger. Fiona spent the next hour trying on dresses and insisting that the girls change as well, while Leo donned the traditional suit worn by an Imperial Professor. He might have been fired from the University of Earth – a very rare occurrence – but no one had stripped him of his professorship. Fiona's one suggestion that Jasmine abandon her uniform for a dress was met by a harsh stare.

Chief Councillor Ron Friedman's house was more like a castle, built out of solid stone and guarded by a number of tough-looking men carrying locally-produced weapons. Leo would have been more impressed if he hadn't spent time with Captain Stalker during the long voyage to Avalon; the guards struck him as thugs, rather than disciplined soldiers. They wore uniforms that made them look uncomfortably like wasps – yellow and black – to make them stand out in a crowd.

"Easy targets," he heard Jasmine mutter. He couldn't disagree with her assessment. "A single platoon would go through them like a knife through butter."

The interior of the house was easily the finest building he'd seen on Avalon, even if it didn't quite come up to the levels of some buildings on Earth. A number of men and women chatted together about nothing in particular, while children ran around or played in the pool just outside the house. Their hostess, a charming woman with a big smile, gently took Mandy and Mindy and put them in the care of her own daughter, who led them off towards the pool. Leo hoped that they'd be all right. It had been years since either of them had swum for pleasure.

"You're from Earth," a voice cooed to Fiona. It belonged to a woman who was quite astonishingly fat, making her way through the crowd like a battleship. "You must tell me, my dear; is that the latest fashion?"

Leo blinked, and then smiled. He hadn't thought of it, but Avalon was so far from Earth that all of its styles would be six months out of date. It hadn't struck him as important, of course, but it would make Fiona happy if she was suddenly one of the local fashion leaders. He watched with wry amusement as the newcomer – he hadn't even heard the woman's name – steered Fiona away to a cluster of other women, all of whom looked thoroughly vapid.

"And you must be Professor Caesius," another voice said. He found himself looking at a middle-aged man, with brown hair and an oversized moustache. "I'm Councillor Friedman. On behalf of my constituents, welcome to Avalon."

"Thank you," Leo said. The man's handshake struck him as limp, insincere. He tossed a nervous look at Jasmine and led him over to a smaller group of men and women. "It's good to be here."

Councillor Friedman laughed, too loudly. "Excellent," he proclaimed, slapping Leo on the back. "Now, you must tell us all about Earth and Imperial politics. We hear so little out here."

And, for the next twenty minutes, Leo did.

Jasmine had once been told that the Marine uniform was not only a sign of achievement, but also a barrier. She was uncomfortably aware of the gazes being tossed at her by people who thought that they were being subtle, as if they weren't quite sure what to make of her. She stayed close to the Professor and listened, pretending to be isolated in her own little world.

Captain Stalker had given her two sets of instructions. The first was to keep an eye on the Professor and his family and effectively act as their bodyguard, should one be needed. The second was to gain what intelligence she could about Camelot and the true state of affairs on the ground. She hadn't objected to going to the Afternoon Tea because it offered a priceless opportunity to carry out her second set of instructions…and it was proving very educational. The men and women gathered around the Professor, she was sure, were most of the Councillors of Avalon. They were systematically picking his brains.

A young man was giving her the eye. Jasmine met his and gave him what Marines called the Stare, a wordless challenge to do battle. He lowered his eyes and walked away, with his metaphorical tail between his legs. Jasmine would have preferred to go out drinking with her platoon, or even to have undergone another punishment duty, rather than spend time at such a party. Everyone was just being painfully polite to one another. There was very little love lost between them.

Slowly, she inched closer to Leo and listened carefully. He hadn't mentioned his own disgrace, but he was talking about some of the Empire's problems. Jasmine silently memorised the reactions, carefully placing names to faces. The briefing notes had warned her that some of the most hated men and women on the planet were on the Council. And now, the most dangerous ones were gathering intelligence – for what?

She shook her head. The deployment was going to be very interesting.

CHAPTER SIXTEEN

> What motivates resistance to the Empire? There are simply too many reasons to list; political, economic, and even personal. The real problem, however, is that the number of anti-Empire groups has skyrocketed in the last five decades. None of them pose a threat on their own. The real danger is that they will get organised as a group if we give them time to develop.
> - Professor Leo Caesius, *The Waning Years of Empire* (banned).

Lucas Trent laughed aloud as he shot his load deep into the girl, and then pulled out of her, ignoring her protests and cries of pain. She didn't have any right to protest, not as far as he was concerned. The stuck-up bitch had once been the daughter of a paid-up settler family, looking down on indents like himself because she'd been lucky enough not to be shipped to Avalon as an indentured labourer. Lucas had suffered more than enough abuse from such bitches – and their families – in the six months he'd spent as an indent to want to spend the rest of his life punishing them for their crimes. And, besides, it was fun.

He stood up and wiped himself, using water from a bucket, before pulling on his clothes. The girl had stopped whimpering and was staring up at him, fearful of what her future might hold. It had only been two days since she'd been snatched from her homestead and she'd been raped at least seven times, slowly breaking her spirit and turning her into a girl any bandit could be proud of. She'd spend the rest of her life in one of the refuges in the badlands, hidden from any search parties that came out so far from civilisation, servicing the gang until she grew old and died. He reached out and pinched her nipple, savouring her scream as if it were a fine wine, and then walked out of the room. The door banged shut behind him and one of the guards locked it. The girl wouldn't be going anywhere.

"Yah, Boss," Steven said, looking up as Lucas strode into what he liked to think of as his operations compartment. In reality, it was just another hidden room, with a pair of maps spread out on the table. "Good ride?"

Lucas leered at him. "The best," he said, with a sneer. "Go try her out yourself sometime."

Steven shook his head. "Wrong plumbing," he said. "You should try out the buck I have in my storage bin."

Lucas laughed, part of his mind marvelling at how relaxed he was around Steven. Back on Earth, he'd hated homosexuals, considering them weak and disgusting pieces of shit. His gang had fought homosexual gangs in the Undercity and never even considered making peace with them, even if they were one gang that would never be fighting over women. On Avalon, so far from the Undercity that it seemed like a dream, old hatreds didn't matter. Steven was tough, dependable and loyal. He made an excellent deputy for the bandit gang.

Earth's authorities didn't know it, but they'd made a serious mistake when they'd sent Lucas to Avalon, rather than simply dumping him on a far less Earth-like world or executing him on the spot. His deportation papers stated that he'd been nothing more than yet another gang member, but the truth was very different; he'd been their leader. Lucas had been born to a mother in the Undercity – he had no idea who his father had been, or that of his brothers and sisters – and he'd never even had a hope of climbing out to the shining towers of the Middle City.

At five years old, he had already been a vicious fighter, working for one of the gang lords in his city-block. At nine, he had started to run whorehouses, pimping girls to his fellow gang members and to richer people from the Middle City, who wanted tastes of things they couldn't have high above. At fifteen, after a brief and bloody gang war, he'd been the undisputed ruler of his city-block and a terror to anyone who knew him.

Lucas had been born with a talent, one that might have taken him far had he been born elsewhere. He instinctively understood how to build an organisation – the Knives – that supported his primacy, and how to maintain it. His lieutenants had known that he would support them as long as they were loyal and that if they were disloyal, there was nowhere they could run to that would keep them safe. He'd bribed the Civil Guard and forced them to turn a blind eye to his people as they raided along the edges of the Middle City. At nineteen, he'd been expanding his power into other city-blocks and considering ways and means of making an assault on the Middle City. It wouldn't be the first time a gang lord had become respectable.

And then it had all come crashing down. The first he'd known of it was when a Civil Guard assault squad had come crashing into his city-block, apparently looking for someone else! The irony hadn't amused him as he'd sat with the other Knives, chained up and awaiting what passed for a trial in the Empire. They hadn't known who they were dealing with. It had been the only thing that had saved him. Like almost everyone else born in the Undercity, Lucas was unregistered. The Civil Guard hadn't made the link between him and the dreaded Knife, leader of the Knives, and merely transported him and some of his men to Avalon.

They had been promised opportunities. They had come, all right; the opportunities to be kicked, beaten and treated like dirt. Lucas had had quite enough of it very quickly and he'd planned their escape with care. They'd escaped one night and slipped into the badlands, encountering other bandits as they fled. And Lucas, formerly a gang lord of Earth, had risen to become a bandit chieftain. The irony was not lost on him.

He shook his head, changing the subject. "Has there been any sign of pursuit?"

"Nothing," Steven said. "The spotters reported that the Civil Guard merely swept the area around the township and went home. We haven't monitored any communications that suggest that they're planning an offensive."

Lucas nodded. It would have horrified the Civil Guard to know that one of their officers had quite happily sold the bandits one of their tactical radios, but as far as he knew, they had no idea that it had happened. The officer in question had been waylaid as he came out of a brothel and knifed to death. At least he'd died happy.

"The other report, however, is more worrying," Steven said. One of the other reasons Lucas tolerated him was because Steven was a great organiser. Lucas knew that it was important to be carefully organised, but it bored him and most of his men. "The men who landed at the spaceport are definitely Marines."

Lucas looked down at his hands. "How much damage can a single Company of Marines do to us?"

Steven shrugged. "Our sources in Camelot claimed that the Marines were the most dangerous men on the planet," he said. "It's hard to know for sure. But then, they do have a good reason to go after us."

Lucas smiled, thinly, thinking about his growing power. He had realised, at a very early age, that there was no difference between the Empire's government and his own gang. The Knives took money or beat up the people who couldn't or wouldn't pay. The Empire's tax collectors took money or jailed the people who couldn't or wouldn't pay. Hell, a third of Avalon's population was so deeply in debt that their great-grandchildren would be working to pay off the interest. There was no moral difference at all. The thought had led to another thought, one that could be applied in full to Avalon.

There were hundreds of homesteads and townships scattered around the badlands, most of them rarely capable of standing off a bandit raid. He'd sent representatives to each of them, offering them the choice between paying tribute and being raided. Some – like Kirkhaven, which no longer existed – had refused, or screamed for help from the Civil Guard. Others, the vast majority, had swallowed their pride and knuckled under. A vast web of fear and servitude was slowly being woven around the townships, holding them all under his thumb. It was a direct challenge to the government in Camelot. They had to respond, if they knew that it was taking place.

"I suppose that they do," he agreed. "Get back in touch with our sources in the Civil Guard. Tell them that I want to know in advance if the Marines so much as fart publicly." Steven snickered. "And then send the tax collectors" – another joke, one with a nasty sting in the tail – "around to warn the townships not to cooperate with the Marines. We can hand out another object lesson if necessary."

He glanced down at the map, considering. "The Marines will be gone soon enough," he added, "and we will still be here."

"Perhaps," Steven said. "Or perhaps our allies at Camelot will try to betray us."

"They'd be fools to try," Lucas said, with a leer. They hadn't kept all of the women and children they'd taken on the raid. A handful had been assigned to a far darker fate. "With everything we have on them, they'll be lucky if they're only beaten to death by an outraged public."

He winked at his friend and headed back out of the room. There were other newly-enslaved women in the complex and they wouldn't deflower themselves. Lucas was on top of the world, the real power in the badlands and in much of the surrounding area. His power was intangible, barely seen unless it was time to give some stupid bastard a clout, but none the less real for all that. What could the Marines, no matter their reputation, do against him?

"Our sources in the Civil Guard were quite clear on the matter," Rufus said. There was a bitter tone in his voice. "Our esteemed Governor's pleas for help have finally brought the Marines."

Gabriella Cracker blinked at the hopelessness in Rufus's tone. The older farmer had been her father, to all intents and purposes, ever since her real father had died when she was very young. He and his family had brought Gaby up as their own, along with their own children, and he'd always been a reassuring presence in her life. To hear him sound broken was startling.

"One Company of Marines," Julian pointed out. His handsome face twisted into a sneer. "We are legion."

Rufus eyed his son with an expression that would have promised a belting, if Julian had been younger. Rufus had survived successive attempts by the Civil Guard to exterminate the Crackers and had learned caution. Julian – and many of the others from the younger generation – was keen for action. They thought that the thousands of Crackers – in both movements – could take on the might of the Empire and win. Gaby knew better. Peter Cracker, her grandfather, had lost his life when the Empire had dispatched a tiny destroyer to Avalon and dropped kinetic weapons on his army.

"We are winning when we are not losing," Rufus said, coldly. "If we attempt to take on the Marines on their own ground, we lose. It's as simple as that."

Gaby stared down at the map, wishing that they would both shut up and let her think. Her father had been young – barely entering his teens – when he'd become the Cracker, the head of the family and head of the movement. He'd had rejuvenation treatments at a very young age, but he'd lived out most of his extended lifespan without making any real progress. He'd married late, had her late…and, when Gaby had been four years old, he'd gone down fighting against the Civil Guard. No one had been more surprised than Gaby when she'd been declared the movement's leader, although she had eventually realised why. The Crackers had split into two factions already. A second set of fissions would destroy the movement more completely than anything the Empire could do.

They didn't dare face the Empire in open combat, no matter what some of the younger fools said about the honour of open battle. They'd be slaughtered. Gaby might have grown up on a farm, but she was far from ignorant about the realities of the Empire's power. The Imperial Army alone included more men than existed on the entire planet of Avalon. If the Empire wanted to crush the Crackers once and for all, they could do it. Gaby believed that while complete independence was impossible, they might be able to work out an agreement that would leave Avalon as an autonomous world. End the debts, end the indenture program, end the endless series of bureaucratic regulations that were killing local industry…Avalon might become a world to remember.

She looked up at Julian and winced, inwardly. She had had to learn the techniques of underground warfare on the job, but she'd learned quickly. Julian had never learned at all, but then, as an officially unregistered child, he'd never had to. He'd moved from his father's farm to the base camps in the badlands and up in the mountains, confident that he could handle anything that the Empire might throw at him. Gaby knew that it was a delusion, but it was hard to convince him otherwise.

"Leave the argument for now," she said, firmly. She'd told the movement's council that she had no intention of being a figurehead, even if there were some people who questioned the wisdom of appointing a sixteen-year-old girl as leader. She wouldn't have absolute authority – that was asking for trouble – but she would be respected and obeyed. "Are the Marines likely to come after us?"

She saw the faint smile on Rufus' face and her lips twitched. He was proud of her, although she didn't know why. She hadn't done anything yet! "I think that that is very likely," Rufus said, finally. "They now represent the single most formidable combat unit on the face of the planet. The Governor will insist that they do something about us very quickly."

"They may go after the bandits first," Julian put in. "Major Grosskopf has been shitting bricks about them, according to our spies."

Gaby nodded. Major Grosskopf was an uncomfortably capable officer. If the Civil Guard had been a real army, she had a nasty suspicion that the Crackers would have been in serious trouble. Even so, he'd pulled off a number of unpleasant surprises, convincing the movement's council to try to have him assassinated. So far, he'd survived everything the Crackers had thrown at him.

"We can only hope," she said. The bandits were the other real enemy. When Avalon belonged to her people, they would be ruthlessly hunted down and destroyed. "That should give us a chance to learn just what they can do."

"Definitely," Julian said, with a grin. It reminded her of the embarrassing times they'd shared when their hormones had gone into overdrive, back when they'd both been teenagers. He'd been attracted to her, but she hadn't been attracted to a boy she'd known since she was a baby. His crush had faded when he'd fallen for someone else, yet there were times when being with him was uncomfortable. "And perhaps we can steer them towards the bandits."

Gaby looked up, impressed. "Devious," she said. She wouldn't shed a tear if the Marines massacred the bandits. The Civil Guard might not be able to track the bandits very well, but the Crackers knew roughly where their bases actually were. "I like that thought."

"On the other hand," Rufus said, "anything that ties the Marines up is going to help us in the long run."

Gaby nodded. "Perhaps we can slip them information through our moles in the Civil Guard, get them more trusted," she said. The Crackers had supplied quite a few men for the Civil Guard, although Major Grosskopf's efforts had limited their effectiveness. "That might even things up a bit."

"Perhaps," Rufus said. "The bad news is that the Marines are going to be moving to Castle Rock. We don't have any sources there."

"We could probably get a few fishermen to take a look at the island," Julian suggested. "Some of them do use it as a harbour during stormy weather."

"They won't be able to stay," Rufus said. "We'll have to give the matter some thought."

Gaby nodded. It would have upset the Governor to know just how badly Camelot had been penetrated by the Crackers, or just how many spies there were operating within the planetary government. Good intelligence was one of the keys to victory – or so she had been told as a young girl learning at the feet of men and women who had fought for years – and she had that. The Marines might be impossible to penetrate – or so legend had it – but they'd need help from the mainland.

"We can afford to play a waiting game," she said, standing up. "We'll watch and wait, maybe pull our horns in a bit and see what they do. Perhaps they're overrated after all."

"Perhaps," Rufus said. "And what if they're not?"

"We could always strike now," Julian said. His voice became more eager as he outlined his new thought. "We have assets in place in Camelot. We could move now and obliterate the planetary government before they call out the Marines."

"Too risky," Rufus said. "We'd stand to lose too much if we lost."

Julian looked unhappy, but nodded.

"Our objective is to win," Gaby reminded them. "Our objective is a free and independent Avalon. That is our goal. We don't need to launch a desperate attack to win. All we have to do is carry on with the plan."

CHAPTER SEVENTEEN

> The Civil Guard is, in theory, meant to provide a local force capable of handling most disturbances. In practice, the Guard is often heavily corrupt and completely useless. Promotion is based on political reliability rather than military competence. This is endemic to almost all of the Empire's combat arms, but the Guard is almost certainly the worst.
> - Professor Leo Caesius, *The Waning Years of Empire* (banned).

"Attention on deck!"

The Marines stood to attention as Edward strode into the briefing room. It had once been a warehouse for storing dried fish and hints of the smell still lingered, but it was usable and far from the worst accommodation the Marines had used. The Governor had been apologetic about the living quarters – the owners of the island hadn't bothered to install more than the basics – but Edward hadn't cared. It would have surprised and horrified the Governor if he'd known that his former Captain had once commanded an operation, quite literally, from a muddy hole in the middle of the battlefield. That had been a clusterfuck to remember!

"At ease," he ordered, as he took his position at the front of the warehouse. Someone had pinned a large paper map of Avalon on one wall and a chart showing the local government officials on another, but the remainder were thankfully bare. It wouldn't be long before the Marines started turning the makeshift barracks into home. "We have been here one week and the Governor is already asking when we intend to take the field against the bandits."

A low murmur ran through the room. They had all seen combat and few of them enjoyed it for its own sake, but they'd heard enough about the depredations of the bandits to want to wipe them out. They had been brought up to understand that the credo of the Marine Corps – and the Imperial Army and Navy, for that matter – was to stand between civilians and those who sought to do them harm. And, besides, they were all bored with unpacking the shuttles and setting up prefabricated barracks and training grounds. The shortage of trustworthy civilian labour was forcing the Marines to work overtime. It was starting to take a toll on the Company's morale.

The former owners of Castle Rock – who had apparently sought to charge the Governor through the nose for the use of their island – wouldn't have recognised it. It had been transformed from a windswept island with only a handful of farmers to a primitive but effective military base. The Marines had loaded most of the supplies into a set of prefabricated warehouses and had placed them under heavy guard, even though no one outside the Marine Corps was supposed to set foot on the island. With some local labour, which Edward intended to bring in once the island had been properly secured, they could expand the base to the point where they could begin training new recruits.

Over the last week, the Marines had explored the island carefully, poking their noses everywhere. With the exception of some wild pigs and sheep, the island was deserted now that the farmers were gone. Given time, the Marines would possess an intimate knowledge of their new base, one that would serve them well if the Crackers ever sought to attack them at home. It would be suicide if they tried, but Edward knew better than to assume that the enemy would know that. Untrained insurgents could be very dangerous, if only because they would sometimes try things that no qualified officer would dare. Sometimes they even succeeded.

"It is my intention to start deployments tonight," Edward continued. The Marines sat up straighter as they confronted the prospect of action. Hands unconsciously checked weapons and utility belts for equipment. "First, Second and Fourth Platoons will take the field against the enemy; Third and Fifth will remain at the base and continue to unpack our supplies. Sixth and Seventh will serve as reserve. We will move fast and get into position to confront the enemy as soon as possible."

He felt Lieutenant Tom Faulkner's wince beside him and carefully concealed his smile. Faulkner had not only passed the Slaughterhouse, but he'd spent two years of his career earning his Combat Engineer's badge. If he hadn't been so eager to transfer into a fighting company, he would probably have remained on Earth, or deployed out to one of the fireman deployments in the core worlds. The Imperial Army maintained separate Combat Engineering departments, but the Marines preferred to blur them together, if only to ensure that they had a reasonable blend of skills on hand. It would take weeks, at best, to bring in a Combat Engineering unit from the nearest military base. Faulkner would have to remain at Castle Rock until the base was properly up and running.

"We will depart tonight under cover of darkness," Edward said. Avalon, thankfully, wasn't covered in cities. It was quite possible to move even a relatively large number of Marines under cover of darkness without someone noticing. The planet's ATC was a part-time operation. They could barely track the Civil Guard's aircraft, let alone the Marines'. "We will board the Raptors and move out to the platoon house. Major?"

He looked over at Major George Grosskopf, who looked up. His reaction to the Marines had been slightly disappointing, for he'd taken them in stride. Edward had had to remind himself that Grosskopf had served in the Imperial Army and had a good idea of the capabilities of Marines and their supporting units. The Civil Guardsmen who had never served off Avalon would be in for a shock.

"This is Avalon," Grosskopf said, nodding to the big map on the wall. "You will notice that there are only five main cities on the planet, all concentrated on Arthur, the main continent. Those cities hold around half of the planet's population. The remainder of the population is scattered over the countryside in townships, which are effectively farming communities intended to develop the planet. Some of them are friendly towards the local government, some are deeply hostile and some are under permanent threat by the bandits, forcing them to pay tribute and keep them informed of our movements. It has so far proven impossible to dislodge the bandits from the countryside."

He pointed with a long stick towards an area of the map that had been shaded red. "The badlands," he said. "The badlands are easily the worst terrain on the planet, perhaps the worst outside an H-Class world or even the Slaughterhouse." Edward smiled at some of the chuckles from the Marines. "Some thousands of years ago, there was a massive series of earthquakes and the ground is all broken up into canyons, underwater pools and exposed mineral deposits. The deposits, in particular, make it hard to use sensors or even primitive navigation devices within the badlands. The terrain is so bad that it is very hard to locate or destroy bandit camps. There could be hundreds of thousands of bandits in there and we wouldn't know a thing about it."

Edward saw his face twist, bitterly. "There are a large number of townships scattered near the badlands, for reasons best known to the ADC," he continued. "In theory, those towns are armed and capable of looking after themselves. In practice, everyone has to work hard to give the town a chance of surviving and it is quite easy for a bandit raid to get into town before the inhabitants have time to react. You cannot imagine the scenes of horror; the bandit gangs loot, rape and burn before escaping back into the badlands. We – the Civil Guard – have been unable to get forces into position to block their escape in time."

"A question," Gwen said. "How many bandit gangs are there?"

"No one knows," Grosskopf said. If he was surprised at her question, he didn't show it. Marines always asked questions during briefings. "Our intelligence suggests that there are many small bands, but some of them cooperate with each other and others try to wipe out their fellow bandits while also raiding us. There have been reports of a super-gang emerging, one that has absorbed or destroyed the smaller gangs, yet we have been unable to obtain confirmation."

Edward frowned inwardly. The Civil Guard had had an astonishing round of bad luck, which suggested that another factor was involved. It hadn't taken more than a quick glance at their records to realise that they never carried out background checks on any of their recruits, particularly the poor bloody infantry. It wouldn't be hard for a bandit gang to slip a few of their members into the Civil Guard, or simply offer large sums of cash for information. If they received advance warning of a raid, they could simply pull up stakes and vanish into the badlands.

"We have, however, been granted an opportunity," Grosskopf said. "My Intelligence Officer has been running a source in one of the bandit gangs, trying to pin down their next move. She believes that the bandits intend to attack Eddisford, a large-sized township five miles from the outer edge of the badlands. Eddisford is lucky in that most of the settlers were actually able to pay off their debts and reinvest in equipment they need – in short, they're not the kind of people to pay tribute to the gangs. We need to catch those bastards in the act and wipe the fuckers out."

"We need to take as many of them alive as possible," Edward injected, quickly. "Now…"

He pointed a long finger at the map and tapped a handful of locations. "This is what we're going to do…"

"Now this is *real* activity," Blake said, as they checked their weapons and armour. The thin humming sound of the Raptors spooling up could be heard in the distance. "How many bandits do you want to bag?"

"Oh, I don't know," Joe Buckley said. "I think it's a bit of a comedown after hunting pirates and storming rebel fortresses."

"The Captain said to take them alive," Jasmine reminded them. She pulled on her armour and studied the reflection in Blake's armour. "That means stunners only at first; lethal force authorised only if they fight back."

"Of course they will," Blake said, turning slightly so he could check his own armour. "Imperial Law demands the death penalty for their crimes. We may take them alive, but only so we can beat the crap out of them for information and then hang them from the nearest tree. What do they have to lose by fighting us?"

"The chance to help our gallant Empire grow and develop," Koenraad said dryly. "How could any self-respecting bandit pass up on that chance?"

Jasmine chuckled to herself. "They're not interested in chances," she said. "They're not even interested in a political cause. They're just interested in what they can take off other people. They're the worst kind of scum."

She scowled down at her helmet, thinking furiously. They'd been shown some of the pictures that the Civil Guardsmen had taken of the aftermath, after the bandits had invaded a town, had their fun and headed off again. There had been bodies everywhere, burning buildings and desecrated churches. Worst of all, at least to her eyes, had been the handful of dead women left on the ground, stripped naked. It hadn't taken much imagination to know what had happened to them. She'd thought about rape, even acknowledged that it could happen to her, yet coming face to face with the reality was sickening. Blake was right. The bandits deserved to die.

Cold discipline, the result of three years on the hardest training ground known to man, forced her emotions down into the small compartment in her head. Yes, the bandits would die, but only after they'd betrayed their friends and allies. They might think themselves tough, yet they were nothing compared to the puniest Marine in the entire Corps. And, when they did die, Jasmine intended to volunteer for the hanging squad. Let the bastards see her tying the knot and yanking them up to break their necks.

"You think that they have links with the big men in Camelot?" Koenraad asked, as he pulled on his own armour. "Wouldn't it be nice to prove that?"

Jasmine smiled, her mind still dark and cold. She hadn't enjoyed the brief time at the Chief Councillor's mansion and her opinion of most of the Planetary Council wasn't high. She'd been trained to observe and she'd seen a number of men and women trying to see what advantage they could wring from the Marines, or trying to decide how the Marines would affect their own plans. Jasmine was cynical enough to know that sometimes the Marines were just sent out on missions because of a political agenda, but not even the Grand Senate had been so blatant. They had to have forgotten that she had ever been there, for they had been quite open in their assessments. The Marines could live or die for all they cared.

"Yes," she said. "It would be nice to prove that and hang half of the bastards."

Forty-one Marines marched out of the makeshift barracks and down towards the landing strip. It had originally been designed for light cargo aircraft, but Marine Raptors could use them without problems. The Raptor was a VTOL aircraft capable of landing almost anywhere, even in the middle of a forest or a sinking boat. The massive tilt-rotors were already chopping at the air. They looked primitive – the technology was almost ten centuries old – but they could do the job. The more advanced skimmers or flyers would have to wait until they were needed.

"This is the Captain," Captain Stalker said. Jasmine had been surprised to hear that the Captain intended to take personal command, but after dealing with the politics of Camelot, he probably felt like killing someone. "Lock your communicators to Frequency Alpha."

Jasmine nodded, keying the command into her suit's processors. The *Sebastian Cruz* had launched a constellation of light satellites into orbit, providing the Marines with a secret – and secure – communications network. She couldn't understand why Avalon had such a primitive communications network in the first place – there was such a thing as taking budget cuts too far – but it wouldn't matter. The locals might know that the satellites had been launched, yet they could only guess at their capabilities. The tiny satellites not only handled communications, but they also provided astonishingly efficient reconnaissance from high above. The bandits, she knew, would wet themselves in shock if they knew just how good the system actually was.

"Good," Captain Stalker said, when they had all checked in. "Board the aircraft."

Jasmine followed Blake's reassuring bulk as he stepped into the lead Raptor, finding a place to sit inside the aircraft's cavernous hold. Unlike a civilian aircraft, or a ground-to-space shuttle, there were no seats for the Marines. When they landed, they would be expected to exit the aircraft as quickly as possible – and, if they were hit, they would be ejected out into the air before the aircraft could explode. Jasmine had been ejected from a Raptor during the Han Campaign and the experience had been the most terrifying of her life. The Marines had all survived, barely. The pilots had given their lives to prevent the remains of their aircraft from coming down on top of friendly forces.

She felt the aircraft jerk as it launched itself into the sky. The Raptor was, despite its crude appearance and technology, the product of hundreds of years of research into aircraft design. It was almost completely silent, drifting through the sky without being detected, unless it was by the naked eye. The bandits, she had been informed, didn't possess active sensor systems. It made sense to her; if they had, even the Civil Guard could hardly have failed to locate their base. The planetary ATC wouldn't be able to track them.

The low humming running through the aircraft almost lulled her to sleep as the Raptor crossed the coastline and headed inland. Many of the other Marines were snatching what sleep they could, knowing that they might be in action as soon as they landed, but Jasmine couldn't quite close her eyes. She wished she could see out of the aircraft, even though she knew she would see nothing, but darkness, broken only by isolated lights. Avalon was barely one hundred and fifty years old. The human race hadn't made much impression on the planet.

"Four minutes to landing," Gwen said, her voice echoing sharply in Jasmine's earpiece. "Anyone resting their eyes had better open them now."

Jasmine realised with astonishment that she had dozed off and hastily checked her weapons and supplies. Everything was as it should be, much to her relief, as the aircraft started to descend. This was always the most dangerous part of any insertion operation – a single ground-based weapon could wipe out an entire platoon of Marines with a lucky shot – and she only relaxed slightly when the aircraft touched down. No hail of fire tore through the aircraft and shredded them. The night was as dark and silent as the grave.

"Go, go, go!" Gwen barked.

Jasmine followed Blake and Koenraad as they raced out of the aircraft, spreading out to secure the landing zone. Their suits of armour exchanged fast signals with one another, confirming that the Marines were alone. She looked up at Merlin, hanging high overhead, yet seemingly so close that she could reach up and pull the moon from the sky. Merlin wasn't much larger than Luna, but it orbited closer to the planet. The briefing had suggested that that might explain the badlands, or the Mystic Mountains in the distance.

"All clear, Captain," she reported. She carried out another sweep of the area, just to be sure. "No enemy contact."

"Good," Captain Stalker said. He sounded reassuringly calm. "Move out."

Chapter Eighteen

> There is a joke that runs 'a nation is a group of people united by a shared delusion of the past and a hatred of their neighbours.' Like many such jokes, there is a hard kernel of truth within the humour. Society is always a consensus, a shared understanding of right and wrong. If 'wrong' becomes 'right' – i.e. behaviour tending to increase a person's chances of survival – then society will be warped and destroyed. This is becoming alarmingly clear all across the Empire.
>
> - Professor Leo Caesius, *The Waning Years of Empire* (banned).

Nelson Oshiro braced himself as he led the small group of Knives down toward Eddisford. It was a larger, more prosperous settlement than the one he'd been sent to after being transported from Earth, but it was alarmingly similar for all of that. It was never certain what reception they'd receive from the farmers and their communities. Some would pay their tribute without fighting; others would refuse to submit until the Knives started to open fire. It confused Nelson, but the Knife himself had issued strict orders and he didn't dare disobey them. There was to be no looting, rape or burning unless the township offered serious resistance.

Eddisford was a small cluster of buildings surrounded by tilled fields and farmhouses. Some of them looked as if they were on the verge of expanding, perhaps claiming additional ground from the Land Development Office and inviting in new settlers. Others looked as if they were permanently on the verge of falling apart, marking out the less successful farmers from their rivals.

He stroked the nag's back gently – it was almost worth being transported, and the kicks and beatings he'd received when he arrived, just to ride the strange alien beast – and urged it forward, down towards the centre of town. He saw a handful of birds rising up as the bandits rode forwards, but there was no sign of any living human beings. A sense he hadn't known he possessed began to sound a warning at the back of his neck. There were always people. The men might be out working the fields, but the women would be at home, while the children would be at school. They should be running from his men now, trying to hide.

His lips twitched as they rode down into the centre of town. Perhaps they were hiding, except they couldn't…could they? Nelson had never been much of a farmer – his former master had thought that he was only fit for brute work – yet he knew that the farmers couldn't abandon their crops. He touched the nag's neck and the beast obediently slowed to a halt, allowing him to slip off the saddle and down onto the ground. It hadn't been obvious over the noise of hooves and the pounding of his own heart, but the town was silent.

"They're gone," Lucky Vin said. Nelson scowled at him. Lucky Vin was one of the former Knives from Earth, assured a high position just by being close to the Knife himself. He was also, he suspected, there to keep an eye on Nelson. It wouldn't be the first time someone had decided to desert the Knives and set up a private operation of their own. "Where the hell have they gone?"

"Perhaps hell," one of the other bandits said. He threw back his head and bawled a laugh into the air, sending more birds scurrying through the air. "Perhaps some other bunch of bastards has come and taken them all away."

Nelson shook his head absently, staring around in disbelief. None of the bandit gangs would take an entire township. They'd take young and pretty women – or perhaps older women, if there were no younger women to hand – and children, but not adult males. They couldn't be trusted and there was no fun in raping them. A bandit attack would have left the town in flaming ruins. Instead, it was empty.

One hand dropped to the flare pistol at his belt. A single red flare would bring the remainder of the force out of hiding and get them into the town, but for what? A green flare would tell them to back off and wait, but they had never considered what might happen if the entire town was deserted. The mystery nagged at him. Had the town decided that they didn't want to live near the bandits anymore and had simply packed up and left?

"Hey," Lucky Vin said, suddenly. Nelson snapped his head around and saw…nothing. "I saw something."

"I bet you did," Nelson sneered. He pushed as much disdain into his voice as he could, if only to cover his own unease. "What do you think you saw?"

"A shimmer in the air," Lucky Vin admitted, uncomfortably. A handful of bandits jeered and others looked as if they wanted to join in. "It was just…there, just for a second."

"Right," Nelson drawled. "And a shimmer is going to hurt us?"

Lucky Vin flushed. His position was at least partly dependent on respect, and that would be comprehensively lacking after today. Even if someone didn't put a knife in him, he wouldn't be able to issue orders to junior Knives. He could beat up as many Knives as he liked and still no one would ever forget.

"It's odd," he persisted. "It could be important."

Nelson turned away from him, deliberately looking towards the church the settlers had built…and froze. Just for a second, he saw a heat shimmer in the air, a distortion that had to be concealing something. The moment of horrified realisation came too late.

One of the other interesting – and classified – attributes of Marine Combat Armour was the chameleon effect. It had its limits, but it allowed a Marine – walking slowly and very quietly – to be effectively invisible, as long as the enemy didn't know what they were looking for. Edward had considered it a worthwhile gamble. The bandits might know about the Marines, but they wouldn't be looking for high tech equipment, allowing First Platoon to get to almost point-blank range before the enemy realised that they were in trouble. On his command, the shimmer faded away, revealing no less than seven Marines standing almost within touching distance of the bandits.

The bandits froze for a second, too long. Four of the Marines carried stunners and played them over their targets, knocking them to the ground. Their horse-like steeds – nags, according to the briefing files he'd memorised – howled under the impact of the stun rays, but weren't badly affected. One of them lifted its hooves and tried to kick its tormentor, only to break its spindly legs on the armour.

The remaining bandits opened fire with their chemical-projectile weapons, only to see the shots bounce off the combat armour and ricochet away. They were rapidly stunned, apart from one who was cuffed to the ground by a Marine and kicked in the chest. Edward smiled inwardly as the Marines cuffed their targets and piled them up in a corner. By the time they recovered, they'd be held back at the platoon house, spilling everything they knew to the interrogators.

"Mission accomplished," Master Sergeant Young said over the private channel. He'd dreamed up the plan and insisted on leading it personally. Edward had seen the common sense at once. Stunners had only limited range and using them too early might have given the bandits a chance to flee. "We have nine hostiles captive, sir."

Edward nodded. Convincing the townspeople to hide in their basements had been simple enough, once he'd explained who and what they were. Not all of them had been eager – he'd seen expressions that reflected fear of the bandits and fear that the Marines would desert them – but they'd complied. The bandits had walked right into the trap.

"Excellent work," he said, relieved. Whoever the enemy leaders trusted to carry out a raid had to be pretty high up in their organisation. Such a person could normally be relied upon to know as much as possible about their gang, if only to use as blackmail information. "Take them back to the platoon house and…"

The sound of shooting breaking out interrupted him.

Horace Netherly had never trusted Nelson, the slimy son of a bitch. He was all puffed up because he was smart and clever, yet he wasn't really one of the Knives. How could he be? He'd been brought up in a mega-city on the other side of Earth and his original gang had been small fry compared to the Knives. The Knife could keep telling and telling them how important it was that they learned to think big, but Horace knew that that was a bad idea. The larger the organisation, the more outsiders; the more outsiders in the organisation, the greater the chance of a betrayal. One of his most trusted lieutenants had quietly followed Nelson and his men into the deserted town, reporting back from the very edge of Eddisford. The town was completely deserted.

It didn't take long for Horace to realise what Nelson had done. The bastard had warned the townspeople himself, warning them to run and hide. It was the only alternative that made sense to him. The Civil Guard wouldn't have been able to even fart without the Knives hearing of it, while the Marines...well, if the Marines were so good, why hadn't they been ordered to clean up the Undercity? Nelson was trying to set up his own organisation in direct opposition to the Knife. It could not be allowed.

He passed his orders down the chain of bandits, each one carrying rifles and grenades, as well as their signature knives. They'd take Eddisford quickly and occupy the town, before torturing Nelson to discover where the locals had gone. They would be found, punished and left in no doubt that defiance led only to death. And then Nelson would die and the Knife would be pleased with him.

"Go," he shouted, and fired a single red flare into the air. A stream of bandits poured out of hiding and started to run towards the town. "Kill the fuckers."

He followed his men down the long road, cursing Nelson's nags under his breath, and watched as they approached the outskirts of the town. Nelson could ride out of the other side of the town and vanish if he acted quickly enough, although he had yet to see a nag that could outrun a bullet. A Gnasher, maybe...

The thought was banished from his mind as he saw the black-clad figures standing in the centre of town. He had only a second to realise that he'd been wrong before a single bullet smashed through his head and killed him instantly.

Jasmine had lain in her position for over three hours, alternatively cursing and blessing her armour for its protection. They'd allowed the first group of bandits to enter the town, but she was damned if she was going to allow a second group to enter…and, now that they had prisoners, there was no need to avoid slaughtering them. The bandits seemed completely insane – they were charging right at the Marines – but to be fair, they had no way of knowing the Marines were there. The first group of bandits would have been horrified to know that the Marines had tracked them with their scopes all the way.

The order, when it came, was almost an anticlimax. "Open fire," Gwen said. "Kill them all."

Jasmine squeezed the trigger on her MAG-74 and had the satisfaction of seeing one of the bandits die, his head exploding like a grape. A MAG-74 was designed to shoot through light combat armour. A human head was nothing to it. Other bandits were falling as the other Marines fired themselves. She switched her rifle to another target and serviced him as well, putting a neat hole through his forehead. A third man jumped up, for some reason best known to himself, and her shot caught him in the throat, blowing out the back of his neck.

The bandits, acting more on instinct than any plan, threw themselves to the ground and tried to fire back. It was pitiful. They couldn't even see where the shots were coming from – the MAG-74 was smokeless – and most of their firing went wild. A handful of the more self-possessed bandits threw grenades towards the Marines, but most of them fell uselessly in the gap between the Marines and their targets. They didn't stand a chance. Jasmine pushed that thought to the back of her head, squeezing her trigger time and time again. It was a point of honour not to miss with a single shot. The sharpshooting badge she'd won at the Slaughterhouse still meant something to her.

We should have set up a MAG-54 and swept them away with a single burst, she thought as she picked off another bandit. Their line had come completely to pieces. Some had thrown down their weapons and were trying to surrender; others were turning and fleeing, only to be shot down in the back. Jasmine saw an overweight man running with a speed that surprised her and placed a shot right in the back of his head. He threw up his hands and crashed to the ground. She didn't smile, but moved on to the next target.

"Men talk about fair fights," her Drill Instructor had thundered. For various reasons, new recruits at Boot Camp and the first year of the Slaughterhouse were segregated by sex. "Men are fools and morons who cannot remember that the purpose of war is to win. You are not being trained to fight a fair fight; you are being trained to defeat the enemies of the Empire! The best chance to give your enemy is none at all. A fair fight is a losing fight. Shoot him in the back, kick him in the balls, play dead till he has his pants around his ankles and then give him hell!"

Jasmine's lips twitched as she saw a bandit who had somehow managed to hide himself behind a tree and was popping away desperately at the Marines with a little hunting pistol. It was more powerful than she would have expected – but then, Avalon's wildlife tended to be dangerous – but it hardly mattered. His shots weren't going anywhere near the Marines. She targeted him carefully, wondering if she was aiming at one of the rapists who had left small and broken bodies behind, and placed a shot directly on his nose.

And, suddenly, it was all over.

"Cuff the survivors and prepare to take them back to camp," Gwen ordered. Her voice was as cold and dispassionate as ever, but Jasmine could have sworn she heard a note of satisfaction hidden behind the commanding tone. If half of the rumours about Gwen's activities were true, the dead bandits were the lucky ones. "I want Fourth Platoon to sweep the area towards the badlands. Now!"

Jasmine exploded out of her hiding place, half-expecting to feel a bullet slamming into her armour. There was nothing, but a bloody field full of cooling bodies. A handful were still moving, suggesting that they were alive, even though they had lost the will to fight.

She didn't blame them. After six months of boot camp, she had thought she was good. The very first battle exercise they'd done at the Slaughterhouse had been a bloody defeat for the new recruits, a humbling and pointed reminder of how inexperienced they were. She smiled at the memory – defeat always taught more lessons than victory – and reached the first captive, a young boy barely out of his teens. He stared up at her, his eyes wide with terror.

She rolled him over with her boot, then grabbed his hands and cuffed them behind his back. He cried out at the new pain, but she ignored him, leaving him lying there for the recovery team to find. The next bandit was clearly too badly wounded to live for long, even with the best of medical care. It was tempting to leave him there to bleed out and die, but what little mercy remained in her pushed her into putting her foot on his head and crushing the remains of his life out of him. It was probably something of a relief.

The next captive had been playing possum, holding a pistol to his chest until she got too close for him to miss. Jasmine watched with detached amusement as he levelled it at her chest and pulled the trigger four times. Four heavy punches slammed into her chest – the armour couldn't block everything – but it was nothing, not compared to what she'd been through without the armour. She reached forward, snatched the pistol out of the bandit's hand, and crushed it in one armoured fist, before rolling the suddenly-subdued bandit over and cuffing him. He didn't offer any more resistance.

"Nineteen prisoners," Captain Stalker said, over the general channel. Jasmine caught herself breathing heavily as she started to come down from the high of battle and carefully forced her breath into steady gulps. "Well done, all of you."

Jasmine shrugged, staring around at the devastation. It had been the single most one-sided battle she'd ever taken part in. Her old Drill Sergeant would have been impressed. Of course, she'd also been a bloodthirsty bitch who had once told her trainees that the quickest way to a man's heart was with ten inches of a monofilament blade, stabbed right through the chest. There had to be nearly a hundred bandits lying dead, yet there was no way to know for sure until a forensic team got out to Eddisford and started putting the pieces together.

"We done good," Blake said, over the platoon's private channel. "We sure kicked some ass today! Even Unlucky over there didn't get into trouble."

"Fuck you, with the greatest of respect," Joe said crossly. "You want to bet that the next time won't be so easy?"

Jasmine privately suspected that he was right.

CHAPTER NINETEEN

The fundamental problem with human rights is that there is no such thing as a human right. By definition, a right is something that is not only self-evident, but impossible to remove. Few, if any, of the human rights cited by lawyers across the Empire meet that definition.

Regardless, it is self-evident that rights come with responsibilities, yet the vast majority of the Empire's population demands the former without the latter. Such a system cannot survive for long.

- Professor Leo Caesius, *The Waning Years of Empire* (banned).

The small barn had once belonged to the homesteaders, before they had abandoned their farm to fear or threats or debt. Edward's Marines had spent a day fixing it up and turning it into a makeshift prisoner interrogation centre – the prisoners themselves would be held in another barn, one that had originally been used to hold pigs or sheep – before setting out on their mission.

The Governor had questioned the expense when Edward had notified him of what he was doing, but Edward had reassured him that they'd take prisoners. The entire battle plan had been based around taking prisoners. The Governor's reluctance to consider the possibility had surprised him, although Gwen had pointed out that most prisoners taken by the Civil Guard were probably released by their captors upon the payment of a substantial bribe.

"Bring in the prisoner," he ordered, as he took one of the two chairs in the barn. The other one had been rapidly turned into a holding chair.

It had been splashed with blood when they'd found it in the corner of the barn, leading him to wonder just what had happened to make the original owners flee for their lives, if they had managed to escape at all. The records had suggested that the homestead had been abandoned and no one had bothered to move in to take over the farm. The owners had simply vanished.

Two Marines, wearing full body armour, marched in the first prisoner. Edward studied him with cold dispassion, noting how the fight had fallen out of the thug as he'd realised that he was up against genuine soldiers. He and his gang had been used to terrorising farmers and their families; the idea of determined opposition had come as a complete surprise to them. The first battle on Avalon's soil – the Marines' first battle, he reminded himself – had been easy. The others wouldn't be anything like as simple.

The prisoner was thrown into the chair and cuffed to the metal. Edward smiled thinly as he recognised the man's features, the racially-mixed features of Earth's Undercity. Edward's own father had been the same race as his mother, but several of his half-siblings had had differently coloured skins and odder features. There were even families down in the Undercity where the taint of incest had begun to take hold, the taboo broken long ago under the pressures of living in such conditions. The whole concept made him sick, yet how could he condemn people who were doing only what they had to do to survive? He'd broken out of the Undercity and never looked back; the young man – boy, rather – facing him had not.

He was tall and badly bruised from his fall, but there was nothing wrong with his mind. The Marines had poured cold water over him to shock him awake, after they'd stunned him and transported him to the platoon house, hopefully disorienting him before they started to ask questions.

Edward knew that stunners were unreliable weapons – a simple layer of body armour could neutralise their effects – yet they seemed to have worked perfectly in this case. The prisoner had been taken alive. Edward doubted that he would have the nerve to suicide anyway; still, they had all been bound and gagged, just in case. The prisoner's eyes rose to meet his and then flinched away, bitterly. This one, Edward decided, would not have made a good Marine.

Edward leaned forward and reached out towards the prisoner's chin, lifting it up to face him. The prisoner flinched away, but he couldn't prevent Edward from touching his face. Edward held his eyes, watching as the prisoner mentally cowered away from him. He knew what to expect, all right, even if he didn't know who'd captured him. The competent Civil Guardsmen would probably quietly dispose of him rather than locking him up and watching helplessly as one of the jailors freed him.

He spoke, finally, and watched as the prisoner flinched again. "Do you know who I am?"

The prisoner swallowed hard. "Fucking Wasps," he said, in a futile gesture of defiance. He cringed, expecting a blow, but Edward only smiled. Wasps was an old nickname for the Civil Guard, who wore yellow and black dress uniforms while on parade. "You can't do this to me."

Edward allowed his smile to grow wider. "I am Captain Edward Stalker, Terran Marine Corps," he said. "My men have slaughtered most of your friends. You are thousands of miles from any hope of rescue" – a flat lie, but one that would be believable to a man who had no idea how long he'd been out of it – "and you are our prisoner. I trust that you are comfortable?"

The prisoner looked as if he wanted to spit, but didn't quite dare. "I want you to understand something," Edward continued. "You have been taken prisoner while engaged in an act of terrorism. Your guilt has been proven beyond all reasonable doubt. Under the Terrorism Act, I am authorised to use any methods required to extract information from you, before summarily executing you for crimes against Avalon and its residents. Do you understand me?"

He held the prisoner's gaze until the man finally nodded bitterly. The prisoner knew what he and the rest of his gang had done to the settlements near the badlands; he knew that he could expect no mercy from the Marines, the Civil Guard, or the local population. His gaze flickered across the array of farm tools placed against one wall, his imagination convincing him that they could – that they would – be used to torture him. Edward took no pleasure in breaking the man, even if there was no need to actually hurt him physically, but there was little choice. They needed information urgently.

"Good," Edward said. "There is no way that you will be able to lie to us. The device on your wrist" – he pointed to a wristwatch-sized gadget that one of the Marines had attached to the prisoner, after they'd cuffed him to the chair – "serves as a lie detector. So far, no one has managed to fool it, even with the best training. They lied so convincingly that everyone listening believed them, but the machine wasn't fooled. Do you want to tell me a lie, just to test it?"

The prisoner shook his head. Edward smiled inwardly, even though the fear in the man's eyes showed that there was no reason to believe that the interrogation would fail. It was a pity in many ways. A few words from him would allow the lie detector to calibrate itself, learning the precise biofeedback patterns the prisoner possessed. The lie detector, like other learning software, grew more accurate as time went on. There was no reason for the prisoner to know that, of course. The more accurate he believed the lie detector to be, the less reason there would be to lie.

"Good," Edward said. "Now…the first time you try to lie to us, we will hurt you. The second time, we will simply inject you with truth drugs and get our answers that way. And if we have to do that, we will have no reason to be merciful when it comes to handing out the sentences. If you refuse to cooperate, we'll just use you as an object lesson and hang you in Camelot City. Do you understand me?"

"Yes, sir," the prisoner said. A sour smell wafted across Edward's nostrils and he winced inwardly, showing no trace of his feelings on his face. The prisoner had urinated on the seat. "You can't do this to me…"

"Yes, I can," Edward said, flatly. He found the whole concept distasteful, but a field interrogation was the only real alternative. He had no prisoner holding pens on Castle Rock. "Now…start talking. Tell us everything you know."

The lie detector had one weakness; it couldn't detect when a prisoner was holding something back. The prisoner might succeed in misleading the Marines even without lying to them, although a skilled interrogator could generally tell when the prisoner was attempting to lead them up the garden path. If the prisoner talked freely, without answering questions, he might suggest new lines of enquiry without ever knowing that that was what he had done. The interrogators would record the conversation, play it back in their helmets and ask follow-up questions. And, once the prisoner had been drained of everything he knew, they'd put him back in the holding pens and start interrogating the next prisoner.

He listened as the prisoner stumbled through a life story that was, more or less, what Edward had expected. He'd been arrested on Earth, walked past a judge whose assistant had reviewed the case file and sentenced him to indentured servitude on a faraway planet and exiled to Avalon, where he'd eventually joined up with the gangs. It was hard to show no reaction as a sickening list of atrocities starting to pour out of the prisoner; looting, rape and mass slaughter. The gang – the Knives, the prisoner called them – had been busy. They'd infested the landscape like vermin.

They would, Edward resolved, be wiped out like vermin.

"So, tell me," he said, breaking into a story about how the prisoner and one of his mates had kidnapped and raped a farm girl, "where is your base?"

The prisoner blanched. Edward didn't need the lie detector to know that the prisoner was agitated. If he betrayed the location of his base to the Marines, his fellows wouldn't hesitate to kill him when they got the chance. The gang was definitely organised on the same system as was used on Earth, where betrayal was punished by a horrible death and there was no such thing as safety, even if the betrayers got away at first. Edward's own childhood had been marred by memories of how gangs had punished their wayward members, in one case systematically torturing a former member's family to death before finally crushing his skull. The prisoner knew he didn't dare answer the question…

"Please don't be a fool," Edward said, coldly. "We have ways of making you talk."

"They'll kill me," the prisoner screamed. Raw panic was written on his face. "You don't understand. They'll kill me!"

"And I will hurt you until you answer the questions," Edward said, dispassionately. The fear ran deep, unsurprisingly. Gangs were held in line by fear and the sheer numbing horror of life. A resident of the Undercity who wasn't in a gang had no safety at all. They were effectively fair game for anyone. His own sister…

He shook his head and pushed the thought aside. "You will talk to us, one way or the other."

The prisoner tried to pull himself together. "And if I tell you," he asked, "will you protect me?"

"Your leaders will never get their grubby little paws on you," Edward assured him. It was even true. After hearing the list of crimes, he had no intention of allowing the prisoner to walk free. His hanging would serve as an object lesson, all right. "Now talk, or do we have to start getting creative?"

He waved a hand at the tools on the wall.

"I'll talk," the prisoner said. Sweat was pouring off his face. "I'll tell you whatever you want to know."

Edward listened carefully as the prisoner started to outline the location of the gang's camp, a sinking feeling spreading through him as he realised what he was dealing with. The gang had a number of bases in the badlands, but the prisoner they'd caught only knew the location of one of them. The gang was operating under operational security. The more he listened, the more he wondered if their leader had greater ambitions than simple banditry. They almost seemed to be developing a separate government near the badlands. If they played their cards carefully, they'd have the townships paying tribute rather than be raided. A few generations and the gang might be running the entire area.

It had a dark veneer, but he'd seen it before – and studied it at the Slaughterhouse. The gangs – or insurgents – would move in, slowly start chipping away at the organised government and replacing it with their own structures. Resistance would be harshly punished. A few object lessons and the remainder of the population would fall into line. How could they fight back, even with weapons, if they had no idea where to attack, or when a gang attack would be underway? It was clever, devious and almost unstoppable.

At least until we get a new army trained up, he thought. The Civil Guard was effectively worthless. The five hundred combat effectives wouldn't be able to spread themselves out any more than the Marines could, and the remaining soldiers would be worse than useless. It was the old classical insurgent problem, with a nasty twist. As long as the insurgents were not losing, they were winning...and their victory would put the future of Avalon into the hands of men who had learned their trade in the Undercity, where government was an enemy and might made right. Avalon's future, although precariously balanced, would be shattered.

"Show the prisoner out," he ordered, finally. He'd be kept in the pens until he could be moved to Camelot for his date with destiny. "Check his story with the others and let me know if they can give us more accurate directions."

Leaving the interrogation team behind, he walked out of the barn and across to the farmhouse, watching with calm approval as a guard shimmered into existence and checked his ID. Only a platoon of Marines had been left to guard the platoon house, but the area was so isolated that he was fairly certain that any newcomers would be bandits looking to try to loot the farmhouse. Once word got around about who had taken it over, there would be no more probes...or perhaps he was deluding himself. If the gangs really wanted to establish a secondary government, one that would eventually separate from Camelot's authority, they'd have to try to evict the Marines.

He smiled as he stepped through the door. The farm might have been overgrown, but the former owners had carefully removed all of the trees from the fields and ensured that anyone approaching the farm would be seen easily, even without the network of sensors the Marines had scattered around the area. A KEW or a long-range missile would obliterate the farmhouse and the platoon of Marines guarding it, but there was no reason to believe that the gangs possessed such heavy weapons. The interrogation had suggested that the heaviest weapons they had were machine guns and, perhaps, home-made mortars. The gangs on Earth had never been known for their fire discipline either. Unless they'd learned how to take care of their weapons, they might not have as much firepower as they thought they did.

"We need to redeploy the forward platoon," Edward said as he entered the briefing room. It had once served as a dining room, but the only trace of the former occupants was a painting someone had left on the wall. No one had had the heart to remove it and so four children, a handsome woman and an ugly man smiled down at the Marines. "We have an approximate location for the enemy base."

He glanced down at his timepiece as Gwen unfurled a map on the table. The badlands had never been charted properly, even after the ADC had realised that its enemies used the ground as a base. The sudden changes in environment made mapping it a difficult task at the best of times. A single rainstorm could change everything. It had barely been four hours since they'd destroyed the gang force at Eddisford. How long would it take their leaders to realise that they'd run into something they couldn't handle? If Edward had been running their operation, he would have left someone far back, in a position to watch without being seen. There had been no radio transmissions, but that meant nothing. The gang might know already.

"Chancy," Gwen commented. Edward nodded. The badlands couldn't compete with the Slaughterhouse, but he had too few Marines to lose any of them. "A quick raid in and out?"

"With the Raptors on standby and missile companies set up here," Edward said, tapping a location on the map. Marines believed in precision operations. If they located the enemy camp, a hail of missiles would soften up the enemy before the Marines moved in for the kill. "Once the operation is underway, contact the Civil Guard; they can move up two of their own companies and cover our backs. Eddisford is going to need additional protection."

"Yes, sir," Gwen said. It had taken time to convince the residents to leave their homes, even if it had been for their own safety. The Civil Guard would have to see to their protection, even if it meant tying down a trustworthy company with the duty. The bandits would certainly try to punish them for their actions. "Will you be leading the operation personally?"

Every bone in Edward's body cried out to go forward with his Marines, but he knew he couldn't, not while he was the senior officer. "No," he said. Gwen knew how much it hurt him to hold back and wait while others went into danger. "I will remain here."

CHAPTER TWENTY

> Each planet offers its own peculiarities; its own unique features and problems. No planet can be treated as any other planet, yet the Empire tries to do just that. Thus we are left with the issue of some planets receiving aid they do not need, while others are starved of items they desperately need to survive.
> - Professor Leo Caesius, *The Waning Years of Empire* (banned).

"It's as hot as that girl I fucked back on Capricorn," Blake commented through the platoon's private channel. "This should be a fun place for a rumble."

Jasmine snorted, feeling the heat even through the armour. The badlands was, among other things, a suntrap, warming up rapidly until she felt as if she was baking inside her armoured shell. If she had been on her own, out for a relaxing hike around the countryside, she thought that she would have worn only a top and shorts, but she knew that there was danger all around them. The badlands was not a place to grow complacent. The enemy could be anywhere.

"I remember," Joe Buckley said, dryly. "Was that the slut who insisted on you paying her first, or the one who wanted your Rifleman's Tab?"

"Fuck you," Blake said, with some feeling. "She really wanted to bag a Marine for some reason."

"I guess she wanted to add you to her collection," Joe said, with an evil chuckle. "She got one Marine who couldn't be bothered to keep his tackle in his trousers. What sort of bragging rights do you think she got?"

"I'll have you know that I lasted all night with her," Blake said, with great dignity. "While you were off chasing that pretty boy in the bar, I was screwing her senseless."

"She was already senseless," Jasmine put in. "She slept with you, didn't she?"

A dull chuckle ran around the platoon. Despite the banter, the Marines watched their surroundings carefully, wondering when – if – the enemy would make its appearance. The badlands were closing in all around them, hemming them in. The handful of paths within the zone had to be known to the enemy. Jasmine privately suspected that the easiest solution to the problem would be to drop defoliant on the badlands and destroy the vegetation, but the Captain would never agree. The Marines didn't need another stain on their honour.

Avalon, like many Earth-like worlds, had received the full package of plants and animals from Earth, released out into the wild to compete with the native vegetation. The badlands was a zone of perpetual conflict between old and new, with trees and vines from Earth struggling to survive in ravines and crevices opened up by massive earthquakes, thousands of years ago. A river ran from the Mystic Mountains to the north, running right through the badlands and down to the sea near Camelot, yet no one ever tried to take a boat up the rapids. The badlands and their treachery extended even to the river. The orbital images of the rapids had fascinated her, even though she wasn't fond of boating. Blake and Joe had been talking about taking canoes up there after the war and really testing themselves against nature.

She glanced ahead as the platoon rotated around in a pattern that – to outside observers – should have been completely random. They were spread out far enough to prevent a single mine from taking out the entire platoon, yet it worried her. The path they were using was a dry riverbed, yet it could come alive at any moment, if the ground shifted or a well-placed explosive charge broke a river's banks.

The armour should protect them, but no one wanted to test it. Marines didn't get claustrophobic – recruits who were subject to claustrophobia were weeded out at Boot Camp, long before they ever saw the

Slaughterhouse – yet Jasmine understood how they must have felt. The trees were closing in. Anything could be lurking, just ahead of them.

A tiny shape flashed across the path and into the vegetation, moving so fast that she could barely bring her MAG to bear on it. The small creature, no larger than a well-fed hamster, was harmless to armoured humans, but dangerous if it was allowed to bite bare skin. The Chatters – as the early colonists had named them, after the noise they made at night – were poisonous to humans and native wildlife alike. Some locals kept them as pets, training them up, but others put down mouse traps and exterminated them on sight. They were too dangerous to have around small children.

"Only a tiny critter," Joe said, as they relaxed. "Now…where were we?"

"Blake's one-night stand," Koenraad reminded him. "I can't remember if we were slapping him on the back or mocking him for it."

"Asshole," Blake said crossly. He paused for a second, staring up at a very familiar bird staring down at the platoon. The red and yellow parrot eyed them disdainfully before flapping its wings and flying off into the distance. "Jasmine; what did you make of the redhead?"

It took Jasmine a moment to realise that he meant Mandy Caesius. "A spoilt brat with an attitude problem," she said, sourly. Chaperoning the Professor might have been interesting, but the older girl had ruined it, just by being herself. "I suggest you concentrate on more interesting girls."

"The Captain has to let us out on leave sometime," Joe put in, seriously. "There has to be a few places in Camelot where Blake can get his ashes hauled."

"I didn't see that side of the city," Jasmine said, before Blake could say anything explosive. "I just saw the wealthy part of it. It felt a lot like Han."

Silence fell as the Marines digested that titbit. Blake, Joe and Jasmine had all been new graduates from the Slaughterhouse, settling into their new platoons, when they'd been posted to Han. It had been supposed to be an easy posting, one that would allow them a chance to get settled in before the company was assigned to a more challenging position. Instead, it had been hell incarnate; Han's autonomous government had been so repressive that when the dam burst, it had washed over everything. They'd found themselves fighting their way out of the capital city and struggling to stay alive until the Empire shipped in reinforcements. Jasmine's view of war had never been the same.

But before the rebellion, the NCOs and the Captain – it hadn't been Captain Stalker then, but Captain McClelland – had suspected that something was up. There had been a brittle feeling in the air, as if something was about to break and break hard. There had been a desperation that had washed away all sense of restraint or social conservatism. The newly-minted Marines had enjoyed themselves, little realising that it was the calm before the storm.

"I hope you're wrong," Blake said, finally. Jasmine nodded inside her helmet. "Jesus…if we have to go through that again…"

"Quiet," Joe snapped. The platoon snapped instantly to combat awareness. "Mine!"

Jasmine followed his gaze, seeing the subtle clues marking the location of a hidden minefield. The bandit camp, according to the prisoners they'd interrogated, should be just over the ridge. The presence of the minefield suggested that – for once – intelligence had gotten it right. It wasn't a fair attitude – Jasmine knew that Captain Stalker and trained interrogators had handled the interrogation – but it was one she held close. Back on Han, intelligence had kept assuring everyone that everything was fine, just before the entire planet had exploded into rebellion.

"I can get through that no bother," Joe muttered. The Marines were spreading out slowly, testing the minefield with senses honed at the Slaughterhouse. The bandits hadn't been particularly subtle. They'd simply strewn a few hundred mines around their base. With a little care, they could probably find a safe path and slip through the net. "Can I try?"

"No," Master Sergeant Gary Young said, firmly. He held a small portable sensor in his hand. "There's a safe path there" – he pointed – "and we're going to take out the guard and slip through it. Jasmine…you're up."

Jasmine nodded and crept forward. The guard looked to be half-asleep, which suggested that he wasn't aware of what had happened to the raiding party the Marines had destroyed. She didn't take chances, but kept moving slowly, watching him carefully. The armour's stealth mode had its limitations and anyone watching closely would notice a slight shimmer in the air.

Good thing we're not wearing heavy armour, she thought, grinning inwardly. *They'd have heard us coming from miles away.*

The guard sat up suddenly, as if he'd sensed something, but it was too late. Jasmine was on him in a second. One hand clamped over his mouth, stifling a scream, while the other twisted his neck and snapped it like a twig. She held him close until the life had faded from his body, and then carefully lowered him to the ground. The others slipped up beside her and advanced towards the ridge, watching carefully for other ambushes. There were none.

She peered over the ridge and smiled inwardly when she saw the bandit camp. It looked as if they'd been hiding tents and even small huts under the foliage. No one would have seen anything from high above. The iron ore and other minerals in the area would disrupt sensors and even Civil Guard communicators.

She keyed her throat mike with an effort. "Captain; bandit camp located," she said, knowing that her words were being relayed through a microburst transmitter to one of the orbiting satellites. It was a risk – the enemy would not be able to break the Marine encryption algorithms, but they might well be able to detect that transmissions were being made – yet it had to be taken. "I estimate seventy-plus bandits…"

Something touched her ear and she winced. "And I hear female screams," she added. "The camp isn't just inhabited by bandits, sir."

"Understood," Captain Stalker said. Bombarding the camp first was no longer an option. In some ways, it worked in their favour, as they'd have a better chance of catching someone important. "Sergeant Young…?"

"We can take them, if the Raptors give us some covering fire," Young said, calmly. He had over forty years of experience in the Marines and had forgotten more than Jasmine and her generation had ever known. "There are three antiaircraft weapons platforms in the camp. We will take them out and then the Raptors can hit their other defences. I'm uploading targeting specs now."

Jasmine felt a moment of pity for Captain Stalker. Twenty-one of his Marines were about to assault the enemy…and he was seven kilometres away, back at the platoon house. She'd served as squad leader several times, long enough to know what responsibility meant, and she didn't envy her commander at all.

"Got them," Captain Stalker said. "The Raptors are in holding orbits. Tactical command is now yours. Call when you need them."

"Lock and load," Young said. His voice was as calm and steady as ever. "Jasmine, Blake, Sally – take out their heavy weapons. Everyone else; cover them."

Jasmine twisted her MAG, selecting the sniper option. The weapon linked into her helmet, with targeting crosshairs appearing in front of her vision, allowing her to target the bandit manning the guns. Her vision focused in on him, showing him laughing and joking with a friend. Her lips twisted in distaste. He showed no sign of discipline at all. The bandits clearly weren't worried about being attacked.

"Fire," Young ordered.

Jasmine squeezed the trigger and the MAG fired a single hypervelocity pellet towards her target. Even if he had heard the shot, and the MAG was silent except at very close range, he could not have hoped to move in time. Only lasers and plasma cannons were faster than MAG-launched bullets. Her target's head exploded in a gratifying burst of blood and skull fragments as the bullet spread out on impact, punching right through his head. Jasmine didn't stop to congratulate herself. She switched to the next target and calmly serviced him as well.

The bandits were caught in a bind, helplessly confused. There were no flashes of gunfire for them to fire back at and no sign of where the Marines were at all. Given time, someone would deduce their location from the firing pattern, but that would require time.

The enemy were firing in all directions, as if they hoped to discourage the Marines through sheer firepower. It wouldn't have worked, not even against the worst Civil Guard unit in existence. And the Marines were just too well prepared.

"Incoming blue," Young said, still unruffled. Jasmine's audio-discrimination system in her helmet picked up the noise of the Raptors as they swooped overhead, launching a handful of precision weapons towards their targets on the ground. A couple of weapons emplacements exploded in sheets of fire, tearing the defenders apart, while gas started to billow out of canisters, knocking out anyone who even caught a whiff of it. There were laws against using it on Earth, Jasmine knew, but out in the colonies…no one would even care. "Blue is withdrawing; go, go, go!"

Jasmine leapt up, following Blake and Joe as they raced down towards the camp. The handful of defenders who were still standing barely saw them coming; the Marines slashed through them before they knew what had hit them. Jasmine tracked another target as she came staggering out of one of the makeshift huts, before she breathed in some of the gas and collapsed on the ground. The target had been naked and unarmed, suggesting that she was a hostage rather than a bandit, but she'd still be checked carefully before she was released. It wouldn't be the first time a bandit or terrorist tried to escape trouble by claiming to be nothing more than a hostage.

Red icons flared up in front of her as a blast of blue-white fire flared out in the distance. Someone with a quicker mind than she had expected had covered their mouth and nose with a gas mask, firing on the Marines with a handheld plasma rifle. God alone knew where it had come from – Avalon's home-grown industry could barely produce primitive computer chips and equipment, let alone plasma weapons – but it was real. Joe's icon in her display was flashing red and blue lights, warning her that he'd been hit and hit badly.

"Marine down," she snapped, as she snapped off a shot toward the newcomer. It wasn't a perfect shot; it went through the plasma weapon before slicing into the newcomer's chest. The plasma weapon exploded in a blinding flash, sending white-hot plasma blazing through its owner's body. Jasmine watched him burning, wrapped up in his own weapon's death throes, and felt nothing. "Cover him!"

"His armour took most of the blast," Sally said, as the Marines swept away the remaining opposition. The relief in her voice was all too clear. They'd all feared losing their lucky mascot. "He's alive, if burned. It's a few days in a regeneration tank for him."

"Blue-one, land for medivac," Young ordered, calling down the Raptor gunship. "Blue-two; provide overhead cover and watch for trouble."

Jasmine pushed the thought to one side as she followed Blake towards one of the huts, covering him as he kicked down the door and burst in, weapon at the ready. He stopped dead a second later, allowing her to see the remains of a man, killed by the four naked women in the hut. Their eyes were alight with a savage fury that eclipsed the scars and bruises on their bodies. They showed no sign of guilt, or remorse, merely a heartfelt relief that it was all over. Jasmine could understand just how they felt.

"Stay down," she said, as gently as she could. The Marines had to be a terrifying sight in their armour. "We've come to get you out of here."

She stepped back outside and realised that the fighting was over. A handful of bandits had tried to flee into the jungle, only to be shot in the back as they ran. Others lay on the ground, having breathed in some of the gas, waiting to be picked up and transferred back to the holding pens at the platoon house. Marines moved among them, cuffing their hands with plastic ties, just in case they proved to have only inhaled a tiny amount of the gas. The former prisoners were treated more gently – they'd be separated from their captors – but they were secured as well. Jasmine didn't complain. It would take days, perhaps weeks, to sort out just who was who.

A second Raptor orbited low overhead, allowing a third platoon to jump down to the ground to reinforce the Marines already present. Jasmine smiled tiredly, doubting that the bandits would try to catch the Marines on the ground, although she was grateful for the help. Joe would be evacuated back to Castle Rock, while his buddies cleaned up the mess. The remains of the bandit camp would be thoroughly searched before it was burned to the ground. There would be nothing left for any of their successors.

"Good work, all of you," Captain Stalker said, on the general channel. "The medic reports that Rifleman Buckley will be fine in a few weeks."

There was a general cheer. "I guess he was still wearing his lucky red shirt," Blake said. He sounded relieved. He might have argued with Joe and the others from time to time, but Marines always looked out for one another. And, on a more practical level, they couldn't afford to lose anyone. Joe Buckley would have been missed even by those who didn't like him. "Did we get enough prisoners?"

"Over fifty," Captain Stalker said. Jasmine smiled. There was a good chance they'd taken one of the bandit leaders alive, then. "And we've captured plenty of their weapons and deprived them of one of their bases. It's been a very good day's work."

CHAPTER TWENTY-ONE

> What is won by soldiers, at a high cost, is often given away by political leaders.
> - Professor Leo Caesius, *The Waning Years of Empire* (banned).

Lucas Trent was a careful man by instinct and training, such as it was. He'd mastered the skills required to stay alive on Earth, in the Undercity, and many of them had proved applicable to Avalon when he'd been transported to the planet. Indeed, or so he told himself, he had never truly failed. The Civil Guardsmen who had arrested him had had no idea who they had caught. They'd thought he was just another thug. Some of his subordinates had thought that he took excessive precautions, but they hadn't dared complain to his face. And now some of them would never have the opportunity.

His headquarters was in a secret location, known only to his most trusted subordinates and the guards he kept around him at all times. The slaves – the women the Knives had kidnapped from various homesteads over the years – were never allowed to leave, although few would dare pass through the badlands without weapons and armour. There were nastier things than human beings lurking in the undergrowth. The last slave who had tried to escape had stumbled into a mud hole and been devoured by a lurking crocodile-like creature. It seemed, now, that all of his precautions might have been insufficient.

"They definitely took out the entire camp," Steven said, after the runner had been debriefed. Literally; the Knives hadn't wanted to believe him at first. "They just walked right up to it and smashed their way into the camp."

Lucas stared down at the table, unwilling to believe what he had heard. His local leader had known – he'd certainly been ordered often enough – to have scouts out on every possible angle of approach, watching for trouble. The Civil Guard might have been largely corrupt, but even they had their dedicated leaders and soldiers, men and women who might brave the badlands to hunt down the bandits. The Marines…the Marines were just inhuman. They'd slaughtered over a hundred gang members and if they'd lost anyone…

He looked up at the naked runner, seeing the sores covering his body from the whipping. The runner had claimed that a dozen Marines had been killed, but Lucas discounted that claim automatically. It was his experience that runners always lied, if only to avoid being punished for bringing bad news to the leaders, and in any case, the camp had had few heavy weapons capable of penetrating even light armour. He'd have to plan on the assumption that none of the Marines had been killed, which gave them a depressingly big advantage. If a handful of Marines could wipe out an entire camp, his grand plan was on the verge of coming apart at the seams.

"The idiot should have had scouts out watching for their approach," Lucas said, trying to put a brave face on affairs. As sure as eggs were eggs, any sign of weakness would have his subordinates thinking about sticking a knife in his back. He trusted Steven, yet even he might be tempted by the prospect of supreme power. It was one of the other reasons for persistent gang warfare in the Undercity. The gang leaders knew that they had to keep their thugs happy or they might revolt. "Have we heard anything from our sources?"

"Nothing," Steven said, calmly. The Civil Guardsmen who had been bribed should have warned them if the Marines were planning anything, yet the whole thing had been assembled and launched terrifyingly quickly. The last time the Civil Guard had attempted to make a showing in the region, it had taken those weekend warriors two weeks to get ready and the bandits had had a month's warning, more than long enough to make preparations. And they'd never dared go into the badlands in force. "Either they didn't know…or they simply didn't inform us."

Lucas frowned. Treachery was part of his daily existence and he always assumed that the same was true of everyone else. He'd had all of his sources warned that failure to deliver would be punished – if only by revealing their activities to their superiors, who wouldn't hesitate to hang them for it – yet they were out of easy reach. One of them might have decided to withhold information in the hopes that the Marines would slaughter the Knives before they could betray them to the Empire. In that, Lucas was sure, they would be disappointed. He had taken pains to leave a dead man's chest behind to make sure that any betrayer was punished.

"All military operations have to be cleared through the Governor," he said, tightly. The Governor didn't completely trust the Civil Guard – not an unwise position – and insisted on approving all operations personally. The sources he had in the Governor's office insured that he would hear about all planned operations in advance. "Could the Marines operate without the Governor's approval?"

"Perhaps the Governor didn't mention it to his staff," Steven suggested. "It's not like you tell us everything you're planning."

"Oh, come on," Lucas snapped. "That idiot of a Governor can't even take a shit without polling his staff and taking opinions from anyone who feels that having a pulse gives them the right to have opinions. He insists on filling out requests in triplicate just to have new pencils forwarded to his office! He'd have run it past at least a few of his most trusted allies and one of them would have leaked."

"And if the Marines can operate nearly independently, we may be in trouble," Steven pointed out. "They could be anywhere."

Both men looked upwards, towards the foliage that hid the base camp from intrusive eyes high above. Lucas had never considered the possibilities of satellite observation before he'd been transported to Avalon, but he'd learned quickly. Cold unblinking eyes, eyes that never tired or lost focus, were watching from high above. The old satellite network had been a joke, yet he was sure that no one competent would allow it to remain that way. The Marines still had a pair of destroyers in the system, according to his source in System Command. They could have rotated one over the badlands and used its onboard sensor suite.

"There are only a few dozen of them," he protested. It might not matter. Horace Netherly had had nearly a hundred bandits under his command, but they'd been rapidly and quickly slaughtered. The camp the Marines had attacked had been built to stand off an attack, yet it had been destroyed. It wasn't easy to admit, but he was starting to realise that his imagination might have been inadequate for the task at hand. If the Marines were really that deadly, the Knives might be totally outclassed. "They cannot be everywhere."

"They can give the locals hope," Steven reminded him. "That would encourage them to call in to the Marines and warn them of our movements. The whole plan might come apart."

Lucas rubbed the back of his head, feeling a headache pounding away at his temples. A protection racket – and that was what government was; a large-scale protection racket – depended on two things. It had to be capable of carrying out its promises – both of protection and of retribution – and it had to be present. If a rival force entered the picture – and he saw the Marines as a rival force – it had to be destroyed before it could break the racket completely. If he pulled back into the badlands, the prudent course of action, the Marines would have all the time they needed to prepare for the next encounter.

"We can push at the locals when the Marines aren't around," he said, firmly. "We'll see how many of those fucking idiot farmers support the Marines when we hit them after the Marines are gone."

"Except that would force us to keep a presence in the area, outside the badlands," Steven reminded him. "We might lose someone to interrogation."

Lucas ground his teeth. Against the Civil Guard, that wasn't so much of a concern, not when all prisoners had to be transported back to Camelot, if they weren't released by the jailers. The Marines might have taken the time to interrogate the prisoners themselves…no, that was wishful thinking. They *had* taken the time to interrogate the prisoners. The attack on the base camp proved that, if nothing else. And the thugs…the Marines could have used drugs or bribes, or simply kicked the shit out of them until they talked, but it hardly mattered. Anyone could be broken, given enough time. The farm girls who now serviced the Knives as if they'd been born to be whores were proof of that.

And if the Marines captured someone who knew more than the bare minimum…the consequences didn't bear thinking about. They could find their way to the main camp and destroy it. He could almost feel a rope around his neck already.

"We pull back," he decided, finally. "Pass the word to the other camps. They are to pull back into the badlands and wait for the Marines to get tired and leave. Once they leave, we can remind the farmers who really rules here."

He smiled. The farmers might be armed, but they couldn't afford to keep a militia on permanent alert, waiting to be attacked. The Knives could choose the time and place of their attacks, striking hard against vulnerable homesteads. The Marines would be gone soon enough, but the bandits would always be there.

"How many prisoners did you take?"

"Fifty-nine," Captain Stalker said. Brent stared at him, noting the calm confidence of the Marine. Fifty-nine prisoners…no one had bothered to take so many bandits alive in the past, not when they knew that most of them would simply be released by their gaolers. Most bandits who fell into the hands of the Civil Guard's more competent formations didn't survive the experience. "Four of them are wounded, but the remainder are fit and healthy."

"Good," Brent said, wondering if it really was good. He looked up at Linda, seeing the expression on her face. She was worried about how it would all play out in front of the Council. "We'll have to hold a trial, of course."

"There's no need for that," Captain Stalker assured him. "They were all captured in battle. We have interrogated their former prisoners and have a comprehensive case against each of them for terrorism and bandit-related activities. Under Imperial Law, they can be hanged at once – and they should be hanged at once."

Brent opened his mouth, and then closed it again, rendered speechless. "You would simply execute them now?" Linda asked, stepping into the breach. "You don't want to indenture them and put them to work?"

"Many of them started out as indentured workers," Captain Stalker pointed out calmly. He didn't seem bothered at all by the implication. "There is no reason to believe that they will revert to being good workers, now that we took them prisoner. Justice needs to be done, Governor, and the punishment has been laid down by Imperial Law. They are sentenced to death by hanging."

His gaze sharpened. "And, besides, if we put them back to work, how long are they going to stay there?"

Brent stared down at his hands, and then up at the map of Camelot his aide had placed on the wall. It was a political map, rather than one reflecting the local population demographics, and it mocked him every time he looked at it. The Council wouldn't be happy if he simply went along with the Captain, but yet…if he refused to execute the bandits, he'd lose whatever remaining support he had from the middle class. They'd know that he had spared the bandits for political reasons.

"Captain," he said, finally. "You must realise that there are political issues here."

"There are none," Major George Grosskopf said coldly. The Civil Guardsman leaned forward, his dark eyes aflame. "Governor, with all due respect, the Marines have just handed out a decisive lesson to the bandits, one that they will not soon forget. We killed over a hundred of their raiders at the cost of one injured Marine. We tracked down and obliterated one of their bases, rescuing – in the process – nineteen women who were being used as sex slaves. This isn't something we should hide as if we were ashamed of our own success. It's something we should shout to the skies. We beat the bandits and utterly smashed them!"

Brent winced inwardly, trying to keep his face blank. The Major was right, even though he was associating himself with the victory. The Crackers fought because they had a political ideology and a political goal in mind. The bandits looted, raped and burned because they could…

and because it was easier than actually having to work for a living. They wouldn't want to continue their activities if they were being hunted relentlessly, even into the heart of the badlands themselves.

"There is also another issue here," Captain Stalker said. "A population will support a war as long as it seems that there is a chance of victory. The problem here is that your population doesn't believe in victory. Executing the bandits will send a very clear signal that you, at least, believe that victory is possible. It will encourage people to sign up for the new army."

He smiled thinly, meeting Brent's gaze. "As for the fact that the captured bandits are still in debt...you should just forget it," he added. "Those debts are never going to be paid off."

Brent scowled at him. It wasn't Brent who cared about their debts, but the men and women who had purchased their debts off the ADC before it collapsed into a shell of its former self. Markus and Carola Wilhelm, among others, would certainly push the issue in the next Council meeting, even though Captain Stalker was right and they would never see any return on those investments. But then, Captain Stalker couldn't be removed from office...legally, Brent couldn't be removed either, but the Council could make governing the planet impossible. Again, he cursed his predecessor under his breath. The man had been a moron. Avalon was nowhere near ready for an independent Council.

"I take your point," he said, finally. He had a nasty suspicion that if he refused his permission, the Marines were just going to go ahead and hang the captives anyway. Abigail had looked up the relevant section of the Imperial Code of Military Justice and had concluded that the Marines owned the prisoners, body and soul, until they chose to hand them over to local authority. "What do you intend to do with them?"

"Two days from now, it is market day in Camelot," Captain Stalker said. "I intend to hang them publicly."

"Are you out of your...there'll be a riot," Linda protested in disbelief. "The bandits have friends within the city!"

"All the more reason to hold the executions there," Captain Stalker said. He sounded amused by her protests. "Their friends should learn the price of supporting the bandits."

Brent stood up and paced over to the window, staring down over his capital city. It wasn't much, but it was his. There would be no other posting for him once he left Avalon, no other chance to make his mark in the history books. He had long since realised that even now, he wouldn't have that chance. Avalon had a habit of taking dreams and sucking them out, leaving nothing behind but the tired bitter shell of a man. Officially, there were no homeless on Avalon. There was enough work for all. Unofficially... things were different.

He looked towards the slums and shuddered. The reports were terrifyingly clear. Every year, a greater percentage of Avalon's population found themselves homeless, so deep in debt that it was hopeless to even dream of escape. The conditions in the slums were appallingly bad. Only the foodstuffs provided by the handful of Church missions kept the population alive. It was a nightmare, one that could never end as long as Avalon remained unchanged. He had once hoped to change it, but now...all he could do was wait and see out his term. The next Imperial Governor might have more authority or backbone.

Oddly, the thought spurred him on. "See to it," he ordered, without turning around. A fishing boat was coming into the harbour and he watched, feeling a moment of envy for the sailors who had so little else to worry about. They could set their sails of silver and head over the horizon, vanishing to one of the unexplored continents or illegal settlements on the Golden Isles. They weren't bound to a city permanently on the verge of collapse. "I want them hanged and I want you to make it very clear *why* they were hanged."

He ignored Major Grosskopf's surprised look, or Captain Stalker's half-smile. "If it is to be done, then it might as well be done properly," he added. Perhaps showing the mailed fist inside the velvet glove would convince some of the Council to moderate their knee-jerk opposition to everything he did. "It may even serve a useful purpose."

"Thank you, sir," Captain Stalker said. If he was pleased at his victory, he showed no sign of it. But then, he barely had to care. "They will be hanged on market day."

Brent barely heard him. He was too busy watching the sailing boat as it docked at the harbour, unloading a silvery horde of fish. Haddock, cod and other Earth-native fish competed uneasily with Avalon's own native creatures. Some of them had to be carefully weeded out, for they were deadly poisonous. Others were a delicacy if prepared properly. His own cook was a past mistress at preparing good meals.

"Thank you," he said, finally. "And well done. Please congratulate your men for me."

Chapter
Twenty-Two

> One of the commonest signs of social decline lies in the separation of the elites from the masses. Where the elites – the leadership – share the concerns of their people, government proceeds smoothly. Where the elites are physically and socially separated from their people, they start designing policies that are actively harmful to the masses. This is nowhere clearer than it is in the issue of criminal justice.
>
> - Professor Leo Caesius, *The Waning Years of Empire* (banned).

Market Day on Avalon had been intended as a special holiday, or so Michael Volpe had been told. The ADC had planned the day so that farmers on the outskirts of Camelot could bring in their produce and sell it directly to the grateful citizens of the city, while taking time to enjoy the city and spend time among its distractions. In reality, it hadn't taken long before the vested interests took over the holiday and started taxing the farmers who tried to break the official monopoly on food transport, leaving Market Day as little more than just another day. Michael valued it only because it served as a chance to make some money on the sly.

He walked from stall to stall, offering his help to the dealer in exchange for petty cash. Some of them would need a strong man to help them set out their boxes; others stared at him suspiciously, as if they suspected he intended to steal their produce and vanish into the side streets before anyone could catch him. It was a depressingly familiar scene, yet what choice did he have? There was no other employment for someone like him.

At seventeen years old, Michael had come to the conclusion that his life was already over. The son of a indent mother and a colonist farmer, he had inherited some of his father's debt, even though his mother had literally owned nothing but the clothes on her back. His father might have abandoned the family just after Michael had been born, yet the debt sharks never forgot. The moment he signed on to work at any official job, they'd start tapping over three quarters of his salary to pay the interest on the debt. Michael was far from stupid and had painstakingly worked his way through the math. If he got a good job, if he worked for over fifty years, he might just pay off the interest alone…by which point more would have piled up. It was a perfect trap. He couldn't work without losing most of his salary; he couldn't even refuse to pay. There was no escape.

He saw a young-looking farmwife with old eyes and paused long enough to help her unload her nag, before accepting a handful of coins in payment. It was dangerous to carry too much – the criminal gangs who also infested the marketplace might notice and take it off him before he could get back home – but a few coins probably wouldn't attract their interest. The coins were the only untraceable funds on Avalon and there were laws against holding too many of them, even though most people simply ignored the laws. Paying money into the Bank of Avalon was a sure-fire way to lose most of it to pay a debt.

"Thank you," he said, accepting an apple she tried to press on him as part-payment. Winking at her, he strode off, looking for others to help. He passed a set of farming tools that had been hand-made by one of the local craftsman and cast an eye over some of the sharper blades, before the craftsman reached for an obvious shotgun under the table. Michael shrugged at him and walked onwards, feeling a tingle running down the back of his shoulder blades as the old man's glare followed him.

An hour passed slowly, but he was in no hurry. His mother would be working herself – in order to survive, she sold herself to men – and his younger half-brother would be out with his gang. It was yet another thing to worry about. The street toughs hadn't forced Michael to join them, as they had some of their other members, but one day he knew they'd call for him. He'd seen the results of gang violence and wanted to stay away from it, yet what other choice did he have? The Civil Guard would laugh at him if they heard his complaint. No one in their right mind would trust them to solve a problem.

As if his thought had called them forth, a group of men dressed in combat uniforms appeared at one end of the market, marching upwards towards the middle of the square. The wooden stage had been intended for live performances of plays, but now…now it was empty.

Michael realised, with a shock, that someone had renovated it, adding a wooden construction he didn't recognise. The soldiers weren't Civil Guardsmen, he saw, as they passed him, but something else. They held themselves with an easy discipline that shouted out that they ruled…and no one else could even challenge them. Their assurance was so powerful that Michael found himself backing away before his mind had even caught up with the thought. A thought seemed to echo through the crowd…

Marines…

Michael felt a sudden bitter surge of envy. The young men and women had everything he ever wanted and more, free of debt and the legacy of a father who had never cared for his son. They walked with their heads held high, as if they had nothing to worry about, without any trace of fear in their stance. He wanted to be them and knew that it would never happen. Avalon's Imperial Navy recruiting station was moribund and had been so for years. Joining the Civil Guard would have been worthless.

And then he saw the prisoners.

Nelson Oshiro struggled against the shackles binding his hands and feet, even though he knew that it was useless. The chains were overkill, intended to make it very clear to both the prisoners and the watchers that they were prisoners and leave no one in any doubt as to what was going to happen to them. He tried to hold his head up high and face the sneers from the watching crowd with determination, but somehow he couldn't maintain the pose. The crowd was hissing them as the truth sunk in. Here, in front of them, were some of the dreaded bandits who had been driving their food prices upwards. They were at the crowd's mercy.

He pulled at the chains on his hands, but he couldn't break them free, even as the crowd started throwing rotten food at them. He wanted to memorise names and faces, yet he knew it was futile. The Marines had interrogated him, drugged him and then had interrogated him again, milking him dry of everything he knew about the Knives. They'd been dumped back in the same holding pen and had tried to come up with a shared story, but it hadn't worked.

The drugs had broken all resistance. A handful of prisoners bore marks from when they'd tried to lie and their interrogators had dealt with it brutally. They had betrayed the remainder of the gang. If the Marines let them go, which didn't seem likely, they would be hunted down and killed by their former comrades for betrayal.

A young girl leaned forward, shouted a curse that was lost in the roar of the crowd, and threw a rotten egg right into his face. Nelson tried to twist, to evade, but it was impossible. The egg struck his chin and shattered, sending a horrifying smell wafting up towards his nostrils. He wanted to vomit, but somehow held it in. He had the nasty feeling that showing any kind of weakness would only make it worse.

The Marines pushed them up a ramp towards a stage and lined them up in front of the crowd. The hail of rotten food had faded away as a new air of anticipation settled over the crowd, with faces exchanging knowing looks that somehow made Nelson feel sick. At first, he didn't understand what was happening, and then a Marine hooked a noose over his neck, drawing it tight. It was suddenly very hard to breathe. He wanted to open his mouth to protest, but it was far too late.

Michael watched as the Marines slowly lined up the prisoners in front of the crowd, tying nooses around their necks. The former bandits didn't look terrifying any more, not after the crowd had shown their fondness for their tormentors by covering them in rotten food. They looked tired and desperate, staring around as if they expected someone to come free them at the last minute. The crowd was in an ugly mood. Michael sensed, somehow, that if the Marines had freed the prisoners and dumped them into the crowd, the prisoners would have been brutally killed by the civilians. No one had any mercy for bandits.

One of the Marines stepped forward, his voice echoing out over the crowd, somehow enforcing silence. "These men were captured in the act of pillaging their local townships, burning crops and raping innocent victims," he said. "They have been found guilty under Imperial Law and have been sentenced to death."

Michael shivered. Rape was one of the local gang's favourite pastimes. One day, it might be his half-sister lying on the ground as the assholes took turns.

The ugly note of the crowd seemed to grow louder. The prisoners, suddenly realising what was going to happen to them if they hadn't known before, started to protest, pleading for help and mercy. No one was inclined to give it to them. The crowd had no time for a loser. Michael had seen street thieves given rough justice at the hands of the crowd before and it made no difference that the new victims were from outside the city. They deserved to die.

"The sentence will be carried out," the Marine said, somehow speaking over the crowd. "May God have mercy on their souls."

———

Nelson wanted to panic, but somehow he held his peace, thinking desperately. If he could think of something important, something the Marines needed to know, perhaps they would spare his life…but there was nothing. The interrogators had pulled everything he knew out of him and drained him dry. There was nothing left to offer.

The Marines had attached the ropes to a single machine at the rear of the stage. It hummed to life, slowly pulling in the rope…and lifting the prisoners above the ground, slowly choking the life out of them. Nelson drew in a breath as the rope came tight, trying to hold on as long as possible. His legs started to stretch as the rope pulled him upwards; somehow, despite himself, he felt the life slipping out of his body…

Faces started to appear in front of him. His mother and father, the ones who had birthed him and abandoned him when he was ten years old, shaking their heads sadly as they walked away. Jenny, the first girl he had admired from afar, a tall brunette who had somehow maintained her smile in the Undercity...until the day he'd grabbed her suddenly and taken her brutally, convinced that that was what she wanted. She'd screamed and screamed, but he'd thought he'd known better, until he found out that she'd killed herself afterwards. He'd dismissed her from his thoughts until her face reappeared in front of him, mocking him, joined by his other victims. His vision was blurring as the faces merged together into one leering shape; a voice was whispering, right at the edge of his mind...

The rope jerked suddenly, there was a snap, and then nothing. Nothing at all.

Michael watched as the bandits died one by one, their bodies jerking as their necks snapped. Some of them had clearly been trying to struggle, others seemed to have accepted their fate, but it hadn't mattered in the end. They were all dead, hanging from the ropes like demented puppets. Silence fell over the crowd as it sank in, and then there was a roar of approval. Michael felt his own voice echoing as he joined in the roar. The rough justice suited the crowd. How could it not have suited them?

The Marines walked from rope to rope, cutting the dead bodies down and letting them fall onto the stage. They looked as if they had died in agony. A Marine pushed up a trolley and the bodies were unceremoniously dumped onto it, left to wait for disposal. They'd probably be taken to the mass grave outside town and buried there, unless they were fed to the creatures in the zoo instead. It was just possible.

"We fought the bandits and won," the lead Marine said. His voice somehow silenced the crowd again. "We proved that they can be beaten. Now we have an offer for everyone. Your planet needs you; we need new recruits for the army we intend to build to exterminate the bandits and rebels alike. If you are interested in joining up with us, please go to the recruiting booth we have opened in the Imperial Office."

He leaned forward, as if he were going to whisper a secret. "And we pay in cash," he added. "Your salary can be paid each month, or it can be banked with the Imperial Bank, rather than the Bank of Avalon. You won't have to pay off any debt-mongers if you don't want to."

A rustle ran through the crowd. He had just told them that they could earn their salary…and keep it, keep all of it. Very few of the city's population had gone into debt willingly, but they had inherited their debt from their parents. Young men like Michael had had no hope, until now. He looked up at the Marines, watching calmly in their uniforms, and wondered if he could join them. Did he have whatever it took to be one of them?

Yes, he told himself. It was an opportunity that would never come again.

"It won't be easy," the Marine said. "It will be the hardest thing many of you will have ever done, but it is worth it. We will allow any of you a chance to come and prove yourselves."

Michael watched as the Marines jumped down and walked off, taking the dead bodies with them. The gallows they left behind, probably for the next group of captured bandits. He walked away, shaking his head; he'd seen death before, but watching an execution was something new. A thought struck him and he broke into a run as he ran towards the centre of town. If the word spread as fast as he expected, the entire city would be trying to sign up.

He reached the Imperial Office – a prefabricated building just north of Government House – and was unsurprised to discover that seventeen people had beaten him to it. Eleven of them were young men like himself, who had grown up on the streets; the remainder were young women, including two who had probably been forced into prostitution to feed themselves. That wasn't uncommon in Camelot, not when prostitutes – too – were paid in cash. The women would have faced the same debt problem as Michael did when they tried to hold normal jobs. As prostitutes, the only person taking a cut of their income would be their pimp.

The queue stretched around the block by the time the doors opened, allowing three of the prospective recruits to enter at a time. Michael waited as patiently as he could for his turn, following a young woman who looked as if she had barely entered her teens into the Imperial Office. A smiling man wearing a uniform he didn't recognise showed him into a private room, where he came face-to-face with a scarred man who scowled at him.

"So," he thundered. "You want to join up, do you?"

Michael nodded, too terrified to speak.

"Take this," the man said, passing Michael a small egg-sized device that he held in his hand. "Understand; the first time you lie to me, I'll boot you out and you can forget about joining anything more worthwhile than the sanitation department. Now..."

He fired off a long list of questions at Michael, who stumbled as he tried to answer them. Some made sense, asking about his family and his father's name, others made no sense at all. Why did the Marines want to know about his political leanings? What political leanings did he have anyway? It wasn't as if he'd ever be able to pay off his debt and claim the franchise. He found himself growing more and more impatient with the list of questions, and then it dawned on him that the questions were a test in themselves. The Marines wanted to know how patient he was.

"Good enough," the recruiter growled, finally. He didn't sound happy, which made him unusual in Michael's experience. Most recruiters wanted as many young bodies as they could get, although he'd never met a military recruiter before. Perhaps there were limits to how many men and women the Marines could recruit. "Do you understand that you will be going into an area where heavy discipline is the norm, where you might be injured in training and where you will be expected to obey all orders, without hesitation?"

"Yes, sir," Michael said. "I understand."

"No, you don't," the recruiter said. "You just think you understand."

Michael said nothing.

"Be at the spaceport in three days, with this card," the recruiter said, holding out a piece of cardboard. Michael was somehow unsurprised to see his picture on the card. "Time and date are on the card. If you don't show up then, don't bother to show up at all. And, if you get your ass shot off, don't blame me."

Michael stared down at the card and then nodded. "Thank you," he said. "I'll be there."

Chapter Twenty-Three

> ...Increasingly, the young men and women of the Empire – those born to the Middle and High Classes, at least – are concentrating on living for the now and not thinking about the future. They sense, however dimly, that the Empire has no future.
>
> - Professor Leo Caesius, *The Waning Years of Empire* (banned).

They heard the music long before they rounded the corner, a thumping beat that spoke of dancing and forgetfulness. Jasmine felt the beat reaching out to her as the four Marines strode down the street, glancing from side to side. The middle-class zone of Camelot was a study in contrasts; in the day, it was all staid and respectable, but in the night the party began. Lighted shops offered everything from pornography to drugs, while hookers waited at lampposts, accosting men and offering their services. The young and desperate thronged through the streets, taking little note of the Marines as they sought the next high, or something else that could make them forget their troubles for a night.

"It sounds like a party," Blake said, cheerfully. Jasmine, who would have quite happily remained in barracks for the night, scowled inwardly. They might have been on leave, but platoon comrades never left each other alone – unless one of them got lucky, of course. Blake and Joe might want to look for suitable partners – and Koenraad had come along for the ride – but Jasmine didn't share their enthusiasm. A night of guiltless sex with someone who had no idea of what she did for a living didn't appeal. "Shall we go gatecrash?"

"It could be fun," Joe agreed, with a wink. "You want to bet on who comes home with the most panties?"

"After those bastards in First Platoon showed them that game, maybe not," Blake said, with a leer of his own. One of the less endearing Marine traditions was picking up a girl each night, or maybe two or three a night, and stealing her panties afterwards to prove that they had scored. Jasmine privately thought that it was a silly tradition and had said so, more than once. "They were boasting about how Camelot girls were easy."

"They probably want a handsome Marine to marry them and get them out of the slum," Koenraad said, unexpectedly. He looked up at their bemused glances. "So I study local politics. You want to make something of it?"

Jasmine shook her head. Marines were expected to have hobbies in their spare time, even though it was the shared belief of every Marine that spare time was a delusion invented by a particularly sadistic drill sergeant. Koenraad had spent his time earning a degree in sociology from the University of Earth, although they had refused to grant him a doctorate as his work was hardly 'non-judgemental and sensitive'. A Marine who had spent his time in various hellholes being shot at by the natives – normally after the Empire's vast army of bureaucrats had gotten something wrong and seriously hacked off said natives – would have a very different view of their culture than a high-browed academic who'd never spent a day of his life off Earth.

"All the better for us," Blake declared, as they passed a line of street toughs. Jasmine braced herself, expecting a fist-fight, but the toughs somehow picked up on their true nature – even through the civilian clothes they were wearing – and wisely backed off. There might have been nine of them, but the Marines would have handed them their heads, even without weapons. "We can have all the pussy we want and no one will say boo to us."

Jasmine rolled her eyes. "Do you ever think about anything apart from women?"

Blake pretended to consider it. "No," he said, finally. "I guess I'm a naughty Blake. Mama Coleman would not be impressed."

Joe chuckled. "Remember," he said, in a passable impression of Sergeant Young, "a soldier who won't fuck won't fight."

"And a soldier who fucks when he should be fighting won't be fucking for much longer," Jasmine said, in a rather less passable impression of her first Drill Sergeant. The fornication excuse for being late back to barracks worked once; after that, it was punishment duties for any repeat offender. "Just remember to pay them in local coins."

"I am *offended* at your suggestion that I might have to pay them," Blake countered, archly. "Why, there are women who pay me to have sex with them."

Koenraad laughed. "If that is true, Blake, why are you still here?"

"Because without me, you'd all be dead by now," Blake said. He snorted dryly. "Who has the local cash anyway?"

Joe reached into his pocket and brought out a roll of paper notes, produced at the Bank of Avalon. Jasmine hadn't been impressed when she'd first seen them. Any halfway competent forger could have produced millions of counterfeit banknotes and used them to wreck an already-unstable currency. They were, in theory, equal to the Imperial Credit and could be exchanged one-for-one, but the Bank of Avalon had tried to overcharge the first Marines who had attempted to exchange their money.

It had been Joe who had come up with the solution. He'd taken an inventory of the songs and tunes the platoon had brought with them from Earth, and then sold them to distributors in Camelot, giving them advance access to the currently-fashionable music from Earth. Jasmine disliked the howling racket that was the height of fashion on Earth – it sounded like an army of cats screeching at the moon while being savaged by wild dogs, in her considered estimation – but it had brought the platoon plenty of local money. By the time the official releases reached Avalon, the music would already be old and forgotten.

"There's enough here to wipe your bottom after eating in the mess," Joe said, as he passed out bundles of notes. Jasmine took hers and stowed it in her inside pocket. "I'm not sure what else it will buy here. It won't be long before they start producing million-credit banknotes."

"Probably," Koenraad agreed. "They're in the middle of an inflation spiral right now and it's only going to get worse before it gets better."

"Hey," Blake said, as they turned another corner and saw the party. "We don't want to know about economics and maths and boring shit like that. We want to go to a party!"

He slapped Jasmine on the shoulder. "And you can play the game too," he said. "We'll let you bring home underpants instead of panties and see who wins."

"Get fucked," Jasmine said, dryly.

"I intend to," Blake countered. He smiled at her. "Come on; live a little. It might be fun."

"I seem to recall that we end up being thrown out of places; that or being chased back to barracks by the wasps," Jasmine said. "If we have to spend the next week cleaning toilets, I'm going to do something awful to you. Something so unspeakably awful that I haven't even thought of it yet."

Blake chuckled and ambled towards the party, followed by the other three. The party seemed to have started in one large hall and spread rapidly into several others. There were hundreds of young men and women dancing in the first hall, while others pushed in and out as they grew tired of the music. Jasmine rubbed the back of her temples as the noise grew louder. She'd been in powered combat armour under fire and that hadn't been anything like so much of a racket. The rate of ear trauma on Avalon, she decided, had to be quite high.

A topless girl danced past with her breasts bobbing as she moved. From the dazed look in her eye, Jasmine guessed that she was on some kind of stimulant, probably something grown illegally in the countryside and shipped into the city. Her hard nipples seemed to mock everyone as she moved from boy to boy, kissing each of them before moving on to the next. From the laughter that followed her, Jasmine had the very clear impression that she wasn't operating entirely of her own volition.

Sparkle dust, probably, she thought. Sparkle dust was banned on almost every world in the Empire, with good reason. Properly prepared, it acted as a mild hypnotic, allowing someone who took it to enter a state where they would follow almost any suggestion they were given. The girl had probably taken it on a dare – or it had been slipped into her drink – and someone had suggested that she act the wanton for the night. She was going to be very embarrassed in the morning.

"I knew we'd have fun," Blake said, as they pushed their way towards a makeshift bar. It looked as if it was going to topple over at any second, although that hadn't stopped people from covering it with barrels and glass bottles of drinks. Avalon might not produce much in the way of marketable goods, but it was generally agreed that it produced excellent beer, although there was little point in exporting it to other star systems. It wasn't cost-effective. "I should have worn my uniform. That always brings in the girls."

He leaned across the counter and smiled at the barmaid, a girl who looked as if she had seen too much in her young life. She couldn't be much younger than Jasmine herself, but her eyes were those of an old woman. "Four beers please," he said, waving the wad of cash under her nose. "We're thirsty and starving."

"We take Imperial Credits only," the barmaid said, tiredly. Blake leaned over and glared at her. Jasmine sighed inwardly, even though she knew that the barmaid deserved it. It was illegal – if good business – to refuse payment in local currency. "All right. I'll pour you four beers."

"And pour one for yourself as well," Blake said, affably. He passed across some of his banknotes. "Please don't try to short-change me. I'll never live it down."

Jasmine smiled inwardly at the barmaid's expression. The woman didn't know it, but one of the many secrets implanted into the Marines was an implant that prevented them from becoming drunk, or even mildly inebriated. A pleasant buzz was the most they could expect from their drinks, even if they drank twenty pints each. She took a long pull at her glass and sighed in delight. The beer was cold and surprisingly good. She'd had drinks on Earth that should have been poured back into the horse.

"I'm going over there," Blake said, pointing towards a table where several girls sat, giggling as they watched the Marines. "Come on; you might find one that's into girls."

Jasmine surveyed the girls and frowned. If what they wore was high fashion on Avalon, it proved that bad taste was truly universal. "I dread to imagine," she said primly. "You go have fun. I'm going to sit here and watch the crowd."

"You don't have to stay here, honey," the barmaid said. "There are other places you can go."

Jasmine shook her head as the crowd swallowed up Blake and Joe. Koenraad had vanished off somewhere, perhaps chasing a pretty girl. Blake and Joe might enjoy being in a party, but Jasmine felt out of place. Her strict upbringing hadn't prepared her for such debauchery and her experience in the Marines meant nothing to the young fools on the dance floor. They would never understand what it was like to crawl through the mud, trying to sneak up on an enemy position, or the costs of her career. Her father had understood, the day she'd told him that she was leaving to go to Boot Camp, but few others outside the Marines knew or cared. They were the only real family she had.

An hour passed slowly as the dancing swirled around her. The music never seemed to stop – she suspected that it was produced by a computer, rather than a human band – and dancers joined or left at will. She caught sight of Joe, locked in an embrace with a pretty girl, and Blake, being… serviced by a girl in public, and recoiled, even though no one else seemed to care. It reminded her of the last days on Han before everything had gone to hell. No one might have said it out loud, but Avalon was a dying world.

She was turning sharply before her mind caught up with what she had seen. There was a girl, over at a table, surrounded by three tough-looking guys. Jasmine locked her eyes on them and realised in a sudden burst of horror that she knew the girl. Mandy Caesius's red hair was almost impossible to mistake.

Silly bitch, Jasmine thought, angrily. The Professor and his family might have finally obtained housing in the richer section of town, but his silly spoilt daughter still had to get her kicks somehow, even if it meant coming right into the seedy area of town without an escort. Jasmine had privately wondered if the Professor had hoped that she'd play Mandy's older sister, but there just hadn't been the time. Captain Stalker wouldn't have bothered to pussyfoot around the issue; if he'd wanted Jasmine to baby-sit the girl, he would have issued orders and left it to her to carry them out.

Her gaze sharpened as she realised that Mandy was in real trouble. One of her male friends was holding up a tab and reaching out towards Mandy's neck, while the other two were holding her arms and pawing at her body. Mandy was laughing, but it was the nervous laugh of prey, caught in the predator's net. Jasmine didn't even think about leaving the girl to suffer whatever fate they had in mind for her. Marines existed to protect people like her and, even if some of them weren't worth the effort, the creed of the Corps wouldn't allow her to walk away.

She stood up and stretched, checking out the area. It was hard to be sure, but the thugs holding Mandy might have more allies in the nearby area. They might have been a street gang, like the ones back on Earth, or they might just have been friends, out to see just how far they could go before someone stopped them. No one was going to stop them, Jasmine knew, unless she intervened. There was no sign of the Civil Guard at all. She glanced around, looking for any of her comrades, before walking right up to the lead thug and yanking the tab out of his hand. Whatever it was – and she had nasty suspicions – she couldn't allow him to inject it into Mandy.

"Hey, bitch," the thug said, wincing. Jasmine hadn't been gentle and had applied considerable force to his hand. He was lucky she hadn't broken it outright. "What the fuck do you think you're doing?"

He meant to be intimidating, but after an endless series of Drill Sergeants, Jasmine had long lost her fear of anyone lesser. "Mandy," she said, ignoring him, "we're leaving. Now."

Mandy looked up at her, astonished. "I…"

"Shut the fuck up, bitch," another gang member said. He looked at his mates, eyes glittering. Jasmine realised that he'd popped a tab of a different drug. "We can have some fun with this one too."

"No," Jasmine said, pushing all of her authority into her voice. Wiser men, or men who hadn't addled their mind with drugs, would have backed away. "I'm taking her out of here. You can fuck off and find a few whores to satisfy your appetites…"

The gang leader roared at such a challenge to his authority and threw a punch. He might have thought that he was tough, but Jasmine saw him as if he were moving in slow motion and she had plenty of time to think of a counter. She stepped to one side, reaching up to snap his arm as he fell past her, before shoving him down onto the ground with a kick. Mandy stared at her as she twisted before a second gangster could grab hold of her, neatly placing a kick right in his groin. The young man folded over and crashed onto the floor. The others howled in rage and closed in. Jasmine braced herself, just before one of them was sent flying right across the room by Blake.

"You should have called," he said, as he turned to flatten a second thug. There was nothing elegant in his punch; he simply smashed the thug right in the face. "I had just finished my business and…"

"We didn't wish to know that," Joe said, appearing out of nowhere. He was grinning a toothy grin. "How much did you have to pay her?"

The gang closed in, unable to retreat. Jasmine instinctively bunched up with the other three, leaving Mandy in the centre, and fell into a combat stance. The thugs had no idea what they were up against. Used to picking on defenceless and drugged girls, or isolated victims, they had no conception of organised violence. The four Marines sliced through them, knocking them all down one by one. Blood flew as several of the thugs drew knives, only to find themselves targeted for immediate suppression.

"You'd better get her out of here," Blake said, over the private communications channel. The crowd was starting to panic, breaking up as the music was mercifully drowned out by screams. The young men and women were trying to run in all directions, knocking each other over as they fled. The injuries would be horrifying on an advanced planet, but on Avalon, comparatively minor damage could be fatal. "What was she doing here anyway?"

"Fucked if I know," Jasmine said. She caught hold of Mandy's arm and hauled the girl up, throwing her over her shoulder in a fireman's carry. Mandy yelped once and fell silent. "I'll get her back to her home and then ask her specifically."

"Good," Blake said, all business suddenly. A thug came at him, waving a length of chain, and he caught it and used it to knock its former owner to the ground. "Go!"

CHAPTER TWENTY-FOUR

> The Empire needs to ensure that its young are brought up to understand, embrace and propagate the values of the Empire, yet over thousands of planets, this simple truth is no longer heeded. They are taught, instead, that there are no consequences to anything they do. The Empire-mandated curriculum has, by replacing the parents, produced a generation of sheep and wolves.
> - Professor Leo Caesius, *The Waning Years of Empire* (banned).

Jasmine held herself together as she ran out of the hall, heading towards the nearest street. A handful of people tried to get in her way and she knocked them down, snapping into close-protection mode. It had been years since she had ever had to serve as a bodyguard to a civilian – rather than a Marine officer, who could be relied upon to know what to do in an emergency – but she hadn't forgotten. The health and safety of passers-by was of no concern compared to the safety of her charge.

"Idiot girl," she growled, as the cold night air struck her in the face. Merlin, orbiting high overhead, seemed to laugh at her in the cold night. The planet's single moon was far more pronounced than Luna had ever been to the early generation of humans. Perhaps it wouldn't have taken so long for humanity to reach the stars if the Moon had been closer to Earth. "What were you thinking?"

Mandy made no reply. Jasmine half-guessed that she might be in shock, but there was no time to stop for a medical emergency. She could hear sirens as the Civil Guard's local force finally responded to the growing riot and hoped that Blake and the others would have the sense to vanish before they could be arrested. Captain Stalker would not be happy if he had to bail them out of some local jail, if they survived so long. The gang probably had an ally in the local service who would help them to take revenge on the Marines.

The stream of people fleeing was growing stronger as the Civil Guard finally arrived, too late to do anyone any good. Jasmine took a breath and ran right towards the first car. The officer who climbed out of it stared at her in surprise. He had enough military training – even if it had been supplemented by civil police service training – to know when he was looking at a fellow soldier.

"Marine Corps," Jasmine said, flashing her Rifleman's Tab at him. The golden badge was unique. It had been made for her specifically when she had graduated from the Slaughterhouse and would be stored there after her death, if it survived whatever killed her. There were a handful of badges in private hands, even though it was illegal. "I need your car and a driver."

"But…you can't be serious," the officer said. "I have to deal with the riot!"

"Take it up with the Governor," Jasmine said, as the Civil Guard began to spread out and head towards the growing riot. "I need your car, now!"

The officer blinked owlishly at her, and then got out, allowing Jasmine to put Mandy down onto the rear seat. Unsurprisingly, the car was luxurious, even though it had been prepared for military service. She closed the door behind her and barked an address to the driver, who clearly hadn't dared to object to her sudden hijacking. The car's engine roared as it slipped into gear and headed away from the chaos.

Jasmine glanced down at Mandy and keyed her implanted communicator. "The Civil Guard is here," she subvocalised. The driver couldn't be allowed to hear her words. "Get out of there and I'll meet you back at the barracks."

There was no response, so she turned her attention to Mandy, picking through her utility belt for her medical bracelet. The device was centuries ahead of anything Avalon could produce for itself – which had worrying implications for when they ran out of supplies – but it should suffice to run a basic medical diagnostic on the young girl. Mandy looked as if she were in shock, perhaps because of the attempted rape and ultra-violence, yet Jasmine feared that there was more to it than just that. The bracelet had no baseline for her – an oversight that would have been corrected, if there had been anything official about her voyage on the *Sebastian Cruz* – but it didn't matter. The results blinked up in front of her and Jasmine swore. Mandy had taken at least one other drug and quite a lot of alcohol.

"You're young," Jasmine told her, as she pulled a small tab out of her belt. "This won't be pleasant, but you should be able to take it."

She pushed the tab against Mandy's neck – hearing a moan of disbelief from the girl – and injected her with a broad-spectrum cleanser. It was a distant relative of the civilian sober-up pills, but where sober-ups were concentrated on alcohol, the cleanser was concentrated on everything. Marines used it to clear their systems of battle stimulants or painkillers and they were never a pleasant experience. Jasmine privately suspected that the whole process was painful just to prevent Marines from becoming addicted to the rush.

Mandy thrashed, half-gagging as her whole body convulsed, but Jasmine held her tightly as the drug worked its way through her system. Mandy had no immunity at all and it was hitting her hard. The car pulled up outside Mandy's new house and Jasmine's eyes narrowed. She had hoped to pass Mandy over to her parents and return to the barracks, but there was no sign of life in the building. She helped Mandy out – the cold air had probably come as a relief to her – and thanked the driver for her services.

"Mandy," she said, as the car drove away, "where are your parents?"

Mandy's eyes were still defocused, but her voice was steadier. "They went out to a party," she said, brokenly. "They didn't care about me. All Mum cares about is her social status and Dad just doesn't care. And Mindy's fucked off somewhere else with her new friend. She doesn't care either."

Jasmine frowned and checked the girl's pockets, finding a set of primitive keys. "Your parents care a great deal about you," she said, as she opened the door and helped Mandy into the living room. The Professor had bought a good house, but it would be a disappointment after their home on Earth. She clicked on the lights and gently pushed Mandy onto the sofa. "Stay there. I'll fetch you some water."

She checked the medical bracelet before she found the kitchen and poured Mandy a glass of water. When she got back into the living room, Mandy was staring off into the distance, her entire body shaking. The bracelet had reported that she wasn't having an adverse reaction to the cleanser, but she clearly hadn't been taking care of herself. Mandy, Jasmine realised, had never had to learn discipline.

"My parents don't love me," Mandy said, between dry sobs. "Dad gets us all kicked off Earth, away from my friends and everyone I knew and love. Mum doesn't give a damn about us. She just wants to be the woman in charge of everything."

"Your father may have saved your life," Jasmine said, quietly. She had liked the Professor, even if babysitting the family had been one of the weirder duties she'd faced. "Earth isn't a safe place…"

"It was my home," Mandy snapped, angrily. "I had friends, I had a life…and suddenly I'm exiled to this fucking dirty rock at the edge of Empire, a place so primitive that they barely have anything remotely fun!"

Jasmine gritted her teeth, wishing that she'd put in for the Training Badge rather than the Sniper Badge, back during her third year at the Slaughterhouse. She had no experience of training recruits, even if she did have some experience with her sister's children, long before she had gone to Boot Camp and never looked back. Dealing with a crying child-woman was a little beyond her. Her homeworld wouldn't have tolerated such an adult baby.

"And so you went out and got stoned," Jasmine said, tightly. She didn't want to snap at Mandy, but the words came out. "What were you thinking?"

"I wanted some fun," Mandy said. "Why shouldn't I have fun? What right did you have to interfere?"

Jasmine controlled herself with an effort. She hadn't had much experience with the middle classes on Earth, but their world was a safe one, barely even disturbed by terrorists or natural disasters. They barely even knew about the Undercity and, when they thought about it, considered it a kind of daring place to visit. It did a gentleman's reputation no harm if he could drop the odd hint of roguish dealings. Mandy could have gone out and gotten stoned in the Middle City and the worst that would have happened would have been a headache the morning after. On Avalon, the results could have been far more disastrous.

"They were going to inject you with Sparkle Dust," she said, sharply. There was no way to be sure, but she thought that it was fairly likely. "Do you know what that would have done to you?"

Mandy shook her head, her defiant eyes meeting Jasmine's eyes and refusing to look away. "I'll tell you, if you like," Jasmine snapped. "It would have turned you into their slave! You would have done anything they told you to do while you were convinced that it was a good idea all the time, or that it was your idea, or some other self-justifying crap! You could have found yourself being gang-raped or fucked by the entire group of bastards, or you could have been sent off with orders to fuck any guy who even looked twice at you. There is a very good reason that that stuff is banned!"

She sat down next to Mandy and put her arm around the girl's shoulder. "What happened to you?"

The story came out in-between sobs. Mandy's new friends from the rich part of the city enjoyed slumming and they'd taken her to a handful of bars in the seedy area. For one reason or another, they hadn't thought to take escorts, trusting in their names to keep them safe. They might have been right, but Mandy didn't have a famous name or a reputation to protect her. The gang who'd picked her up had gently but firmly pressured her into coming to the party, giving her free sniffs of several drugs to help make her pliable, and kept pushing away at her. By the time it had entered her dulled brain that she was in trouble, it had been far too late. If Jasmine and her comrades hadn't gone to the same party, she would have been raped and murdered.

"You're an idiot," Jasmine said, flatly, when Mandy had finally finished talking. "You wanted to get some pleasure and walked right into a trap. Why...?"

"You cannot understand," Mandy snapped at her. "You're surrounded by handsome men who would do anything for you. I'm...I'm just the daughter of a political exile."

Jasmine blinked at her, profoundly shocked for the first time. Mandy could not have been more wrong. It was strictly forbidden to have sex with Marines from the same Company. It had been hammered into their heads time and time again. Sex within the same Company destroyed unit cohesion. There were breaches of regulations that would be winked at, with the regulations considered guidelines rather than hard laws, but the no-fraternizing edict was not one of them. A Marine who was caught breaking that particular regulation – and it was impossible to keep something like that a secret for long – would be lucky if he or she wasn't dishonourably discharged from the Marines. The idea of sleeping with Blake, or Joe...she had to admit that they were handsome, but they were her brothers in arms.

"So you went off and went looking for someone to fuck," Jasmine said, feeling her mind reeling. Didn't Mandy have any sense of responsibility at all? Or, for that matter, a sense of self-preservation? "Why couldn't you find someone from the upper crust here?"

"Because they all laugh at me," Mandy cried, shaking Jasmine's arm free. "They think that mum is a social climber, even if she is from Earth and knows all the fashions. They just laugh at me and treat me like a silly girl..."

"You *are* a silly girl," Jasmine said, dryly. A few years at the Slaughterhouse would teach the girl discipline, if she managed to pass through Boot Camp. Mandy probably didn't have the determination to even get through the entrance exams. "You have no idea how lucky you are, yet you're bitching because your life has changed...your father might have done you a favour when he brought you here. Earth won't be safe for much longer."

The memories of the Nihilist attack and its aftermath rose unbidden in front of her eyes. "What do you think," she demanded, "will happen when Earth collapses? People like you will be butchered as blood runs in the streets. Out here, you have at least a chance of a future."

"I hate this place," Mandy screamed. Tears were flowing down her cheeks. "I hate my family. I hate you! I wish I was dead!"

"Enough," Jasmine said, coldly. Part of her mind told her that it was a losing battle, but she felt that she owed the Professor something, even if it was just an attempt to save his daughter from doing something stupid. "If you insist on acting like a child, I'll treat you as a little baby…"

Mandy raised her hand and aimed a slap at Jasmine's face. Jasmine saw it coming and skimmed through options. Anything she did to stop the blow would injure Mandy, perhaps break her arm…she allowed the girl to slap her, recoiling slightly at the pain. It was nothing compared to unarmed combat practice back on Castle Rock. The Sergeants believed firmly in learning through pain. Jasmine caught her arm as Mandy pulled back from the blow and made her decision.

"Come here," she snapped, catching hold of the girl's upper body. "I have had enough of you."

Mandy yelped as Jasmine pulled her across her lap. She was stronger than Jasmine had expected, but Jasmine had learned to fight with the best. There was no question of who would win in a struggle, yet Jasmine had to be careful. Inflicting permanent harm on the girl, even by accident, would not look good on her record. Mandy started to protest aloud, demanding that she be released, until Jasmine landed a hard smack on her rump. She gasped in pain and recoiled from the blow.

"You can't do this to me," she protested, in horror. Jasmine ignored her, reaching for the girl's shamefully short skirt and flipping it up, revealing a pair of near-transparent panties. "Let me go and…"

Her voice trailed off as Jasmine yanked her panties down to her ankles, exposing her rear to the air. "If you had been brought up by my family," Jasmine snapped, lifting her hand into the air, "your mouth would have been washed out with soap before the real punishment started, just for your filthy language."

She brought her hand hard down on Mandy's behind. The girl screamed in pain as a gratifying red handprint appeared on her pale bottom. Jasmine smacked her again and again, moving from cheek to cheek in a slow rhythmical pattern, pausing long enough to slap the back of the girl's thighs every time Mandy tried to dislodge herself from Jasmine's knee. Mandy forgot all dignity as she screamed and kicked; exposing everything she had to cold dispassionate eyes. It had been years since Jasmine had been spanked herself, by her parents as she had turned from a child to a young lady, yet she remembered what it had been like. The pain, the humiliation…and then, finally, the acceptance.

It crossed her mind that spanking the girl might have been considered abuse, or assault, on many worlds, including Earth, yet she didn't care. Fiona Caesius was simply incapable of disciplining her daughter. It might get her into real trouble, but it might also teach Mandy the meaning of discipline. If she'd been taught that from when she was a child…yet Earth no longer taught children how to behave. Mandy's shocking behaviour was proof enough of that. She had wanted instant gratification, had thrown a tantrum when she hadn't received it quickly enough to suit her and had completely ignored the risk. A spanking was mild compared to what could have happened to her if Jasmine hadn't been there.

She paused, resting her hand on the girl's warm bottom. "You could have gotten yourself killed today," she said, feeling rather like a mother for the first time. If she had wanted kids, she would never have joined the Marines. She couldn't have children until her enlistment expired, assuming she didn't try to make officer or become an NCO. "You put your life at risk, for nothing."

Mandy's sobs were real, now. Jasmine held her for a long moment, and then pulled her up and hugged her tightly, the way her mother had hugged her back when she was a child. She would have been pushed into a corner and told to wait, with her hands on her head and her rear exposed, yet that would have been too much for Mandy's first real experience of discipline. The girl had kicked her panties free and right across the room, but her skirt fell down as she stood up, covering her rear.

"Don't sleep on your back tonight," Jasmine advised, dryly. Mandy looked at her with an injured expression on her face, as if she couldn't quite comprehend what had happened. Her hand rubbing her injured rear was almost cute. "I'll be here when you wake up."

She took Mandy upstairs and tucked her into bed, leaving her dressed. The girl fell asleep almost instantly, suggesting that she'd been tired out and emotionally drained even before the spanking. Jasmine watched her for a long moment, and then headed back downstairs. When the Professor arrived home from wherever he was, she would have to tell him what had happened, and why. He wouldn't take it calmly.

But at least his daughter survived, she thought. *He could have been coming home to a dead body.*

CHAPTER TWENTY-FIVE

> The aim of the Imperial Elites has moved from obtaining power – and using power responsibly for the good of the Empire – to holding on to that power at all costs. This is not surprising – they would be torn apart by their outraged victims – yet it is stagnating the Empire's development. In short, the elites are unable to accept the possibility of other – newer – elites.
> - Professor Leo Caesius, *The Waning Years of Empire* (banned).

"You cannot be serious," Carola Wilhelm demanded, her imperious voice echoing through the room. "This is an outrage!"

Brent leaned back in his chair, suppressing a desire to cover his ears. Carola was loud and shrill and very angry. She looked twenty years old, a strange mixture of Cascadian and Oriental features, but she was much older, even though she relentlessly attacked anyone who suggested she was over twenty-five. Somewhere back in the past, she'd had some very good regeneration treatments and it showed. Her classified file suggested that she was nearly seventy years old, yet she could have easily passed for her husband's daughter, rather than his wife.

"An outrage," Brent repeated. "And what, pray tell, is such an outrage that you have to burst into my office and demand explanations?"

Carola glared at him. "A Councillor has the right to visit the Imperial Governor at any time and demand an explanation for Imperial policy," she said, tartly. "The Council is most concerned over your recent activities."

"I see," Brent said. He knew perfectly well what had her so angry, but he chose to play the innocent for a few moments more. "And which of my activities has you so angry? I went to the scene of the riot yesterday and commended a pair of Civil Guardsmen for their bravery in preventing the riot from spreading further. I then visited the flower show at Imperial Heights and presented one of the ladies with a prize for her ingenious arrangements. And then I…"

"Don't be a bloody fool," Carola snapped at him. "I'm talking about the recruiting effort! The Council was not consulted on either the public hangings or the recruiting policy!"

"The defence of the planet is a reserved issue," Brent pointed out, calmly. "The Council doesn't actually get a say until it evolves into an autonomous government. Even after it becomes a government, it still has only limited authority and that over only the Civil Guard. I imagine that one of your lawyers would have known that before you burst in and disturbed poor Abigail."

Carola dismissed his comments with a sniff. She barely regarded her servants as human, let alone anyone else's servants. Brent had heard rumours – none of them had been confirmed, of course – that Carola treated her servants badly, whipping and beating them at the slightest provocation. He'd considered launching an investigation that might have provided the ammunition to get her off the Council, but the rest of the Council would never have allowed it to happen. They knew they had to hang together or hang separately, just as the former bandits had been hanged.

"The Council was still not consulted," Carola reminded him, "and I might remind you that you have consulted the Council in the past when making changes to the Civil Guard."

"I have no obligation to consult the Council about anything relating to the defence of the colony," Brent said. "The lines are blurred on Avalon, I concede, but I am still under no legal obligation to consult with anyone apart from the Civil Guard commander. The fact that I have done so in the past" – something he had rapidly come to regret – "does not create a future obligation to do so."

"That is as may be," Carola said, leaning back. "You have, however, chosen to ignore a direct law. All local transactions are to be done in local currency. All businesses are to use the Bank of Avalon for their payments.

The new recruits, or so I am told, will be paid in cash. That is completely beyond the pale."

Brent sighed inwardly, feeling overcome with a sense of cold despair. It said something about the general condition of Avalon that the planet couldn't muster a working satellite network, or possessed a barely-functioning communications datanet, but it had a first-rate banking system, supplied by Carola and the other debt sharks. They had manipulated the law to ensure that they collected what they were owed first, discouraging businesses from hiring any indebted workers from signing up.

The black market thrived; the official businesses, even the monopolies established by the ADC, were fading away. Carola might just find herself the queen of nothing when the system finally collapsed, if she wasn't assassinated first. The bodyguards she'd brought with her testified to her reputation as the most feared and hated woman on the planet. Even Gabriella Cracker didn't have such a terrifying reputation. Brent knew men and women who would have risked everything just to take a shot at her, not that it would have mattered in the long run. Her husband would simply have taken over the business and kept going.

He felt a flicker of admiration for Captain Stalker. In one neat move, he had found himself with more willing volunteers than he could handle…and, just incidentally, given the local economy a boost. Without such high levels of taxation – the banking system taxed wage packets automatically, when they were uploaded into the computers – the volunteers could spend money freely, while the businesses wouldn't have to declare all of their earnings. It would give the economy a shot in the arm…no wonder, then, that Carola wanted to squash it before it could get out of hand. It would weaken the Council's grip on the local economy and therefore weaken their power base.

"I said that it is completely beyond the pale," Carola repeated, seeing Brent drifting off. "What are you going to do about it?"

"Nothing," Brent said, calmly. "It is out of my hands."

Carola's face darkened. "You are the Imperial Governor of this planet," she snapped. "You are the supreme authority on this godforsaken rock. You can do anything."

Brent considered pointing out that the Council, ever since his predecessor had called it into existence, had spent most of its time denying that that was true, but decided against it. The temptation to rub her nose in her own failure was overwhelming. It would even be true.

"That isn't strictly true," he said, keeping his voice calm when he wanted to gloat. "The Terran Marines operate under the authority of the Emperor himself." He nodded towards the framed portrait of the Childe Roland on the wall. It was out of date by at least seven years, but no one had bothered to change it. It could wait until an official painting was produced when he reached his majority and took the throne formally. "They have independent authority over military deployments in the system."

"That's absurd," Carola protested, angrily. "You're the Governor."

Brent snorted gently. "I am the Governor of a planet with a serious insurgency," he said, deciding not to point out how Carola and her allies had hobbled the Civil Guard, making it harder for the Guard to actually fight the bandits, let alone the Crackers. "I am a very small fish compared to the Sector Governor, let alone the Grand Senate and the Emperor. If they choose to grant a Marine Captain freedom of action…who am I to say no?"

He shrugged. "And, besides, an officer from the Marines or the Imperial Army would officially have seniority over anyone from the Civil Guard," he added. "Captain Stalker, like it or not, is the *de facto* senior military officer in the system. The best that I" – and your puppets, he carefully didn't add – "can do is advise. If he decides he wants to recruit volunteers and pay them in cash, he has the legal authority to do so."

"The Council will not stand for this," Carola said. "The Council…"

"Has no say in the matter," Brent cut in, sharply. He saw her eyes widen and cursed his own mistake. She had thought him a fool. Now she would be taking him seriously. "The decision was made by Captain Stalker and I cannot gainsay it. If the Council refuses to co-operate…well, at best, it won't slow him down at all. At worst…the Council could find itself charged with treason."

"A Councillor has immunity from all charges," Carola pointed out.

"There is no such thing as immunity against a treason charge, even among the Grand Senate," Brent countered. He looked down for a moment, studying the map on his desk. "The best advice I can give you is to cooperate and make what profit you can on the sidelines."

"They're hiring workers to build barracks," Carola said, changing the subject. "Those contracts should be issued by the Council and given to those who need them. That is very definitely a civilian issue."

Brent snorted. She meant that the Councillors would give the work to businesses they owned, rather than allowing companies to bid for the contracts and undercut the Council. It was a common trick and explained why so much of Camelot was in bad shape. If there was no need to compete against a rival firm, a business had every incentive to cut corners and use poor materials. Who would dare make a complaint against a business backed by the Council?

"Castle Rock is their territory now," Brent said. He'd seen to that. "They can determine everything from the building codes to the wages – what and how the workers are paid. If it works out well for them, I may even ask the Council to review the business-related policies in Camelot and the other cities."

Carola's eyes sharpened. She was no fool and read the underlying threat easily. If the Marines paid well for good work, they would create new businesses that would undercut the Council…and, if the Council moved to crush them under a mountain of red tape, they might face massive civil unrest. For the first time since the colony had been settled, hope was spreading through the air. The Crackers would not be slow to take advantage of any sudden changes. Carola's power was limited, even though she pretended otherwise. A massive explosion in Camelot would see her and the Council dead.

"I formally protest," she said, sharply. "The Council will meet to discuss the issue."

Brent silently dismissed it as the empty threat it was. "I look forward to it," he said. Carola couldn't be trusted to pass on an accurate account of their conversation to the other Councillors; he'd have to see to it himself. "Until then…"

Carola bowed angrily. "This isn't over," she said, as she turned to depart. "We are the elected representatives of the people, empowered to act in their best interests. Don't forget that."

"I won't," Brent told the door. Carola had slammed it shut as she stormed out. A roar of engines from outside told him that her private car had departed at high speed, heading back to her mansion. "I won't forget anything."

He shook his head and turned back to the endless paperwork that needed his signature. Some homesteads, abandoned since the bandit attacks had begun, had been claimed by new settlers, who wanted to try to turn them into prosperous farms again. The Civil Guard wanted to up its signing bonus for new recruits, although Brent doubted that that would get far. The Civil Guard still paid wages directly into the banking system. He signed it anyway, knowing that the Council would block any attempt to pay the Civil Guardsmen in cash. They did have authority there.

"Idiots," he muttered, as he finished signing the papers. "Stupid idiots."

It would have upset the Governor, Edward knew, if he had known that his office was bugged. Colonel Kitty Stevenson had scattered a handful of modern surveillance devices throughout Government House, using them to keep tabs on the Governor and his senior staff. It was barely legal, as she'd acknowledged when Edward demanded to know just how much authority she had, but there was no other choice. Governors of stage-one and stage-two worlds tended to be corrupt and the various intelligence services were charged with rooting out corrupt officials.

"I think she means trouble," Kitty said, once she had finished replaying the recording. "You've managed to hack off the entire Council."

"You say that as if it were a bad thing," Edward said. Castle Rock's facilities were still being developed, the new recruits would be arriving in two days…and he simply didn't have the time to waste on political manoeuvrings. Two of his platoons were still out near the badlands, backed up by the Civil Guard. "We need those recruits motivated."

"I'm not disputing that," Kitty said, impatiently. "The problem is that you're smashing up the local power structure. The Wilhelm Family and their allies won't let you get away with it without a fight. Sure, legally you're in the right, but they can keep hammering away at you until you break."

Edward shrugged. The Governor had been right when he said that Edward was the senior officer in the system. The closest officer who could overrule him was at the sector capital, several weeks away even under Phase Drive. It would take months before any countermanding order arrived, if one was issued. Carola Wilhelm might be a big fish on Avalon, but her concerns would hardly register elsewhere. Why would they care about her?

"And then she might try something really stupid," Kitty continued. "What happens if she starts trying to have you assassinated?"

"Lieutenant Faulkner assumes command and Carola Wilhelm ends up dead," Edward said. He knew enough not to take the threat lightly – mindless bravado wasn't a Marine tradition, although legend suggested otherwise – but it barely registered compared to the other problems he faced. The equipment they'd brought from Earth had to be protected at all costs, yet once the starships pulled out – and he'd delayed them too long already – it would be much harder to safeguard Castle Rock. "It really isn't a concern at the moment."

He smiled up at her. "Keep an eye on them for me," he added. "Can you get any bugs into her mansion?"

"I've tried," Kitty admitted, "but she has some really sophisticated counter-surveillance systems. I think she must have purchased them before she came to Avalon and kept them to herself. I can't get a bug inside for long and none of the ones I have deployed have reported anything useful before they were removed. I don't know if she knows we're the ones watching her."

"Her friends are probably watching her as well," Edward said. Marine counter-surveillance teams swept Castle Rock's facilities every day, looking for any surprises. "A nicer crowd of smiling backstabbers you couldn't hope to meet."

"Yes sir," Kitty said, with a shrug. "I'll do my best, but I don't think she's going to rest on her laurels and wait for you to take her power away from her."

Professor Leo Caesius finally came home in the early hours of the morning, his face tired and wan. Jasmine, who had been waiting patiently – reading a copy of his famously banned book to pass the time – stood up to open the door and beckoned him inside. His eyes widened when they saw her – he hadn't known that she was going to be inside – and she saw the fear in his eyes. He wasn't scared of her, but of what she might tell him. His wife or daughters might have been hurt. Jasmine motioned him to the sofa and, in crisp brief words, explained exactly what had happened, leaving out nothing.

She had considered simply telling him about the spanking and nothing else, knowing that she would have hated for her father to know everything she'd done when she was that age, but the Professor had to know the full story. Mandy could have gotten herself killed – or worse – while her father did…what? She still didn't know what the Professor did now that he lived in Camelot.

"I see," he said, finally. His voice was calm, but Jasmine's sensitive ears could hear a quiver. He loved his daughter, even if she could be a pain at times. It reminded her of when she'd told her father that she was leaving for Boot Camp and how he'd tried to be brave for her. He'd been more nervous than Jasmine had been! "I understand…"

"If you want to report me to the Captain, you can," Jasmine said, flatly. She glanced down at her timepiece, considering. She still had several hours before she had to report back to the spaceport or be declared AWOL. "He will probably not take it calmly."

"No, no, it's all right," the Professor said, stumbling over his own words. Jasmine realised that he had been in quiet despair over his daughter for a long time. But then, Mandy was the product of her environment, just as the Professor himself had been before he'd broken out and realised the truth. "I...thank you, I think. Will you stay for breakfast?"

Jasmine would have preferred to leave, but she chose to stay as the Professor puttered around his kitchen, boiling water and brewing tea. He could easily have hired servants, yet instead he chose to do it on his own, without help. Jasmine wondered just what he did for funds; his private bank account back on Earth, which would have gone a long way on Avalon, had been frozen by the government. She took the tea gratefully and then stopped. Mandy was standing in the door. She had changed into a pair of shorts and a shirt, yet she looked pale and wan. One hand kept rubbing her behind.

"I'm sorry," she said, and sounded – for once – as if she meant it. "I didn't mean to...I'm sorry."

"Live and learn," Jasmine said, and felt a surprising burst of sympathy for the girl. "It could have been worse."

CHAPTER
TWENTY-SIX

> Basic Training – be it for the Marines or the Imperial Army – is designed to accomplish just one thing. It is designed to break down a new recruit and build them up again into the image of a proper soldier. Once broken down, recruits learn discipline and weapons skills along with the ethos of their new service.
>
> - Major-General Thomas Kratman (Ret), *A Civilian's Guide to the Terran Marine Corps.*

The bus lurched to a halt outside the spaceport and opened its doors. Michael Volpe felt a tingle of excitement running through him as the new recruits poured out, gaping around at the spaceport – which they had never seen in their lives – and the handful of transport aircraft parked on the tarmac. It wasn't much, not compared to the pictures he'd seen of Grand Central Spaceport back in the early days of spaceflight, but it was hellishly impressive to his eyes. Other buses arrived and disgorged their own passengers, all young men. The young women seemed to have gone elsewhere. A wave of chatter swept over the crowd as they stared around, suddenly unaware of what to do next.

"ATTENTION," a voice bellowed, loudly enough to be heard even over the chattering. "You will see lines painted on the ground. Line up facing me on those lines!"

Michael ran forward and found a place on the front row, squashed between two other recruits. The shouter – a short man wearing a blue uniform studded with badges and a Rifleman's Tab on his collar – was pacing backwards and forwards, tapping his baton against his thigh in irritation. The recruits finally managed to line up and stared nervously at their new master. The man seemed to have muscles on his muscles. Michael had seen cartoon superhuman characters with magic powers who were less intimidating than the man facing them.

"I am Drill Sergeant Jared Barr," the man thundered. His voice was no quieter, even with the recruits too terrified to breathe. "For my sins, I am the official Drill Sergeant for you recruits. My job is to whip you into shape and make soldiers of you all. I'm not here to be your friend. I am here to turn you into soldiers. You are going to hate every last minute of the next few months. Most of you will quit. That is good! It is my job to sort out the quitters and get rid of them before we have to trust you on the front lines. You think that you understand me. You don't. You won't until you go through training.

"You will address me as 'Sergeant'. You will not call me 'sir!' I actually work for a living."

Michael winced as the Drill Sergeant's gaze seemed to stab into him before he passed on to the next recruit. "You are the sorriest bunch of recruits I have yet seen on this planet," he said. "You are in this course for one purpose; you are here to become soldiers, the first real soldiers your planet has yet seen. In twelve weeks, we will break you down and build you up again into soldiers. Don't bother crying to your mommy or whining about your pappy; they're not here and they can't help you. You volunteered for this."

His eyes swept across their ranks. "You are under military discipline now," he thundered. "You can be punished under the Codes of Military Justice and if necessary sentenced to death by field court-martial. There is no point in whining about lawyers and due process. You're in the Army now. In order that you know what you should not do, we will list the offences against military order every day. You will learn them off by heart. You will not commit them. Understand?"

A ragged chorus rose from the recruits. "Yes, sir," they stammered.

"You will not call me 'sir,'" Barr thundered. "All of you; drop and give me twenty push-ups, now!"

Michael stared at him and then dropped to the ground, beginning his push-ups. Barr marched from recruit to recruit, barking out advice and a few orders. "Keep your back straight," he barked at Michael, when he passed him. "Concentrate on lifting yourself above the ground!"

The recruits slowly finished their exercise and staggered back into line. A few looked shocked, as if they had expected an easier induction into the service. Others were breathing heavily, badly out of shape. They'd spent their last night as free men drinking and carousing and were paying for it now. Michael didn't feel any better. His heart was pounding and his breath was coming in fits and starts.

"By the time you finish this course, you will be doing hundreds of push-ups and thinking nothing of it," Barr informed them. It sounded like a particularly sadistic joke. His gaze flickered along the line of recruits. "Keep your shoulders straight. You're not with your mother now."

Michael winced inwardly as Barr's gaze swept over him again. "Now… offences against military order, listed as follows; insubordination, use of drugs, tobacco and alcohol, possession and/or consumption of food outside designated eating periods, possession of any contraband, failure to perform duties as assigned to you by lawful authority, being absent without leave and, last, but not least, fraternisation. To repeat; any of those offences will get you a punishment that may range from heavy exercise to being summarily discharged from the army. You will have those offences read to you every day, along with the definition of each offence. You will have no excuse for committing any of them!"

He paused long enough to measure their reaction. "Many of you will have brought drugs, or alcohol, or even food into the spaceport," he said, coldly. "When you are taken to be assigned your uniform and regulation-issue underclothes, get rid of them. This is your one warning. You may think that the civilian police wouldn't charge you with a crime if you are in possession of illegal drugs, but this is the army. If I catch any of you possessing or using drugs during training, that person will wish that he had never been born!"

Michael felt his head spin as Barr kept thundering at his cowed audience. "Insubordination; wilfully disobeying, insulting, or striking a senior officer. Absent without leave; leaving the base or your unit without permission, or failing to report back to your unit at the end of a leave period without permission. Fraternisation; sexual relationships with any of your fellow recruits, or senior officers, or anyone within your military unit. The remainder should require no explaining. If they do, you're in the wrong line of work."

His gaze swept across them again. "That building there holds the medical personnel and the outfitters," he said. "Form a line and march into the building, two by two!"

Michael, his ears still ringing, followed the other recruits into the building. A dark-skinned man wearing a medical uniform checked his ID and then ordered him into a smaller room, where a male nurse told him to strip before running through a brief but very thorough medical examination. The nurse took blood samples and inspected every one of his orifices, even though Michael couldn't imagine what half of the tests were actually for. The brief sight and hearing test, at least, made sense. The nurse kept muttering under his breath, before finally clearing Michael for duty.

"Get rid of any drugs and shit you have in the next room," he warned. Michael blinked at him. "Get moving; you're in the Army now!"

Michael moved, heading out of the door into the next compartment. Seven bins stood there, inviting him to empty his pockets of anything illegal, although he hadn't brought anything with him. He glanced inside, out of curiosity, and recoiled when he realised how many recruits had brought something illegal with them to the spaceport. He hoped that they all had the sense to discard everything, no matter how much they wanted to keep it. Somehow, he doubted that Barr would be kind when he caught anyone stupid enough to keep their stash with them.

"Take a seat," another man ordered. Michael sat down, puzzled. "Hold still…"

The barber rapidly cut his hair with an electric buzzer. Michael had no time to protest before it was finished, allowing him to stand up and see his face in the mirror. His hair had been cut back sharply, leaving nothing but a tiny amount of stubble. It would take weeks to grow his locks back, although he suspected that he'd be expected to keep it cut down to the bone. He stared. Was that tough-looking stranger really him?

"Yes, that's you," the barber said impatiently. "Get along to the next room."

The next room contained a pair of harassed-looking clerks and a pile of clothing. "Strip," one ordered, and Michael hastened to obey. The clerk swooped around him with a measuring tape, checking out every last part of his body, before picking up a pile of clothing and tossing it at him. "Put them on and then report back to be checked."

Michael dressed slowly. The Army-issue clothing felt odd compared to the clothes he'd worn as a civilian, even though it was clearly new and not handed down from older boys. Other recruits came in to dress and he did his best to copy them, pulling the tunic over his head. Somehow, with the uniform properly fixed, he felt taller. The clerk gave him a brief once-over, placed his old clothes in a storage box for when he left the spaceport, and shoved him back out into the sunlight. A line of recruits was already gathering in front of the Drill Sergeant, who was eying them with a gimlet eye. Michael had the uncomfortable feeling that nothing they did would be good enough for the man. There would always be room for improvement.

"You will notice footprints on the ground in front of you," Barr barked, once the first row had filled up. "Place your feet on them and stand to attention. You will learn how to do that as naturally as breathing."

Michael followed his orders. Perhaps it was the uniform, but he didn't feel any sense of the absurd as he posed with the others. Some people had spent the last two days mocking military pomp and circumstance, but he was starting to realise that it all had a place. Drill Sergeant Barr added others to the line as they came out of their own medical examination and dressing, forcing them to pose. He showed more patience than Michael would have expected, nothing like the teacher he'd been forced to pay attention to at school. The man had been unable to teach Michael and his fellows anything they actually wanted – or needed – to know. It had taken years for him to realise that the Empire's mandated curriculum hadn't been designed to create thinking youngsters, but more peons for the elite.

"Acceptable," Barr said finally. "Now" – he pointed a hand towards one of the transport aircraft – "you will march into the aircraft for transport to Castle Rock. March; not run."

Michael followed his new comrades towards the aircraft. He'd never flown before and, despite the surroundings, he was quite looking forward to it. The aircraft, he discovered to his disappointment, only had a handful of windows, but he was lucky enough to sit next to one. He stared out as the aircraft accelerated down the runway and climbed into the sky. It all felt worthwhile, somehow.

Edward stood on the prefabricated control tower and watched as the four transport aircraft floated down out of the sky to land on the runway. Hiring labour from Camelot was a risk, yet there had been no choice; the Marines and their auxiliaries couldn't do everything they needed to do in time to open the base. Once he'd started paying the labourers in cash, they'd worked with enthusiasm; indeed, he rather suspected that some of them would try to join the Marines. It would offer them a better life than working for fixed wages back in Camelot.

Although that might change, he thought, grimly. The vast mass of civilians in Camelot had had no future and no hope of a better life, until the Marines had come along and started to show them that things could be better. Kitty was right; the political elite would try to slam the lid back down, but he suspected that would be impossible. The civilians in Camelot might be largely unarmed – although the city did have plenty of illegal weapons – yet the same couldn't be said for those who lived outside the city. An alliance between the Crackers and a similar group inside the cities would be disastrous. And the Marines had started the ball rolling.

He watched as the aircraft landed and the new recruits were urged out of the aircraft and rapidly formed up into lines. Drill Sergeant Barr and a handful of Marines who had served as training officers at the Slaughterhouse had organised themselves to deal with the first wave of recruits, but Edward was all-too-aware that they were spread thinly. There were five hundred recruits in the first wave and that was pushing the Marines right to the limits.

He'd seriously considered borrowing some Civil Guardsmen with training experience, but Major Grosskopf had dissuaded him. Far too many of the training officers had two masters. They simply couldn't be trusted. Besides, the majority of the competent Civil Guardsmen were out along the badlands, patrolling with the Marines and hunting for bandits.

Edward scowled as the recruits were introduced to Castle Rock. There had been only a handful of reported bandit sightings since the brief and bloody battle in the badlands, which suggested that they'd either wiped the bandits out in one fell swoop or that they were hiding and keeping their heads low while they waited for the Marines to get bored and go away.

The media on Camelot – owned, like the rest of the planet's business, by the elite – had been claiming that it was the former, but Edward would have been astonished if that were true. It was far more likely that they were plotting something. They'd invested too much time and effort in their grand plan to take over half of the continent to back away now.

And then there were the Crackers, who had been keeping very quiet. How long would it be until they joined the fight?

He glanced down at his timepiece and turned towards the ladder. It was time for the oath.

The heat struck them as soon as they stepped out of the aircraft, a wave of heat that was almost physical in its intensity. Michael recoiled and then stepped forward, feeling sweat trickling down his back. The aircraft had been air-conditioned, but it had only served to leave them unprepared for the heat of Castle Rock. He stumbled slightly as he moved forward, hunting for the lines before realising that there were none. They had to form up without any aids at all. Drill Sergeant Barr watched, his face turning darker and darker with every little mistake, until he finally barked a series of orders. The new recruits formed up and waited under the blazing sun.

"Stand to attention," Barr said, as a newcomer appeared at one end of the field. "Captain Stalker will now give the oath."

Michael tried to stand up straighter as the Captain paced from recruit to recruit, his eyes passing from face to face. He wore a dress uniform with at least a dozen decorations, although Michael had no idea what they all represented, if anything. Apart from the Rifleman's Tab at his collar, they were all meaningless to him so far. The Captain's stripes on his shoulder only made sense when he realised what they had to stand for.

"The Marine Oath has remained unchanged since the Empire itself was founded," Captain Stalker said. There was an air of calm competence in his voice, the voice of a man who didn't have to prove himself, or scare the recruits shitless for their own good. Barr had commanded obedience through shouting; Captain Stalker claimed it as his right. "Its basic form goes all the way back to the days before the Federation, before Earth itself was united under one government. It is living history. It is also your last chance to back out. If any of you have changed your minds, now is the time to leave."

There was a long pause. No one left. "Good," Captain Stalker said. "Repeat the Oath after me, inserting your own name at the beginning. I, Edward Stalker, do solemnly swear that I will support and defend the Empire against all enemies, foreign and domestic; that I will bear true faith and allegiance to the same; and that I will obey the orders of His Imperial Majesty the Emperor and the orders of the officers appointed over me, according to regulations and the Imperial Code of Military Justice. So help me God."

"I, Michael Volpe, do solemnly swear…"

Michael felt…odd as he spoke the words, as if a thousand generations were looking over his shoulder. He had never seen it in the Civil Guard, but then, the Civil Guard of Avalon was barely a hundred years old. The Terran Marine Corps dated all the way back to the days of the Terran Federation and then all the way back to Old Earth's pre-spaceflight era. It was older than the Empire, older by far than Avalon itself, older than he could imagine. The various military forces that had given birth to the Marine Corps dated back centuries even before spaceflight itself. History itself was tapping him on the shoulder.

He felt a lump at his throat as he finished the Oath, before standing to attention and saluting the Imperial Flag waving from one corner of the field. It wasn't a perfect salute – Barr had promised them that they'd be spending as long as it took to practice – but somehow it meant more to him than it had before.

"Welcome to the Marine Corps," Captain Stalker said. It was impossible to imagine him as a young recruit, yet he must have been one, years ago. If he could do it, so could Michael. "Dismissed!"

CHAPTER
TWENTY-SEVEN

> Freedom of information is one of the Empire's fundamental tenets. Indeed, by law, every colony world has to have a branch of the Imperial Library established in its capital city, free for all to enter and use. And yet, the Empire has grown more and more restrictive of information over the last few decades, concealing everything from economic data to political statistics. It is therefore very hard to draw a comprehensive picture of the Empire's overall state. It is even harder out on the Rim.
>
> - Professor Leo Caesius, *The Waning Years of Empire* (banned).

Leo sat at his desk in the Imperial Library, staring down at a sheet of paper without actually reading it. The Imperial Library should have been bustling with life, like the famous Library of Earth or the planet-sized Library of Alexandra, but there were only a handful of visitors. It wasn't surprising. Avalon's Council had pulled a fast one and banned anyone who had any debt at all from claiming any of the Imperial services that were theirs by right. Knowledge was power, after all, and the Council had a good reason to keep the rest of the population as powerless as possible.

The Imperial Library was one of the prefabricated buildings constructed in the centre of Camelot, built out of heavy battle steel. It should endure for centuries, even without human care and attention, and could survive anything short of a direct nuclear hit. In the early days of interstellar spaceflight, Leo knew, colonies had failed and their populations had fallen back to barbarism.

The Empire, in a bid to prevent the loss of knowledge that might have saved them, had ordered that each new colony play host to a branch of the Imperial Library, which would store all of humanity's hard-won experience. The farmers and miners of Avalon should have been visiting the library regularly, searching through its vast databanks for information that would be useful to them, or would make their farms and mines more productive. Avalon was a new colony and it was quite possible that any problem encountered on the planet had been encountered before, by other human colonies. The Library existed to help the human population survive.

It had been Fiona, desperate to find her husband something to do, who had asked her friends for suggestions. Avalon didn't have a university yet and it was unlikely Leo would have been allowed to teach there in any case, not after his exile from Earth. One of her new friends had suggested the Imperial Library, pointing out that the last librarian had quit in disgust and caught the first starship back to the sector capital. Leo had been delighted at first – if nothing else, he would have access to research materials for his future works – but it hadn't taken him long to realise that it was a dead end. The library's restricted nature prevented most people from coming and using the massive files.

The Imperial Librarians would be furious when – if – they found out, he knew. In many ways, they were just as determined and coherent as the Marines, devoted to ensuring that the spark of knowledge remained alive right across the Empire. Their Imperial Mandate would certainly prompt them to action, yet they might not be able to do anything. If the former librarian hadn't been able to convince them to intervene, protests from an exiled professor wouldn't get any further. Avalon was so far from Earth that it might be impossible to do more than issue orders and hope that they would be obeyed.

He stood up and paced over to the small coffee machine the previous librarian had left behind. It had been imported from a more advanced world at considerable expense and still worked perfectly, although the coffee grains had decayed long ago. Leo had replaced them with grains grown on Avalon itself and put the machine back into service, although the taste wasn't quite up to the standard of Earth's coffee. But then, the Imperial University had always had the best, demanding – in exchange – that professors and students didn't think for themselves. Leo himself had lost himself in academia until it had been too late.

The small office held nothing, apart from a desk, a computer and a small row of printed books. In theory, Avalon should have set up a printing press long ago and started to copy all of the manuscripts waiting in the massive library databanks, but Leo hadn't been surprised to discover that only a handful of books had been reproduced. Most of them were fictional works, rather than practical books that might aid the planet's population, distributed to distract them from their problems. Leo had added a picture of his family and nothing else.

He sat back down and sipped his coffee, wincing at the taste. The job was boring because there was nothing to do. Anything that might have required his services had already been done before the last librarian quit. There were few visitors to attend to. Fiona might have wanted him out of the house, or she might have believed that a librarian would have enjoyed the same sort of social cachet as a Professor at the University of Earth, but he was bored. He could feel his mind slipping away into hopeless boredom. The job didn't even pay that much.

Mandy's picture seemed to wink at him and he smiled, even though his daughter was a constant worry. He'd known that she had had an active social life on Earth – even though he hadn't wanted to know the details – but he'd also known that it was safe, unless she was insane enough to walk into the Undercity. On Avalon…she'd come far too close to being raped and murdered. The thought kept running through his head.

He could have lost his daughter barely two weeks after they'd landed on their new home. Colonists had experienced hardships throughout history, of course, but nothing like that – or so he told himself. Mandy had walked quite willingly to her own doom. If the Marines hadn't been there…the consequences didn't bear thinking about, yet he couldn't *stop* thinking about them. Horrible visions kept rising up behind his eyes.

Leo knew parents who would have screamed the place down if their daughters had been punished by a stranger; indeed, on Earth, it would have been regarded as physical abuse. He could only be grateful, for it had caused a change in Mandy. She was more subdued and thoughtful than she had been in years, although that might also have been because of her lucky escape. A few nights sleeping on her tummy was infinitively preferable to being raped and murdered. Who knew... perhaps she would grow into some form of maturity. Or perhaps he was just dreaming. He knew from his own studies that if a child wasn't taught right and wrong from a very early age, the behaviour would never truly improve.

The Marine communicator he'd been issued buzzed. "Professor," a voice said, "would you be able to come to Castle Rock at your earliest convenience?"

Leo smiled. He was so bored that an invitation to visit anywhere would have been welcome. "Of course," he said. "Where do I go to be picked up?"

"The spaceport," the voice said. Leo was sure that he knew the speaker, although he couldn't put a name to the voice. "There are flights from the spaceport every hour on the hour."

Leo stood up and walked out of the library, closing and locking the doors behind him. The library position came with a car and driver – the car burning primitive gasoline rather than using batteries – who waited outside every day. Leo had suggested that the young woman spend time in the library herself, but she had refused, being more interested in watching some of the vision shows on her terminal. They were, in fact, copies of shows that had been fashionable on Earth years ago, designed to help keep the population's mind off their own affairs. Leo's position had caused him to be aware of the various social dampeners operating within the Empire, trying to prevent internal strife. They had been breaking down for years.

The driver drove like a manic, leaving Leo silently praying for safety as they roared out of the city and down the long road towards the spaceport. Every so often, he'd been told, the Crackers slipped a team into position and fired on any official-looking vehicle, just to remind the Governor that they existed. They'd been quiet since the Marines arrived, although that might change in a hurry. Captain Stalker's success against the bandits and the new recruits would tip the balance of power against the Crackers, unless they acted swiftly to counter the threat. Leo knew, from his own studies of insurgent warfare, that it wasn't going to be easy.

"Here we are, sir," the driver said, as she pulled up outside the spaceport. "I'll have to wait for you here."

Leo scowled as he passed through the security checkpoint and was pointed towards a small VTOL aircraft that had probably been picking up Marines who had gone on leave. They'd proven surprisingly popular in the city, if only because any thugs who tried to pick on them rarely survived the experience. Mandy wasn't the only girl to have been saved from death or worse; indeed, the Civil Guard had even started to shape up and patrol properly in the wake of the Marines. The Council had had a long list of complaints about Marines taking the law into their own hands, yet they could do nothing. The Marines didn't set out to find trouble; it just found them.

He reflected on that as the VTOL took off and headed over the blue sea to Castle Rock. The last time he'd seen the massive island, there had only been a few buildings, mainly former homesteads that had been abandoned when the Marines moved in. Now, it had mushroomed into a military base, with dozens of buildings scattered around and guarded by armed Marines. He caught sight of new recruits training in a field as the VTOL came in to land and found himself hoping that they turned into good Marines. There simply weren't enough Marines to make a major difference, not yet. The aircraft touched down with a bump and he had to go through another security check before he was escorted into the new office block. It was, thankfully, air-conditioned.

"Captain," he said in greeting. "Do you need all of those security checks?"

"You'd be surprised," Captain Stalker said, from the window. The building looked down onto the training yard. A hundred men, stripped to the waist, were going through exercises under the command of a man barking orders. Leo looked at them and felt distinctly fat and podgy. "Some people have tried to slip in through the security checks and we've turned away a couple of fishermen who tried to land. It's rather worrying."

Leo followed his logic. "Because the Crackers might try to slip people onto the island," he said. "Were the fishermen Crackers?"

"I'd be surprised if they didn't have Cracker sympathies," Captain Stalker said dryly. "How is your family?"

Just for a moment, Leo wondered what – if anything – Captain Stalker knew about recent events. "Fiona is having…a great time amidst the social whirl," he said, slowly. "Mandy is improving and Mindy has decided that she wants to join the Marines when she's sixteen."

"I'm sure we could find a place for her," Captain Stalker said. "We had to separate out male and female recruits here, at least for the first few months of their training. There's more raw material here than I thought, but they're almost completely undisciplined."

Leo blinked. "I thought segregating the sexes was illegal," he said. "The Civil Guard doesn't do it."

"Put men and women together without proper discipline and sex will start complicating the picture," Captain Stalker growled. "Men will do anything for sex; women will learn to use their sex to get ahead. Men will ask the obvious question; was she promoted because she was good at her job, or because she put out for a superior officer? Women will wonder if they're being treated differently because of their sex."

He shook his head. "Boot Camp and the Slaughterhouse always segregated the sexes until the new recruits had completed their first year of training and had the rules firmly drummed into their heads," he added. "The designers of the training program were practical men. They went with what worked, rather than some idealised version of the universe."

"I see," Leo said. It was a way of looking at the world that would have shocked the old him, although the new Leo understood. "Mindy will have fun if she survives that long."

Captain Stalker shrugged. "True," he said. "Tell me something, from your civilian point of view. Does this planet have a future?"

Back on Earth, Leo would have given a smart answer to any student who had posed that question, but Captain Stalker deserved a proper effort. "No," he said, bitterly. He had brought his family to another dead end. "As long as the current social system survives, Avalon is not going to have a future. The Governor cannot deal with the challenges or push through reforms against the entrenched interests, reforms that must be made if the planet is to have any chance of long-term survival. And, because the entrenched interests have made themselves so unpopular, any popular revolution is likely to be bloody and rapidly replaced by a dictatorship."

He spoke for thirty minutes, feeling like he was finally doing something useful. "There is no prospect of a peaceful transfer of power on Avalon," he concluded. "The Crackers – or some urban resistance movement – will have to take power by force. When they do, the old elites will be strung up and left to die – and they know it, hence the private armies they have been building up and their attempts to take over the Civil Guard and co-opt it to their own purposes. If they could hold on long enough for the Imperial Navy to get here…but they can't hold on. They'd be at war against the entire planet."

"That was pretty much what I was thinking," Captain Stalker said, wryly. "So, Professor, what are we going to do about it?"

Leo considered it. Only one answer came to mind. "Destroy the elites first," he said, flatly. "Break up the monopolies, forgive all debts and reform the Council. Is that going to happen, Captain? Do your orders give you that much latitude?"

"No," Captain Stalker admitted. "On the other hand, perhaps we can press matters in the right general direction. If you are interested, Professor, I have a job for you."

"So we definitely cannot get people onto the island?"

"No," Nomiki Dimitris said. The fisherwoman looked up at Gaby, her dark eyes furrowed. "We attempted to land on Castle Rock, as we had done before the Marines arrived. We were intercepted by a patrolling aircraft which ordered us to return to the mainland and not to attempt to land on Castle Rock. We thought it best to comply with their orders. A later attempt, with a damaged engine, only resulted in the Marines towing us back to the mainland. The crew was not allowed to set foot on the island."

Gaby listened grimly. The Marines had played it smart; just by establishing a base on an island, it would be almost impossible to get someone onto the island to spy on them, much less launch sabotage attacks. They could be up to anything there and the Crackers wouldn't be able to do anything about it. The resistance couldn't launch an assault across miles of open water.

"Very nice of them," she said, finally. "A Civil Guardsman would be more likely to sink the boat rather than offer aid."

She watched the fisherwoman head out of the room – she'd be smuggled back to one of the smaller fishing towns overnight – and turned to Rufus. "They've checkmated us," she said, flatly. "How do we get a force over to the island?"

It was a rhetorical question and both of them knew it. "We can't," Rufus said, gravely. "We'd have to wait until they started deploying their new forces over on the mainland."

"By which time the odds might start tipping against us," Gaby said. She had scant respect for the bandits, but she had to admit that they knew how to hide. The Marines had located and destroyed one of their bases and – if the local media was to be believed – had done it without losing a single man. The Crackers were amidst the local population, yet how easy would it be to hide when the Marines started active patrols? "We need to move operations forward, quickly."

Julian grinned. "We could always try to capture one of the Marines and ask them a few questions," he said. "We know that they are allowed to go on leave in Camelot. One of them, perhaps one lured away by a girl, would be vulnerable to being taken alive."

Gaby considered it. "It might work," she conceded, "but we'd have to be careful. The Marines have a reputation for not leaving their comrades behind."

She looked down at the datapad they'd liberated from one of the wealthy debt sharks. One of her agents, a man without debt, had taken it into the Imperial Library and downloaded everything they had on the Terran Marine Corps. Even allowing for exaggeration and propaganda, it made depressing reading. The Marines made the Civil Guard look like incompetent bunglers.

"And then we might need to consider moving up Operation Headshot," she added. "All of a sudden, time is no longer on our side."

"It would be a risk," Rufus warned. "The presence of the Marines alone confirms that the Empire hasn't lost interest in us."

"Yet we have no choice," Julian said. "Father…what happens if the Marines deploy vast new numbers of trained men?"

"We lose," Gaby said, flatly. "I will not let that happen."

CHAPTER TWENTY-EIGHT

> Marine training is based around a very old military truism. Easy training, hard mission; hard training, easy mission. A certain amount of injuries – and even death – is the inevitable result of this process. It may seem unacceptable to the civilian mindset, but it is required to produce the finest fighting troops the galaxy has yet seen.
>
> - Major-General Thomas Kratman (Ret), *A Civilian's Guide to the Terran Marine Corps.*

"Get down!"

Michael hit the ground as a burst of brilliant tracer flew over his head. The defenders – a group of hostage-taking insurgents – had dug into the hill and the training platoon had orders to capture or kill them all, yet it was starting to seem impossible. Every nook and cranny seemed to hide a sniper, a hidden machine gun, or an enemy trap. The heat wasn't making it easier. Sweat poured down his back as he hefted his own weapon.

"They're using live ammunition," someone protested. Michael couldn't help but smile, despite the pain. The Sergeants had warned them that live ammunition was included in the training program, even if few of the recruits had believed them, at first. Michael couldn't quite believe that any of the training cadre, as sadistic as they seemed, would deliberately take aim at one of the recruits, but accidents happened. A week into the training program and four recruits had already been dispatched into the base's growing hospital.

"Stay down," he barked, cursing the other recruit under his breath. The assault line was coming apart, ever since the nominal commander had been 'killed' by the enemy force. No one knew who was supposed to be in charge now, yet the trainers hadn't ended the session. The recruits seemed to be expected to charge up the hill and die gloriously, yet that somehow didn't seem right. "Keep your fucking head down now!"

He heard the sound of mortar fire seconds before an explosion billowed up far too close to the small group of recruits. It was terrifyingly real...and then it struck him that it *was* real. The Sergeants had rigged the entire training ground to teach their charges how to fight and if a few of them got hurt or killed...well, that was part of the price. The longer they cowered in the depression, the greater the chance that they'd fail outright and be humiliated in front of their fellows.

"Follow me," he hissed, keying his radio and running a brief check. A fully-trained Marine could do several things at once, but Michael had barely even mastered the SAR-23 he carried. Barr had told them that the SAR was the most practical design for an assault rifle in the entire history of humanity, but Michael wasn't sure if he believed him. The weapon seemed crude and almost heavy enough to use as a club, if they ran out of ammunition. "Come on!"

The hill had once had a spring flowing down from high above, or so he guessed, a spring that had dried up in the wake of the summer heat. It had left a gully behind, one that should provide cover for the recruits as they advanced up towards their goal. Michael crawled towards it, hearing the sound of shooting growing louder as he reached the gully, and peered carefully up it. A sniper lay there, bringing his weapon around to bear on Michael's head, and Michael shot him reflexively. The sniper twitched and lay still.

Michael would have grinned, but he was too tired to grin. The training suits they all wore had one purpose, registering and enforcing a kill. The weapons they carried didn't shoot real bullets, but beams of laser light which would trigger the suits, sending the person wearing the suit falling to the ground if they didn't drop quickly enough to simulate death. He'd been trapped in his own suit a few times and the experience wasn't one he wanted to repeat. It had been terrifying, as if he had been completely unable to move anything below his neck.

He checked the gully anyway, looking for signs that might have suggested a buried mine or an explosive charge, before leading the way up the gully towards the top. A line of small stones rattled down from high above as he caught sight of a cat-like creature staring down at the humans who had invaded its territory, but it clearly wasn't an enemy soldier. A thought struck him and he stared at the creature, who stared back disdainfully before walking off, twitching its tail. It could have been a surveillance robot in disguise…

A line of rockets seemed to explode in the sky, deafening him as he reached the top of the gully. He used hand signals to get three of the other recruits to move up beside him, then produced a line of sonic grenades and threw them over the top. The grenades were non-lethal weapons, normally used for crowd control, but they also triggered training suits. The howl of the grenades covered the noise as they scrambled over the edge and ran right into a group of defenders on the ground.

Their suits were all blinking red, showing that they were officially dead, but Michael checked them all anyway. It wouldn't be the first time they'd been punished for taking anything for granted. A few minutes of being shouted at by a Sergeant, they'd been told, was far better than spending weeks in hospital having their legs regenerated, or worse. They'd been shown images of Marines who had been wounded on active duty and some of them had never recovered, regardless of the best medical treatment the Empire could offer.

"Nice one," one of the other recruits said. Michael was already looking for the way up towards the top of the hill. The gully seemed to end with a dried pool, where once a boy could have gone swimming with a girl. The heat had dried it up, leaving the remains of a handful of dead fish baking on the ground. "Where do we go now?"

Michael pointed up towards a sheer cliff. At first sight, it had seemed impossible, but he was confident that they could climb up it. He motioned for four of the recruits to stay back and cover them, while he led the other four up to the cliff and started to climb up it. It was easier than he expected. There were plenty of handholds and places to put his hands and feet. It occurred to him, too late, that one of the holes could play host to one of Avalon's nastier forms of insect life, but there was no going back. He scrambled up as quickly as possible and peered over the top. There was no sign of any enemy force.

"Come on," he hissed, helping the next recruit over the edge. "We have to move…"

A line of explosions shook the entire area, almost sending him plummeting back over the cliff and down to certain death. Somehow, he caught himself and managed to remain stable, even though he was badly shaken. He unhooked his rifle from his shoulder and looked around, but there was still no sign of the enemy. Had they killed them all…no, he corrected himself; if they had, surely the Sergeants would have told them.

He kept moving forward as the others spread out and was narrowly missed by a beam of red light that flickered out from a hidden cave. Three of the other recruits fell to the ground as their training suits activated. Michael fired desperately into the cave – there was nowhere to hide – and sighed in relief as the red light winked out. A brief glance confirmed that one of the defenders had hidden in the cave with a machine gun.

He glanced back and swore. He was alone. Common sense suggested that he should call in to the HQ and report what had happened, but he wanted to press on. He kept moving, flitting from tree to tree, until he stepped into a clearing. A girl was sitting at the other end, her hands hidden behind her back. She was so self-evidently tied up that it didn't occur to him to question it; she had to be the hostage the briefers had told them about. A sense of chivalrous determination came over him and he ran forward, intending to cut her free…and then she produced a small pistol from behind her back. Michael had no time to react before she shot him and his training suit sent him sprawling to the ground.

Jasmine smiled down at the young recruit, whose eyes glared reproachfully at her. It was quite understandable, even though a fully-fledged Marine wouldn't have made the mistake of assuming that she was innocent, just because she looked to be tied up. If the recruit had surveyed around the clearing first, he would have seen Jasmine holding a hidden pistol and would have known that she was just another of the defenders, rather than an innocent maiden hoping to be rescued by a modern-day St. George. The civilian clothes she'd worn only added to that impression. He had probably taken one look at her tits and concluded that she couldn't possibly be a Marine.

"Sorry," she said, as her radio buzzed, signalling that the exercise had come to an end. "If it is any consolation, I fell for the same trick myself at Boot Camp."

It wasn't entirely true – Jasmine had been fooled by a baby who had actually been a robotic doll linked to an explosive charge – but perhaps it would be some consolation. She held out a hand as the recruit's suit unlocked and helped him to his feet. Down below, the attackers would be mustering to hear the Drill Sergeant's opinion of their efforts. The recruit she'd shot had been the only one to reach so high; perhaps Barr wouldn't be so hard on him. Or perhaps she was deluding herself. Young recruits didn't learn through kindness, but through blood, tears and sweat.

She headed off down the hill and, after a moment, the recruit followed her.

"You lost," Drill Sergeant Barr thundered, as soon as the recruits had mustered. They were all tired beyond measure, but he somehow expected them to remain on their feet and at attention. "You lost every single one of your lives up that hill. Do you know how you managed to lose so badly? You made mistakes!"

Michael wanted to protest that it was only their second week and they barely knew anything, but somehow he was sure that interrupting Barr was a bad idea. There were times when he expected – demanded – that the recruits asked questions and answered them as patiently as possible, and times when he chewed the poor recruit out in front of the entire training squad.

"You knew that the hill was held by the enemy, yet you walked right up to it," Barr continued, singling out the former leader for special abuse. "What were you thinking? You got seven of your men killed along with your own worthless ass! What were you thinking?"

The unfortunate squad leader quailed under his gaze. "I was thinking that we might have a chance to surprise them before they were ready for us," he said, finally. It sounded reasonable to Michael, except it had failed. Badly. "We could have caught them out of place and…"

"Bullshit," Barr exploded. "You're trying to stick a cherry on top of a bowl of shit and telling me it's ice cream! Are you in the habit of lying when you fail at something, or are you just trying to get out of punishment duties?"

The squad leader said nothing. "I shall assume that it's the latter, as the former would be too horrible to contemplate in trainees," Barr said. "Now…"

His gaze slid across the recruits until it lighted on Michael. It felt like staring down two heavy gun barrels. "And what," Barr demanded, "were you thinking when you took over command?"

Michael braced himself for an explosion. "I thought that everyone else who was in the chain of command was dead," he said. The chain of command within the training squads was fluid. Barr changed it every day, just to force them to keep up with it. A recruit who had been leader one day might be bottom of the heap tomorrow. It didn't get any easier when they graduated. According to the training material they'd read, the rank of Corporal seemed to come and go at whim. "And someone had to take over command."

"How true," Barr sneered. "And then you took horrendous risks. You could have got half of the remaining squad killed, for real!"

"Yes, Sergeant," Michael said. The recruits had fallen out of the habit of calling Barr 'sir' within the first day. "It nearly worked."

"It nearly worked," Barr repeated. "It may interest you to know, *recruit*, that the most expensive thing to have in all of human history is the second-best army in the world. Being the second-best only means that the best will destroy you, does it not? It nearly worked…but it didn't work. What were you thinking when you walked up to the girl wearing civilian clothes?"

Michael flushed, despite the heat. "I was thinking that she needed help," he admitted. "I was wrong."

"Well, at least you're honest enough to admit it," Barr drawled. "And now you have a chance to reflect upon it, what should you have done?"

Michael had realised *that* a second after his suit had locked up. "I should have checked around first, before assuming that she was helpless and harmless," he said, slowly. "If I'd checked, I might have been able to avoid being shot when she produced her weapon."

"Good," Barr said. "At least you managed to learn from experience."

He looked up, his gaze moving along the line of recruits. "Understand this," he said. "A person who looks helpless may not be helpless. A person who looks harmless may not be harmless. A weapon can be anything, or hidden anywhere. Back on Han, we lost several soldiers to women who hid monofilament blades up their cunts and produced them at the worst possible moment. There are an infinite number of tricks that an enemy force can carry out to lure you into a trap. Learn to recognise the signs when you see them and perhaps that trap won't cut off your cocks when you fall into it."

Michael nodded inwardly, remembering some of the early training exercises they'd done. Even ground that looked untroubled might hide a nasty surprise; a mine, or an IED, or even something really inventive. A primitive weapon, used properly, could be utterly devastating even against the most powerful military force. A weapon was only as good as the person using it. He'd been told that Marines who went in for the Weaponmaster Badge were expected to be able to handle any weapon, without hesitation. He had already privately determined that he was going to try to qualify for it.

"Report to the shooting range," Barr ordered, finally.

Michael winced; they were all sweaty and smelly, yet they still had to carry on with the training. "It's time to shoot holes in a few more dummies!"

The Marines, he had explained the first time they'd handled weapons, had a very progressive attitude to expending rounds during training. Michael, who had never handled a weapon before joining up, had fired off thousands of rounds during the first week alone, learning to handle the

SAR. Barr marched from recruit to recruit, teaching them the value of fire discipline and careful targeting, rather than just pointing the weapon in the general direction of the enemy and opening fire. That way, he'd warned them, accidents happened…or, worse, nothing effective was done.

"There are times when you have to force the enemy to keep their sodding heads down," he'd thundered, "and there are times when you need to conserve ammunition. Learn to tell the difference!"

Night was falling and Merlin was rising in the sky when the recruits were finally allowed to go for food and then hit their bunks. Michael had a private suspicion that the Marine food – which wasn't actually bad and there was always plenty of it – contained drugs and vitamins designed to help build their muscles and flush their bodies clear of any past history of drug abuse. It was certainly healthier than anything he'd had before joining up with the Marines. If the Marines had promised good food and a proper diet, he knew hundreds of mothers who would have been delighted to urge their children to sign up.

The barracks were air-conditioned, although they'd been warned that they'd soon have to start sleeping out in the open air. The bunks themselves were small, barely large enough for one person, although it wasn't as if they were going to be sharing bunks. There were no girls around at all, even though he had run into a female Marine. If there were any homosexuals in the unit, they were keeping their heads low. He lay down, placed his head against the pillow and closed his eyes. Seconds later, or so it seemed, Barr started bellowing orders for them to get up and get out onto the parade ground. By now, dressing at a rush was almost second nature.

"They're not doing badly," Gwen observed, as they watched the recruits stumbling back out onto the parade ground. "We could probably start recruiting the second batch now."

Edward shook his head. "We're going to be spread too lightly," he said, checking the map. "I don't want to recruit any more newcomers until we can afford to pull the platoons away from the badlands and we won't be able to do that for a while."

Gwen scowled. "We don't have enough, sir," she said. "The ships are leaving tomorrow."

"I know," Edward said. He was still mulling over his conversation with the Professor. "And then things get interesting."

CHAPTER
TWENTY-NINE

As power and responsibility become ever more separated, those with power will act in an increasingly irresponsible fashion, perhaps even neglecting the very source of their power. Why should they not? Surely, they think, their power lies apart from any responsibility.

- Professor Leo Caesius, *The Waning Years of Empire* (banned).

"You are sure of this," Carola Wilhelm demanded. "The starships have definitely departed?"

Her informant, a man who worked part-time at the local System Command, such as it was, bowed his head. "They departed orbit earlier today and headed out on a least-time course to the Phase Limit," he said, with a bow. He owed his cushy position to Carola's patronage and knew that lying to her would have unfortunate consequences. "We couldn't track them once they were outside the satellites' range, but there is no reason to believe that they remained within the system. I understand that Captain Yamato was eager to return to the sector capital and meet up with other Marine starships."

Carola nodded, staring out of her window over her grounds to the wall beyond, preventing any of Camelot's less-advantaged citizens from finding their way onto her territory. A handful of men from her personal guard were roving through the grounds, watching for anyone brave or stupid enough to try scaling the wall. Carola knew better than to trust the Civil Guard to protect her and her property, despite the care and attention she had lavished on her clients within the Guard. Besides, her own personal guard had no divided loyalties between her and the Governor.

"We cannot track ships outside the satellites' range," her informant continued, mistaking her silence for an order to carry on. "They could have doubled back and…"

"That will be all," Carola said, airily. "You may go."

She watched as the informant departed before looking up at the map of Avalon she'd placed on one wall and decorated with her own notes. It wouldn't have made sense to anyone else, but to her it was easily readable, a reminder of everything the cartel had…and everything it had to have before they could become the absolute rulers of the planet.

Between them, the Council – the important members, at least – owned most of the planet and controlled the rest of it through an unbreakable voting bloc on the Council. Once the Governor was removed for incompetence – and they had been working towards that end for years – they could put their own person into office and take control directly. Carola longed for that day. Avalon didn't have much to recommend it at first, but given a few years of absolute rule, they could transform it into a first-rank world. The ADC had already made the heavy purchases before they ran out of money and collapsed. Carola and the Council would merely inherit their work.

Carola and her husband had been born with enough money to make them part of the Empire's upper crust, but not enough to make them part of the aristocracy. They might have been the richest people in the sector, yet their fortune barely registered compared to the Earth-based industrialists or the Grand Senators, who had unparalleled opportunities to loot. They could have been comfortable for the rest of their lives, but Carola wanted power…and she didn't care what she had to do to get it. While others in their set had been spending money like water, Carola had been hoarding it and waiting for her opportunity. It had come sooner than she had expected. Desperate for money, the remains of the ADC had been selling off the corporation's assets for years and Carola had purchased most of their debts. The mere possession of a strip of paper had made her the single most powerful woman on Avalon.

It didn't look like much, not when she was realistic enough to know that most of those debts would never be repaid, but it didn't end there. Carola had watched with interest as the Empire's investment in the sector declined and realised that the decay extended all along the Rim. There were fewer starship patrols, fewer troop deployments and fewer investments. Years ago, it would have only taken the Empire a few months to confirm the appointment of a new Sector Governor. Now…it had taken years, as if no one on Earth cared enough to put one of their proxies into power. The thought had been terrifying, when it had finally burst into her mind, yet it had been inescapable. What would happen if the Empire withdrew from the sector altogether?

Working with her husband, Carola had studied the entire sector, looking for opportunities. There had been several possible worlds, but most of them were firmly controlled by various organisations already, or simply lacked any form of space-based industry at all. The ADC hadn't been the only corporation to have financial trouble after the Tyrant Emperor had been assassinated. Avalon hadn't seemed like a likely prospect at first, but it had opportunities and Carola and her Cartel were perfectly placed to take advantage of them, if they could get rid of the Governor.

She looked up and out the window, staring towards the haze on the horizon. Camelot's climate lent itself to long summers and growing seasons, even though it was quite uncomfortably hot at the worst of times. Somewhere, hidden within that haze, was Castle Rock, the new home of the Marines and their trainees. Carola had bid for several of the contracts to expand Castle Rock's facilities, but the Marines had turned her down, preferring to work with newer and hungry industrial concerns. Carola cursed that decision under her breath, as much as she cursed the decision to pay their workers and recruits in cash. Just by doing that, they had undermined the whole basis of the Cartel's power, threatening everything Carola had built. Her plan to eventually become Queen of Avalon had been badly weakened.

The Marines bothered her, and not just because they weakened her grip on her indebted assets. They were formidable – they'd proved that when they went up against the bandits – and they were beyond her influence. The Governor's comments when she'd spoken to him suggested that they were beyond *his* influence as well, which was worrying. Even if he could command them, they weren't...influenced by the Council, not like the Civil Guard. Carola had spent enough time and money putting her proxies into high-ranking offices within the Civil Guard to be fairly sure that the Guard would obey the Council – apart from the Major and his handful of loyal men – but the Marines wouldn't obey her. A military force she could neither control nor influence was a dangerous possibility. She had no illusions as to how long her personal guard would last if they had to go up against the Marines.

She felt, more than heard, the door open as Markus Wilhelm stepped into the room. Like her, he'd been born rich and determined to become richer. Their partnership was a natural one. They even still slept together sometimes, even though they both wanted power more than they wanted each other. She smiled at the goatee he'd cultivated since they'd arrived, knowing that he was under the impression that it gave him a faintly sinister air.

"They just finished sweeping the house again," he said. Mansion it might be, but Wilhelm always referred to it as a house, reminding her of the castle he intended to build once they held supreme power. They had grown up in the shadows of the houses owned by the local aristocrats on their homeworld. "We found three new bugs and stomped on them."

Carola shrugged. One of their advantages was that they had brought a surprising amount of modern technology with them when they'd moved to Avalon, including some devices that hadn't trickled down from the Imperial Army to the Civil Guard. She wasn't too surprised to learn that their house was being bugged, even though it was impossible to say who was trying to listen in on their conversations. The parties she threw every second week allowed too many people into her house.

"Some of them were definitely military-grade technology," Wilhelm added. "Our noble friends and allies in the Council couldn't have provided them, but the Marines could have sent them here."

"Could be," Carola agreed, as if it were a very minor matter. The Marines would definitely want to spy on them, but as long as they could keep the bugs out of the secure rooms, it wouldn't matter. "Of course, if they had managed to gather evidence against us, they'd have come bursting in here by now."

She turned and looked up at the map. "I think we're going to have to urge the Knives to move now," she said, slowly. "The longer the Marines have to train new recruits, the harder it will be for them to make any headway at all."

"They lost the last time they went up against the Marines," Wilhelm reminded her. "What makes you think that they will want to risk everything and move against them openly?"

"There are only ninety-odd Marines," Carola said. She'd taken pains to cultivate Fiona Caesius as an intelligence source, but the wretched woman simply hadn't bothered to learn the fundamentals, or even gather information that could be useful. Her husband hadn't been interested in spending time at Carola's parties and had been bored stiff the few times he had attended. "They can be weakened if they are lured into a trap."

She smiled. "And besides, given what we have on him, I'm sure the Knife will want to move openly," she added. "Just think of what we can offer him as a reward!"

"A dangerous game," Wilhelm said. "If it gets traced back to us, the next Marines we'll see will be the ones breaking down the wall and coming to arrest us, dead or alive."

Carola looked up at him. "What do you think will happen if the Marines succeed?"

She answered her own question before he could speak. "They already have more recruits signed up than they can handle," she said. "They will be taught how to fight and given confidence, the confidence they will need to stand up to the Civil Guard and our proxies within the Government. Our power only holds as long as we hold on to the government and we will lose it if the people have the mindset needed for a rebellion. We're not exactly loved out there."

Wilhelm nodded. If they weren't the most hated husband and wife on the planet, it wasn't for lack of trying. In order to build up their power, they had entrapped thousands of families in an endless web of debt and obligation, placing their investments carefully to ensure that they had influence everywhere. As long as they controlled the government and its monopoly on force, they were safe...which was why they had worked hard to prevent any threat to that monopoly. If the Crackers took over, they would both be the first against the wall.

Working with the bandits had been a risk, but a worthwhile one, for the growing problem called the Governor's competence into question. If the bandits kept pushing, there would be grounds to press for his removal, allowing the Council a chance to take complete control of the planet. The Knives themselves were expendable. If they refused to cooperate afterwards, the Council – which would be in full control of the Civil Guard – would see to their extermination. It was a risk, yet they had no choice.

"And you know what's been happening when the Marines go on leave," Carola added. "How long will it be before they start sending their recruits on leave?"

"Yes," Wilhelm agreed. The Marines who had gone on leave had been mugged – or, rather, muggers had tried to rob them. The results had been several fatalities and at least thirty would-be muggers in the hospital, recovering from the beatings they had taken. The Marines, unlike the Civil Guard, hadn't hesitated to hand out broken bones, if only to make their point. Various criminal gangs had responded by putting out contracts on the Marines, but so far they'd had no takers. No one wanted to see what would happen if they managed to kill a Marine. "They'd start cleaning up the city."

They contemplated the possibility of an armed citizenry demanding better civil government for a long moment. It wasn't a good thought. In theory, the new recruits would remain in debt and would be unable to vote, but there was no guarantee that they would accept it. Worse, the Marines were paying them well...they might even pay off their debts and claim a vote. If that happened, the Council's monopoly would be shattered beyond repair. It could not be allowed to happen.

"I'll send the messenger," he said, finally. A Council-issued pass would take someone out of the city without being questioned, yet if one of the honest Guardsmen caught sight of it, it would raise questions they would prefer not to be asked. "And then I think we'd better pull our heads in and wait to see what happens."

"I'm going to keep working on Fiona," Carola added. "The silly woman might just know something useful after all."

Lucas Trent rubbed the back of his neck as he stood up, feeling the sweat running down towards his waist. The heat in the badlands had always surprised him, ever since they had first set up the hidden camp and he sometimes wondered why the badlands didn't simply catch fire and burn to the ground.

The explanation was simple enough; the network of underground reservoirs that fed most of the plants in the badlands helped keep their temperature down. It might have been normal for a native resident of Avalon – if such mythical creatures had ever existed – but it was uncomfortable as hell for a human.

The girl stared up at him blankly as he pulled on his trousers. Her mind was long gone now, leaving only an automaton that followed orders and just lay there when he wanted sex. There was something about the heat that made him horny – it had never been so hot on Earth, where the Undercity had been dank and cold – and he could indulge himself as often as he liked. He touched the girl's chest with his foot and rubbed her breast for a long moment, before turning and heading out of the cave. There was business to be done.

He peered through the foliage that hid the camp, even from the Marines and their sensors, towards another hidden cave. The messenger from their friends in Camelot was waiting there, served by a pair of girls Lucas and the Knives had taken from a homestead near the badlands. They might have had to pull in their horns and hide since the Marines had shown up, but there was no point in sparing themselves the creature comforts – besides, it kept the man's mind focused. One day, Lucas had every intention of killing their friends at Camelot – who he was sure would change sides when the pressure grew too high for them to bear – but until then, he would work with them. He needed what they were offering.

Carefully remaining under the foliage, he made his way into the cave and dismissed the two girls. They weren't broken yet and had to be escorted everywhere, just to make sure they didn't do anything stupid like lighting a fire in the middle of camp. The messenger looked up and smiled at him, but Lucas could taste the man's fear. He had never expected to find himself playing for such high stakes, in a game where he was nothing more than a pawn. Lucas could have killed him at any moment and he knew it.

"So," he said, without preamble. "Your masters want me to hit our new friends as hard as possible."

"Yes," the messenger said. "They believe that there is a window of opportunity to hit the Marines now, before they can build up their forces and start pressing against the badlands."

"How lucky for them," Lucas said, dryly. "And what can they offer to convince me to take my men out of the badlands and attack the Marine base?"

"They have pulled some heavy weapons out of Camelot Garrison," the messenger said, referring to the Civil Guard base near the city. "They believe that you will find them useful."

Lucas kept his face blank, trying not to show how eager he was to get his hands on the weapons. It was easy to obtain small arms and rifles, but heavier weapons were harder, even with the Civil Guardsmen being so easy to bribe. It showed how much importance his patrons placed on the attack, for heavy weapons could easily be turned against them as well. Lucas was sure that they expected him to turn on them one day – after all, he expected the same. Treachery was part of the human condition. They wouldn't be keen on his plans to set up a kingdom out near the badlands.

"Very well," he said, making his mind up quickly. "When will the weapons arrive?"

"In five days," the messenger said. "I have been told to inform you that they will be dispatched by a roundabout route and handed over at Point Alpha. They wish you to attack as quickly as possible."

"Do they indeed," Lucas said. A plan was already forming in his head. Attacking the Marine platoon house was suicide, but perhaps there was another way. "They can wait until the heavy weapons arrive…and then we'll see."

The messenger smiled. "Thank you," he said. He looked more than a little relieved that it had been so easy, but then, the Knives were going stir crazy in their lair. They weren't used to hiding. "They were quite happy with the last shipment you sent into the city."

"I'm sure that they were," Lucas said. He grinned. "A shipment of whores and drugs would have made their day."

CHAPTER THIRTY

War is a democracy in the truest possible sense. The enemy gets a vote.
- Major-General Thomas Kratman (Ret), *A Civilian's Guide to the Terran Marine Corps.*

"I have the latest reports from Company Delta, sir," Lieutenant Ryan Spencer reported. "They're on their way back to the Fort."

Major George Grosskopf nodded. Fort Galahad – the Arthurian theme couldn't be escaped, even outside Camelot itself – was the main Civil Guard base near the badlands, even though it was too far away to have any immediate influence on the surrounding area. It had been built before the badlands and their nature had been fully understood and, so far, the Council had refused to allow the Civil Guard to construct any bases closer to the badlands. It made little sense to George – the Council needed the homesteads intact until the homesteaders paid off their debts – but the precise reasoning hardly mattered.

The Fort was actually his favourite place on the planet, untouched by politics and the officers he'd been forced to promote at the Council's strong urging. He'd reinforced the garrison after the Marines had smashed the bandit raiding party three weeks ago and urged the Fort's CO to organise a regular patrol schedule, patrolling the surrounding area and trying to deter any retaliation from the badlands. Four hundred Civil Guardsmen, his most capable soldiers, now inhabited the Fort. Having so many men so far from Camelot worried him, but the Council had been sanguine about the risk. Didn't they have the Marines to call upon in case of emergency?

He scowled down at the map, thinking cold thoughts. The Council had refused his request to pay his own men in cash, even local credits. The Civil Guard had always had a surplus of recruits, even if they did lose half of their monthly pay to the debt sharks, but now that surplus was drying up. Young men were signing up to join the Marines instead, adding their names to the lists and awaiting the call-up to the training centres. George knew that several of the more competent Guardsmen were talking about refusing to reenlist and, instead, trying to join the Marines. Why should they not? The Council didn't give a damn about them.

The Marine platoon house was thirty kilometres to the north, far too close to the badlands for comfort, even if they had been left alone so far. Of course, the bandits – unlike the Crackers – were cowards. They were happy picking on unarmed homesteaders, but less inclined to take on someone who could and would fight back. Fort Galahad itself had never been attacked by the bandits, although the Crackers had attacked it on several occasions, reminding the men in the fort that they existed. George envied the Marines their position, even though two platoons of Marines would be seriously overstretched if they ran into trouble. A bandit gang leaving the badlands might be detected and attacked before it could kill any helpless civilians.

"Tell them to take their time," George ordered. If nothing else, Delta Company could sweep through the local area and remind the bandits that they existed. "There's no need to hurry."

"Yes, sir," Spencer said. "I'll send the signal at once."

George shrugged and returned to his brooding, allowing the younger officer to slip away. The Marines had served as a goad to his competent officers, pushing them to start patrolling much more aggressively than they had done before the Marines arrived. The less competent officers had taken the time to mock the Marines, asking who was going to clean up the mess after the Marines were gone and what would happen when the Crackers finally launched their mass attack on the government, particularly now that their starships had departed. It didn't bear thinking about.

An alarm rang. "Major, we just picked up an emergency transmission from Morgan," Spencer said, bursting back into George's office. "They're under heavy attack."

George pulled himself to his feet and strode into the dispatch room. "Report," he barked. "What's going on at Morgan?"

"The report says that at least a hundred bandits appeared out of nowhere and started attacking the town," the dispatcher said. "The signal was lost moments later and I have been unable to raise them."

"Poor bastards," George said. The bandits were finally striking back in response to the loss of their base. It was brute force on an unforgivable scale. "Mobilise Alpha and Beta Companies; tell them I want them ready to depart in five minutes."

"Yes, sir," the dispatcher said. Alpha Company had been on Quick Readiness Alert; they should be ready to depart by now, with Beta Company just behind. They might not have been Marines, but their reaction time was commendably fast. "Delta Company is reporting in and asking for orders."

George glanced up at the map, mentally placing Delta Company's position in context. He swore under his breath. Delta Company was out of position, even though they were armed and ready to move. It would take longer to get them to Morgan than it would to move both of the QRA companies at Fort Galahad.

"Tell them to double-time it back to the Fort," he ordered. "We'll use them as backstop if we run into trouble."

"Yes, sir," the dispatcher said.

"Pass the alert up the chain to Camelot and Castle Rock and tell them that we need some helicopter support out here," George added. "And tell them that I'm taking command personally."

Spencer blinked. "Sir?"

"It's not debatable," George snapped, still studying the map. They couldn't get to Morgan in time to prevent the bandits from sacking the town, but if they moved fast, they *could* get into position to block the bandits from escaping. With the other townships alerted, they'd have to be careful not to run right into a trap. "You are to remain here; keep sending updates back to the city."

"Yes, sir," Spencer said. "Good luck, sir."

―――――

Eric Passover watched, grinning openly, as Morgan died. The township hadn't been very important, even though it served as a crossroads for the network of roads that stretched out of Camelot and up towards the badlands. It had fallen into a moribund changelessness that drove young men and women away to other homesteads or down to the city, leaving it occupied by the very young and the very old. The farmers had paid their taxes to the government, their debt interest to the debt sharks and their tribute to the bandits, which was one of the reasons why they had been so badly surprised when the bandits appeared and opened fire. They hadn't realised that they'd just been pawns in a greater game.

He felt his mouth fall open in delight as the flames licked higher into the sky. Unlike many of the other bandits, Eric had little time for rape and less for looting – it was the pure art of destruction he craved. It had been impossible to destroy one of the city-blocks on Earth – they'd been built so solidly that a nuclear warhead wouldn't do more than scratch their paint – but on Avalon, everything burnt. The wind blew and sheets of flame spread rapidly, jumping from house to house. The ground shook as an underground store of fuel caught fire and exploded, sending a billowing fireball raging up into the air. Eric laughed out loud, feeling his inner self jumping for joy at such destruction. The flames would spread into the fields and burn the crops to the ground. Who knew how far they would spread in the hot weather?

"Hey, Eric," one of his men shouted. "Come and have some fun with this babe here?"

Eric followed his gaze. Three of the bandits were holding down a girl from the homestead, having torn away her clothes and exposed her body to their gaze. They'd already had her, fucking her despite her screams and protests, and would have her again once Eric took a turn, *if* he took a turn.

THE EMPIRE'S CORPS

He looked at her and, despite the almost sexual excitement of the blaze, shook his head. There was something pure about burning a township to the ground, while raping a girl was just…squalid.

The bandits shrugged and returned to their fun, while Eric walked outside the township, passing the untouched buildings on the way. The blaze shifted and a wave of heat struck him in the face, just before the remaining buildings suddenly caught fire. He saw a woman's face in one of them, her face contorted in agony, before the flames swept over her and she was gone. Perhaps it was the smoke, or the lack of oxygen, or perhaps she'd been burned to a crisp instantly. It didn't matter. Eric had killed her and destroyed her home.

His radio buzzed once, a warning. The Civil Guard had finally responded to the atrocity and they were on their way. He took one last look at the destruction and pulled a whistle out of his pocket, blowing it as loudly as he could. All over the ruined township, the bandits dropped whatever they were doing and ran for the edge of town. Behind them, the girls they'd been raping crawled away, hunting blindly for a safety that no longer existed. Eric's grin grew wider as he contemplated their feelings. Their lives had been ruined and it had all been because of him.

"Come on," he shouted, at the handful of stragglers. The Knife had put him in command simply because he *wouldn't* waste time raping when it was time to run. "We don't have time to waste!"

He was still laughing as they fled towards where they'd hidden the nags.

Edward had been trying to plot out the next training schedule when Gwen poked her head into his office. "Captain," she said, "there's been a report of a township coming under heavy attack. The Civil Guard is moving to intercept the bandits."

"Put the ready platoons at the platoon house on alert," Edward ordered, although he was sure that Gwen would have already seen to it. There were certain orders that always had to be issued. "Have they requested support from us?"

"No, sir," Gwen said. "Major Grosskopf has requested helicopter support from the spaceport, but he's made no direct request for our involvement. That may change, of course."

"Of course," Edward agreed. He checked his personal weapons out of habit. "Get the Raptors up and ready to fly if we have to move in support." He glanced up at the training roster and swore. "Contact Jared and tell him to terminate the current exercise; we're going to need Fourth Platoon to join Third on QRA. The trainees can practice something else for a while."

"Yes, sir," Gwen said. "I took the liberty of warning him that that might be coming."

Edward scowled. Real battles didn't end when one side found it convenient, nor were they terminated because the opposing side had to go fight elsewhere. It couldn't be helped, but it was sending the wrong message to the new recruits. He briefly considered putting them on the defence line and adding Fifth Platoon to the QRA force, but they couldn't be trusted, not yet. Castle Rock would come under attack eventually – it occurred to him that the bandit attack might be a diversion – and by then he intended to be ready.

"Good," he said. The waiting was always the hardest part of any military operation. "Keep me informed."

George winced as the Rover Armoured Fighting Vehicle ran over a pothole, shaking the entire vehicle badly enough to make him feel sick. The Rover was locally-produced, built by one of the industries owned by the Wilhelm Family from a design that had been old when spaceflight was young. George wouldn't have been surprised to discover that Patton, Montgomery or even Lee would have ridden to war in them, even though the Empire had added additional armour and protection for their troops. The masters of lightning warfare would have understood the problem he faced, all right; the Imperial Army had always had the advantage of overwhelming firepower and a stupendous logistic chain. That wasn't true of the Civil Guard.

He peered out of the vehicle as they bounced along the road. By his admittedly imprecise calculations, the bandits would have to pass through a certain area before they could reach the badlands and safety. Alpha Company's vehicles were moving faster than the bandits could move on their nags and should be able to block them before they escaped. Alpha Company might be only lightly armed compared to a Marine unit, but the bandits wouldn't have any heavy weapons with them at all. He cursed the terrain as they kept moving forward, knowing that it was closing in on them. The local townships were meant to keep foliage cut back from the roads, but as they weren't paid for the duty, they did it with little enthusiasm, when they did it at all.

The road itself had been going out of shape for years. The indentured workers had constructed it – often escaping and running off to join the bandits – and it was poorly maintained. The ADC had been interested in establishing secure lines of transport into the interior of the continent, yet they hadn't been interested in the investment required to produce solid roads. The indentured workers and their supervisors had cut corners wherever possible and the roads were decaying badly. George wasn't particularly surprised – it was typical of Avalon – yet the Council had refused to do anything about it. It was as if they wanted to limit communications between the cities and the outlying farms.

Perhaps they just don't want people running away to the cities, he thought, sourly. It was something they would have to deal with, somehow. *Perhaps…*

A massive explosion shook the entire convoy. A mine had detonated right under the lead vehicle, sending it exploding in a ball of flame. No, he realised, it was more than just a simple mine; they'd emplaced a colossal bomb under the road. Some of the bandits would have worked on the roads and remembered their skills. A moment later, he heard the telltale sound of incoming mortar rounds, just before they started landing on his vehicles. The bastards had the entire area zeroed in!

He dived out of the vehicle and took cover as heavy weapons started to sound out in the distance. God alone knew how the bandits had gotten control of them, but they'd caught all of Alpha Company in a trap. One of the armoured cars drove up on the ridgeline, hoping to provide cover, and exploded as it ran over another mine. George drew his pistol and looked for targets, but the bandits were well dug in, pouring fire down on the trapped soldiers. An armoured car tried to retreat and to find a way around the trap, but a heavy shell landed directly on top of it and blew it to rubble. Was that sheer bad luck…or a smart round? There was no way to know.

Alpha Company started to return fire as training reasserted itself, but George could see that it was already too late. With wrecked vehicles on both sides of the ends of the road, they couldn't get the other vehicles out until they managed to clear the roads, which would be difficult under fire. The bandits weren't acting like normal bandits at all; they were acting more like soldiers or insurgents. They had Alpha Company pinned down and helpless.

He keyed his radio. "We made enemy contact," he reported, hoping that the enemy couldn't jam his signal. Beta Company was nearby and Delta Company would be nearing the Fort. They could probably punch their way out if necessary. "Lieutenant, have Beta Company rerouted to…"

"Beta Company is pinned down, sir," Lieutenant Spencer reported. "The Fort itself is under attack!"

George felt his mouth fall open. They'd badly underestimated the bandits if they could pull off a successful attack at three different locations at once. The plan struck him as a textbook plan, one guaranteed not to work so well in real life, except he'd allowed his contempt for the enemy to blind him and he'd walked right into it. The bandits probably intended to just keep dropping shells on them until they were wiped out, or perhaps they intended to take the Civil Guardsmen hostage. They had a plan and the ball was firmly in their court.

His radio buzzed. "Sir, this is Hellfire-Three," a new voice said. "We are inbound to your position; ETA one minute, forty seconds. What are your orders, sir?"

The helicopters, George realised. Pinned down as he was, it was impossible to get any sense of the enemy positions, but they had to be dug in all around Alpha Company's position. Had all of the bandits come out to fight? Intelligence's best estimate was that there were upwards of ten thousand bandits in the badlands, spread out over a wide area. Even a few hundred could have pulled off such an attack, if they had planned it carefully and had access to heavy weapons. Where had they come from?

"I want a full missile spread around our location, danger close; I say again, danger close," he ordered. There was no time for half measures. "Make one pass and then assume orbit and prepare to give fire support."

He heard the noise of the helicopters as they flew closer, two massive black objects hanging in the sky. The two helicopters parted, spreading out to start targeting the enemy, when a streak of light shot up from the ground and blew one of the helicopters into a massive fireball. George barely had time to realise what had happened before the second helicopter went the same way. The bastards had HVM missiles! There was only one place on Avalon where they could have gotten their hands on those, he knew, and he swore that if he survived the ambush, he'd tear the Civil Guard apart to find the traitor who'd sold them to the bandits.

But for now, he was trapped.

And the most competent soldiers of the Civil Guard were trapped with him.

Chapter Thirty-One

> Superior speed and firepower combined are the keys to victory. One alone may grant you victory; two combined will offer certain victory.
> -Major-General Thomas Kratman (Ret), *A Civilian's Guide to the Terran Marine Corps.*

"The Civil Guard is in trouble, sir," Gwen said.

Edward nodded, studying the display in front of him. It was easily the most advanced system on the planet – the Civil Guard was bottom of the list for new equipment – yet it wasn't easy to make out what was going on. His team had vectored two satellites to positions from which they could observe what was going on, but nothing seemed to quite add up. The bandits had set a carefully-planned ambush that had, so far, worked perfectly. It wasn't like them at all.

"They had HVM missile launchers," Edward said in disbelief.

He swore. HVM launchers were fire and forget weapons, simplified to the point where a total novice could use one with a few minutes of instruction, yet they were well beyond anything the bandits could have produced for themselves. There were only two places on Avalon where they could have obtained such weapons and both of them were meant to be under strict tight security. The implications of losing launchers from either of them were disturbing as hell. The Civil Guard's security had to be worse than he had dared imagine.

"And smart warheads for their mortars," Gwen added. "There's no way that a total novice of a fire team could have dropped such an accurate shot on the Civil Guard, not without an unbelievable amount of luck."

Edward nodded. "They don't have very many of them," he agreed. It made sense, or so he thought. If the bandits had had more than a dozen such rounds, Alpha Company would have been wiped out. The bandits might have been able to produce mortars on the planet, but they couldn't have produced the smart warheads. There was only *one* place on the planet where they could have found those. "Get me a link with the Raptors."

The display altered, revealing the Raptors racing out towards the mainland as fast as they could fly, each one carrying a platoon of Marines to reinforce the platoon house and the Civil Guard. Edward couldn't understand why the bandits had set an ambush and then set out to destroy – rather than delay – a pair of Civil Guard units, but they wouldn't last long against armed Marines. They were going to be chopped to pieces…

He looked up at the display and swore as the pieces fell into place. "They're not gunning for the Civil Guard at all," he said, angrily. The sheer chutzpah of the enemy plan was stunning, fully the equal of a hundred other plans Edward had seen developed by armchair generals. "They're gunning for us!"

Gwen stared at him, astonished. "They'd have to be out of their minds," she protested, surprised. "They can't take us on in open combat."

"Look at the map," Edward said, tapping it with a long finger. "They set a pair of ambushes along the obvious approach routes for the Civil Guard and pin them down, rather than fleeing for the badlands as they normally do. The Civil Guard takes the bait because they *expect* the bandits to be fleeing, except the bandits have set an ambush and the Civil Guard blunders right into it. So why haven't the bandits tried to break off or destroy the Civil Guard before we can get to them?"

"They're the bait," Gwen said. "They can't hope to pull it off, can they?"

Edward shook his head, trying to project confidence. The enemy had produced a nasty surprise, but he had confidence in his Marines to adapt and react to the new threat. The more he looked at the map, the more he saw the weaknesses in the enemy plan…if his Marines lasted long enough to take advantage of them.

"Pass a general message to all units," he ordered. "I want all of us to be using a strict microburst-only policy, nothing else. No radio transmissions of any kind. I bet you that if they have access to Civil Guard military equipment, they have access to their communications gear as well."

"No bet," Gwen said. "They could have far more heavy weapons in reserve than we've seen."

"Probably," Edward said. He keyed the map as the satellites came into position to observe the fighting on the ground. Unsurprisingly, the Civil Guard companies were still hemmed in by rather less accurate mortar fire. The first shot had to have been with a smart warhead then, or perhaps they'd had a dose of beginner's luck. There was no way to know now. "I want the Raptors to land here and the Marines are to proceed overland to relieve Alpha Company."

"Yes, sir," Gwen said, neutrally. "They'll have to swing around the area, sir. That will slow us down before we can deploy."

"Ten gets you twenty that the enemy have dug-in antiaircraft weapons platforms along our most likely approach path," Edward said. It was basic tactics; Marines on the ground were tough formidable fighters, but Marines in aircraft were vulnerable to a simple missile. He'd seen entire Marine units wiped out on Han when enemy aircraft had engaged their transports during one of the early battles. That had been a clusterfuck to remember. "They can't have too many of them, or they would be in Camelot dictating terms to the Governor."

His hand traced out an angle of approach on the map. "I want the Marines from the platoon house to leave Alpha and Beta Companies alone and head to here," he said, tapping another location. "When the bandits realise that their ambush has failed to produce the desired effect, they'll try to break off and retreat. I want our people in position to block their retreat before they can get out of sight and into the badlands."

"Yes, sir," Gwen said. "Do you have any other orders?"

"Warm up my command vehicle," Edward added. "I'm going out there personally."

"No you are not," Gwen said, firmly. She fixed him with a gimlet stare. "You are the senior officer on this station and you are not to put your life at risk. You have a capable command team on the ground and they can handle anything the enemy might deploy against us."

Edward nodded sourly, knowing that she was right. Part of him wanted to suit up and get stuck into the bandits who had looted, raped and killed all along the perimeter, but his duty was to remain on Castle Rock and coordinate the response from a place of safety. His lips parted in a humourless smile. Marines normally didn't graduate to REMF – Rear Echelon Mother Fucker – status until they reached the rank of Colonel and even then a Colonel might be expected to serve on the battlefield. Only Major-Generals, the highest permanent rank in the Corps, never saw the face of battle. A lowly Captain who avoided battle would have been a scandal anywhere else. On Avalon, she was right. His place was out of danger.

"Yes," he said, flatly. "Warn everyone; the enemy may have heavier weapons than we have yet seen. Tell them to be on their guard."

Jasmine braced herself as the Raptor tilted sharply and fell out of the sky in a controlled crash dive…or at least she hoped that it was a controlled crash dive. The young men and women back at Castle Rock has no idea how lucky they were, for Castle Rock's limited facilities couldn't even begin to match the facilities available at the Slaughterhouse. Jasmine had dived out of more aircraft in a month than she'd ever had to dive out of in her entire active career. In the process, she had learnt a deep and abiding respect for the crazy pilots who flew Marine aircraft. They might have been Auxiliaries, and therefore not pureblood Marines, but there was no doubting their bravery.

"Landing in ten seconds," the pilot said, through the intercom. "Please put your vomit back in your tummies and thank you for flying Sick Comet Airlines."

The usual chorus of insults and catcalls failed to materialise as the aircraft touched down and Marines lunged to get out of the plane before the enemy started firing on the grounded aircraft with mortars. Jasmine joined the exodus and sprinted out into the sunlight, wincing slightly as her HUD updated with datastreams from the other Marines. They were spreading out around the aircraft, just in case the enemy knew where they were going to land and had arranged a welcoming committee. It should have been impossible, but any Marine who had made it through the Slaughterhouse knew to have a healthy respect for the Demon Murphy. It wouldn't have been the first time Marine forces had accidentally landed on top of an enemy nest.

"No contact, no contact," Lieutenant Faulkner reported. Jasmine heard the whine from behind her as the Raptor lifted off and headed back to a safe LZ some kilometres away from the battlefield. They'd be there when the Marines needed them, once the Marines had suppressed any remaining HVM threat. A Marine Raptor was a tough bird, but a direct hit from an HVM would be lethal. "There are no enemy forces on our LZ."

"Understood," Captain Stalker said. His voice sounded odd through the encrypted microburst channel. "Good hunting."

Jasmine put an audio-discrimination program into primary mode as the Marines spread out, moving through the fields with a speed that would – hopefully – shock and awe their opponents. Even without powered combat armour, any Marine could have won a long-distance marathon race with ease…and wearing the armour, they could move with the speed of graceless leopards. Jasmine remembered the first days of wearing the armour, when she had been able to jump into the air and leap small buildings in a single bound, before they'd been taught that any fool who showed herself that clearly would be killed by the enemy. The program, working on the suit's receptors, warned that there was shooting and gunfire in the distance.

"Seems kind of hard on the farmers," Joe observed as they entered a field of corn and started to trample through it. "What will they do when the crops fail because of us?"

"Would you rather head up the roads and get blown to hell when a mine detonates?" Blake demanded. The usual banter was gone, wiped away by the HVM missiles that had destroyed the Civil Guard helicopters. The bandits were suddenly no longer a laughing matter. "I'm sure that the

Captain will do his best to ensure that we pay proper compensation and save them from having to go even further into debt."

Jasmine scowled inwardly as the first group of Marines leapt over a wooden fence, one she could have jumped even without the suit. The internal map on her visor was reporting that they were closing in on Alpha Company's position, yet they had seen no sign of the enemy, even on the live feed downloaded from the drones that the Lieutenant had launched as they deployed. Each of the drones cost upwards of twenty million credits each, yet he'd launched them without hesitation, a worrying decision in the circumstances. He expected to run into real trouble.

A flicker of energy in the distance popped up on the display, a moment before a flare of blue-white light shot past her, narrowly missing two of the Marines. She threw herself down and started to bury herself in the soil as pulse after pulse ranged towards them, daring them to keep moving forward and impale themselves on the plasma bolts. Her suit provided an intelligence estimate as she crawled towards the edge of the field, warning her that at least four medium-sized plasma cannons had been emplaced ahead of them. Jasmine had used the weapons herself and knew their limitations – they had a nasty habit of overheating when they were fired too quickly – yet it was evident that their new owners had never even heard of the concept. They were firing too rapidly for that.

"We could just stay low," Joe said. There was an odd quiver in his voice and Jasmine winced, wondering if he was truly healed after his last encounter with a plasma cannon. He should have stayed in regeneration longer, but very few Marines would stay in the tank any longer than they absolutely had to. "We give them seven minutes and the bastards will blow themselves up."

"Not before they get lucky and rip us to shreds," Blake growled. He didn't sound happy, but Jasmine could hear the note of concern in his voice as well. The platoon was her family and something that affected one of them affected all of them. "One shot in the wrong place and your family will be getting a sealed casket for your remains."

"As you were," Lieutenant Faulkner ordered. "Prepare to start throwing grenades."

"Yes, sir," Jasmine said. A grenade fell out of her suit's storage compartment and into her armoured hand. She cocked her wrist, running through possible trajectories with the suit's computer systems. "Ready..."

"Now," Faulkner snapped. A line of twelve grenades flew towards their targets. Two went wide, but the remainder detonated near the plasma cannons. The explosions blew the enemy position into flaming ruin, vaporising the bandits before they had a chance to escape. Jasmine ran forward with the rest of the platoon, looking for targets, but there was no point. The entire bandit position had been wiped out.

"Camouflage netting," Blake said, as he tripped over something on the ground. There was a rare note of wonder in his voice. "They hid their guns under fucking camouflage netting."

"Clever," Jasmine said, as her suit registered incoming mortar rounds splashing down around the platoon. The enemy fire wasn't very accurate, but a single hit would cripple a Marine, even if it didn't kill him outright.

"Take them," Faulkner ordered. "Move now!"

Jasmine triggered her suit's systems and charged right across country towards the second bandit position, lowering her weapon and firing round after round towards the mortar operators. The others followed her, sweeping through the bandit position and tearing it apart. A handful of bandits turned to run, only to be shot down as they tried to flee, while others threw their hands up in desperate surrender. The noise of incoming rounds shifted as another enemy position tried to bring its weapons to bear on the Marines, but they hadn't laid their weapons properly. The shells went wide.

"They timed this well," Blake said, as they overran a smaller position. The bandits were scattering now, feeling the weight of the Marines as they moved faster than the bandits could react. "If the destroyers had still been in orbit..."

Jasmine nodded bitterly, concentrating on shooting down a bandit who was carrying what looked like a homemade antitank rocket. The destroyers could have ended the whole battle by dropping killer crowbars from orbit onto the heads of the bandits, but then...no one on Avalon would ever underestimate the firepower of a single Imperial Navy destroyer. A lone destroyer had ended the Cracker Rebellion; two of them could have scorched the badlands from orbit.

"Second Platoon, this is Third Lead," a voice said on the general frequency. "The bandits are starting to break, but they're pushing harder at the Guard's Alpha Company as they leave."

"Advance on Alpha Company and relieve them," Captain Stalker ordered, grimly. Jasmine could understand why. The Civil Guard wasn't particularly competent by Marine standards, but Alpha and Beta Companies were among their best. Losing them would be painful as hell. They would certainly be impossible to replace within the next few years, at least until the Council dropped its short-sighted insistence on paying its recruits electronically. It wouldn't be the first time that local authority didn't seem to know that there was a war on, but this example was particularly odd.

"Understood," Faulkner said. First and Second Platoons reformed and jogged rapidly towards the enemy firing positions, ducking as the enemy brought their heavy weapons around and fired rapidly, trying to keep the Marines back. Jasmine felt the impact of light chemically-propelled weapons and winced, even as she kept moving. They would need something heavier than that to break through even light powered combat armour. "I'm switching to loudspeaker now."

Jasmine heard him even though the suit. "THIS IS THE MARINES," Faulkner thundered. "DROP YOUR WEAPONS AND PUT YOUR HANDS ON YOUR HEADS. ANYONE HOLDING A WEAPON WILL BE SHOT!"

A handful of bandits threw down their weapons, but others continued to try to fight or run, knowing what would happen to them once they entered custody. A handful of the surrendering bandits were shot down by their own side, if only to discourage further defections. Jasmine and her platoon moved to cover them, keeping a wary eye on the surrendering bandits as they did so. Any fool who picked up a weapon after surrendering would get all of his fellows killed, for nothing.

She winced as a mortar shell came down on top of them, knocking some of the Marines to the ground and killing some of the surrendering bandits, just before they crested the ridge. It was immediately evident that

Alpha Company had driven right into a trap. Jasmine would have picked the same place herself if she'd been planning the manoeuvre. They had restricted fields of fire and limited options. Without the Marines, they would have had to charge their opponents, or die when their ammunition ran out. No one in their right mind would have surrendered to the bandits.

"Alpha Company is liberated, sir," Faulkner said. "We're moving to beat out the remnants of the bandits now...."

A drone picked up the emission signature, too late. A flare of brilliant white light blazed out of a hidden enemy position and struck a Rifleman dead on. His suit glowed bright white and failed. A second later, he was dead.

CHAPTER THIRTY-TWO

> We don't leave anyone behind, ever. We account for all of our men. If they are abused in enemy hands, we seek to ensure that the abusers are held to account for their crimes. If they are killed by the enemy, we avenge their deaths. We ask for great sacrifices from our Marines. The least we can do is ensure that their lives – and their deaths – have meaning. A civilian will never understand, but a Marine always will.
> -Master Sergeant Jackson Hendry (Ret), *The Meaning of a Marine.*

"Marine down," a voice snapped. "Captain, we have a Marine down!"

Edward swore, angrily. It wasn't the first time that men and women had died under his command, but it was never easy to accept. It was worse, somehow, because he hadn't been in *direct* command. Would a young man's life have been saved if he'd been in command, rather than one of the Lieutenants? Edward had known that it wasn't going to be easy to deal with the bandits, not as long as they had modern military-grade firepower, yet…he pushed the feelings of rage and grief into a corner of his mind and locked them away firmly. There would be time to deal with them later.

"Confirmed," Gwen said. Her voice had gone icy cold. "We got a distress squeal from his suit before it was destroyed. There's no hope that he survived the blast."

Her bluntness helped Edward to focus. Alpha Company had been saved from certain destruction, but that still left Beta Company and then there were the snipers harassing Fort Galahad. The Civil Guard's Delta

Company was trying to assemble to hunt them down and not having much luck. Edward silently dismissed them from his thoughts and studied the map. The enemy were breaking off and trying to run, but they wouldn't be allowed to escape. Not now, not after they'd killed a Marine.

"I want the platoons to move in and relieve Beta Company, and then act as beaters, driving the bastards into our waiting arms," he ordered, sharply. Hammer and anvil was a military tactic as old as the human race itself, yet the sheer level of firepower available to the Marines and the Civil Guard took it to a whole new dimension. "Warn Lieutenant Faulkner to watch out for ambushes. Those bastards might be trying to lead us into another trap."

He studied the map, wondering just what his counterpart was thinking. The ambush of the Civil Guard had been brilliant, yet the enemy plan had fallen apart as soon as it had met the Marines. It spoke of a mind that didn't have much military experience and had developed a plan that was, simply, too complicated. Edward had gone through the Slaughterhouse OCS and had had a lesson drilled into him; never, even, forget the KISS principle. Keep It Simple, Stupid; his instructors had made it very clear. If your complicated plan is working perfectly, they had warned, you are about to lose. The bandits hadn't realised just how fast the Marines could move across rough ground.

"And get additional surveillance assets up there," he added. "I think the bastards have built us a Kratman's Hill."

Gwen blinked, but understood his point. Major-General Thomas Kratman had been Senior Training Officer at the Slaughterhouse four hundred years ago and had been responsible for introducing a number of new training programs. Danger Hill – it had been renamed after him several years after he had died – was, on the surface, a fairly simple training exercise. The Marine squad had to make their way up the hill and capture the flag on top. The first time the exercise was run, squads knew nothing about the hill's defenders, but when they reran the exercise the following day, they discovered that nothing had changed and they could use their previous experience to know exactly where the defenders were and how they could get up the hill. By the third time, the recruits could have picked the defenders apart for no losses at all…

And, on the fourth time, the defenders would change everything. They'd reposition their guns, lay new minefields and hide new surprises. A squad that was smart enough not to take anything for granted would probably still be able to take the hill. A squad that didn't think that anything would have changed – after all, it had been the same three times in a row – would be rapidly destroyed, and then humiliated by the Drill Instructors, who would point out with loving detail just where they had gone wrong. The bandits had built a reserve Kratman's Hill and had hammered the Civil Guard hard. The Marines had nearly fallen into the same trap.

"And as long as we think they might have HVM launchers left, we can't bring up the Raptors," he added, sourly. "Tell them to stay on the deck for now. They're out of the war until further notice."

It was a bitter thought, but it had to be faced. A Raptor couldn't be constructed on Avalon, not when the best the planet could produce was armoured helicopters from a bygone age. There was no hope of any replacements, not with the Empire largely unconcerned about what happened outside the Core Worlds; a single lost Raptor would have an adverse effect on his command. And, by raising the spectre of antiaircraft missiles lying in wait, the bandits had forced him to take his aircraft out of the game without even shooting down a single Raptor.

"Yes, sir," Gwen said.

Lucas stared in disbelief as his plans fell apart around him. He hadn't realised just how fast the Marines could move…hell, he hadn't realised that the Marines wouldn't be dumb enough to land where they were supposed to land. If they'd followed his plans, just as the Civil Guard had done, they would have been destroyed…or, at the very least, bled white, giving him time to get the rest of his men out of the combat zone. Now the Marines had saved one Civil Guard force and were moving towards saving the other force.

He keyed his radio. "Fox, this is Knife," he said. It wasn't the most professional of codes, but he was still experimenting with the radios. Now the

Marines knew about the shit he'd been sent from Camelot, by his backers, it wouldn't hurt if they knew about the radios as well. What harm could it do? "Get out of there and start heading back to camp. Now!"

An explosion billowed out in the distance as the Marines overran one of his positions. It had been a good plan, he told himself, and it had almost worked. He would have to make sure that everyone knew that it had almost worked, or one of the Knives would try to stick a knife in his back. There was no safety or security in being a gang leader. He had had to lead his men onto the battlefield, or they would have refused to stand and wait for the inevitable response from the Civil Guard, let alone the Marines. He might as well have placed his head in a noose.

Upper-class fuckers, he thought, as he turned to run. *If they betrayed me, I can betray them in turn.*

The thought made him smile, for he knew enough about his backers to know that they were important people, too important to risk leaving him in a position to spill his guts to the Marines. They'd rescue him if the Marines took him into custody, if only to prevent him from telling his captors everything. All he had to do was surrender and wait to be liberated on some technicality. He'd certainly been able to recover men from the jail before, just by working with his allies. Smiling, he started to run. Behind him, the noise of explosions grew louder.

Lucas had never heard of a stealth remote drone, nor did he know just how effective the sensors mounted on such a drone could be. Lieutenant Faulkner had launched several such drones into the air and one of them was floating high above him, too high to be seen by the naked eye. It was almost invisible to mil-grade sensors; there was literally nothing in the Civil Guard's arsenal that could have picked up on it, even if they had known that there was a drone in the area.

"We got a single enemy contact using a radio," the operator said. She was sitting back in Castle Rock, staring through her drone's sensors and sifting for useful data. "They're using Civil Guard-issue tactical radios, but they're not using an isolated frequency or encryption."

Edward smiled tightly. It had been apparent that the bandits had somehow managed to loot a Civil Guard facility…or, more likely, simply bribed the quartermasters to give them whatever they wanted and report the equipment as having been lost. The bandits couldn't have that many radios, which suggested that the person holding the radio was someone he wanted alive, very much so. And, with the drone following him, taking him alive would be easy.

"Mark him out for capture when he hits the blocking force," he ordered. "Pass the word to all of the Marines; I want him alive."

The bandits were running now, some even dropping their weapons as they fled, if only to move quicker. Jasmine wasn't entirely surprised, although she kept a close eye out for any traps that might have been left in their path. A Marine platoon that was retreating would – naturally – try to strew booby traps around, if only to delay anyone in pursuit. The bandits didn't seem to have thought of that particular trick. She focused on the pursuit, lifting her rifle and neatly shooting one bandit in the leg, sending him falling to the ground. Leaving traps behind required a certain presence of mind that – so far – the bandits seemed to be lacking.

"I'm moving the remains of Alpha Company up behind the Marines," the Civil Guard Major said, over the general frequency. Jasmine scowled inwardly – Captain Stalker had specifically ordered no radio transmissions, if only to prevent the enemy from intercepting the signals – but the Civil Guard had no other choice. Their equipment didn't do microburst transmissions. "We'll pick up the prisoners and cart them off to the Fort. You can keep pushing at them."

Jasmine checked the update from the satellites as she kept moving, watching for any straggler who tried to go to ground. The bandits attacking Fort Galahad had finally been driven off, even though there had only been a handful of them with primitive weapons. The bandits must have considered them expendable because they hadn't stood a chance once the Civil Guard had gotten organised. They hadn't even been armed with plasma weapons. That would have given them a fighting chance.

"Just like hunting birds back home," Blake said, grimly. Jasmine heard the undertone, a restless demand for revenge, and nodded inwardly. One of their family was dead, murdered by assholes who had looted, raped and burned when they could have been building a future for their kids. People like them were what the Terran Marine Corps existed to destroy, people driven by the primitive barbarian mindset that lurked in the back of the human mind, people who had found it so much easier to take than to build. The bandits would pay for their crimes. "We keep beating; they keep running."

Jasmine nodded, consulting her visor as the Marines kept spreading out. The blocking force from the platoon house was in position now, ready to start shooting the bandits as they were flushed out towards it. They'd be firing with stunners at first, but if the bandits had managed to obtain body armour – even a basic protection mesh – from the Civil Guard, they'd have to switch to lethal weaponry. No one would want to wear a protection mesh in this weather – it was far too hot for wearing heavy outfits – but they wouldn't have any choice. Professional rioters on Earth and the other Core Worlds had been known to wear them, just so they could force the Civil Guard or local police forces to use violence against the protestors. The media blew such incidents completely out of proportion.

A flicker of light made her duck as a burst of plasma fire erupted from a shrub. She put an explosive round through the camouflaged position and smiled as her visor automatically darkened, protecting her eyes from the flare of light. Plasma cannon were notoriously unreliable at the best of times and it looked as if the Civil Guard hadn't bothered to maintain them properly. It was galling to be grateful for incompetence, yet it had probably saved their lives.

"I think you got him," Blake said, dryly. The remains of the fire would have to be left to smoulder. Perhaps, when the fighting had finished, they'd have to deal with a blaze as well. Her lips twitched. Accidentally setting off a fire that raged out of control would be embarrassing and very definitely no laughing matter. She still remembered the pair of idiot male cousins back home who had tried to hold a barbeque without adult supervision and had nearly set fire to the entire compound. They'd been in disgrace for months. "We'll have to pick up his remains with tweezers."

"That's enough of that," Faulkner growled. He designated a line in front of them on their visors. "We'll hold there and let them run right into the blocking force. Keep an eye out for anyone dumb enough to think that they can get past us."

Corporal Jody Cochrane lay in the hollow and watched as the bandits ran right towards her, utterly unaware of her position…or of the other nine members of the platoon. They were clearly panicking, thinking only of getting back to the badlands and safety, rather than watching where they were going. They shouldn't have been able to see the Marines – Jody was camouflaged behind a chameleon field – but if they had the time to take a sweep with a proper sensor, they would realise that they were running right into a trap.

"Place your stunners on wide beam," she ordered, calmly. Half of the bandits were bare-chested, proving that they weren't wearing any protection…or that they'd discarded it in their desperate attempt to get away from the Marines. Stunners lost their effectiveness rapidly as the range opened, but the bandits were running *towards* her. "Fire!"

She triggered her own stunner, sweeping it over the oncoming wave of bandits. They were completely surprised, falling to the ground in shock, sometimes hit several times by the same stunner. It wouldn't do them any harm in the long term, but some of them would wake up with terrible headaches. Jody couldn't find it in her to care. She'd seen the videos of what they did to their victims. If they all had splitting headaches for the rest of their lives, which wouldn't be very long if she had anything to say about it, it would be less than they deserved.

Some of the bandits tried to turn back, realising that they'd suddenly run right into terrible danger, but it was far too late. Stunners didn't work like conventional weapons; they could be played over their targets time and time again, sweeping them down like ninepins. Jody smiled inwardly as she realised they'd caught nearly seventy bandits in their little trap.

They'd all have to be cuffed and marched back to the Fort, or a secure holding area nearby, but they'd never threaten the peace and security of the area again. Morgan and their other victims have been avenged.

"We knocked them all down, sir," she said, keying her radio. "What do you want us to do with them?"

"Hold your position and stun them again if they get twitchy," Captain Stalker ordered. "Let the others sweep up the stragglers."

———

Lucas had been falling behind as they fled, unwilling to be too obviously fleeing for his life. As he saw the first bandits start to fall, he realised what had happened and threw himself into a ditch. It stunk to high heaven of animal scents – the smell, instantly familiar to anyone who spent time in Avalon's countryside, warned him that there might be a Gnasher nearby – but it was safety, of a sort. He forced his trembling legs to keep propelling him forward, unaware of the watching drone high overhead that kept a careful watch on his progress. The noise of hunting Marines behind him – no longer trying to be stealthy with their movements – provided all the incentive he needed. If he could just get out of their view, he was sure they couldn't catch him…

A heavy shape thumped down in front of him and he looked up, right into a leering smile. The Gnasher's teeth, sharper and nastier than any purely terrestrial animal, seemed to shine in the sunlight. Lucas froze, knowing that it was all over. The creature was merely playing with him before it closed in for the kill. He could smell its warm breath as it glided closer to him, opening its mouth wide. Warm liquid trickled down his leg as it prepared to bite…and then it recoiled. Lucas turned his head, knowing that he was dead anyway, and saw two armed Marines right behind him, one of them pointing a long rifle at the beast. Time seemed to freeze…

And then the Gnasher turned and vanished, moving faster than the eye could see.

Lucas looked up at the Marines and tried to speak. One of them pointed an armoured finger at him…and darkness crashed down.

Jasmine retracted the stunner and picked the bandit up. In her armour, he weighed almost nothing.

"We got him, sir," she said, keying her communicator. "What do you want us to do with him?"

"Hand him over to Corporal Cochrane and get back to the Raptors," Captain Stalker ordered. "Your services may be needed in Camelot."

Chapter Thirty-Three

> What will happen to our Empire, if I may ask, when the military leaders take matters into their own hands? Already, discontent with the current situation is growing within the military and there are unconfirmed reports of mutinies and attempted mutinies within the outer systems. What happens if a large military force decides that it can no longer follow the orders of the civilian leadership?
> - Professor Leo Caesius, *The Waning Years of Empire* (banned).

"So," Carola asked. "What happened?"

"I don't know," Wilhelm admitted. "The ambush should have gone off three hours ago, but we've heard nothing specific from our sources in the Civil Guard. The ATC team reported that the Marines launched four of their VTOL transport aircraft towards the badlands moments after the first reports came in…and then nothing. I don't know what happened at all."

Carola stared down at the table. It was real wood and would have been worth a fortune on Old Earth, but on Avalon wood was as common as dirt. It was a shame it wasn't really worth the effort of exporting wood to Earth, yet perhaps it was for the best. If Avalon had produced something of interest to the Core Worlds, the Empire-backed trade cartels would have moved in and frozen her out of the market. It also reminded her that something that looked strong, like an old oak tree, might have rotted away inside and come to grief in a powerful storm.

"The Civil Guard said nothing to their home base," she repeated, puzzled. The Marines had very good communications security, but the

Governor kept the Civil Guard on a tight leash. They were supposed to seek his approval for any moves outside the prearranged battle plans, which would have passed through the layer of functionaries – and Carola's agents – before the Governor was even consulted. Her spies would have known to inform her as soon as anything changed. "They didn't even tell the Governor?"

"Not as far as we can determine," her husband replied. He was playing with a knife he'd brought from their homeworld, one that had been in his family for generations. He'd told her that he intended to pass it on to their firstborn child, but Carola had had no intention of getting pregnant, not until she was the undisputed mistress of Avalon. A child was nothing more than a burden, or a hostage to fortune. "There's a total communications blackout up near the badlands."

Carola considered it, looking down at the single sheet of paper on the table. It was a petition, signed by the majority of the Council, for the Governor to relieve Major Grosskopf of command and pass the duty to another officer, one nominated by the Council. Used properly, issued in the wake of a devastating defeat, it would have undermined the Governor's own position, leaving him with little choice, but to comply. If the Civil Guard and the Marines had been defeated, it couldn't fail…or so she told herself. But if they had actually *won* the battle, issuing the petition would weaken the Council's position; it would certainly turn them into a laughing-stock.

"We could push the Governor now and see if he fell," she said, slowly. They exchanged a long look. If they tried and failed, it would mean public humiliation, even if nothing worse happened. "Or we could hold on to the petition and wait to see what actually happened up there."

Wilhelm gave voice to one of the darker possibilities. "What happens if the bandits lost the fight?"

Carola scowled. The weapons they'd arranged to fall into the bandits' hands should have come as a complete surprise to their opponents, yet she knew enough to know that mere possession of a weapon didn't make someone dangerous, let alone invincible. The links between her faction and the bandits weren't obvious, certainly nothing to provoke a full Imperial Investigation, but it wouldn't be hard to work out where the weapons had actually come from. If the Governor traced the line back to their friends in the Civil Guard, all of their plans could rapidly come unravelled.

"It's time to put Jackie to work," she said, shortly. She had decided that the particular Civil Guard ally had to go just after he'd smuggled the weapons out to the bandits; it would be easy to move matters up a little. Their assassin could deal with him before the Governor's investigators caught up with him and started asking him questions. "And then, I think, we'll have to wait."

She turned to peer out the window, towards the looming shape of the Mystic Mountains in the distance. What *had* happened out there?

Major George Grosskopf braced himself as the helicopter swooped down towards the LZ, a bare two kilometres from the main Civil Guard Supply Depot on Avalon. The complex was the largest military base on the planet – although the Marines would probably turn Castle Rock into a larger base in the future – and held most of their weapons and supplies. It had been placed near to the spaceport for ease of transport, as well as allowing the garrison to react quickly to any crisis that needed their intervention. Over the years, as the quality of the Civil Guard had continued to decline, it had ended up as a dumping ground for officers who couldn't be trusted on the battlefield. The results had probably been inevitable.

He silently cursed the Governor's weakness – and those of his predecessors – as he jumped out of the aircraft and exchanged salutes with Captain Bertram of Alpha Company. The Captain of Beta Company had been injured in the ambush, but George would deal with him later. The soldiers who had survived were in an evil mood and it had taken too long to calm them down before transporting as many as possible to the main supply depot. He was uncomfortably aware that he was about to make history; his unit would be the first Civil Guard unit in the Empire's entire history to assault its own supply base.

"I've combined the units into one Company," Bertram informed him, as the next set of helicopters came in to land. "As per your orders, we have enforced a blockade around the supply depot and arrested anyone trying to get out of it, regardless of their rank. The prisoners are currently held in that field."

George followed his pointing finger and saw a number of senior officers, their tailor-made uniforms glittering in the sun, squatting in the dry field. Their hands were bound and they were guarded by a handful of soldiers who had made it absolutely clear that if their former superiors got out of hand, they would be cut down without mercy. In the long run, George was grimly aware that he was initiating a major social change on Avalon, if not launching a mutiny against lawful authority. It would all depend on which way the Governor – and Captain Stalker, for that matter – decided to jump.

"Good," he said, as Alpha Company started to form up around their position. "How many personnel do you believe are still in the complex?"

"Around seven hundred at most, including Kappa Company," Bertram said. They exchanged glances. Unlike Alpha, Beta or Delta Company, Kappa Company was commanded by political appointees and had the lowest combat ratings in the Avalon Civil Guard. George would not have bet good money on the soldiers trying to resist overwhelming force – the CO of Kappa Company hadn't tried to develop loyalty among his men – but it was something to watch. "As far as I know, no one from Camelot knows that we are here."

George shrugged. It wouldn't matter. The supply depot was military territory and no civilians were allowed to enter without a pass and an escort. He'd convinced the Governor to declare a two-kilometre exclusion zone around the depot years ago, allowing the defenders licence to engage anyone found in the zone without warning. The Crackers had to have their eye on the massive military stockpile within the depot, which made it all the more galling that he had to leave its defence to a bunch of politicians in uniform. So far, they'd only launched harassing attacks against the garrison, but George doubted that that would last. If they took out the Civil Guard's supplies, they would gain a decisive military advantage.

"Good," he said, finally. "I want you to assemble four platoons, along with the armoured cars and two heavy tanks, and move them up to the gates. I want them to see what's coming at them."

He watched as the vehicles slowly moved forward, following in their wake. He – as the Civil Guard's supreme military commander – should have had total access, but he had a feeling that if he had come alone, he might have walked into a trap. As it was, Alpha Company might not have matched the Marines for firepower, but he would have bet on them against Kappa Company, if Kappa Company dared to put up a fight.

"Major," Corporal Van Diamond called, "I have Captain Stalker on the line for you."

George keyed his personal radio. "Captain," he said. "What can I do for you?"

"We're currently transporting the prisoners back to secure housing," Captain Stalker said, calmly. George didn't miss the edge in his voice. "I also have two platoons heading towards the spaceport. Do you require their support?"

"Not yet," George said, although he was tempted. "This is something the Civil Guard has to do for itself."

"Understood," Captain Stalker said, at once. George was almost surprised. He had expected an argument. "Call us if you discover you need us."

George looked up as the connection broke, watching as the massive Main Battle Tank glided towards the barricade. There were only a handful of tanks on Avalon and normally they remained in storage, but he'd had four of them deployed to protect the city in the wake of riots two months ago. They might not have been first-rank machines, not up to the standards of those he'd used in the Imperial Army, yet they were hellishly intimidating. They hadn't built the supply depot to stand off a single tank. He lifted his binoculars and saw the guards staring at the tank, unsure of what was going on, but convinced that it wasn't good. The odds were high that whatever corruption had affected the senior officers hadn't reached them, yet George couldn't take chances. Soldiers had no civil rights and everyone on the post was going to go through a full lie detector test before he was satisfied that they could return to duty.

"Give me the loudspeaker," he ordered, keying his radio. "THIS IS YOUR COMMANDING OFFICER. YOU ARE ORDERED TO PUT DOWN YOUR WEAPONS AND PLACE YOUR HANDS ON

YOUR HEAD. THIS COMPOUND IS NOW UNDER MY DIRECT COMMAND."

He smiled at the reaction. The guards had probably alerted the compound's CO as soon as they realised that Alpha Company was bearing down on them, yet if he knew Colonel Smuts, he was still panicking. Smuts had gotten his rank because of a few hefty bribes paid by the Wilhelm Family and had very little use at all, at least as far as George could see. He couldn't handle logistics, let alone command a unit under heavy fire. A handful of the officers who had been put in place by powerful patrons had their uses, he grudgingly admitted, but Smuts was an imbecile. Throw him into a pit of gold and he would somehow come out covered in shit.

"No response, sir," Bertram reported. "I think they're not convinced of our sincerity."

"Bring the main gun to bear on the gate," George ordered, keying the radio again. "IF THE COMPOUND DOES NOT STAND DOWN AT ONCE, IT WILL BE DECLARED TO BE IN MUTINY AND SMASHED FLAT!"

It was partly a bluff – they needed to secure the supply dump, not destroy it – but the guards didn't hesitate any longer. As George watched, they threw down their weapons and held up their hands in surrender, one of them keying the gate to open automatically. Captain Bertram barked orders and Alpha Company moved forward, collecting weapons and taking prisoners as they went. The former defenders were ordered to lie on the ground and had their hands bound, where they would stay until they could be transported to a POW camp and run through lie detectors. The experience would be humiliating for the innocent men, yet there was no choice. George would quite cheerfully have opened fire if the compound's defenders had tried to fight.

"We have the gate, sir," Captain Bertram reported. "And we have seventeen prisoners."

"You know the drill," George ordered. "Spread out by platoon; arrest anyone you come across and secure them until they can be taken away. I want the entire base secured as quickly as possible."

He followed one of the platoons as they headed into the HQ Building. The clerks who made the supply depot run stared as the heavily armed soldiers burst in, before being roughly rounded up and made to assume the position. Protests were dealt with quickly and brutally. The men on the front lines had little use for the clerks, even if one of them hadn't sold heavy weapons that had gotten far too many good men killed. The senior clerk, clearly recognising his ultimate commander, started to stutter out a confession that would have been very interesting, under other circumstances. George motioned for him to join the rest of his clerks and keep his mouth shut. They'd have time to interrogate him properly later.

The lead soldiers raced up the stairs to the main office and George followed them, no longer expecting any serious resistance from the REMFs. He glanced from side to side as they burst into the offices of high-ranking personnel and scowled, taking in just how luxurious they were, even by Avalon's limited standard. It was expected that some senior officers would be allowed to decorate their own offices, provided that they were decorated at their expense, but they'd taken it far beyond the permissible. The money they'd wasted in creating a comfortable working environment could have been spent on better equipment or recruiting new soldiers. He heard female shrieks up ahead and realised, to his horror, that some of the senior officers had brought their mistresses to work. What the hell had they been thinking?

"Put them with the others," he ordered, when the women were finally secured and dragged out. He held up a hand as he recognised one of the women, a girl who served as Smuts' private secretary. The few times they met, she'd struck him as dumb, blonde and barely fit even for whoring. She didn't possess the motivation necessary to reach such a post. "You; where is your boss?"

"I don't know," the girl said, shaking against the soldier who held her. "I don't…"

"Don't give me that shit," George snapped. "Tell me where he is or I'll have you injected with truth drugs and then we'll get an answer out of you."

The girl wilted, cringing back against her captor. "He's in his private office," she said, bitterly. "He's been in there for hours. I don't know what he's doing there."

George could guess. Smuts had set up a private office that included dedicated phone lines, one linked directly to the Council Chambers. He was probably trying to get in touch with his patrons and beg for their support, although it wouldn't work; Alpha Company's lead elements had cut the lines and isolated the base before moving into view.

"Good," he said. He nodded to the soldier. "Cuff her to that sofa there and come with me."

Leaving the girl behind, they walked up the third set of stairs towards the final office. George keyed his radio, listening briefly as reports came in reporting that the remainder of the base had been secured, and smiled briefly. The prospect of a bloodbath – or, worse, of civil war – had been averted, barely. His career might not survive what he'd done today, not if the Governor chose to disapprove, but his men would be safe. They had all followed his orders.

"Start moving the prisoners out to the camp," he said, once all the units had reported in. "I'll deal with Smuts personally."

It wasn't wise but he was determined, for if anyone had been involved in the corruption, it was Smuts. The man might have been useless for any military purpose – except perhaps as a live target, a nasty part of his mind whispered – but he'd been a past master at ruling a bureaucratic empire. He had to have known what was going on in his base, even if he hadn't been the prime mover. He had to have known…

The doorway was ajar and George moved in, holding his sidearm at the ready. A moment later, he lowered it as he took in the sight before him. Smuts was seated at his desk, a bloody hole blasted right through his head. One of his hands held a gun. He was very clearly dead.

"Took the easy way out, did you?" George growled. Even with Imperial medical science, there was no hope of saving his life. "I'll find the rest of your friends and they'll pay too."

"It wasn't suicide," the medic said, an hour later. The compound had been completely cleared and a group of logistics officers were going through the inventories and comparing the records to reality. "There was no trace of propellant on his skin."

George saw the implications at once. "Someone killed him to silence him," he said, flatly. "Who the hell killed him?"

"I don't know," the medic said. "We don't have a proper forensic team or even a WARCAT unit on Avalon. It may go down as a complete mystery."

"Fuck," George said, coldly. It wasn't hard to guess why Smuts had been killed. Logically, he could have led investigators all the way back to his backers. "Bag up the body and prepare it for transport to Camelot. I have to go see the Governor."

"Good luck, sir," Captain Bertram said. He looked uncomfortable. "Sir, after this…"

"Everything changes," George agreed. They shared a moment of silent understanding. "I know just what you mean."

CHAPTER
THIRTY-FOUR

The Marine Corps is a family. When one of the family dies, we all mourn, once we are free to mourn without being distracted from our work.
-Master Sergeant Jackson Hendry (Ret), *The Meaning of a Marine.*

The word had come down from the Drill Instructors; two days ago, a Marine had died. Michael had known that *something* had happened – the sudden spate of activity had been impossible to miss – but they hadn't been told what, not until Barr had called the recruits together and told them the truth. It had brought home to many of them just how dangerous their chosen profession actually was and Michael, along with most of the others, had found himself searching his soul for answers. When the shit hit the fan, he asked himself, could he truly stand up and fight? The armoured warriors who had boarded their Raptors had looked invincible. The bandits had just proven that they were not.

"You are invited to attend the ceremony in two hours," Barr had said, in tones that had made it very clear that it was an order. "Until then, you should spend your time in silent contemplation, or weapons practice. One of the family has died."

The odd contrast had made no sense at first, but as he'd sat on his bunk, he had started to understand. The contemplation was for coming to grips with the fact he could die; the weapons practice was to burn off steam afterwards. The lectures on what it meant to be a Marine had been empty words until he had finally understood just what Barr had been trying to teach them. The Marine Corps was a family and even bastard sons like the new recruits were part of something far greater than any of them were individually.

He'd never seen the parade ground so full, nor had he been allowed to wear his dress uniform in public before the tragedy. The unfortunate Marine's platoon were standing on the front row, wearing a black version of their standard uniform, while the other platoons were wearing their dress uniforms with black armbands. Michael did a quick headcount and realised that at least two platoons were not taking part in the ceremony, although he had no idea why. The Company was a family, the only family most of the Marines had, and all of them would want to be present when they said goodbye to their brother. They had to be on deployment. He couldn't imagine anything else that would have kept them away.

The cap felt itchy on his head, but he'd been ordered to wear it and not remove it until the Sergeant ordered them to uncover their heads. Michael hadn't been religious in the conventional sense, but his mother had tried to develop a sense of religion in her children's lives, sending them to church from an early age. He'd stopped going as soon as he'd been old enough to make his decision stick, having concluded that the money his mother paid the priest was better spent elsewhere. The church was never short of money and the family often barely had enough to eat. It just hadn't seemed fair.

Now, staring at the silent Marines, he understood the depth of their faith. It wasn't in God, but in themselves and in the integrity of the Marine Corps. Barr's comment – that some political leaders were terrified of the Marines – suddenly made sense. The Marines presented themselves as beyond corruption or intimidation. They could be killed, but they couldn't be scared.

He wanted to speak to his fellows, but the entire area was silent. No one had ordered silence; it had just fallen, with no one speaking aloud at all. He heard footsteps from behind him as someone entered the parade ground and twitched his eyes, catching sight of Captain Stalker and a short woman wearing a Sergeant's dress uniform and a sword. Her stripes proclaimed her to be a Command Sergeant. Barr had told them that Command Sergeants were, in a way, the actual second-in-command of their units, whatever the Table of Organisation might say.

Captain Stalker marched up to the front row, paused in front of the casket, and then stepped around it, taking his place on a podium. He stared down at his men for a long moment and then, still silently, reached up and removed his cap, placing it neatly in his uniform pocket. A rustle ran through the air as everyone uncovered their heads, holding their caps in their hands. The ceremony, Michael realised, had begun.

"One of our brothers is dead," Captain Stalker said. His voice was very composed, but Michael was sure he could hear…something behind the calm, a hint of bitterness and anger. The dead Marine might have served in Stalker's Stalkers for years, developing relationships with his fellows that transcended the rights and duties of rank. The Marines seemed oddly informal at times. Perhaps the dead Marine had been Captain Stalker's friend, as well as his subordinate. "He died on the field of battle, among his brothers and sisters, as a Marine should. His death will be avenged."

He spoke for nearly ten minutes, speaking about the dead Marine in a manner that somehow made him alive again, if only long enough to say goodbye. Michael hadn't known him, not personally, but he felt a lump in his throat as he gazed at the casket. It had been sealed shut and there was no way to see inside, which didn't look good. Most injuries that weren't immediately lethal could be healed, given time, but Barr hadn't hidden the truth from them. They were training to be soldiers and soldiers sometimes got injured in battle, directly and indirectly. It wasn't unknown for Marines to survive as cripples, shadows of their former selves, or to develop mental problems as they grew older. The Slaughterhouse tried to weed out vulnerable personalities, but it didn't always work. One day, Michael himself might be in a casket while his friends said goodbye. It wasn't a pleasant thought.

"It is traditional for a Marine's body to be transported back to the Slaughterhouse, with his Rifleman's Tab placed within the Mausoleum to be stored for all time," Captain Stalker said. "We cannot transport the body back now, but I swear to you all that the body *will* be transported one day, so that he may rest in peace among the thousands of other Marines who have given their lives in the line of duty. The Honour of the Terran Marine Corps demands that we who knew him when he was alive do his corpse the final honour. We will stand on Flag Hill and pay our final respects to his soul."

There was a long pause, long enough for Michael to feel uncomfortable. "I would like to read to you from the words of Major-General Thaddeus Carmichael, the founder of the modern Terran Marine Corps," Captain Stalker continued. "Carmichael was appointed the first commanding officer of the mixed force that the Terran Federation had assembled from its most prestigious military units. It was Carmichael who, against all opposition, turned the ramshackle force the Federation had created into what we call Marines, the finest soldiers in the known universe. The Corps has changed over the years and he would no longer recognise our organisation or even our technology, but his wisdom still lives on.

"We few, we happy few, we band of brothers…we came together from across the world," he quoted. "When we were pulled together, after the burning blaze of the Third World War, they told us that we were outdated, that there would be no need for the Marine Corps in the brave new world we had won for them. They were wrong. The world may have advanced, but yet it stayed the same and the values of the Corps – honour, loyalty and integrity – remain of value. When we were pulled together, we were just men, but when we fused together, we were Marines. To be a soldier is to be part of a world that a civilian can never understand or enter, to be part of a brotherhood that transcends time itself.

"And, as the years go on, we look to the past to remind ourselves of where we came from. The old guard – we who were there at the beginning – grow older, yet our memory lives on. And, as long as a single Marine remains alive, our memory will never fade. Out of a culture that practices democracy and self-determination, we embody the best of that society. We fail in that charge at our peril."

He looked up, staring down at the assembled Marines. Just for a moment, his eyes met Michael's and they seemed to share a moment of communication, of understanding. "We will not forget our brother, who gave his life so that we may live," Captain Stalker said. "Sergeant, assemble your men."

A Sergeant Michael didn't recognise stepped forward, followed by his platoon. Silently, in perfect formation, they marched apart and lined up on each side of the casket, producing their rifles and pointing them into the sky. Michael realised what was about to happen just before the Sergeant barked the first command and the rifles fired, so close together that it seemed that only one shot had been fired. The Marines fired a second volley, and then a third, before returning their rifles to their shoulders and picking up the casket. As a lone trumpet played, they carried the casket off the stage and out of the parade grounds.

"We will not forget," Captain Stalker said. His voice seemed quieter after the shooting. "You are all dismissed."

Michael followed Barr as he assembled the recruits and marched them back down towards the shooting range. Part of his mind realised that Barr wasn't giving them any time to brood, but he couldn't help thinking about the dead Marine…and about a tradition that had lasted for over a thousand years. Barr had made them study the history of the Marine Corps – somehow, he expected them to read massive volumes in their *abundant* spare time – yet it had all been dusty words, until he'd realised what the tradition *meant*. It would never die, not as long as men like Captain Stalker kept it alive.

"Here's to David," Blake said, as Second Platoon gathered in their barracks. "God rest his soul."

Jasmine took her own plastic glass and sipped the fine brandy carefully, enjoying the taste as it rolled off her tongue and down her throat. David Robertson's wake wouldn't be the grand carouse it would have been on the Slaughterhouse or a more mundane deployment, but he would understand. The brandy had been shipped all the way from Old Earth, which made the bottle Blake had produced expensive as hell. The Marine who had donated it could have sold it to the locals and made a fortune – in local currency, at least – but instead it had been preserved for a wake.

"God rest his soul," she echoed, as she took another sip. There was no hope of seeing another bottle like the one they were drinking until they returned to Earth, if they ever returned to Earth. The brandy was so far ahead of the local rotgut that it wasn't even funny. "May he always be remembered by us, wherever we may wander."

There was a long pause as the platoon drank, remembering the dead. Jasmine remembered being partnered with Robertson for a brief scouting mission back on Han, when she'd been the new shrimp from the Slaughterhouse, convinced that she knew it all. Robertson hadn't been interested in promotion, or graduating to become an NCO, but he'd been patient with the newcomer and taught her the tricks the Slaughterhouse had never shown her. Like the rest of the Company, he'd been her sibling in every way that counted, apart from biology. She would miss him.

She'd seen other Marines die, of course, but back on Han she hadn't had time to make friends with her new comrades before the shit had hit the fan. Afterwards, back when she'd woken up and discovered that she was a veteran, she had bonded with the rest of her unit, only to lose some of them when they were killed in action. It never got easier. Jasmine had hoped that Second Platoon would have a chance to crack some heads when the Civil Guard hit their own supply depot, but the Civil Guard had handled it themselves. She held them in contempt – they'd met far too many Civil Guard units that broke at the first sniff of enemy action – but she had to admit that they'd handled themselves well, once they'd realised that they'd been ambushed.

The brandy aftertaste was fading and she took another sip. The aftermath of the battle had been confusion incarnate, but once they'd realised that it was all over, the Marines had settled down to hashing out what had happened and assimilating the lessons – getting their stories straight, as Blake had joked at the time. It was never easy to put together what had happened during a battle, but a comprehensive picture had slowly begun to emerge. The Civil Guard had followed a predictable path and walked right into an ambush, one that had threatened to snare the Marines as well. The lessons had been hammered home by the Sergeants; take nothing for granted, they'd warned, and watch for advanced weapons that shouldn't exist outside the Civil Guard, or the Marines themselves.

Always learn from mistakes made by other people, her first Drill Sergeant had bellowed, after verbally tearing apart a particularly disastrous exercise. *It's much cheaper than learning from your own.*

"He saved my life during the Hangchow extraction," Blake said, slowly. He'd been a shrimp then too, but he'd grown up rapidly. "Without him, I wouldn't be here today."

"He used to play chess with me," another Marine said. "We'd spend some of our off-duty time playing together, competing endlessly for victories. We even invented our own form of chess and tried to market it on Earth."

Jasmine smiled slowly, sipping her drink as more stories emerged. One day, they'd give her the same wake, telling the new recruits stories about her life before she finally bought the farm. She wondered just how many of the young faces staring at her would be alive to see her off at her wake, or if they would all die together, going out in a blaze of glory. If nothing else, Han had proven that Marines could die just as easily as civilians, when their transports were hit by missiles and destroyed.

Blake poured the last of the brandy into their plastic glasses and threw the bottle against the wall. "That's the last of it," he said, quietly. It was odd to see him so subdued. "It's the local piss-water now."

Jasmine shook her head as the bottles were offered around. It had always struck her as odd that drinking wasn't discouraged in the Marine Corps, although rendering oneself unfit for duty was an offence against military order and heavily punished. If necessary, the Marines would inject themselves with sober-ups before they returned to duty, although the experience wouldn't be pleasant. Running the Gauntlet for being unfit for duty would be worse. She'd heard of Civil Guard units that had spent their entire tours in a permanent drunken stupor, and then had been surprised when all hell had broken loose in their sectors.

"Leave it," she said, and put the glass down. "I'll see you all later."

She stood up and walked out of the barracks, heading towards the shooting range. She had an urge to blow off as much steam as she could, yet there was no one in the practice ring who could give her a bout. The targets would have to face her wrath.

Edward watched one of his Marines heading to the shooting range, and then turned back to the communicator. "So the Governor didn't order your immediate arrest, then?"

"No," Major Grosskopf said. "I think he was a little scared of the public reaction after rumours of what happened to the Civil Guard started to leak out. We may not be entirely popular on the planet, but our soldiers do have friends and relatives in the cities. And we smashed a bandit ambush and killed or captured over two hundred of the fuckers. It's not all bad news, even if I did…exceed my authority."

Edward smiled at the understatement. He'd signed off – unofficially – on the Major's plan and had even stationed Marines nearby to help if Kappa Company had decided to try to fight rather than surrender, but he'd half-expected to hear an urgent message from the Governor demanding that he move to suppress a Civil Guard mutiny. That would have been awkward, to say nothing of placing both Grosskopf and himself in a very dangerous position.

"The bad news is that Smuts was definitely assassinated," Grosskopf added. "There's a good chance that we swept up the assassin in the purge and we'll get him when we pass him through the lie detector, but for the moment we've hit a blank wall…as far as anyone on the outside knows."

"The bandit we captured with the radio," Edward said. They shared a long look. Officially, no bandit leaders had been taken alive, or so they'd informed the media, knowing that it would get back to the right ears. "We were going to start interrogating him tomorrow."

"And find out if he knows who was behind this," Grosskopf agreed. "He has to be important if they trusted him with a radio."

Edward wasn't convinced of that – someone *important* would have known that the radio transmissions could be tracked – but he held his peace. "We'll see," he said. "How are your men coping?"

"Morale is surprisingly high after we invaded the supply dump," Grosskopf said. "I think we could probably turn the whole thing around in a few months, if we have the time."

Edward nodded. "I'll let you know what our friend knows once we're finished with him," he said. "And then we can decide what to do next."

CHAPTER THIRTY-FIVE

The dividing line between legal and illegal combatant is blurred and – like all other such principles – is effectively determined by the winner. Given the nature of the wars we fight, expecting an enemy to conduct themselves according to the Azores Conventions of 2052 is foolish. We can therefore define a 'legal' combatant as one who attempts to spare civilian lives, where possible, and an 'illegal' combatant as the opposite. The latter, under the Articles of War, have no rights whatsoever. This does not sit well with civilians – or, rather, it does not sit well with civilians who are isolated from the war.
-Major-General Thomas Kratman (Ret), *A Civilian's Guide to the Terran Marine Corps.*

Lucas sat back against the wall of his cell and tried to make himself comfortable. It wasn't easy. His leg had been firmly shackled to the floor and it could barely move, while a cold draft blew under the door and sent shivers down his spine. He was naked; the Marines, or perhaps the Civil Guard, had stripped him after he'd been stunned and then dumped him in the cell. Somehow, despite knowing about his backers, he found it hard to remain optimistic. He didn't know how they'd done it, but they'd somehow identified him as an important person. How much did they know?

The question ran around and around in his mind as he settled back, cursing the heavy chain under his breath. It was overkill – a short look at the door had told him that he wouldn't be breaking out any time soon – but it wasn't there to keep him imprisoned. It was there, he knew, to make sure he knew beyond a shadow of a doubt that he was a prisoner and his fate was completely in someone else's hands. Lucas had used similar techniques himself back when he'd been a gang leader on Earth, even before becoming one of the Knives, for the human psyche often refused to realise that a situation was truly hopeless.

He'd seen women, kidnapped from the homesteads, slowly fall into new thought patterns, ones that allowed them to remain sane in the face of sexual abuse from their new masters. The thought of someone doing the same to him – making him think that he was where he should be, no matter how much it hurt – was intolerable, yet he was no longer sure that he was sophisticated enough to resist it. He knew what they were doing… and it was working anyway.

He had no idea how long he'd been in the cell. It could have been bare hours since he'd been stunned and captured, or it could have been days or weeks. The single light, burning down from high above, never went out and there were no windows, depriving him of anything he could use to measure time. He'd tried to keep count of when he'd fallen asleep, yet he had rapidly lost track of time. The food supply, a handful of ration bars someone had placed in the cell along with a single water tap, didn't provide any clues. Besides, the ration bars tasted suspiciously like someone had made them out of shit. He'd heard stories of farmers in the outlying regions who had starved to death rather than eat ration bars on a regular basis. Just now, trapped in the cell, the stories seemed quite believable. He had had to force himself to swallow even a single bite.

His backers had failed to materialise, he realised, or perhaps they were in trouble themselves. There had been no way to conceal the fact that the Knives were deploying advanced weapons, weapons they could only have obtained from the Civil Guard, and their only hope of preventing investigators from drawing a line from their source to the backers was to kill the source before he or she could tell all. There was no hope that the source would remain silent, either; the Marines or the Civil Guard could simply have injected him with truth drugs, or perhaps they would have resorted to good old-fashioned torture.

Lucas had tortured men and women himself back on Earth and knew that anyone could be broken, given enough time. They could be building a case against him right now…and there was nothing he could do about it. He'd shouted, claiming his rights under the Imperial Charter and demanding to see a lawyer, but there had been no response. In many ways, that had been more frightening than an official thug entering the cell and beating the shit out of him. If his civil rights had been suspended…how much could they do to him?

I have things they want, he reminded himself, trying to remain optimistic. *I still have room to bargain…*

The door to the cell clicked loudly as it was unlocked. Lucas looked up as the door swung slowly open, revealing two men wearing unmarked black tunics. There was nothing to say who they were or which particular organisation they worked for, but they had to be soldiers. They held themselves in a military manner, although he couldn't have pointed to exactly what had tipped him off. They didn't show any fear of Lucas either. Of course, he reminded himself, with one leg chained firmly to the floor, all they had to do was remain out of reach and there would be nothing he could do to them.

"Well," he said, as the two men rapidly inspected his cell. He'd assumed that there were pick-ups in the cell as a matter of course, just to see if he said anything incriminating while alone, but perhaps not. "Are you going to take me to my lawyer?"

"No," one of the men said. His accent was very clearly not an Avalon accent, which suggested quite strongly that he was a Marine, rather than one of the Civil Guard. Lucas felt his blood run cold. He had allies among the Civil Guard, men who would risk their lives to save him rather than risk him blowing the whistle on their covert activities, but he had no allies among the Marines. For the first time, he realised deep inside that he might not be able to get out of the trap. "You have a different appointment."

The men finished their sweep of the cell and drew back. "Stand up," the leader ordered, "and place your hands on your head."

Lucas glowered at him for a long moment, and then reluctantly complied. It wasn't as if resistance would have gotten him anywhere. They could simply have hit him with a stunner and then dragged him wherever they wanted him to go. It was better to be awake and aware, he told himself; perhaps he would see something that he could use to leverage his escape. A moment later, one of the men moved behind him and cuffed his hands firmly behind his back. The cuffs were so tight that Lucas rapidly lost all feeling in his hands.

"You will come with us," the leader informed him, as he unlocked Lucas' chain. "Do not attempt to escape."

His companion took one of Lucas' arms and started to push him towards the door. Helpless, Lucas allowed him to keep pushing at him, looking around with interest as they stepped out of the cell and into a darkened corridor. It took him a moment to realise that he was looking at a prefabricated building; a *new* prefabricated building. His heart sank. The only place on Avalon that could be expected to have new prefabricated buildings was Castle Rock, the home of the Marines.

The warning was unnecessary, for Lucas had already realised that escape would be impossible. The building should have been a simple design, yet he lost track of just where they'd taken him very quickly, as if they were leading him through a maze. The corridors were so interchangeable that they could have been taking him in circles and he would never have realised it, or perhaps the building was larger than he had thought.

The only other prefabricated building he'd seen had been a colonist barracks, back when he'd first come to Avalon. It had been dingy and decaying; this one was new and apparently massive. Even guessing what they had done provided no relief. There was still no hope of escaping his captors, let alone finding his way off the island. He would have to remain calm and focused on the only chips he held. They were his only hope.

A door opened up in front of them on an unseen command and the Marines marched him into a small room. At first, Lucas thought they'd simply returned him to his cell, after giving him some demented version of exercise, but then he saw the chair that had been placed in the exact centre of the room. His escorts pushed him into it and secured his cuffs to the back of the chair; a second later, before he could do anything, they locked his legs firmly down as well. A band went around his throat, making even the smallest movements uncomfortable. He could barely move.

"Good work," a new voice said. Lucas blinked in shock. There had been other men in the room and he hadn't even noticed them in the shadows! Marines, it was rumoured, had enhanced eyes, allowing them to see in the dark like cats. Even if it wasn't true, they might well have far better eyesight than Lucas or any of the Knives, allowing them to fight in the dark as easily as fighting in daytime. "Let's see what we've got, shall we?"

The new speaker came into view, a tall man with short blond hair and an expression of cold, dispassionate fury that reminded Lucas of his first Gang Boss. That man had been as safe to play with as unstable explosives and had once ordered one of his whores to be lowered feet-first into a vat of acid for some imagined slight. Lucas had been terrified of the man and even when he had managed to carve out an independent existence for himself, thoughts of that first master still haunted him. The newcomer wore no insignia, yet Lucas was somehow sure that he was looking at the Marine CO. He held himself not only as if he expected to be obeyed, but as though the issue were completely beyond argument.

"You," Lucas said. It was hard to talk with the band around his throat, which made him wonder if they simply intended to execute him, rather than interrogate him to find out what he knew. Had they drugged and interrogated him in his sleep? "I want to deal."

"Yes," the Marine said. His voice was cold and flat, yet there was a hint of underlying amusement, as if he were a cat playing with a mouse. Lucas swallowed his pride and lowered his eyes, knowing that he couldn't afford to play his cards poorly. He had never been in so much danger in his entire life. "You want to deal."

He waited. Lucas wanted to out-wait him, but he didn't quite dare. "I have information that you need to know," he said, realising that there was no way he could out-wait the Marine. "I also know that you cannot interrogate me using drugs or torture. You have to bargain with me for the information."

The Marine smiled. "Really?"

Lucas shivered at the tone. "I have a nerve-burst implant in my head," he said. "If it detects that I am being interrogated by force, it will kill me and you will be unable to learn anything from my body. It is impossible to remove and…"

"We scanned your head when we brought you in," the Marine said. His smile suddenly had a very cruel edge. "You have no such implant. You have nothing, apart from a handful of colourful tattoos on your body and an Indent ID number tattooed on your ass. You have no way of preventing us from draining information out of your head by force."

His lips twitched. "As if a gang lord would have access to such technology," he said, mockingly. "I doubt that you were ever that important."

Lucas scowled inwardly, struggling against a tidal wave of despair. If Earth's Civil Guard had known who they had arrested, he would have been lucky to have been merely dumped on a hellish world with minimal supplies and no hope of survival. But they hadn't known and his records, of course, had shown him as just another indent, perhaps a little smarter and healthier than most. His few chips had been knocked from his hand.

"We know that you were important because you had a radio and were giving orders," the Marine said. Lucas flinched as he realised how easily he had been caught. "You know what we need to know, so we're going to make you an offer. Tell us everything – and I mean everything – that you know and we'll indenture you again rather than tossing you off a boat and leaving you to the dagger fish."

Lucas blinked. Being indentured again wouldn't be any fun, but it would hold the possibility of escape and a return to the badlands. It had to be a bluff, a cruel way of making him talk.

"I don't believe you," he said, stubbornly. "You're lying."

"I swear to you, upon the honour of the Marine Corps, that you will merely be indentured, rather than executed," the Marine said. Lucas heard the sudden shift in tone and realised that he was serious. "It's the best offer you're going to get, but…"

Lucas braced himself. Here it came. "You're hooked up to a lie detector," the Marine warned. "Lie to us once and the deal is off and you will simply be…disposed of, once we no longer need you. Start talking."

They had him in a bind, Lucas realised. He didn't understand why they hadn't moved to use the truth drugs at once, yet if their offer was sincere the Marine was right; it was the best offer he was going to get. His allies should have freed him, but it was becoming increasingly clear that they weren't going to be able to help him, let alone save themselves. They were expendable now. He gathered himself and mentally composed his words. Perhaps he could keep a few surprises in reserve.

"I came to this planet a few years ago," he began, "and…"

Edward listened carefully as the bandit – the supreme bandit leader, according to his testimony – started to talk. It stuck in his craw to make deals with such scum, but lives were at stake and truth drugs had their limitations. Even a skilled interrogator could miss something while digging into a subject's mind, for while drugs encouraged a person to be honest, the subject needed to be led to the right issues. He hadn't realised just what a gold mine had fallen into their hands until the man began to speak, but now…now he knew just what they were up against.

The Knives hadn't just been attempting to organise a government; they were working with elements of the official government, even before the Marines had arrived. Treachery on such a scale was appalling, yet it seemed to be merely the tip of the iceberg. Just how far did the rot go?

It was easy to accept that the Civil Guard had plenty of bad apples, for Edward was used to dealing with such issues. It was far harder to realise that at least seven senior officers had not only been subverted by the bandits, but had been actively assisting them. At least one reasonably honest officer had been assassinated, just to allow one of the corrupt officers to take their place and assist the bandits. A handful of bandits had even gone through Basic Training with the Civil Guard before deserting back to the badlands! It was unbelievable.

George will have to be warned, he reminded himself, realising just how dangerous the entire situation had become. It was far more than just another bandit plot; it seemed to him that the mysterious backers had managed to subvert part of the Civil Guard, giving them enough firepower to take over the Government. If they had intended to ambush and wipe out both Alpha and Beta Companies – along with the Marines – they would have controlled the single strongest military force left on the planet. With that, and their bandit allies, they could have taken over Camelot and declared themselves the new government. It should have had no hope of success but, with the Empire in such disarray, they might just get away with it.

"All right," he said, as the prisoner paused. He had told the truth – or, he had to remind himself, the truth as he knew it to be. His backers could have easily lied to him. A lie detector could only recognise a lie when the speaker knew that it was a lie. "I assume you knew who you were dealing with. Who were your backers?"

The prisoner looked up and paused, a faintly cunning smile spreading out over his face. "You'll never guess," he said, and named a string of names. The lie detector confirmed it. "I had half of the Council on my side from the very first day."

Edward felt as if someone had punched him in the chest. He had had his suspicions after realising that the heavy weapons could only have come from the Civil Guard, yet he'd hoped that he'd been wrong. Legally, he could do pretty much whatever he wanted to the prisoner, but it was far harder to deal with political leaders. It would require absolute proof to convict even one of them and testimony from a bandit leader, even under a lie detector, might not count. They would certainly refuse to be interrogated without a warrant and one couldn't be granted on such grounds.

"Shit," he said. He'd have to speak directly to the Governor. His authority could open doors, if he could be convinced to use it. Edward stood up and looked at the interrogators.

"Keep working on him," he ordered. "I want to know everything he knows by evening."

CHAPTER
THIRTY-SIX

It is an undeniable fact that Marines have been known to make life better wherever they go.
-Major-General Thomas Kratman (Ret), *A Civilian's Guide to the Terran Marine Corps.*

Jasmine stood outside Professor Caesius' house and contemplated the note in her hand. It had been delivered through Avalon's postal service and she'd picked it up at the spaceport, just before she and her platoon had been sent on leave. Or perhaps it hadn't been leave at all, not in the conventional sense; they'd been told to keep their weapons with them and their armour had been stored at a safe house on the edge of the city. It sounded as if Captain Stalker was expecting trouble and was placing his Marines in position to deal with it, yet it was unlike him not to warn them of what they might be facing. He'd even told them to have a good time on leave.

She read the note again, puzzled. It was simple enough; Mandy had invited her to visit when she next had leave in Camelot. Jasmine hadn't expected to hear anything from the girl; indeed, she hadn't *seen* the girl since the last time she'd been on leave and rescued her from being raped and murdered. It had taken a certain kind of courage for Mandy to write to her at all and she knew that it would have been disrespectful to allow it to pass, yet…what did she want? Despite herself, Jasmine seriously considered turning about and heading back to her platoon, before steeling herself and walking up to the door. She knocked firmly on the knocker and, a moment later, Mandy opened the door.

The girl had changed, Jasmine realised, or perhaps she was just seeing her without her fashionable make-up and perfume. Her eyes were just ever-so-slightly apprehensive as she realised that Jasmine had actually heeded her note, leaving Jasmine wondering just what she had wanted. None of the ideas spinning through her head seemed to make sense, even when Mandy smiled nervously at her. What did one say to a girl one had spanked a week ago?

"Come on in, please," Mandy said. She sounded rather more respectful as well, leaving Jasmine wondering just what her father had said to her after Jasmine had left her last time. "I wasn't sure when you would be coming."

"Your note did ask that I came on my next leave," Jasmine said, slowly. Mandy looked...as if she was working up to something bad. No, perhaps not something *bad*, but something she might be denied. "How are you feeling?"

Mandy's hand twitched, half covering her rear. "Weird," she said. "I've barely been out of the house since" – her face flushed bright red, in a manner Jasmine found rather endearing – "well, you know."

"I know," Jasmine agreed, patiently. She might not have had any kids of her own, but she had worked with enough teenage girls to know that the key was patience; they would come to the topic on hand eventually. The more awkward a topic was, the longer it would take. "Have you been focusing on your studies?"

"It's not easy to do that here," Mandy said, seemingly glad of the change in subject. "I was going to go to the University of Earth once I turned eighteen, but there is no university here and my father says that it will be years before one is founded, if it ever is. The most advanced school here is a technical school for the handful of engineers, and places there come with strings attached."

Jasmine could guess. Avalon had a permanent shortage of trained personnel in all fields, from medical care to construction engineering. They had the facilities to train new experts in any given field, but at the price of putting those new experts into debt, a debt that would be piled on their old debts. The relative handful of youngsters who grew up without debt wouldn't be keen on taking it on, not against such poor odds of ever escaping permanent debt. It was a badly flawed system. Children would get their mandatory eight years of schooling, as laid down by Imperial Law, and would then be cast off and ordered to find their own destinies. Avalon's population was therefore both literate and ignorant, a dangerous combination.

"I see," she said, finally. "You couldn't just pay in advance?"

"It's not just the money," Mandy said, flatly. "If I tried as an orbital engineer and passed the course, I would be expected to spend at least five years working where I was told to work, perhaps longer, at whatever wages they chose to give me. I spoke to a few people who did go through the technical school and they all warned me against it."

Jasmine frowned, studying Mandy carefully. It was obvious that she was building up to something, yet Jasmine didn't have the faintest idea of what it might be. She felt an odd wave of almost sisterly feelings towards the younger girl, yet she wasn't related to Mandy and the girl was certainly not in her charge. Saving her life once didn't actually make her permanently responsible for Mandy's future.

Mandy shook her head. "Thank you for saving my life," she said, nervously. "I didn't realise just what I was getting into until you pulled me out of it."

"And you didn't recognise what was getting into you," Jasmine agreed. If the girl had just wanted to thank her, surely she could have just written that on the note. "That is pretty much the story of the human race."

Mandy nodded. "I haven't been out of this part of the city since…you know," she added. "I just couldn't leave. It wasn't something I could do."

"So you came face to face with a danger and escaped," Jasmine said, wryly. "Just think about how many people aren't so lucky."

"And I wanted to thank you for…everything else as well," Mandy said, as if even getting the words out was a struggle. "I deserved everything you gave me."

Jasmine smiled in sympathetic understanding. "If it's any consolation, I got the same treatment or worse as a child myself," she said, seriously. "No one ever taught you real discipline. Your life among the middle class on Earth didn't prepare you for the real universe. I grew up on a world where children had to learn discipline from a very early age."

"My father said the same," Mandy said. "My mother doesn't know. She didn't even notice that I winced when I sat down. She's too occupied with her new friends."

She looked up, suddenly. "Would the Marines be willing to sponsor me through the technical school?"

Jasmine blinked. That *was* a reverse. "I have no idea," she said, honestly. She'd never heard of such a program, although she knew that the Corps did encourage newly-minted Marines to learn additional skills, ones that might come in handy on deployment. "What do you think that we can do for you?"

"I figured that I had to do something with my life," Mandy admitted. "Just before I sent you that note, I attended a party – no, don't worry, the party was in this district. I looked at the young men and women there, *really* looked at them. They were indolent, people who would never amount to anything in the future, just living off their parents. That could have been me."

"It is you, at the moment," Jasmine said. On her homeworld, children were encouraged to work from a very early age, even if it was just a tiny job. Money didn't come from nothing, after all, and learning to handle a budget had been an important step towards maturity. Mandy had grown up on a world where, even if her family ran completely out of money, they could just go on welfare and spend the rest of their lives at government expense. "Tell me something. Just how serious are you?"

Mandy looked up and met her eyes. "Very serious," she said. "I'll do whatever it takes to get into the school without going into debt."

Jasmine smiled. "I really wouldn't mention that to Blake," she said, dryly. Mandy flushed bright red. "If you're serious, I will mention it to my superior officers and see what they make of it. They may reject it out of hand. They may tell me to go back to you and tan your hide again. Still want me to mention it?"

Mandy's eyes went wide. "Do they know about…you…disciplining me?"

"They might," Jasmine said. "Sergeants know everything there is to know about their units."

Mandy's flush deepened. "They're going to be looking at me and thinking about it," she said. Jasmine snorted. It wasn't really that important. "Yes, please talk to them about it and let me know what they say."

Jasmine smiled. "I'll do my best," she said, "but you might want to remember something. If you make a deal with the Marines, you will be held to that deal, whatever it is. Do you understand me?"

Felicity Bardwell adjusted her dress before stepping into the bar, ignoring – with the ease of long practice – the wolf whistles from the young wolves who had gathered outside the bar. They would have been inside the bar drinking if they had had any money, yet without it all they could do was wander around the city, unless they had the nerve to sign up with the Marines. At other times, she would have been fearful for her safety, but since the Marines had arrived the city had become much safer. The gangs had pulled back rather than risk losing more of their thugs to the Marines.

She smiled nervously, trying to project the image of an innocent young girl stepping into a place of sin, even though everyone would know that it was a lie. Almost every teenage girl in Camelot, apart from those born to the upper class, had at least considered turning tricks for cash, creating a glut on the market. Felicity had always found that amusing, even though she had never prostituted herself until now. It was a step from covert intelligence gathering to actual operations and, despite herself, she was nervous. Everything could go wrong terrifyingly quickly.

The Governor would have been horrified to know just how deeply his city had been penetrated by the Crackers. The intelligence network – of which Felicity was a tiny part – had been watching the Marines ever since they had arrived and worked hard to identify as many as possible. There had been no way to access their personal files, but they were hardly needed; the Crackers knew which Marines could be approached safely and which ones wouldn't be interested. At least, unlike some Civil Guardsmen, they didn't seem to be interested in rough or sadistic sex.

She adjusted her smile slightly and headed towards a Marine who was standing at the bar, quaffing down beer as if it was going out of season. Up close, he was massive, far larger than she had realised from the photographs...and every inch of his exposed flesh was muscle. The media had been making snide remarks about Marines having muscles on their muscles ever since they had arrived, but Felicity was starting to realise that the newspapers – purely due to the laxity of the editors, no doubt – had actually gotten something right. Just for a second, she considered backing away and retreating. She didn't delude herself that she stood a chance if something went wrong.

The Marine looked down at her, taking in her dress in one easy glance. Felicity knew what he saw; a young girl wearing a sweater that exposed the tops of her breasts and a skirt that barely reached halfway down to her knees. Her dark hair fanned out around a heart-shaped face and a pair of lips that – in her own considered opinion – were very kissable. She saw the spark of attraction in his eyes and smiled at him, adjusting her position slightly to give him more of an eyeful.

"Hi," the Marine said. There was a note of confidence in his voice that she found oddly repulsive, before she realised what it was. He didn't think that he was God's gift to womankind, but he was very confident in who and what he was. "Can I buy you a drink?"

"I thought you'd never ask," Felicity said, with a glowing smile. He smiled back at her. "A single drink would be fine."

Their eyes met in silent communication as they found a table and sat down. Felicity had taken a stay-sober tab before entering the bar and the beer had little effect on her, but the Marine – his name, he'd told her, was Blake – kept drinking without showing any ill effects. Playing her prostitute persona, Felicity enquired lightly if he would still be able to perform when the time came and Blake assured her, with a wicked grin, that he was all man. Felicity giggled as they chatted for the next hour, neither of them keen to move too quickly. Under other circumstances, she could almost have enjoyed herself. The Marine was a far more fascinating person than she had thought, back when she'd planned this mission. Eventually, she stood up, walked around the table, and kissed him neatly on the lips. His arms went around her and she was suddenly very aware of his strength. He could have broken her in two without even trying.

"I have a place nearby," she whispered, trying to sound as seductive as she could.. "Would you like to come and have a drink with me?"

The Marine nodded, almost as if the issue *had* been in doubt. Felicity smiled and took his hand, leading him out of the bar and down the road towards the cheap accommodation that had been constructed years ago by a business owned by a Councillor. The quality was appallingly bad, but that would hardly matter…and besides, they served as excellent bases for intelligence gathering. They were kissing as they climbed up two flights of stairs – the elevator was not only out of service, but had been out of service for years – and his hands were roaming all over her as soon as they entered her flat. Strong hands reached under her shirt and clasped her breasts, massaging them lightly. She gasped as she felt her nipples respond to his touch.

"Go into the bedroom," she breathed, as his hands started to move down towards her skirt. "I'll be along in a moment."

She watched as he left, aware of the massive bulge in his pants, before reaching for the make-up bag she'd left on the table. It was easy to touch up her lipstick with a few brief touches, feeling her lips go slightly numb as the lipstick started to sink into the skin. If she hadn't taken the antidote a few hours ago, she would have been flat on the floor within seconds. The lipstick was a very powerful sedative.

"I'm coming," she called, as she pulled off her shirt. The lacy bra had cost more local credits than she cared to think about, but it would give him something to play with and to keep his mind off other matters. Smiling, she stepped into the bedroom and saw him standing by the edge of the bed. His eyes went wide when they saw her.

Felicity knelt in front of him, gasping slightly as his hands returned to her breasts, and started to unzip his pants. His member burst out as she pulled them down and she smiled, brushing her breasts against him. A moment later, she lowered her head and started to kiss her way down his penis, allowing the lipstick time to melt into his skin. His hands continued to play with her breasts as she kissed the way back to the top of his member and carefully took it into her mouth, sucking him as deeply into her as she could.

If he was affected by the drug, he didn't show it, leaving her wondering if he'd taken something to counter it himself. He'd drunk enough alcohol to flatten an elephant. He leaned back on her command, allowing her to suck him harder as his hands reached down inside her skirt. She gasped like it was good, like she was more aroused than she actually was, while her mind worked furiously. What if he was somehow immune to the drug?

He pulled back, pulling himself out of her mouth, and picked her up almost effortlessly, laying her down on the bed. Strong hands removed her skirt and panties, before his tongue started to lick at her, slipping inside her and making her gasp with genuine arousal. She had a horrified vision of him going on top of her, going inside her, just before he collapsed, but it was too late to escape. He climbed on top of her and slowly pushed his way into her. She held him tightly as he started to move inside her, feeling her own arousal building up to a climax, seconds before he shot his load deep into her. His face, bare millimetres from hers, went slack, just before he rolled off her and collapsed. His own thrusts had rubbed the drug deeper into his system.

"Thank God," Felicity said. The Marine hadn't been bad in bed, and under other circumstances she would have enjoyed herself, but if the drug hadn't worked so well…she had no illusions about the outcome. The Marine could have snapped her neck before he collapsed. She pulled herself off the bed and found the injector she'd placed in the bedside drawer, pushing it against his neck and injecting him with a stronger sedative. He should be completely out of it for at least a day.

She stood up and reached for her clothes. The rest of the cell had been waiting in the other flat. As soon as they arrived, they would have to start moving. She had no idea how long it would be before the other Marines realised that one of their comrades had vanished, but she was sure that the moment they realised, they'd start an intensive search.

The Crackers had to be long gone before then.

CHAPTER
THIRTY-SEVEN

> Throughout history, hostages have been taken in order to use them as bargaining chips. This only works as a tactic when the hostages are important enough for their lives not to be risked. It is therefore a known principle of Imperial Law that we do not bargain for the recovery of any hostages, although this principle has been ignored on occasion.
>
> -Major-General Thomas Kratman (Ret), *A Civilian's Guide to the Terran Marine Corps.*

It was the single tensest meeting that Governor Brent Roeder could remember. After a week of chaos – the bandit attack and the Civil Guard's sudden purge – the major players had finally condescended to talk to him about it, after the fact. Brent was old enough to remember when an Imperial Governor's word had been law, yet that certainty – like so many others – had fallen on Avalon. It galled – and worried – him that there hadn't even been a *sniff* of what the meeting was about, even from the Civil Guard. They were keeping it all very close to their chests.

He gazed from face to face. Linda was looking as calm and focused as ever, although he could detect an undercurrent of worry that manifested in her posture, ever so slightly tense. A person who hadn't known her for years wouldn't have picked up on it. Captain Stalker looked…grim and very determined, even though his face was a tight mask of perfect control. Colonel Kitty Stevenson looked oddly relaxed – she'd insisted on sweeping his office for bugs before the meeting began – which begged the question of just what was going on. And Major George Grosskopf, the commanding officer of the Civil Guard, was in a state of barely-controlled fury. It didn't bode well for the subject, or the outcome.

"Very well," Brent said, as they took their seats in front of him. He'd decided to remain seated behind his desk as a reminder of his position, even though he suspected that it was a waste of time and none of his visitors would be impressed. "You wanted this meeting, so…just what the hell is going on under my nose?"

The last line sounded weak and defensive to him, but if they noticed, they gave no sign. "Treason," Grosskopf said, flatly. "We are dealing with treason most foul."

Brent looked up, sharply. The formal phrasing hadn't escaped his notice. Treason most foul was a legal phrase used only when the safety of the Empire itself was at stake. Unlike other legal forms, it was rarely used outside of High Treason and never outside the legal profession. Brent, who had trained as a lawyer before entering the Civil Service, had never heard of it being raised. Treason was normally dealt with directly by the Grand Senate, the ultimate power within the Empire…under the Emperor, of course.

"Treason," he repeated, feeling dazed. He'd heard rumours, everything from a bandit attack that had slaughtered the Civil Guard to a planned coup mounted by Grosskopf or the Marines, but treason…? He hadn't expected treason. "Who has committed this treason?"

Grosskopf nodded to Captain Stalker, who spoke with clear precise words. "We captured over ninety bandits in the aftermath of the Battle of Morgan," Captain Stalker said. His voice was very calm. "One of them turned out to be the leader of the local super-gang, an organisation that controlled and directed the activities of many smaller gangs. His interrogation yielded a number of interesting facts."

"That was not the first clue we had that something was badly wrong in Camelot," Grosskopf added. "Alpha and Beta Companies were ambushed by bandits armed with modern heavy weapons, weapons that came out of the Civil Guard's war stocks…weapons, I need not add, that were never authorised for distribution outside the Guard. Those weapons caused the deaths of over fifty Civil Guardsmen and one Marine."

"Under a lie detector, he named seven people within Camelot who had been working with the gangs for at least the past five years, perhaps longer," Captain Stalker continued. Brent realised that he was being hit on both sides, suggesting that they'd planned the discussion beforehand. "Those people intended to set all three military units – Alpha Company, Beta Company and my Marines – up for slaughter. Their plan came alarmingly close to success."

Brent held up a hand before they could say anything else. "Who do you accuse?"

Captain Stalker met his eyes. "Councillor Sally Park, Councillor Frank Wong, Councillor Cole Smith, Councillor Markus Wilhelm and Councillor Carola Wilhelm," he said. "The other two named suspects are not members of the Council, but are closely connected to its leaders. One of them runs a supply company that has been used to transport weapons and supplies from Camelot and, in return, brings in women and stolen goods taken by the gangs. They are all guilty of treason against the Empire."

Brent felt his senses reel. "You can't be serious," he said, in disbelief. He could imagine any of the more troublesome councillors being ruthless enough to set the Marines up for slaughter, but actually dealing with the gangs…? "They wouldn't do anything of the sort."

"We were not *gentle*," Captain Stalker said. There was a cold fury in his voice that sent chills running down the back of Brent's neck. "We used lie detectors, and then we drugged them unmercifully until we were sure that we had the truth. There was not an iota of doubt left in the interrogators' minds that the few senior gang lords we had were telling the truth. They are guilty. They need to be arrested, now."

"They are also responsible, I suspect, for the death of Smuts, the former commander of the supply depot," Grosskopf added. "He was unquestionably assassinated, yet we have been unable to identify and locate his killer, even though we secured the base only a few minutes after he died. Our arrival could have been the sign to the assassin to act. We have, however, traced orders through the base's chain of command that resulted in delivering hundreds of thousands of credits worth of advanced weapons to the bandits."

His lips twitched humourlessly. "If nothing else, Governor, we will have to account for all that equipment when the Imperial Inspectorate checks their records and starts asking questions," he said. "Smuts committed grand theft on a massive scale."

Brent remembered Smuts, the son of a wealthy landholder who had been promoted into his position over the objections of the Civil Guard's last CO. The man had been both greedy and stupid, yet there had been no choice but to take him.

"Smuts," he repeated. "Are you sure that it was him?"

"Apart from him, everyone who could have issued the orders went into custody and through a lie detector test," Grosskopf said, impatiently. "Smuts was the one who issued the orders. We also uncovered several dozen corrupt officials, nine Cracker agents and a number of illegal gambling rings. Kappa Company may have to be disbanded completely. Their CO spent absolutely no time on training and apparently decided to keep the training budget for himself. Morale in the Civil Guard, I must add, is at rock bottom. First we get our heads kicked in by the bandits, and then we discover that the bandits were aided and abetted by one of our own."

He looked up. "Sir," he said, "I intend to seek the death penalty for the traitors. They should be arrested at once, before they can do more harm."

Brent sighed. They weren't going to like what he had to tell them. "We can't," he said. "We don't have the evidence required to sustain a charge of treason in a High Court."

"Nonsense," Grosskopf said. He waved a hand at the Marine, whose eyes had narrowed sharply. "We have the recordings of the interrogation, don't we?"

"That isn't enough proof," Brent said, tiredly. Just once, he wished he hadn't trained as a lawyer. Acting in ignorance of the law might well have worked…and it would certainly have been more satisfying. "The bandit might have been lied to and merely told you what he believed to be true, or someone else could be trying to set them up and get them off the planet. We could not arrest them under this evidence, let alone put them through a formal interrogation of their own. The Grand Senate's Edict on Treason rules that out."

He quailed mentally before their expressions. The Tyrant Emperor had been fond of using the treason charge to get rid of his enemies, for dealing with treason had been in the sole hands of the Emperor. In his brief reign, hundreds of inconvenient people had been rounded up, charged with treason on flimsy grounds, and summarily executed. He had terrorised most of the Empire into remaining silent, backed up by the New Men and their allies, until he had been assassinated by a lone gunman. In the wake of his death, the Grand Senate had moved to take treason charges firmly into their own hands, demanding a colossal level of evidence before a suspect could be arrested, interrogated and tried.

Any halfway competent lawyer would have been able to get them released once the case was put in front of a High Court. The Empire's legal system was so convoluted that it was possible to cite almost anything as a precedent, using cases of dubious relevance…or even none at all. The Empire's fastest-growing industry was the legal profession, and yet there would never be enough lawyers to cope with the demand. If it were handled badly, they might have been proven guilty at a later date…and they would still have to be freed.

"That is unacceptable," Grosskopf snapped. "We *know* they're guilty!"

"No, we don't," Brent said, wondering if he was about to be the first victim of a military coup. *If it happens*, he decided, *it happens*. "All we *know* is what we were told by a bandit, who might have only told us what he believed to be true."

"They killed a Marine," Captain Stalker snapped. His voice had risen sharply. "That is not a laughing matter!"

Brent lowered his eyes. "If we arrest them now, without proper proof, the rest of the Council will revolt against us," he said, sharply. "Avalon will grind to a halt. Their guilt has to be proven conclusively before we can move."

"We cannot be seen to let this pass," Grosskopf insisted, angrily. "The men in the Civil Guard are not exactly morons, *sir*! They know that the weapons had to come from our stores, even before I led the remains of two companies to secure the supply base. If we don't take steps, someone else might."

"And while we're tied up in political chaos, the Crackers will take advantage," Brent said. "Arresting them might bring Avalon to a halt."

"Perhaps I can suggest a compromise," Kitty Stevenson said, sweetly. Brent eyed her suspiciously. "We can agree that there are strong grounds to open an investigation, so perhaps that is what we should do. We are not, after all, required to notify them that they are the subject of an inquiry. When we discover the proof, we can ram through a suspension of their powers and arrest them before they can react."

"It is also possible that they have other allies within the Civil Guard," Grosskopf said. "I am organising wide-sweeping lie detector checks of my senior officers and I will not allow anyone to refuse them, unless they offer me their resignation on the spot. I strongly advise you to do the same, starting with the people closest to you."

He looked up at Linda, who smiled demurely back. "I have nothing to hide," she said, "but even asking people to undergo a loyalty check – and that is what it will be – is against the Imperial Charter. They did not agree, when they were hired, to undergo random tests to determine if they were loyal. We could not even legally ask for volunteers."

"Perhaps you should set a good example," Captain Stalker said. His voice was very cold. "Would you like to be the first person to be tested?"

Linda refused to flinch from his eyes. "I would have to refuse," she said, dryly. "You have no legal grounds to insist that I take a test."

Brent rubbed his temples, feeling a headache coming on. Linda was right; with techniques that could extract the truth out of a person, willing or not, there were strong regulations built into Imperial Law that governed when a person could be forced to undergo such a test. There had to be strong evidence of a crime, or a reasonably small body of suspects, and even then the suspect had to be tested in the presence of a lawyer of their choosing. It was intended to avoid abuse, yet it could be a burden at times. Military personnel signed away their right to refuse such a test when they joined up, but outside the military it was rare to have mandatory loyalty tests.

"If we don't uphold Imperial Law," he said, tiredly, "what are we?"

"In trouble," Grosskopf said. "I intend to complete sweeping through the Civil Guard and…"

He broke off as Captain Stalker's wristcom buzzed. "Trouble," he said, glancing down at it. "I'll be right back."

Edward strode into the antechamber, fighting to get his temper back under control. The urge to hit the Governor as hard as he could, right in the face, had been bubbling up ever since the man had pointed out that they *didn't* have a strong case after all. With a thousand years of legal changes, precedents and endless red tape, it would be harder than he had hoped to simply arrest them. *He* had every confidence in his interrogators, yet the Governor had none. They needed swift decisive action, not sneaking around and trying to produce the evidence that the Governor thought they needed to act.

"This is Stalker," he said, keying the wristcom. Gwen wouldn't have interrupted the meeting unless it was something truly important…and, after years of working with her, he trusted her judgement. Anything she couldn't handle herself had to be bad. "The area is clear; report."

He smiled at his own words. Kitty had told him, just before the Governor had returned to his office and greeted him formally, that she'd pulled no less than *nine* bugs out of the room. They had all been late-generation military-grade tech, which raised the question of where they had come from and who had emplaced them in the room…and why? No; the answer to that was obvious. Edward had learned the value of good intelligence over the years and it was too much to expect that the Council would have failed to learn the same lesson.

"Sir," Gwen said, "we have a problem."

Edward winced. The last time Gwen had spoken in that tone, it had been to inform him that the Company was being sent into action against the Nihilists without proper protection or support. It never boded well.

"Understood," he said, harshly. "What's happened?"

"Rifleman Blake Coleman has failed to make his scheduled check with his platoon," Gwen said. It wasn't – quite – going AWOL, but under the circumstances it was definitely a chewing out offence. "I attempted to raise him on his implanted communicator and received no response."

Edward swore. A communicator implant was impossible to ignore, unless a Marine had been so badly sedated that they would sleep through anything. He had bitter memories of being woken up after he'd picked up a girl for the night and being ordered back to his station, after some military emergency had broken out. If Blake Coleman had found a girl and gone to bed with her, it would have been a minor matter; ignoring his communicator was not. There was only one circumstance in which a Marine would be unable to reply…and that boded ill.

"Ping his communicator and get a location," he ordered. The implanted communicator would send back a signal and a DF system would track him down. "Once you find him…"

"I tried," Gwen said, sharply. "There was no response from his communicator at all."

He's been abducted, Edward thought, in horror. If Blake had been unconscious or even dead, his communicator would still have been able to send back a location pulse. He had to be somewhere where a communication's signal couldn't reach, which meant that he was in a secure room… or a travelling compartment. Either way, this wasn't a random kidnap but a carefully-planned assault.

"Recall all of the Marines on leave and get them to confirm their locations," he ordered. "Scramble the alert team from the spaceport – armour and all – and get them ready to go after him as soon as we track him down. Start looking at the last place we found him and…no, belay that; get his platoon mates to accomplish that. They'll be more motivated to find him."

"Yes, sir," Gwen said. "I'll deal with it right away."

"I'm on my way now," Edward said. If nothing else, it would provide a distraction from worrying about the Council. A direct attempt to abduct a Marine was hardly their style. It was far more likely that it was the other enemy faction. "Get in touch with the Civil Guard and start looking at how they might try to take him out of the city. We have to get him back before they take him to the badlands or even the outlying farms."

He mentally skimmed through the map of Camelot he'd memorised. There were only four roads heading out of the city. Perhaps they could set up roadblocks in time to be effective. He'd never had one of his people abducted before, but he knew the theory – and the Empire's policies on hostages. If they couldn't recover Blake Coleman in time, he would be deemed as expendable...

"Not on my watch," he vowed, checking his weapons. His bodyguard was downstairs, waiting for him. "Not this time."

CHAPTER
THIRTY-EIGHT

> The first twenty-four hours of a kidnap/hostage situation are always the worst. The kidnappers will want to get their hostage to a safe and secure location from where they can bargain for their hostage's life. The security forces, by contrast, will have the greatest chance of picking up a lead and locating the hostage before the kidnappers have a chance to make a clean break. This ensures that both sides are in a high state of nervousness and the hostage may be killed if one side panics.
>
> -Major-General Thomas Kratman (Ret), *A Civilian's Guide to the Terran Marine Corps.*

"Jesus, look at the size of him," Carl said, as he came into the room. "My masculinity is *so* threatened."

"Big guy too," Janice agreed. She wasn't looking at his height. "How did it feel going in?"

"Shut up and get the coffin in here," Felicity snapped. She was going to endure a lot of good-natured ribbing from the other Crackers for sleeping with a Marine, even though she hadn't had much choice in the matter. She had lured him to her apartment with the promise of sex and seeing he had inconsiderately failed to collapse before things could get that far, she'd had to go through with it. It was hardly the worst thing she'd done for the cause…and, besides, he hadn't been all that bad in bed. "Hurry!"

Carl nodded and opened the door, pulling in the massive metal box, clearly marked USED FOOD. For some reason, the Council had ruled that any spare food from the Farmer's Market had to be returned to the farms, rather than simply handed out to the poor or used as fertiliser near the city. It was yet another thing the Crackers intended to change, but for once it worked in their favour. Struggling, sweating and cursing, they moved the Marine's colossal body into the box and sealed the lid.

"Done," Janice announced, as she put a padlock on the coffin and locked it tight. Street thieves sometimes tried to steal the leftover food and had to be dissuaded, particularly now. The thought of one of them stealing the entire box and opening it, only to discover a comatose Marine, made Felicity smile. It would be rather less funny if he was awake at the time. "Come on."

Picking up the coffin, even between the three of them, wasn't easy, but somehow they managed to get it down the stairs to the van waiting outside. It was a local model, hired out – at exorbitant rates, of course – to one of the more distant farms, one run by a family who owed allegiance to the Wilhelm Family. If the Marines managed to trace their lost comrade that far the family – who had managed to alienate the entire district – would have to answer some tough questions from the Marines. It wouldn't be a pleasant experience for them.

"Get the van doors open," Carl ordered. Julia, who was barely twelve years old and undersized for her age, got out of the van and leapt to open the door. The thinking had been that a preteen girl would help divert suspicion away from them, although Felicity hadn't been convinced of the value of her presence. The Civil Guard could normally be bribed to allow the van to pass without being inspected – although, after the big shake-up a few days ago, even that was in doubt – but the Marines wouldn't be fooled. Julia might end up in a detention camp for small kids, even if they had to build one just for her.

Getting the coffin into the van was hard enough, but finally they managed to shove it into place. Felicity stepped into the rear of the van and picked up a small spray, using it to stink out the van. It wasn't an unpleasant smell to someone who had been born on a farm, but someone who was from the city who smelled it would recoil in disgust. It would certainly discourage an inspector from attempting to open the box. Her mind slipped to the makeshift weapons hidden inside the van and she winced. If the inspectors did try to open the van, the Crackers would have to take them out quickly and brutally…and that might be impossible.

The van's engine roared to life as she slipped into her seat. Carl took the wheel and guided them away from the apartment and out towards the city limits. She had no idea how quickly the Marines would react – or even when they would realise that they had a missing comrade – but she had a feeling that they needed to be out of the city as quickly as possible. They had worked hard to turn her rented apartment into one that might be used by a young student of the technical school – yet she had no idea how much of it the Marines would notice. They weren't from Avalon and it might not occur to them that she was dangling clues right in front of their faces. Irritatingly, they might miss the misleading trail completely.

"We're off," Carl said, with more cheerfulness than Felicity could muster. She was used to acting and playing a role, but this would be the hardest role of her life. "West Gate, here we come."

"Yep," Julia said, with a toothy smile. She'd been born on a farm and hated the city, claiming that it stank. The city-dwellers said much the same about the farmers. One of the reasons the Council refused to do much about the bandits, or so Cracker propaganda would have it, was because the city-dwellers generally disliked the farmers more than the bandits. It made little sense to her, so it was probably the right answer. The Council wasn't known for logic and reason. "We're heading home!"

Felicity said nothing.

Jasmine had been chatting about nothing to Mandy – the girl, she had decided, could be pleasant company when she wanted to be – when her implanted communicator had gone off right in her head, sounding the general recall signal. She had been halfway to the door before Mandy's mind had caught up with her eyes and the girl demanded to know what was going on. Jasmine gasped out an explanation, already preparing her body for the run ahead, and dove out of the door. She'd been a runner on her homeworld, years ago, but service in the Marines had honed her skills well past anything she would have believed possible. Running at top speed, she covered the distance from Mandy's house to the rendezvous point in bare minutes. A handful of civilians stared as she ran past, a pair of teenage louts making out as if they were going to try to trip her up. She clipped them hard enough to leave them with broken bones and kept running. One of her comrades needed her.

Gwen kept speaking through her implant, updating her on the developing situation. Blake was missing…and, worse, he was not answering his communicator. Jasmine knew that that meant trouble. Being late back to base was a minor offence, one that might be punished by washing out toilets or digging field latrines, but refusing to answer an urgent call was a far more serious offence. And, if his communicator didn't respond to a ping, Blake was clearly unable to respond at all. He might not be dead – or so she kept reminding herself – but he was out of it.

She ran around the corner, not even breathing hard, and saw Joe and Koenraad standing there, waiting for her. They wore civilian clothes, of course, but no one would have mistaken them for civilians, even without the weapons they had buckled on to their belts. Marines had automatic authority to carry loaded weapons anywhere, even in purely civilian areas. It was a precaution that Jasmine had never fully understood, until now. Whatever trouble Blake had run into hadn't been prevented by whatever weapons he'd been carrying, but his team-mates might still be able to find him.

"This is Stalker," a voice said, in her head. "Track his movements and see if you can locate him. Inform me if you find anything."

"Yes, sir," Jasmine said. The rest of the platoon, a quick check revealed, were still on their way. Jasmine doubted that they'd run into anything that three Marines couldn't handle, but it was well to be careful. "Blake was in that bar, trying to drink them out of horse-piss. We'll check there first."

She walked in as if she owned the place, one hand on her pistol. A handful of young bucks that had seen her civilian outfit and sweat-stained blouse took one look at the weapon and headed out in the other direction. Jasmine glanced around the bar, looking for possible threats, and then walked right over to the bartender. A number of customers decided that they had urgent business elsewhere and left at great speed. The room had probably never been so quiet since the bar had been opened.

"I'm looking for a friend of mine," Jasmine said, clearly. The bartender looked as if he would have liked to start running, but didn't quite dare. "A massive black man, very tall, very well built..."

"He went out with a girl," the bartender said, clearly relieved that she had asked a question he could answer. Jasmine scowled inwardly. What was it with Blake and girls of easy virtue? "She's one of the whores who have rooms in a nearby apartment block, where they take their men for everything they can get."

Somehow, Jasmine doubted that it was that simple. "Where does this girl...take her men?"

The bartender rattled off an address. Jasmine exchanged glances with the other two and they departed. She didn't think that he was lying, but if they found nothing, a team of Marines could arrest the bartender and put him through a formal interrogation. She had considered holding him prisoner, yet there was really no point. He couldn't take the bar with him if he ran from the city.

"A girl couldn't block his communicator," Joe said, as soon as they were outside and walking towards the apartment building. Even from a distance, it didn't look welcoming, as if it was permanently on the verge of collapsing and a single strong gust of wind would blow it down, smashing lesser buildings in its wake. "It's more serious than that."

Jasmine updated Captain Stalker and kept walking. If Blake was still alive, if Blake was there, they'd find him. If not, they'd find clues to his location. The search would go on as long as necessary. Marines didn't abandon their comrades, ever.

"Inspectors," Carl warned, as they headed out of the city. The Civil Guard normally established a roadblock on each of the four roads, if only to ensure that the farmers didn't take anything in or out of the city they hadn't bought legally, but this group seemed thin on the ground. The shake-up at the supply base must have been worse than the Crackers had realised. Perhaps it had been a wasted opportunity for an attack. "Remember, stay calm and we'll get through this alright."

The Civil Guard didn't bother waving down every vehicle that tried to get in or out of the city, but they normally checked out farmers and their vehicles. Felicity wasn't entirely surprised when the van was pulled over and forced to stop by the edge of the road. Two Civil Guardsmen, their faces untroubled by any alert from within the city, sauntered over, allowing the farmers to get a good look at the guns they carried. They wouldn't want to encourage any trouble if it could be avoided, but relations between the farmers and the Civil Guard had never been very good. It wasn't unknown for unlucky inspectors to wind up stabbed to death.

"Get out of the van and kneel down, hands on your heads," one of them ordered. Felicity shrugged and complied, watching grimly as Carl explained to Julia what she had to do. The little girl was treating it as a game, but it was one that could turn deadly serious at any moment. "This won't take a moment."

They were surprisingly professional as they ran their hands over Felicity's body, something that bothered her. She didn't like being groped, any more than any other girl enjoyed it, but a grope would have reassured her that she wasn't dealing with professionals who might obey any orders to inspect the van's contents despite the stink. Julia protested loudly as one of the Guardsmen searched her gently, until Janice warned her to be quiet and wait until it was all over. It was humiliating, but it was also as gentle as it could be, a far cry from some of the horror stories Felicity had heard. There had been one teenage girl who, after having been rude to a Guardsman, had been strip-searched – even including her cavities – in public, or so the story went. It could just have been propaganda.

"You're all clean," the lead Guardsman assured her. Felicity shrugged inwardly. Kneeling on the ground, she had the uncomfortable feeling that someone intended to shoot her in the head. "We'll just check the van and then you can be on your way."

He pulled open the van's door and recoiled. "Fuck me," he said, loudly enough for Julia to hear and giggle nervously. "What the hell do you have in here?"

"Rotting fruit," Carl explained. If he was nervous, he didn't show it. "The Council insists that we take it back for disposal."

"No wonder they all stink," the second Guardsman said, with a disdainful glance at Felicity. "The stench has gotten into their very skin."

Felicity felt her cheeks flush, but said nothing. "I think that that's just a way of keeping men like you off them," the lead Guardsman said wryly. He slammed the door shut and turned back to Felicity. "I think you can go…"

"But we have to inspect everything for the missing Marine," the second Guardsman protested. Felicity braced herself. If it all went to hell…

"There's no point," the lead Guardsman said. "If you want to go rooting through rotten fruit, be my guest." He chuckled. "I didn't think so."

He motioned for Felicity to stand up and relax. "You're free to go," he said. "Have a safe trip back home."

"Thank you, sir," Felicity said, as they climbed back into the car. She spoke the age-old blessing with genuine feeling. "May God bless you and your children and protect them from fear and harm."

She didn't breathe easily again until they were well away from the Guardsmen. "They know about the Marine," Carl said. "They could be tracking us now."

"And if they were, we'd be dead by now," Felicity said. "It's time to relax. We have a long drive ahead of us to the switch-over point."

Jasmine braced herself as they slipped into the apartment block and headed up the stairs. Her nose twitched as the stink struck her, a mixture of piss and shit and helplessness that reminded her of the worst she'd seen on Earth. Mandy had told her that her mother was making friends with people who wanted to learn about the latest fashions from Earth, yet they didn't want to hear the worst of the homeworld. If they had spent a few seconds in the Undercity, they would have been a lot less eager to have Avalon go the same way.

"In there," Joe subvocalised. Jasmine drew her weapon and moved into a support position as he inspected the door, and then picked the lock with a Marine multitool. The three Marines burst into the apartment, only to find it deserted. The scent of raw heady sex floated in the air, mocking her. "At least we know he was here."

Jasmine followed his gaze and saw the small pile of clothes on the floor. They matched the ones that Blake had been wearing before he'd left them at the bar. A quick check revealed that his personal weapon had been abandoned along with the clothes. Whatever had been going on, there was no sign of a struggle and only one thing would have made him abandon his weapon willingly. She noticed red stains on the bed and leaned over, relaxing slightly when she realised that it wasn't blood. It looked more like lipstick.

She pushed the matter out of her mind and activated her communicator. "Captain, we have located the apartment," she said, once the connection was established. "Blake was unquestionably here, but there are no clues that might lead us to his current location, at least none that we can see. We're going to need a WARCAT team out here."

"We don't have one," Captain Stalker reminded her. War Crimes Assessment Tribunals were rare outside sector capitals or major fleet deployments, yet at a pinch they could be pressed into forensic service and put to work as detectives. She rather doubted that Camelot had a local police department worthy of the name, not if they were using the Civil Guard to patrol the streets. "I've found two Marines who served as bodyguards to a WARCAT team on Han; they may be able to assist."

Jasmine winced. It was a long shot, at best. "Yes, sir," she said. She shared a glance with her team-mates, coming to an understanding without speaking a single word. "We request permission to carry on with our own search."

There was a long pause. She knew what had to be going through the Captain's head. Blake was already lost, perhaps beyond recovery…and risking three other Marines would be reckless, at best. Yet he, like all Marine officers, had come up through the ranks and he would understand her feelings. Blake was her brother and it was her duty to try to recover him – or his body – if it was possible. He would do the same for her.

"Permission granted," Captain Stalker said finally. "I'm diverting the remainder of your platoon to the spaceport, where they will pick up their armour before they meet up with you. Once you're armoured up, you have my permission to investigate. And good luck."

"Thank you, sir," Jasmine said. "We won't let you down."

CHAPTER
THIRTY-NINE

When held captive, according to the Articles of War, a captured soldier can only be asked for name, rank and serial number. It is well known, however, that most captors will ask more and back up their questions with proper interrogation measures, like torture. It is for such situations that Marines are trained to resist interrogation and, if it proves impossible to refuse information, to commit suicide at will.

-Major-General Thomas Kratman (Ret), *A Civilian's Guide to the Terran Marine Corps.*

"So we found nothing?"

"No, sir," Gwen said, solidly. "Second Platoon managed to follow a number of leads, but they all proved to be dead ends. The private eye we found" – Avalon might not have had a police department worthy of the name, but it did have a handful of private detectives – "suggested that most of the leads were intended to misguide us. The DNA traces found in the apartment could not be traced back to anyone in the database, apart from Blake himself, of course."

Edward winced inwardly. Blake Coleman, the report had made quite clear, had been seduced and then drugged. The Marines had treatments that were meant to counteract most sedatives and interrogation drugs, but there were limits, if only to allow medics to sedate an injured Marine. Blake had apparently not realised what was happening to him until it had been far too late, for the apartment hadn't been shielded and an emergency call would have been picked up, if one had been made. He'd never live it down after he was recovered – if he was recovered. Edward hated admitting defeat, but at the moment, Blake Coleman was a needle inside a very large haystack.

"It had to be the Crackers," he said. The Council's tactics had shown a degree of desperation that was lacking from the abduction. It had clearly been carefully planned and prepared. Their plan, he was starting to suspect, might have survived even if Blake had proven a tougher customer than they'd expected. Perhaps they'd watched the Marines, picked the one most likely to fall for the charms of a lady of easy virtue, and laid their trap. "He could be well outside the city by now."

"Unless that's what we're meant to think," Gwen pointed out. "They could have hidden him somewhere within the city."

"Yes," Edward agreed, slowly. There was no way to know for sure. Searching the entire city would be a difficult task, even if the Civil Guard helped out and the Governor raised no objections. He wondered if it could be used as an excuse to get inside the Council's different houses and peek around, but the Governor would never agree to that. Edward could sympathise with the man's position, but only up to a point. "I take it that all of the Company has been summoned back to their deployment positions?"

"Yes, sir," Gwen said, as if it had ever been in doubt. "First Platoon is at the spaceport, Second Platoon is working on the search and the remainder are on Castle Rock, waiting for orders."

"Good," Edward said. "We're going back to the Rock ourselves. Inform the officers that I am calling a full Council of War and invite the Civil Guard to send a pair of representatives. We cannot allow this challenge to pass unanswered."

"Yes, sir," Gwen said. She hesitated. "It is my duty to warn you that any hasty action we take may mean Coleman's death."

Edward nodded bitterly. The Empire – facing an endless series of insurrections on hundreds of different worlds – had evolved a code for dealing with hostage-takers. The hostage would be counted as dead, even if they'd kept him alive, and his abductors would face the death penalty when they were tracked down, after failing to use their captive to gain any advantage. The Company would pay no ransom, nor would they make any political concession, whatever else happened. The abductors could not be allowed to think that the tactic would work, even once.

And yet, Blake Coleman was one of his Company, one of the men under his command. He could not be abandoned, even on purely cold and pragmatic grounds, not when there were so few Marines on Avalon. They'd keep hunting for him until he was recovered, or until they located a body, but they couldn't allow his position to prevent them from taking any action. It was a precedent, Edward knew, that could not be set. The war on Avalon would only get worse if he allowed Blake's fate to affect his actions. He kept telling himself that…and yet, somehow it didn't make it any easier. A clean death would have been easier to handle.

"I know," he said. Gwen was just carrying out her duty. "We'll do whatever we can to get him back."

"Big bastard, isn't he?"

Gaby looked up at Doctor White, a pale-skinned man with reddish eyes. Unlike most of the other Crackers, Doctor White had been born in Camelot and graduated from the technical school, before discovering that Crackers were human too. He'd abandoned his position – and his massive debt, of course – to help one of the Crackers escape government custody and join them in their fight. He couldn't be allowed to fight directly – a trained doctor was too valuable to risk – but his services had proven invaluable over the years.

"Very big," she agreed. Blake Coleman lay on the table, his hands and feet firmly chained down and a metal glove covering one of his hands. It looked like one of the dungeons the Wilhelm Family was reported to keep under their mansion, where they tortured any of their servants who displeased them, a comparison that galled her. If it had been possible to treat the Marine with any dignity, she would have done so. "Is that a natural growth?"

"I think so," Doctor White said. "He's not a saner version of Giant Non, not as far as I can tell. Giant was a genetic freak from the Undercity, but this guy is merely at the peak of physical development, probably among the top point-one percent of humanity. There may be some genetic improvements in there, yet I'm inclined to think that he's a pure-blood human who has been training heavily since he was a teenager."

Gaby nodded. Giant Non had been an indent from Earth, a teenage boy with a massive oversized body – he had barely fitted into an apartment room – and the mind of a child. Despite his appearance, he had been gentle and kind to everyone and, unlike almost all of the other indents, had been well-liked by the farming population. No one knew how he'd ended up so large and yet so simple, although Doctor White had believed that he was the result of a genetic engineering program that had failed spectacularly. Giant had died four years ago and had been buried in a family plot, the highest honour that the farmers could bestow. He'd deserved it.

"He does have a number of implants within his body," the doctor continued. "There's one in his spinal cord, another one down in his pelvis, two in his head and one in the tip of his finger. I think that that one is actually an implanted weapon and so I've gloved his hand to prevent him from using it. The others…I cannot even identify, let alone figure out how to remove. I suspect that they will be booby trapped to make it impossible to remove them while keeping the Marine alive."

Julian looked up at him. "You don't even know what they do?"

"I can offer you a few guesses, if you like," Doctor White said dryly. "The equipment I have here is not exactly the best that Avalon has on hand. The Empire's medical tech is two to three generations ahead of anything Avalon can produce for itself. I cannot look inside the implants or figure out what they actually do, with what I have on hand. I cannot even tell you if one of them is a communicator of some kind."

Gaby frowned. "Are we sure that this building is safe?"

"We rigged it to block all signals," Julian said, shortly. He'd led the team that had carried out the work. "If anything can get a signal out of here, it's something as exotic as a neutrino generator and I doubt that even the Empire could implant one of those in a human body. Anything else should be unable to get a signal out of here."

"The weapons implant is an odd one," Doctor White said. "I think it's actually a nerve-burst implant, one that would cause instant death to anyone who was targeted at close range. The weapon itself is mounted in such a manner as to prevent any of the blast from striking the Marine himself, assuming that my theory is correct. I think we're looking at one of the most dangerous men on Avalon."

"Yeah," Julian said, looking back down toward the Marine. Gaby wondered, in a flash of insight, if he felt his masculinity to be threatened. It wasn't as if he was a weakling or a coward, but he wasn't anything like as strong as their captive. "He wasn't so dangerous that we couldn't capture him."

"We caught him with his pants down," Gaby reminded him. "I doubt that that trick will work on Marines in the field."

She looked back at Doctor White. "Can you awaken him?"

"Of course," the doctor said. "Are you sure that you want to be in the same room as him?"

Gaby narrowed her eyes. There were times when she found the over-protectiveness of her so-called subordinates irritating. "Do you think that I wouldn't be safe?"

"There are several implants of unknown capabilities within his body," Doctor White said. "We have no way of knowing what he could do. Escape is impossible…but what if he decides to blow himself up, along with the rest of us? It's quite possible."

Gaby dismissed his concerns with a wave of her hand. "Wake him up, Doctor," she ordered. "I will be here."

"Put on your mask," Julian said. Gaby scowled at him, but he was making sense. "We cannot let him see your face."

Doctor White pushed an injector tab against the Marine's head and injected him with a standard stimulant. Gaby watched with interest, wondering how long it would be for it to take effect. She'd had to use stimulants herself in the past, and had always enjoyed the rush of energy that had raged through her body. It was easy to see why there were people who became addicted to them.

"His vital signs are increasing," Doctor White said. "He should be awake…"

The Marine's eyes shot open and he glanced from side to side, his entire body shaking as he tested his bonds. He'd either realised that he was being kidnapped in the final moments of freedom or figured out the truth in microseconds after waking up. Either way, it was an impressive performance. She watched his muscles flexing and shivered inwardly, reminding herself to never go within arm's reach. He could break her apart like a twig.

"Good morning," she said, as the Marine relaxed on the table. It couldn't be a comfortable repose, but there was little choice. "Welcome to our lair."

The Marine's eyes locked on her. She felt a sudden chill running down the back of her neck, almost as if she were staring into the eyes of a furious Gnasher intent on tearing her apart and feeding her to its pups. The Doctor hadn't exaggerated when he'd said that the Marine was in peak condition. He looked like a human wolf among sheep.

"Blake Coleman, Rifleman, Second Platoon, serial number…"

"We know your details," Gaby said. She would have smiled at his expression, if there had been any point. "We want to talk to you about your fellow Marines."

"Go to hell," Blake Coleman said. There was no give in his voice at all. "Who are you people?"

Gaby exchanged a glance with Julian. Common sense suggested that they should tell him as little as possible, yet she knew that if he managed to escape, it would all be over anyway. His fellows would have figured out, by now, that he hadn't been kidnapped by mere bandits. They would have deduced that the Crackers had taken their friend.

"We are the Avalon Liberation Front," she said, calmly. "The planet's population generally calls us…"

"Crackers," Blake said. Gaby smiled inwardly. "I've been briefed on your people. You're just another bunch of terrorists seeking to wreck the planet, like so many others on so many other worlds."

Gaby felt a hot flash of anger that she firmly suppressed. Beside her, Julian took a step forward before she placed a hand on his arm, holding him back. The Marine, she realised with a flicker of quiet amusement, was trying to get them mad. Either he thought he could do something to them when they were close, or he wanted to die…it didn't matter. They couldn't afford to lose their temper with him.

"We are trying to free the planet from the shackles of debt imposed on people who never went into debt," Gaby explained, calmly. "We wish to talk to you about the true situation on this planet."

"You could just have asked," Blake pointed out. "I don't think you understand the Corps very well. They're not going to stop looking for me, even if you cut off my balls and send them to the Captain as a warning. My life became expendable the moment you managed to get me out of the city."

Gaby's eyes narrowed sharply. How the hell had he known he'd been moved out of the city? It wouldn't help him locate himself if he somehow managed to escape, yet it was alarming and a cold reminder that Blake Coleman was far from stupid. He might have been seduced by a young girl, but that proved nothing. The doctor had said that he was among the highest-rated human population. He might be far more intelligent than he looked. No, he *was* far more intelligent than he looked. No one could have survived the Slaughterhouse, according to the files they'd downloaded, without having a fair degree of intelligence.

"Your best course of action would be to return me at once," Blake continued, calmly. He didn't shout at them, or start screaming, like so many other men she'd known would have done. "At least you wouldn't be charged as abductors when we finally caught up with you."

"You don't get to lecture us," Julian snapped. He would have taken another step forward if Gaby hadn't caught him in time. "You're upholding an evil system and that makes you compliant in the system's evil. You're a prisoner of war and we can do anything to you, anything at all. We can even inject you with some of those truth drugs you Marines find so useful and see what you tell us."

The Marine snorted. "Nothing," he said. "Standard truth drugs won't work on me."

Gaby looked over at Doctor White, who nodded. "It's quite possible to immunise someone against truth drugs with the proper equipment," he said. "The drug would either have no effect at all, or he'd have a major allergic reaction and die."

"He could be lying," Julian pointed out. "And then we could always inflict pain on him…"

He broke off as the Marine *looked* at him. "Do you really believe that you can inflict more pain on me than my trainers did back at the Slaughterhouse?"

"I could have a damn good try," Julian snapped. "You're just a man."

"The recruits call the Slaughterhouse the Torturehouse, sometimes," Blake mocked. "On my third day there, we were lined up and used as punching bags for the upperclassmen, who needed to teach us how to take a punch. The bastard who punched me struck me right in the chest, and then in the jaw. I picked myself up and then he kicked me in the groin. By my third month, I had scar tissue everywhere but my eyes. I could take a blow to anywhere and keep going even without drugs. I saw recruits lose their legs in training and keep going, because the fighting doesn't end when someone gets a bloody nose. Do you really think that you can match that?"

Gaby wasn't sure if she believed him or not. The documents she'd studied had gone on and on about how Marine training imbued a new Marine with a tradition that stretched back over a thousand years, but they had been curiously silent on just how that miracle was achieved. The handful of reports she had read were…oddly elliptical, as if they hadn't wanted to say anything at all. It was almost as if the Marines had something to hide.

"I survived the Slaughterhouse without becoming one of the Slaughtered," Blake said. "Can I offer a suggestion?"

"No," Julian said.

"Go on," Gaby said, giving him a sharp look. "What do you suggest?"

"Open up lines of communication with the Captain," Blake said. "You might find that you can come to an arrangement. The Council may not be ruling Avalon for much longer and their fall would create a power vacuum, one that might allow you to find a role that didn't include fighting to liberate millions of people." His eyes narrowed. "Or are you just the kind of bastards who delight in inflicting pain and don't care who you inflict it on? I saw terrorists on Han mowing down their own people, just for supporting the wrong side. What would you do if you actually won?"

"I like to think that we'd find a way to live together," Gaby said. The interrogation wasn't going to go anywhere, which left them with a dangerous liability. "For the moment, you are our guest. Behave yourself and we'll take care of you."

Blake smiled. "Can I get out of these chains?"

"I'm afraid not," Gaby said. "And I am sorry."

"I'm sure that you are," Blake said. He sounded sincere, at least to her ears. "Believe me, though; you're going to be a lot sorrier."

CHAPTER FORTY

> A Council of War is only called when the CO feels that it is time to make a major change in strategy and consists of all the senior officers and NCOs in a given unit. Although the CO is under no obligation to accept their advice, it is generally considered politic to do so, once the Council has been called. In turn, the officers are obliged to speak freely and air whatever doubts they might have.
>
> -Major-General Thomas Kratman (Ret), *A Civilian's Guide to the Terran Marine Corps.*

"The first Council of War on Avalon is called to order," Gwen said, as the door was closed. "God save the Emperor."

"God save the Emperor," the guests said.

Edward smiled as he took the seat at the head of the table. Marine Councils of War were traditionally informal, although the presence of two Civil Guardsmen and Linda – who was representing the Governor – gave an odd air of formality, despite the cups of tea and coffee that had been placed on the table. He glanced from face to face, taking in his Lieutenants and senior NCOs. A wise Captain knew when to listen to his subordinates – and, also, when the subordinates had to be ignored.

"Please be seated," he said. "Are there any immediate issues that need to be addressed?"

"I spy strangers," Jared Barr said. Edward scowled inwardly. "Why are they here?"

"Because they were invited," Edward said, patiently. He had expected the objection from Barr; Drill Sergeants had a far stronger sense of tradition than any other rank. Marine Councils of War were generally Marine-only, with lesser units only being told about decisions after the fact. "They are welcome here."

He tapped the table when no one else raised any objections. "It has been a day since Rifleman Coleman was kidnapped," he said. Gwen and a handful of others already knew, but the remainder had to be informed and updated on the progress of the search. "We have been unable to locate him and suspect that he may have been taken out of the city entirely. His communicator implant has either been blocked or removed."

"It would have to have been blocked," Doctor Leila Lopez said. The Marine doctor met his eyes unflinchingly. Every Marine had some degree of medical training, but those who trained specifically as battlefield medics were among the most respected of the Marines. Edward had seen her perform surgery under fire on Han. "I doubt that they could remove the communicator without triggering the safeguards and killing their captive."

"Unless they have tried and killed him, explaining why we have not received a ransom demand," Lieutenant Howell growled. "They might not have realised the danger in time."

"We will proceed on the assumption that he is alive until we have some reason to believe otherwise," Edward said. "So far, our mystery abductors have played it very smart; the kidnap shows a degree of planning that was missing when the bandits attacked the Civil Guard. I believe that the abduction was carried out by the Crackers and that they are finally emerging from hiding, now that they have our measure."

"They don't have our measure," one of the Sergeants said. "If they had, they would have dug themselves a deep hole and hidden in it."

Edward shrugged. Over the weeks before the Marines had arrived, the Crackers had mounted a harassing campaign against the Civil Guard and the Planetary Government, a campaign that had come to an abrupt halt when the Marines had arrived. The Governor had been grateful for the peace, but Edward found it ominous. It suggested that the Cracker leadership had a far greater degree of control than he had thought possible. The peace might just be the calm before the storm.

"Regardless, we must face up to the fact that we now have twin problems to deal with," he said. "We hit the bandits so hard that they may not be able to recover for years – at least to the point where they can pose a major threat to law and order – but their backers remain in place, at least for the moment. We need to watch and wait for an opportunity to deal with them, while we must also move against the Crackers before they can capitalise on the Civil Guard's sudden weakness."

Major Grosskopf looked uncomfortable, but didn't dispute Edward's statement. The Civil Guard had been badly demoralised and parts of it were coming apart at the seams. Hundreds of officers, fearing what might happen if they were interrogated, had handed in their resignations or simply deserted, heading back to their powerful patrons and begging for shelter. Several units that should have been able to put up a fight had been discovered to have been starved of training time and equipment and could barely be rated a cut above civilians. The best units had held together, but they'd taken heavy casualties when the bandits had launched their ambush and their morale wasn't particularly good. Ironically, given a few months, the Civil Guard might become stronger than it had ever been…if they had those months.

"They may already realise that they have a window of opportunity and Rifleman Coleman's abduction might simply be the first shot in the resumed campaign," Edward continued. "I therefore intend to force them on the defence and take the war to their territory as soon as possible."

He looked over at Barr. "Sergeant Barr," he said, "what is the current status of the training companies?"

Barr looked uncomfortable. "We've spent eight weeks ramming them through a very basic training course," he said. "Half of them would probably not survive the first month at the Slaughterhouse, but they're definitely above most of the Civil Guard units; if nothing else, they have fewer bad habits to unlearn. I wouldn't rate them as anything above basic infantry – apart from a handful who would benefit from advanced training – but we have been pushing them hard and the chaps have responded well. It helps that they made pretty much every mistake in the book during combat training and learned from them."

He smiled. "And one makeshift company managed to pass Kratman's Hill," he added. "They did very – very – well, although I couldn't tell them that too openly. I've known people who went through the Slaughterhouse who wouldn't have done so well."

Edward smiled. "Was that through care and attention, or a lack of imagination?"

"I think they took the lessons to heart," Barr said. "If you're asking if I think they're ready to qualify as Marines, the answer is no; they don't have anything like the level of training that was hammered into us over the two years we spent at the Slaughterhouse. They have weaknesses that would rapidly see them discharged from a standard Marine platoon and their level of ignorance is terrifying. They would make good infantrymen, but not good Marines."

"We could not brand them as Marines anyway, not without passing them through the Slaughterhouse," Edward admitted. If communications were reopened between Avalon and the rest of the Empire, he'd be able to recommend some of the local recruits for the Slaughterhouse, allowing them the chance to earn Rifleman's Tabs of their own. "But as part of the new Army of Avalon, they'd have a chance to earn real honours."

"Yes, sir," Barr said. "They need practical experience and the only way to get that is to actually go out on patrol."

"That does lead to another question," Howell said. "Do we give them a Last Night?"

"I hardly think that we should deny them the chance of taking part in a grand old tradition," Gwen said, with an evil grin. "What are we going to give them in place of a Rifleman's Tab?"

"A Knight," Edward said. He glanced over at Howell. "The fabricators we brought along can produce individual badges for each of the new soldiers. They won't be Rifleman's Tabs, but one day they will be as famous."

"The Knights of Avalon," Grosskopf said. He smiled in droll amusement. "I like it."

"Good," Edward said. He stood up and stepped over to the map on the wall, his finger marking out small towns and homesteads. "Once the new recruits have graduated, we're going to establish bases here, here and here. The Civil Guard stopped patrolling that area because they kept coming under heavy attack; we're going to go there and dare them to do their worst. They will either have to attack us or accept that we are in a position to impede their activities. Once we get established, we will start offering help and support to the locals."

His eyes swept around the room. "It's not going to be easy," he said. "We cannot offer them – yet – the one thing that will win us their hearts and minds. We can offer quite a bit, including paying for everything in cash, whatever the Council may say. I expect everyone to remember the ultimate rule of counter-insurgency warfare; softly, softly until we are hit…and then give them hell.

"We'll partner with one of the Civil Guard units and maintain joint patrols," he continued. "As new recruits graduate, we'll add them into the patrols and keep sweeping upwards towards the Cracker strongholds in the Mystic Mountains. We will keep applying pressure until we can separate them from their people, the source of their support. I do not expect to win quickly, but I do expect to win. Now…"

He smiled. "The floor is open," he said. "What do you all say?"

On a command from Barr, the recruits were summoned from shooting practice and ordered onto the parade ground, where they stood to attention. Michael, wearing the stripes of a Training Corporal, led his platoon into the ground and lined them up in order, very aware that if the Sergeant inspected his men and found anything wrong with them, it would be Michael who got his ass chewed out for it. There were times when he loved being a Corporal – although he'd been warned that a Training Corporal had no authority over graduated Marines – and times when he hated the responsibility. Being publicly humiliated for his own mistakes was bad enough, but being publicly humiliated for someone else's mistakes was dreadful.

And yet, he'd been taught that Marines looked after one another and supported each other. He'd learned how to check a person's battledress and weapons, while trusting them to perform the same check for him. The lessons and tests – including some he suspected had been designed for them to fail, on the grounds that they learned more from failures than from successes – had hammered trust and cooperation into them. A test where they had each been given part of a map – and, to add to the confusion, half of them had been given false maps – had been insolvable until they'd compared the maps and realised that they'd been misled. Barr hadn't been too impressed by their complaints, pointing out that false intelligence was part of the game and they shouldn't take anything on trust.

On command, the recruits snapped out a salute as Captain Stalker strode onto the parade ground. He was wearing his dress uniform, which meant…he didn't know what? The last time they'd seen him in dress uniform had been during the funeral, but no one else had died. There were no black banners or armbands in evidence. The Captain stepped up on the podium and stared down at them, his face carefully composed.

"It has been eight weeks since we accepted your applications and brought you to Castle Rock," he said, calmly. "During that time – and the tests beforehand – we weeded out the ones we felt would be incapable of completing the course." Michael blinked. How had he missed that? Far more recruits had come to the spaceport than he'd seen on Castle Rock? Had a few hundred of them been rejected, or gently urged to wait until the next time? "You have all completed the course."

His voice darkened. "If it were up to us, we would have given you a far longer training period," he continued, "but it is no longer up to us. We have decided that you have all graduated and are ready to take up positions in the Army of Avalon."

Michael felt a burst of pride…and then fear. The training course had been harsh, but there had only been a handful of accidents and only two of them had been fatal. Back on the Avalon mainland, deployed as part of a unit, they would be shot at with live ammunition and perhaps killed. The Crackers – the ones who had interfered with food supplies to the cities often enough, threatening his family with starvation – had to be put on the defensive. He couldn't think of anything else that required the Marines to graduate the first class ahead of time.

"Recruit Ted Aardvark," Captain Stalker said. "Step forward."

Michael watched as the first recruit stepped forward, allowing Captain Stalker to pin a silver badge on his collar and welcome him formally to the army. Recruit after recruit stepped forward in alphabetical order to receive the badge. Michael felt his stomach churning as his turn finally came and he stepped up, convinced that he would trip over his own feet. Captain Stalker shook his hand and pinned the badge on his collar, before smiling at him and pushing him towards the group of newly-graduated soldiers. Looking at him, Michael realised that he had gone through it himself and knew exactly how Michael felt about graduating.

He studied the badge as soon as he could, surprised that Barr hadn't immediately called them back to order. It was small, about the size of a ten-credit piece, with an etched image of a knight on horseback waving a lance in the air. If it was like a Rifleman's Tab, it would have been made for him personally – a check revealed that his name had been etched into the underside of the badge – and would include a tiny amount of medical information on a hidden chip inside it. He knew the Marine traditions surrounding their Rifleman's Tabs and hoped – knew – that the Army of Avalon would develop similar traditions. Their mentors had taught them well.

"Form ranks," Barr bellowed, at volume. Training took over and Michael found himself in line before he realised quite what was going on. "Present...arms!"

Michael's body clicked into position and he held his rifle at the ready. It dawned on him suddenly that he had not only passed his hump, the moment when all the torment and effort of the training course suddenly became worthwhile, but that he was also a graduated soldier. His mother would be so proud of him...and he liked to think that his father would have been proud, if he had any idea of what Michael had achieved.

"Congratulations, all of you," Barr said, once Captain Stalker had returned their salutes and left. "You will be transported to Camelot, where you will have twenty-four hours on liberty and then report back to the spaceport for deployment orders. Remember that one of us was abducted from the city and take extreme care of yourselves. Look after your buddies and remember…you're in the Army now and you represent it to the world. Good luck."

He dismissed them for the final time, urging them to make their way towards the landing strip to board one of the transport aircraft. It would only be the fourth time that Michael had been on one – he'd been up twice to in the course of parachute training, where he'd been tossed out of the aircraft with an automatic parachute – but it no longer felt strange. The training camp on Castle Rock felt…smaller, somehow, and then he realised why. He had surpassed it. He touched the badge again and smiled, tiredly. It had all been worthwhile.

The trip back to the city passed in a blur and, before he knew it, he was standing with his platoon outside a bar. "Come on," one of the new soldiers said. "Let's go show off."

Michael smiled again, realising that he was still carrying his rifle. He hadn't noticed that no one had made any attempt to take it away, for they were now allowed to carry arms anywhere, unless ordered otherwise by a senior officer. If the uniforms they wore weren't enough of a deterrent to any thugs who might want to rob them, the rifles – and the fact they knew how to use them – would put off all but the suicidal. He checked his pockets and produced a handful of coins.

"Why not?" He asked, as he led the way inside. The smoky interior of the bar was just like coming home. The thought reminded him that he would have to visit his mother at some point and reassure her that he was fine. Barr's old phase, the one he spoke at every mealtime, rose up in his mind and he smiled. "Eat, drink and be merry, for tomorrow we may die."

The platoon chuckled as they reached the bartender and ordered drinks. Michael took his pint and gazed around the bar, wondering why it looked so…strange now. When he'd been younger and he'd earned some illegal money, he had often spent it in bars…or on cheap prostitutes, for there had been little else to spend it on. Now…he had plenty of money, yet he didn't want to waste it all. God help him…had he grown up over eight weeks?

He caught sight of a group of upper-class boys, slumming it in a lower-class bar, and smiled inwardly. Once, he would never have dared pick a fight with them, for their parents controlled the Civil Guard and could make him suffer for anything he did, even if they started it. Now…now the power was elsewhere; it was no wonder the Council hadn't wanted to encourage the Marines to seek more recruits, or even to expand the Civil Guard. The skills they had been taught on Castle Rock would work just as well against the Council, perhaps better.

They're scared, he thought, and took another sip of his beer. It was an odd sensation. *They are scared of me…*

CHAPTER
FORTY-ONE

> An insurgency, in contrast to any other military force, is limited by the nature of the war it fights. It must operate on a decentralised command structure, yet it must somehow also maintain a coherent force and a coherent military objective…or it will fission apart and eventually become little more than a bandit gang. This weakness is easy to exploit with luck; breaking one cell can lead, given time and proper interrogation methods, to another cell, breaking the entire network – hopefully.
>
> This does not, of course, address the fundamental issues that gave birth to the insurgency in the first place.
>
> -Major-General Thomas Kratman (Ret), *A Marine's Guide to Insurgency.*

The sky was dark, lit only by bursts of lightning that flickered out in the distance, followed rapidly by the noise of thunder, echoing off the mountain peaks. Gaby hunched down and pulled her coat tighter as cold rain washed down from high above, turning the mountainside into a nightmarish muddy swamp. Streams of water ran past her and down towards the lakes, feeding into rivers that wandered down towards Camelot and the sea. The Mystic Mountains had storms fairly regularly throughout the year, often enough that this one would pass unnoticed. They also made the perfect hiding place for the Crackers.

Only a few hundred humans lived in the Mystic Mountains and most of them were isolationists who had moved there to get away from the ADC and, later, the Government. They built themselves huts, helped each other out when required and otherwise kept themselves to themselves. The area produced little of value and so the Council was barely aware of its existence. A handful of tax inspectors had tried to make their way up into the mountains and had never been heard from again. Gaby believed that they had been killed by the Mountain Men, who defended their homes from all possible enemies, but it was just as possible that they'd been caught up in a storm and swept away. The Mystic Mountains had their own weather system and sane people tried to stay away from it. Only a handful of climbing fanatics would challenge some of the higher peaks.

I guess I'm insane then, she thought, as the rain broke, just for a second. The sky remained as black as ever and it was impossible to accept that it was the middle of the day. The heavy clouds would restart the downpour soon enough, but as long as they remained overhead the Crackers should be fairly safe from orbital observation. The Marines, or so they had been warned, had deployed their own orbital observation satellites high overhead, models far superior to anything the ADC had deployed on its own. If they were good enough to track individuals through the storm, the Cracker Rebellion was on the verge of being defeated, whatever they did. Answering the summons to the conference would have identified them to the Marines and signed their death warrant.

She smiled wryly as the hut came into sight, half-hidden among the massive timbers that covered the mountain. Once, when she'd been in hiding from a Civil Guard sweep, she'd spent a few months in a similar hut, the reluctant guest of one of the Mountain Men. He'd told her, in the few moments he could bear to stand with her, that the trees were dug in so deeply that even the worst storms couldn't blow them over, helping to keep the soil in place. The hut was literally worked into the forest, using their strength to hold it in place with the trees. The younger Gaby had fantasised about the hut growing out of the trees, but the older wiser woman she'd become knew better. It was still a fascinating sight, if not one someone who lived in a city would have understood, or appreciated.

The skies opened again as they staggered towards the hut and she walked faster, cursing the rain under her breath. Despite the coat, she was soaked and knew that her two bodyguards would be in the same condition.

It was hard to keep focused on the hut as the rain grew stronger, with the wind blowing cold sleet directly into her face, but somehow she made it.

The solid wooden walls of the hut rose up in front of her. She pressed herself into them gratefully, before finally finding the door and stepping inside, careful to keep her hands in view at all times. The Mountain Man who owned the hut might have been one of the few who were willing to take an active hand in the struggle, but he still had the attitudes of his fellows, including a certain degree of paranoia where visitors were concerned. Unexpected visitors rarely meant well.

"Welcome," he growled, after checking her face. "Your friends have already arrived. Spare clothes are in that pile there."

He turned and stalked out, barely able to tolerate her company for more than a few seconds. Gaby shrugged and started to undress, pulling off the sodden coat and clothes gratefully. Whatever body modesty she'd once possessed had been lost long ago, living hand to mouth while avoiding Civil Guard sweeps. Her bodyguards did the same, although they allowed her to dress first and leave them to finish changing in peace. If it were a trap, as Rufus had pointed out when they'd received the message, they were dead anyway. She picked up her clothes and took a few moments to place them in front of the fire, in hopes that they would dry before she had to make her way back down the mountainside, and headed into the main room.

The Mountain Men had no access to the planet's electric network and relied upon burning wood and natural gas for lighting. It cast odd flickers of light over the faces waiting for her, five men and two women, the heart and soul of the Cracker Rebellion. The damage wreaked upon the network by the Imperial Navy – not the Civil Guard; never the Civil Guard – had fragmented the movement, forcing them to develop a cell structure that would prevent another disastrous defeat. Gaby was aware – Rufus had pointed it out, in exaggerated detail – just how dangerous it was to meet openly with her counterparts, even in one of the most inaccessible places on the planet. The Marines might have tracked them and could be waiting, even now, to swoop down on the meeting place and scoop them all up as prisoners.

"Welcome," one of the men said. "We did not intend to call a meeting on such short notice."

There were few names in the movement's upper ranks, although Gaby was fairly sure she knew who at least three of them were in their civilian roles. She tried not to think about that. Unlike their Marine prisoner, she had no implants or immunisations that prevented her from being interrogated. She certainly knew nothing about the locations of their bases, or fighting strength, or anything else that might be useful to their hunters.

And there were times when being Peter Cracker's granddaughter had its advantages.

"I did not intend to spend two days travelling from where I was to here," Gaby said, tightly. The new clothes felt uncomfortable against her skin and she was aware, too aware, that she looked like an overgrown scarecrow. "Your messenger said that it was important."

"It is," one of the women said. "We have received two pieces of disturbing news from Camelot."

Gaby scowled inwardly. The different subsections of the Cracker Rebellion had their own intelligence sources within Camelot, officially so that if the Civil Guard cracked open one spy ring, others would remain untouched. It was something that annoyed her, for good and timely intelligence was often delayed before it was passed down through the network, which opened up its own risks. The more people who knew a given secret, the greater the chance that the Civil Guard and the Marines would know it as well…and be able to use it to identify the source, opening up the risk of false information being passed down the link. There were times when she envied the Marines and their ability to operate openly. If the Crackers had been able to act in the open, the war would be over by now and they would have won.

"Our source is very well placed within the Governor's office," the other woman said. "The source became privy to a disturbing piece of information. The recent smashing of the bandits near Morgan" – there were some amused looks; the Crackers had never cared much for the bandits, knowing that they would have to be wiped out when Avalon gained its independence – "led to them uncovering links between the bandits and certain of the upper personages within Camelot and the Council. They were effectively using the bandit movement as a tool in their political struggle. They even gave them advanced heavy weapons to use against the Marines and the Civil Guard."

Gaby felt as if someone had punched her in the chest. She had known just how corrupt and unfeeling the Council was, how it manipulated local politics to their best advantage, but she hadn't realised that they were capable of running the bandits. It made no sense at first…and then it dawned on her. The bandits, just by their mere presence, kept the townships and homesteads scared, unwilling to commit themselves to the Crackers or even to start their own resistance groups. The Crackers had little penetration near the badlands, if only because of the bandits…and all of a sudden, she saw the shape of a plan that someone had carefully put into place, using the lower elements of society to keep the vast majority of the population under control. No wonder the Civil Guard had never been able to wipe out the bandits. They'd been carefully hobbled right from the start.

"The evidence of this was found by the Marines and brought to the Governor's attention," the woman continued. "The Marine Captain branded it high treason and demanded that the Governor deal with the matter, but so far the Governor has refused. We cannot place any faith in the Governor to deal with this matter."

"As if we ever could," one of the men muttered.

"I see," Gaby said, slowly. She would have to consider the implications carefully and discuss them with Rufus and Julian. "And the other piece of news?"

"The Marines graduated their first class of new recruits three days ago," the woman said. "It is their intention to deploy forces out into the countryside and challenge us directly, hammering away at our support network. This is a challenge we cannot afford to turn down."

"Of course we can," Gaby said. She would have smiled at their expressions, but she was too tired. "We pulled in our horns once the Marines landed and waited to see what they would do. Apart from the abduction stunt, we did nothing to incur their wrath."

"That alone probably puts us on their shit list," one of the men said. "They don't leave their fellows behind."

"We are strong when we are not losing," Gaby said. "Let us pull in our horns and let them make their patrols in peace. They will lose interest eventually and we can regain lost ground."

"It may not work out that way," one of the women said. "The Marines have been creating a new Army of Avalon, one that is far more…motivated than the Civil Guard, for they have been paying their new soldiers in cash. Assuming they continue to churn out new units, they will be able to rapidly deploy thousands of infantrymen to the countryside and shift the balance of power permanently against us. The Marines may be recalled to some other world within the Empire, as the Imperial Navy starship was recalled, but the Army of Avalon will remain, building up its fighting power and intelligence links. They may possess the ability to defeat us.

"Worse, the Civil Guard has been going through its ranks and uncovering many of our spies, cutting off links that we have cultivated for years. They may soon cleanse themselves entirely of our intelligence sources, leaving us blind, while they also dispose of their corrupt officers and even their incompetents. They may soon become a far more dangerous enemy, one that knows the ground upon which they fight. How long will it be before they start paying their men in cash too? It will motivate them like nothing else."

"And the locals will respond to that," one of the men said. "They may feel closer to the new Civil Guard."

"Particularly if we do not terrorise the local population into supporting us," another man said. "Perhaps we should use fear on those who might waver."

"No," Gaby said, flatly. She had no words to express how disgusted she was. "If there is anything that will ensure our defeat, it is convincing the local population that we are a clear and present danger to them, far more than the debt sharks and the Council's stupid laws. They will betray us to them and scream for them to wipe us out as dangerously insane terrorists – and they will be right."

There was a long pause. "You have a Marine prisoner," one of the men said. "What have you learned from him?"

"Very little," Gaby admitted. "We have been unable to get much out of him, beyond name, rank and serial number. He did suggest reaching out to their Captain and trying to see what we can work out…"

"The Marines are compliant in a system that holds the entire planet in bondage," one of the women snapped. "How can we trust them?

"It gets worse," she added, a second later. "My source was quite specific; they offered the captured bandits indenture in exchange for information and, so far, they have not moved against the Council or the network of lower-class scum who work for them. There are brothels staffed by women taken from the townships…and nothing has been done about them, even about the preteen children used as sex slaves! How can anyone argue that the Marines are here to make things better?"

"It seems that we have a choice," one of the men said. "We can do as she suggested" – he nodded at Gaby – "and pull in our horns, offering no resistance…or we can fight. If we fight, we risk losing; if we pull in our horns, we risk losing."

"We might win," one of the other men said. "Am I the only one to be encouraged by the fact that visits from Imperial Navy ships are few and far between?"

"No," Gaby admitted. She took the steaming mug of hot chocolate she was offered and sipped it gratefully. "My cell has been working on a plan to take advantage of the Civil Guard's weakness and hit Camelot itself. A long drawn-out war is not in our interests."

"A battle in the open is not in our interests either," one of the men pointed out. "A Marine Company possesses more firepower than we have been able to amass, even with help from our other friends."

"Assuming that they have a chance to deploy it," Gaby agreed. Operation Headshot had been planned to minimise the effects of Marine firepower. It had originally been designed to take on the Civil Guard, but Rufus and Julian had updated it to counter the Marines as well. It was risky, but the sheer nerve of the move might stun the enemy, if she decided to risk it. "We remain, I see, caught between the devil and the deep blue sea."

"Yes," one of the men said. He glanced from face to face. "Shall we vote?"

"Yes," another said. "All those in favour of challenging the Marines and their new army, raise your hands."

Gaby counted, quickly. Six hands were raised in favour. "I do not feel that this is the best idea," she admitted, "but we have little choice. If the Government is unwilling to respond to actual cases of high treason on the part of its supporters, we must assume that they never will and that things will never get better. It looks as if we're going to war."

The hut shook slightly as a particularly strong gust of wind caught it, sending pebbles crashing down on the roof. She glanced up, despite herself, and then looked down into the flickering fire. She wouldn't live permanently among the Mountain Men, even if the alternative was death or permanent indenture. Perhaps, at bottom, the Marines would understand; Avalon was her home and she would fight for its freedom, for they hadn't given her another path. Independence or autonomy. Either one would be far better than rule by a weak Governor and a corrupt Council.

Two and a half hours later, she pulled on her damp clothes and rejoined her bodyguards, heading back down the mountain. The rain had abated slightly, allowing them to make better progress down towards the little town in the hollow, even though it was merely the first stop on their long trip home. The entire population of the town, such as it was, took absolutely no interest in anyone else's business. The Crackers were fairly safe there, as long as they didn't bring down the Marines on their heads. The inn they'd booked for the night would have a warm bath, a comfy bed and then they could start making their way back to their base. Behind them, the others would be doing the same, heading back to their own cells. The Marines might smash one without smashing them all.

Just as they reached the hollow, the clouds started to break up, allowing the sun to shine down on the mountains. Gaby looked back, smiling as the sunlight warmed her face and hands, casting the mountains in a whole new light. They looked almost as if they had come out of a fairy tale. Their name had been well chosen.

And they hid their secrets well.

CHAPTER FORTY-TWO

There is a very old saying that runs something like this. You can bomb a patch of ground, burn it, coat it with chemical weapons, poison it, irradiate it and destroy it...but you don't own it until you have a man with a rifle standing on top of it. In dealing with counter-insurgency, it is important to remember that the insurgent will have freedom of movement wherever that man with the rifle is not.
-Major-General Thomas Kratman (Ret), *A Marine's Guide to Insurgency.*

"So," the Marine said. She was wearing her armour and it was hard to tell that she was a woman, or even that she was human at all. Michael looked at her and felt very exposed in his battledress and helmet. "Have you ever driven one of these babies before?"

Michael followed her pointing finger to the LAV, an armoured vehicle that managed to look intimidating even without the roaring lion someone had painted on the side of the machine. He'd been told, back when they'd been taught how to drive, that the vehicles were capable of standing off all light weapons and many heavy ones, but they didn't provide full protection against plasma cannon or heavy antitank weapons. They'd also practiced leaping from the vehicle and deploying while under fire, something he wasn't looking forward to trying in real life. The LAV might have been designed to specifications that had been tested in battle time and time again, but he found it hard to trust it.

"Only in training," he said, somehow unwilling to admit that he'd never driven anything more complex than a cycle bike before joining the army. There were few privately-owned vehicles on Camelot, although most of the farmers owned vans and produce trucks. "I don't think I was very good at it."

"You'll only get better with practice," the Marine said. She pointed him towards the hatch leading into the driver's seat. "Get in there and start the engine."

Michael complied, ruefully aware that while he might have been granted the provisional rank of Corporal, he wasn't in charge of the unit. The Marines had pushed a handful of their own people into temporary command ranks until the Army of Avalon produced its own officers, something that he'd been warned wouldn't happen for at least a year. He had hoped that training and evaluation would be over now that they had graduated – he touched the silver badge at his collar to remind himself – but he had rapidly been disabused of that thought. They would be evaluated and judged for the rest of their careers.

The driver's seat was more comfortable than the ones in the vehicle's passenger compartment, although that wasn't saying much. Unlike the interior passengers, he could at least see out of the vehicle, allowing him to see where he was going. It wasn't a perfect view and went a long way towards explaining why they'd been warned never to operate LAV vehicles without either AFV or infantry support. A single sneaky enemy with an antitank rocket could get into firing range and destroy them before they saw it coming. He keyed the command switch and started the engine, smiling as he felt it rumbling into life.

"Come onboard if you're coming," the Marine bellowed, urging the platoon to scramble to get into the LAV before it departed, leaving them to explain themselves to the post commander. "Let's move!"

Michael nodded. The base had been rapidly constructed near the spaceport itself, allowing the newly-minted soldiers a chance to learn what it felt like to march through civilian-occupied areas. He had learned rapidly that something that looked threatening might not be…and something that wasn't threatening might be a nasty surprise, just waiting for one of them to step on it before detonating. They'd run through exercises over the last few days in a deserted village, play-acting encounters, conversations and enemy attacks. He had never felt so capable and yet so scared. A single mistake could have disastrous consequences.

The Marine pulled herself alongside him and winked. "Not too shabby," she said, as the hatches banged shut and were checked, and then checked again. A loose hatch could become deadly in a battle situation. "Shall we depart?"

Michael reached for the wheel, and then shook his head. "No, sir," he said. 'Sir' seemed to be the default for Marine officers, male or female. "We haven't been ordered to leave by the convoy's commander."

"Good," the Marine said. Michael realised with a flush of embarrassment that it had been another test. "I'm afraid that it's just going to be hurry up and wait now. The more things change, the more they stay the same."

"I see," Michael said. Marines were encouraged to be informal, but surely there were limits. "Can I ask a question?"

"You can ask anything you like, although I don't promise to answer," the Marine countered. "Didn't your Drill Sergeant beat that into you?"

Michael nodded. Barr had told them, time and time again, that if they didn't understand something, they had to ask and ask again until they understood. The Marines hadn't been interested in training up rote automatons, but soldiers who could actually think, and plan, and understand the reasoning behind their orders. The mission they'd been given was actually a case in point. They were being deployed away from Camelot to threaten the Crackers and challenge their control over the countryside. It was almost certain, they'd been warned, that they would come under fire.

"A question, then," he said. "Why are there swords included in the weapons package we've been given?"

The Marine grinned, her face completely transformed by the smile. "Did no one tell you?" She asked. Michael shook his head. "Those are not swords. Those are Zombie Decapitation Devices."

"Get away," Michael said, automatically. "There's no such thing as zombies?"

"And how do you know that?" The Marine asked, dryly. "On some planet in a faraway sector, there was a Marine Regiment stationed there for some leave when suddenly the dead kind of rose up from their graves. They rapidly ran out of ammunition and had to resort to hacking the dead apart with swords. After that, they became part of the standard weapons package and had to be included in every deployment, just in case it happened again."

"I don't believe you," Michael said. "It's a joke, right?"

"It's hard to say for sure," the Marine admitted. "You know that every battle the Marines have ever taken part in is studied endlessly on the Slaughterhouse? There are very few sealed records, but the records relating to that particular deployment have been very carefully sealed. There are quite a few odd stories from deployments out along the Rim, so I wouldn't be so quick to dismiss it as impossible."

She grinned. "And besides, it makes for a few good stories," she added. "Now…"

The radio buzzed. "LAV-4, this is the CO," a voice said. "Follow LAV-3 out of the complex, keeping at least ten meters between your vehicle and theirs. Acknowledge."

"Acknowledged," Michael said, keying his radio. He gunned the engine as LAV-3 moved out ahead of their vehicle, heading towards the gate and the great outdoors. Slowly, carefully, he followed LAV-3 and passed through the gates. The whole world opened up in front of him.

"Easy on the acceleration," the Marine warned, as the military convoy turned onto one of the roads leading up away from the city. "We don't want to crash into another vehicle. I've seen convoys take hours to cross ten miles merely because the drivers hadn't had time to practice driving together."

Something crossed Michael's mind. "The Crackers are going to know that we're coming," he said, as they passed a group of farm vans heading down to the city. "They're going to have plenty of time to prepare an ambush."

"Yep," the Marine said, with a grin. "Hang on to that thought. It will keep you alert."

Michael looked up at her, and then returned his gaze to the road ahead, suddenly feeling very exposed. Anything could be out there, waiting for them.

Jasmine watched the young soldier's face and knew that it was sinking in. No one who hadn't spent any time in the countryside could grasp, intellectually, just how large it was. Experienced soldiers hated the thought of MOUT – Military Operations in Urban Terrain – yet fighting out in the countryside could be just as dangerous. They were horrifically exposed in their vehicles, escorts or no escorts, and she had little faith in the drones or satellites to pick up something truly dangerous. She kept her eyes on the road and silently blessed the workers who had cut the foliage well back from the tarmac. It would be hard to launch an effective ambush, even if they did somehow force the convoy to come to a stop.

The trip passed slowly, but she kept alert, knowing that she had to set a good example to the troops. Marine Companies were generally over-officered compared to the Imperial Army, but then the Imperial Army rarely operated in less than Regimental strength. Captain Stalker had had to spare some of his officers to mentor the soldiers Barr had picked out as POM – Possible Officer Material – and even some of his Riflemen, like Jasmine herself. It had crossed her mind that it was an attempt to distract her and the remainder of Second Platoon from worrying about their missing comrade, but that wasn't a Marine tradition. They could lose someone to death or abduction, yet they would still have to carry on. Wherever Blake was, he would have to take care of himself.

It was possible that he would escape, she told herself, although it would require luck or a mistake on the part of his captors. If they bought into the 'Marines-as-Supermen' myth, they'd have him chained down and probably drugged. Given time, the implants in his body would help him build up an immunity to whatever they were giving him, but by then they'd probably decide to release him, kill him or attempt to use him as a bargaining chip. Jasmine knew the rules as well as anyone else; there would be no negotiations. The thought ran round and round in her mind. They couldn't allow Blake to be used as a bargaining chip.

She scowled as she tapped her helmet, linking into the live feed from the drone high above. There was no sign of anything that might threaten them…but then, there had been little sign of anything when the bandits attacked, either. If the bandits could get access to weapons from the Civil Guard, why couldn't the Crackers do the same? Or, perhaps, get weapons from off-world. Before the Marines had arrived, the handful of orbital systems in orbit around Avalon could hardly have detected a single shuttle landing somewhere in the hinterlands. A hidden mortar, set to fire on automatic, or perhaps even home-made rockets…they'd suffice to slow the convoy and delay the operation. If she was in command of the enemy forces, and there was no reason to believe that the Crackers were stupid, that was exactly what she would do, if only to damage morale.

"Keep your eyes on the road," she warned, as the driver's eyes began to slip. There was only so much training could prepare a new recruit for, and a tension-filled drive through hostile country, every nerve on alert, wasn't one of them. "You never know what might happen if you take your eyes off the vehicle in front."

Under other circumstances, Gavin Patel's little hiding place was used to hunt for birds, mainly the ducks and other waterfowl that used the lake beside the road as a resting place. The ADC had introduced them to the local ecosystem and they'd taken to it like a duck to water – quite literally, in their case. Now, he lay in the hide and peered down towards the road, watching and waiting for the first military vehicles to come into view.

The road itself was a remarkable achievement on Avalon. It had been ordered by the ADC and constructed over the years by indents and, later, by conscripted farmers and indebted slaves. It had survived the years surprisingly well, even though the farmers rarely bothered to do any maintenance work and the only people who did were indentured work gangs marched out of Camelot for a few days and then sent back to their normal working habits. It was the work gangs that had turned the young Gavin into a Cracker, after one of the indents had gotten free and cornered little Sabena Patel in a field. His sister's death had radicalised him as nothing else could have, pushing him to join the Crackers and launching a series of attacks on indent work gangs. They were nothing more than brutes in human form.

A flash of light alerted him as the first military vehicle appeared in the distance. It was a small AFV, bristling with machine guns and observation ports, suggesting that it could fire in multiple directions at the same time. The part of Gavin's mind that had once hoped to be an engineer was impressed with the simplicity of the design, even as the rest of him hated its existence and mere presence in his territory. The next set of vehicles came into view and he identified them as transports, each one capable of carrying up to twenty soldiers. He counted them rapidly and concluded that over three hundred soldiers – counting the drivers of the AFVs – were heading towards Sangria. Three hundred soldiers would be more than enough to dominate the area and impede Cracker operations.

"Damn you," he muttered, as he keyed his camera and started to take photographs. All of the Cracker leaders he had met had been keen on gathering intelligence, but his cell leader was positively obsessed with collecting everything, even information that seemed to have no bearing on the war. The camera alone meant certain detention if he were caught with it, particularly once they saw the pictures he'd taken, but she had insisted. "We'll fix you all, one day."

Once he'd finished taking pictures, he slid away from the hide, pausing long enough to set the anti-personnel mine he'd emplaced to help conceal his secrets. If someone stumbled across his nest, they'd be in for a nasty surprise before they died. Taking a last look towards the advancing convoy, he turned and headed down towards the town. It was time to blend in with the townspeople again.

Behind him, he heard the first shots ringing out.

Michael, despite himself, had been losing his concentration when the first bullets slammed into the LAV. The sound of them pinging off the armour jerked him back to full wakefulness, clutching the steering wheel as if his life depended on it. The pinging sound didn't fade as someone hosed the convoy with bullets, but there was no danger, not yet. Shamefaced, he concentrated on steering, waiting for orders from the CO.

"Just a machine gun, perhaps two," the Marine said. She seemed unbothered by the shots, but then, she'd been in far worse positions. "I think it's just their way of welcoming us to Sangria."

"I feel so loved," Michael growled. His heartbeat was pounding madly in his ears. "I think they don't love us very much."

"No," the Marine agreed. Michael muttered a curse under his breath as he saw a bullet strike the ground ahead of the LAV, sending up a spurt of dust from the road. "Do you blame them?"

"All units, this is the CO," a voice broke in. "Hold your course; I say again, hold your course. There's no reason to panic."

"Unless, of course, the bullets are meant to distract us from the minefield up ahead," the Marine said. "Or perhaps we're meant to go charging into the undergrowth after them and running right into a field of fire. We've used both tricks in the past ourselves."

The sound of shooting suddenly ceased. "They've stopped," Michael said. "Do you think they ran out of bullets?"

"They could have done," the Marine said. She nodded towards the steering wheel. "Keep focused on driving down into the town and leave the overall situation to the CO. It's what he's paid for. You're paid to drive and command a platoon, nothing else."

Michael gripped the steering wheel so tightly his hands went white. "I've got a lot to learn, haven't I?"

"Yep," the Marine said, with a grin. "On the other hand, you are smart enough to realise that you have a lot to learn. You'd be surprised how many soldiers never realise that, before it's too late."

An hour later, they drove into Sangria.

"They weren't deterred," Julian said. "They kept coming and took up a position in the town."

Gaby shrugged. The images Gavin had taken had been carefully studied, although he had overestimated the enemy strength. They had 'only' two hundred and fifty soldiers. The odds hadn't improved that much, although the missing fifty soldiers would be sorely missed by the enemy CO.

"Did you think they would be deterred?" Rufus asked, dryly. "We just sprayed a few bullets at them. They get more of a threat from their own training exercises."

Gaby held up a hand before they could start arguing. "We wanted them to know that they wouldn't be unopposed," she said. She hadn't been keen on the idea, but she'd agreed to it to prevent the young hotheads from going and doing something stupid. They had wanted to greet the military convoy with a hail of fire, just incidentally exposing themselves to the enemy. The Marines and their new recruits would have torn then apart. "Now they know that, it's time to start hacking away at them and keeping them on their toes."

"Of course," Rufus agreed. His hand traced out the new positions on the map. If the source in Camelot could be trusted, the Marines would be running out new bases daily, daring the Crackers to come out and fight. "When do we start?"

Gaby scowled. "Tomorrow," she said. "That should be long enough to get all of our people in place."

CHAPTER
FORTY-THREE

To understand just how poorly the educational system of the core worlds have failed their subjects, it is necessary to realise that of the children who go through the system, over half of them are unable to read, write or handle basic math. They are ill-prepared to work at anything other than brute labour, let alone handle complex issues like voting and galactic politics. The erosion of the Empire's skilled workforce has contributed to the decline in the Empire's industrial infrastructure.
- Professor Leo Caesius, *The Waning Years of Empire* (banned).

"So you're finally in command of a full-scale military deployment," Leo said, as he was waved into the War Room. He wasn't entirely sure why Captain Stalker had asked him to meet him there, rather than in his office or somewhere in Camelot, but he had to admit there was a certain kind of fascination about it. The historian in him looked at the big table, with the detailed satellite map of Avalon's largest continent lying on top, and saw history in the making. "How does it feel?"

"Stressful," Captain Stalker admitted, studying one of the deployments on the map. "The urge to move forces around on the map is overwhelming."

Leo smiled. He'd studied areas of history where the leader, often a man isolated from reality by a sycophantic court, had believed that the map truly *was* the terrain. It might have worked where magic was concerned, but military deployments didn't happen by magic, even though he knew that members of the Grand Senate believed otherwise. At least

Captain Stalker seemed free of that particular delusion, even if he was chafing at the bit to get out and see some action.

"I never realised just how badly it affected the Colonel, or the Lieutenants who were rated as Not Suitable for Independent Command," Captain Stalker admitted, looking up. "They found themselves in places where they had to give orders, and then sit back and wait for their subordinates to bring them victory or defeat. I would probably never have seen anything like this level of authority if I'd remained on Earth or the Core Worlds and all of a sudden I want to abandon it and go chasing Crackers personally."

Leo nodded. The urge to go after danger, rather than getting the hell out of its way, was something that he would never understand, but it was part of Captain Stalker's character. Marines were Riflemen first and foremost, something that had made no sense to him until he had seen them in action. They were trained to stand between the civilised universe and the barbarism that threatened the survival of the Empire. It was hard to be optimistic, particularly for him, for he was aware of just how badly the Empire was falling apart, but as long as men like Captain Stalker existed, the Empire would not die.

"Not that I can, of course," Captain Stalker added. "The sum of my success is that I am now trapped on Castle Rock while my subordinates go out and take it on the chin for me."

"If this works, the Empire may assign more Marines to the planet," Leo suggested. "You might find yourself outranked and back in the front lines."

"I doubt it, not with the Empire in such a state," Captain Stalker said. "It's far more likely that we'll end up being recalled or sent somewhere else that needs a fireman deployment."

He shook his head and led the way out of the War Room, into his office. "There's been little enemy contact over the night," he said. "Apart from their greeting cards, they haven't tried to impede our operation, which is worrying. It suggests that someone on the other side is playing it carefully and with forethought, rather than rushing into battle and trying to smash us by force of arms. I imagine that when we begin regular patrols we'll run right into trouble."

"Perhaps they've decided to be reasonable," Leo said. "If you keep producing new soldiers, won't they find themselves outnumbered?"

"All the more reason for them to act now," Captain Stalker said, taking his seat and tapping the smaller map. "They *cannot* let us keep producing new soldiers and patrolling the countryside, or their operations will be impeded – we might even stumble over where they're hiding Coleman."

Leo frowned. "Are you sure that he's alive?"

"In the absence of any evidence to the contrary, yes," Captain Stalker said. He glanced out the window towards the blue sea. Out there, Leo knew, fishermen were sailing the waters, catching fish and trying to sell them to Camelot, where they would be sold on to the population. "I received an odd request the other day."

Leo lifted an eyebrow. "Oh?"

"Oh, indeed," Captain Stalker agreed, his voice carefully even. "Rifleman Yamane – who escorted your family on your first day on the planet – has informed me that your eldest daughter wishes to use our sponsorship system. Do you have any feelings on the matter?"

Leo blinked. "Your sponsorship system, Captain?"

"We sometimes sponsor promising young men and women in exchange for first call on their services after they graduate," Captain Stalker explained. "It's not something we use very often and is generally only used for Marine Auxiliaries, men and women who have flunked out of the Slaughterhouse and still wish to work with the Marine Corps. There is no legal reason why we should not offer it to Mandy, although I confess I do have my doubts."

"She never mentioned it to me," Leo admitted. The thought was galling, even though he knew that Mandy had told him almost nothing of her life since she had hit puberty. Part of him was relieved and didn't want to know; the remainder knew how close Mandy had come to death or worse and wanted to lock her up for the rest of her life. "What does she want to study?"

"Engineering and spaceship design, apparently," Captain Stalker said. "The technical school here does offer a few such courses, although they won't be first-rank Imperial Standard programs."

"Very few are these days," Leo said, feeling his head reel. "If you pay for her schooling, she won't have any debt afterwards, will she?"

"I believe that that was her motive in making the request," Captain Stalker said, seriously. "She *would* be in hock to the Marine Corps for a few years, though; we might call on her for service here or elsewhere. She might well go into danger."

"I thought that she wouldn't be a Marine," Leo protested. The thought of his daughter in danger…but then, she'd placed herself in worse danger than anything the Marines had ever done to her. "Would you have to take her?"

"If we needed her, we'd have to take her," Captain Stalker explained. "You might be surprised at how many different specialities we need from time to time. The premier brain surgeon in the Empire is a Marine Auxiliary who works for us when we need him. I must admit that we could use a trained engineer in the future."

"Ah," Leo said. "So you are going to agree to this?"

"I do not know," Captain Stalker admitted. He looked up and met Leo's eyes. "If she qualifies and does well, we could use her, but her history is not one to inspire confidence."

Leo wanted to defend Mandy, but the Captain was right. She had done as little as she could get away with on Earth, while on Avalon she'd practically been allowed to wander free, at least until she'd received a sharp wake-up call. Mandy was smart and intelligent – the tests proved that, even if he'd doubted it – but she was untrained and naive. He'd failed her as a father, even though he might have saved her from being caught up in the chaos that would engulf Earth, sometime in the very near future.

"I understand," Leo said. "What do you want me to do?"

"I am disposed to agree to this, if she still wants to go through with it," Captain Stalker said. "What must be impressed upon her – what you must impress upon her – is that she won't be able to wiggle out of it. Once she signs on the dotted line, she's committed."

"I understand that too," Leo said. "I'll make sure that she understands."

He looked down at the floor, trying to change the subject. "Tell me something," he said. "You're paying everyone in cash, right?" Captain Stalker nodded. "Which is good, because it's giving the local economy a boost that it wouldn't have if you paid them electronically, but what happens when you run out of cash? I don't think you brought an entire transport starship of cash with you."

"You might be surprised," Captain Stalker said. "During the campaign on Brace, cash was one of the main weapons of war, bribing people into staying out of the firing line until the rebels were crushed. It was more effective than shooting them, according to the General in command."

He shook his head. "Let me worry about that," he added. "It's not going to be an immediate problem."

Leo frowned. In his experience, financial problems rapidly became immediate problems, even if the people in charge chose to pretend otherwise. Still, it wasn't something he wanted to push any further, not now.

"That does leave the matter of the Council," he said, changing the subject again. It was impossible to avoid realising that the Council *had* to be removed. "What are you going to do about it?"

"So far, we're still working on the proof we need to take to the Governor," Captain Stalker said. "Once we have that proof, we can take action against them and arrest them before they do something drastic. If we'd caught the assassin…but we didn't. We can't pin Smuts and his death on anyone, not yet."

Leo frowned. "I thought that the base had been sealed," he said. "How did the assassin get out?"

"Oh, that would have been easy," Captain Stalker said. "The bastard would have worn a chameleon suit. The Civil Guard isn't generally equipped to watch out for them, so the assassin could have just walked out past them."

Leo smiled. "I was wondering," he said. "You have enough evidence to convict them on a charge of treason, right?"

"Not enough to convince the Governor," Captain Stalker explained. "Treason is one of those charges that have to be proven and proven again before anyone will take it seriously."

Leo nodded. Over a hundred years ago, a junior prince had murdered his brother and become the Heir to the Throne, or so legend had it. No one knew for sure, because the whole affair was covered up, allowing the new Heir to succeed to the Throne and become Emperor.

His faction at Court – the New Men, who had believed that the entrenched power interests in the Empire were dragging it down – had capitalised on his success and started a reign of terror that had paralysed the Empire. The Tyrant Emperor had crushed all opposition and had been on the verge of creating a new and bloody age when a lone assassin had breached the defences of the New Imperial Palace – a free-floating structure orbiting Sol – and blown it to smithereens with an antimatter bomb. The Tyrant Emperor was dead and the entire galaxy had breathed a sigh of relief.

In the wake of his rule, the Grand Senate had moved rapidly to secure the levers of power and prevent such an Emperor from ever ruling again. As the charge of treason had been used to break the Emperor's enemies, they ruled that treason had to be handled by the Grand Senate itself and all such cases had to have absolutely ironclad proof before they were touched. They might have legislated with high ideals, but as the Empire started to crumble – at least partly because of the aftermath of the Tyrant Emperor's reign – it had made it harder to legally deal with genuine traitors and secessionists.

"Assuming that you can convict them," Leo asked, "what happens to their property?"

Captain Stalker frowned. "The property of a convicted traitor is forfeit to the crown," he said. "Avalon's government would take possession of it."

"Yes," Leo said, "and that includes the debts they are owed."

"Yes," Captain Stalker agreed. "And then the Governor will probably try to sell them off again."

"It doesn't have to be that way," Leo said, expounding on his idea. "Why not cut the knot and tear up all the debts?"

He smiled, waving his hands in the air as he tried to outline the solution to Avalon's problems. "You know as well as I do that that money is never going to be repaid," he said. "For half of the people in debt, it isn't even a trap they fell into willingly, but one passed down from their parents or siblings. Why do you expect anyone to repay their debt when they didn't even have the pleasure of spending the original money?"

"You're preaching to the choir," Captain Stalker said. "The Governor wouldn't like it."

"You'd undercut the Crackers in one fell swoop," Leo pointed out. "Just by giving people back their independence, they'd have a chance to reject the Crackers and all that they stand for. If you give them what they claim to want, you could separate the irredeemable from the redeemable and make it easier to wage war on them."

Captain Stalker chuckled. "A neat idea," he said, seriously. "I'll run it past my command staff and see…it might just work."

"And so you fled," Carola Wilhelm snapped. "What exactly do you expect me to do for you?"

The cringing man in front of her claimed to come from a high-born family. In Carola's experience, the claim had about as much validity as the claims that a mad scientist had successfully discovered the secret of long-range FTL communications and needed to go into partnership with someone saner in order to market it to the universe. It was, of course, a con trick intended to separate a fool from her money…not that Carola disapproved of that, of course. It was just another way of separating the smart from the stupid. Besides, the highest-born child of Avalon wouldn't even qualify for membership in a cadet branch of Earth's aristocracy.

"But I had to leave," he pleaded, desperately. "If they had put me through the lie detector, they would have known about everything I'd done and then I would have been disappeared, like the others. I would have vanished and my family would never have known what had happened to me…"

Carola fixed him with a look, unable to tolerate his cringing any longer. She had arranged for the young man – already overweight and unhealthy – to join the Civil Guard as a favour to his mother, who was one of her strongest allies. A man in his position who kept his eyes open and his mouth shut could have been a valuable asset, but he hadn't even been capable of doing that. And, when the Civil Guard worm had turned, he had fled rather than face interrogation. The irony was overwhelming. He hadn't done anything that would have provoked his arrest – apart from being grossly under-qualified for the job – but by going AWOL, he had guaranteed that the Civil Guard would want to ask him a few questions when they finally caught up with him.

"And so you fled," she said, repeating herself. This time, he got the message and shut up. "What use are you to me? No, don't bother; I already know the answer. You're no use at all and there's no point in giving you any help."

She half-turned away, and then turned back to him. He wasn't a pretty sight. If she had managed to get him a combat command, at least the Crackers or the bandits would have killed him and improved the human gene pool a little. His mother was a tough bitch with ice water in her veins, but she had a massive blind spot where her children were concerned and tolerated all of their foibles. The one cringing in front of her was the best of a bad bunch. One of them was simply too stupid to organise a gang-bang in a brothel, let alone work within the Civil Guard. Another had tastes that made even Carola shudder in revulsion.

"Or maybe there is something you can do for me," she added. "You still have your codes for the Civil Guard's mainframe, right?"

"Yes," the man said. He looked up slightly, sensing the first ray of light at the end of the tunnel. Unluckily for him, Carola knew, it was an oncoming train. "I still have the access codes I was given…"

"Good," Carola said. "I want you to pull out the details of Major Grosskopf's schedule for the next few days. Get them back to me as soon as possible."

"But…"

He broke off at her look. Either he did it or he failed. Carola didn't care. "Go," she ordered, and, having applied the stick, added a little carrot. "If you do this for me, I will see to it that you never have to want again."

———

It had been a long time since Kitty Stevenson had had to carry out surveillance on her own, but she had to admit that she was enjoying the experience. Identifying one of Carola Wilhelm's sources had taken more time than she had expected – the wretched woman was good at covering her tracks and sheer luck had played a part – but it had all paid off. The recording she had taken might not convince the governor, but she knew who it would convince…

She looked towards the lighted mansion and the guards patrolling the grounds. Carola had to have been feeling paranoid, for she'd doubled the guard force over the last two days. Or perhaps she felt as if she had dodged a bullet. It didn't matter anyway. One day soon, if Kitty had her way, she was going to go down hard.

CHAPTER FORTY-FOUR

> The insurgent and the counter-insurgent battle for the hearts and minds of the civilian population, who are caught in the middle of the fighting. It is a war of perceptions more than reality, where the appearance of weakness can rapidly become real weakness, or where a rumour of atrocity can destroy years of painstaking work. Learning to eat soup with a knife? Rather more like trying to count all the grains of sand on a beach wracked by windstorms.
> -Major-General Thomas Kratman (Ret), *A Marine's Guide to Insurgency*.

"I never knew what hate was," Private Tom Crook subvocalised, as the platoon slowly made its way through the marketplace. "I feel like someone is drawing a bead on my back."

Michael felt the same way. Sangria was a relatively small and prosperous town in the countryside, far cleaner and safer than Camelot itself, but the population hated the soldiers and resented their presence. The sheer psychic hatred was almost overwhelming and without the training he'd gone though he would have been walking with a hunch, refusing to make eye contact with anyone. The population – many of whom were in debt themselves and struggling to make ends meet – refused to have anything to do with them if it could be avoided. The patrol had barely been outside the compound for ten minutes and they had already had four incidents that could have proven fatal.

He had never been outside Camelot before signing up with the army and Sangria was an eye-opening experience. The Council had been telling everyone about how the evil farmers had been deliberately starving the cities and supporting the Crackers, for no better reason than sheer unadulterated evil. In reality, Sangria was almost paradise, one that the farmers were willing to fight for, one that the Council kept threatening to destroy. The situation puzzled him, even as he kept a wary eye on the nearby locals; he, a young man born into a debt he had no hope of escaping, was enforcing the rule of the Council on others. He'd signed up expecting to fight bandits and terrorists, not threaten ordinary citizens. The farmers weren't monsters at all.

His helmet felt heavy on his head as the sun poured down from high above and sweat trickled down his back, but they had been warned in no uncertain terms not to remove any of their armour. The Marines had armour that was tailored to them individually, but the Army of Avalon didn't have access to such technology, at least not yet. The body armour they wore might be the end result of literally centuries of human research and development, but it was still hot, sweaty and uncomfortable. The netting that held their supplies, including a handful of grenades and clips for their assault rifles, seemed to be dragging them down. It seemed a high price to pay for protection when no one was shooting at them.

Sangria had been designed as the centrepiece of an expanded community, one that stretched out over forty square miles. The farmers occupied their individual homesteads, using the town as a social centre, marketplace and knowledge base. The small library in the town might not have anything like the contents of the Imperial Library in Camelot, but it concentrated on materials the farmers would need for expanding their footholds in the soil. The permanent population of the town was over a thousand…and all of them seemed to be packing guns. Apart from the preteen children, Michael had yet to see a person without a gun. The gangs who preyed upon helpless civilians in Camelot would have been rapidly wiped out in the small town. There were laws against the private ownership of firearms in the city, but the farmers were vulnerable to the nastier wildlife out in the countryside. They needed their guns.

And, if the Crackers appeared and started shooting, it would be impossible to tell friend from foe.

He shook his head as he caught sight of a pretty girl. She was pale, with strawberry-blond hair, wearing a shirt and tight shorts that exposed everything she had to best advantage, even the rifle slung across her shoulders. She looked so much more…alive than anyone in the city that Michael felt his heart skip a beat, not out of desire or lust, but out of anger. A proper diet might have saved thousands of lives in the city, but the Council just didn't care.

The girl looked at him and met his eyes, and then her face darkened, as if she had smelled something unpleasant. She sauntered away, swinging her hips mockingly, although Michael could read a certain tension in her pose, wondering if the soldiers were going to try anything stupid. Michael had reviewed the files of the last Civil Guard unit to be based out so far from Camelot and they hadn't made cheerful reading. It had been alarmingly clear that they had treated the local population badly and made far more enemies than they could handle. The surprising fact was that they'd lasted as long as they had before finally being recalled back to Camelot.

"Bitch," one of the soldiers subvocalised. "Hey, Corporal, you want us to go after her and teach her a lesson?"

"As you were," Michael snapped. He was chillingly aware of the danger and found himself wondering just what the Marines had had in mind when they'd sent him out in command, an inexperienced NCO leading equally inexperienced soldiers. On the face of it, they had made an absurd mistake. "You know the rules as well as I do."

There was some subvocal grumbling, but no one broke ranks. They had been warned – again, in no uncertain terms – not to fool around with the local women, no matter how willing they were. The horror stories that had backed the warnings up should have kept their cocks in their pants, but the combination of heat and sheer physical desire made it hard to remember the danger. At least a dozen Civil Guardsmen hadn't survived encounters with local women, often in circumstances that made it hard to know just what had happened, or who had truly been to blame.

He glanced down at his timepiece and then led them onwards, part of his mind noting that civilians were thinning out the further they moved from the marketplace. The outskirts of Sangria were dominated by a handful of small shops and a couple of large warehouses, but they seemed to have been abandoned, something that sent warning bells sounding in the back of his mind. Camelot had hundreds of abandoned shops and they had all been taken over by the gangs, or used as drug dens for the thousands of addicts who wasted their lives smoking or injecting shit into their bodies. Sangria had no gang problem, but maybe…

Something whistled through the air. He had barely a second to realise that they'd stumbled into an ambush when fire started to pour down on them from high above. He swore and ducked for cover, feeling a pain in his chest as a bullet impacted directly with his armour, but he somehow managed to take cover beside the walls. A figure appeared on the opposite roof, a man carrying a rifle and a stack of grenades and Michael fired at him, striking him on his first shot. The man stumbled and fell to the ground, no longer within Michael's sight.

Time seemed to slow down, just for a second. He'd taken part in hundreds of exercises, but he had never killed a man in real life, not until now. The Cracker had been a living man, a man who had loved, hated, feared and mourned…and now he was dead. The training hadn't prepared him for the gut-wrenching realisation that he and he alone had ended a life. The enemy combatant would have had no qualms about shooting him, or so he told himself, but somehow it failed to convince. The sound of shooting was growing louder as enemy fighters emerged from hiding, coming after the soldiers.

"This is Charlie-one," Michael snapped, keying his radio. They'd trained for that as well, luckily. The training kept him from panicking. "We have major enemy contact; estimate thirty-plus enemy fighters, closing in from all directions."

He swore as a bullet pinged off the wall bare centimetres from his head, so close that he felt dust spraying against his face. "Get the door open," he snapped, to two of his men, as he returned fire towards the enemy positions. "We need cover."

We got lucky, part of his mind whispered. A few seconds later and the platoon would have been caught in the middle of the street and been riddled with bullets before they had any idea what was going on. The Crackers, for reasons unknown, had opened fire too early. He took a silent moment to thank God for their mistake as the door was rammed open and they streamed into the deserted shop, hunting for cover.

"Understood, Charlie-one," the dispatcher said. "We have drone coverage of your position. Seventeen enemy fighters are on screen."

"Just seventeen," Michael muttered, as the shooting dimmed. He waved for his men to take up positions at the windows. If he was in the enemy's shoes, he would have started to throw grenades through the windows, rather than rushing the shop and being shot down for his pains. "Seventeen men and we fled from them like little girls."

The dispatcher didn't bother to respond to that comment. "Help is on the way, Corporal, but it may be delayed," he warned. "Secure your position and await orders."

Michael swore as the shooting intensified. They seemed to be wasting bullets, which made no sense to him, for they'd been warned – time and time again – not to waste ammunition during a battle. The Crackers had more experience with their weapons than he had with his, so why were they wasting bullets? They could produce bullets for themselves, but could they produce enough to spend them like water?

A nasty thought occurred to him and he swore. "You, you, and you stay here and keep firing from time to time to discourage them," he said. One explanation made far too much sense. The Crackers intended to pin them down while they brought up the heavy artillery. "The rest of us are going to search this building and then get up onto the roof."

The ground floor of the shop was nothing special, apart from a cage that had once held a parrot or some other large bird. It looked more occupied than he had expected, raising the question of just what had happened to the original owners. Had their business failed and they had left, or had they only cleared out for the day to allow the ambushers to go about their work. Climbing up the stairs, every sense on alert, Michael heard…whimpering? It didn't sound hostile, but more like someone was terrified out of their mind. He exchanged silent glances with his men and advanced towards the source of the noise, gently pushing the door open with his foot. It crossed his mind – too late – that it could be a trap, but no IED exploded in his face. The whimpering was replaced by screams, terrifyingly loud at such close range.

"Stay here," he muttered, and carefully peeked into the room. Two girls, barely entering their teens, were clinging to one another, their faces distorted by sheer terror. It dawned on Michael that he had to look terrifying to them, a stranger, his face hidden under a helmet and combat goggles, entering their house. There was no sign of their parents or anyone else that might have looked after them.

"It's all right," he said, as calmly as he could. The girls had stopped screaming, but they were shaking madly, clearly expecting a horrible fate. Cracker propaganda warned that the Civil Guard would do horrible things to anyone young, pretty and female they caught, or even someone merely young and pretty. The Civil Guard had provided them with any number of real incidents to bolster their claims. "Calm down. What are you doing here?"

It took nearly five minutes to get a coherent story out of the girls. It would have been easier if they'd had a female soldier with them, but the handful of female soldiers in the Army of Avalon had been assigned elsewhere, leaving the girls to be terrified of hulking evil-looking men. They owned the shop themselves – Michael didn't believe them at first, but one of his men who had had a friend from outside Camelot confirmed that it did happen – and they worked to keep themselves going. He still didn't believe it – how could a pair of preteen girls run a shop, he asked himself – but at least they hadn't lured the soldiers into a trap.

"Remain here and stay on the floor, lying down," he ordered, harshly. The Crackers hadn't known that the girls were there, or so he told himself, feeling as if he had aged twenty years in the space of a few minutes. They hadn't meant to put the girls in danger. "If we can get you out of here, we will come back for you."

It didn't look as if they believed him, but at least they followed his orders. He glanced at them, realising that they were probably going to have problems in the next few years…assuming that they survived the coming hours. The shop was well-built, but it wouldn't stand up to a mortar or rocket attack…and the Crackers were known for having both. He took a final glance at them, wondering if they had been telling the truth all along, and then left the room.

Back outside, he checked the remainder of the house and then started to slip up to the roof. The sound of shooting was growing louder, but luckily no one had tried to block the hatch that would have allowed egress. Carefully, using the Marine knife he'd been issued, he unscrewed the hatch completely and lowered it into the room, rather than opening it and warning the enemy that they were coming out. In their place, he would have had someone on the roof from the start, but perhaps they'd been lucky…

He drew his pistol and stuck his head up, realising that they'd been far luckier than they deserved. There *was* an enemy position on the roof, but the gunner hadn't realised that they'd been coming out, perhaps because the noise of the shooting had prevented him from realising that the hatch was being unscrewed. Michael took aim quickly and shot the gunner in the back, before pulling himself onto the roof and shooting down towards the next gunner. Machine gun bullets ricocheted over his head as the other Crackers realised the danger, only too late. A bullet pinged off his helmet and sent him sprawling to the roof, but did no harm. One of his platoon mates was less lucky as a high-powered rifle shot hit him right in the face. Blood spewed out of his body as he toppled to the ground. Michael felt sick, but there was no time to mourn or even avenge his death. He had no idea where the bullet had come from.

For the first time, as the other four soldiers deployed and started providing covering fire, he had a chance to take in the overall situation. A black cloud of smoke was rising up from the direction of their base, the converted Civil Guard garrison they'd arrived at yesterday. Other clouds of smoke could be seen in the distance, suggesting that they weren't the only patrol that had been attacked.

A handful of bodies – Crackers, he hoped – lay sprawled on the street, already being savaged by a handful of local birds. The Bloodsuckers hadn't been scared off by the shooting, for humans rarely shot at them. The briefing had warned that Bloodsuckers might be omnivorous, happy to eat both Avalon's native animals and the ones imported from Earth, but they tasted bad, even to a desperate human. Apparently, their blood chemistry had some potential commercial use, but Avalon simply didn't have the resources to explore the possibilities.

"Disgusting," one of the soldiers breathed, as a Bloodsucker landed on the rooftop, eying them with beady red eyes. A rag of suggestive red meat hung from its mouth. "Can I shoot the little bastard?"

"Don't waste your ammo," Michael said. The Crackers had fallen back, leaving the platoon alone, or so it seemed. He wished, not for the first time, that he had a Marine-issue terminal, something he could use to link into the drone systems and study the live feed directly. The Marines hadn't brought enough of those from Earth for everyone. "If the creature tries to eat Robin, shoot it; if not, leave it be."

He keyed his radio quickly. "This is Charlie-one," he said. "Enemy contact appears to have receded, but we remain trapped. Assistance would be welcome."

The dispatcher didn't respond for a long moment. "There are multiple attacks coming in all across the board," he said, finally. "Almost every garrison and patrol we had out there is coming under attack. Are you safe for the moment?"

Michael glanced around, dubiously. "For the moment," he said, grimly. It didn't seem possible that they wouldn't be compromised soon enough. Although they had managed to drive the Crackers off the rooftops, they were still keeping the soldiers trapped. "We may be able to break out if necessary."

"Negative," the dispatcher said. There was a grim note in his voice that sent a shiver down Michael's spine. "Hold your position. Drones report that you are surrounded and probably isolated. Helicopters are inbound."

Michael scowled. "Everyone get under cover," he ordered. He'd seen the helicopters at work before. "Get the girls to the ground floor and under whatever cover they can find. Helicopters are inbound."

On cue, he heard the sound of rotor blades in the distance.

CHAPTER FORTY-FIVE

The key to winning a conventional war is heavy firepower, applied liberally onto any enemy position that makes itself a target. The key to winning an insurgency is to apply minimum necessary firepower onto the target, taking extreme care to avoid collateral damage.

-Major-General Thomas Kratman (Ret), *A Marine's Guide to Insurgency.*

"Incoming!"

Jasmine threw herself to the ground as the first mortar rounds started exploding on the shields. The small base had been designed by the Civil Guard to stand off indirect attacks, but judging from the number of explosions, the Crackers had smuggled at least four mortars and firing teams up close to the base. It hadn't been designed for outright bombardment and the attackers might get lucky.

She crawled rapidly towards the observation tower, donning her helmet as she moved. The Marines had been held back as a QRF for the Army of Avalon, but it was starting to look as if the new soldiers were going to be on their own. The enemy weren't using smart rounds – a relief, as a concentrated attack with smart warheads could have wrecked the base fairly quickly – but the longer the bombardment continued, the greater the chance that they would get lucky. They seemed to be lobbing bombs into the base at random, perhaps hoping to keep the Marines pinned down. At least they weren't trying to storm the gate.

The base itself hadn't been designed with a major attack in mind. It had appalled her when she'd first seen it, for the Civil Guard had definitely been taken for a ride by the contractors. It consisted of one large three-story building, a heavy wall that wouldn't have stood up to a heavy plasma cannon for a moment and a set of observation towers. The four gates – one on each side of the base – could probably have been knocked down by a determined or suicidal driver in a truck. At least the Crackers didn't seem to be resorting to suicide attacks, although part of her mind warned that they hadn't done it yet. The Marines had learned to hate suicide attacks a long time before the Phase Drive had been discovered and humanity started to expand outside the Sol System.

"Enemy forces are concentrating on the north gate," her helmet buzzed. The sound of shooting – heavy machine guns and rifles, as well as the incessant mortar fire – grew louder. Jasmine could see, in hindsight, just how the Crackers had managed their attack. They'd hidden in the nearby houses and deployed once the first patrols were too far from the base for effective support. "All Marines, sound off."

Jasmine acknowledged her position as she started to scramble up the observation tower. The enemy might have seen her climb, but she knew that she would be a difficult target, unless they had a sniper out there with a high-powered rifle. That wasn't so unlikely, she had to remind herself, but no one shot at her until she reached the top and started to peer through the slits. There were at least four columns of smoke rising up in the distance, each one – she guessed – marking the position of the four patrols that had been dispatched, thirty minutes ago. It had taken that long for the situation to degenerate into sheer hell.

She keyed her communicator as she moved from slat to slat, looking for targets. "I can make out at least one mortar team firing from a concealed position," she said, as a new round of shells crashed down on the shields. The heavy blocks the Marines had placed to provide additional protection were certainly proving their value, leaving her to wonder why the Civil Guard hadn't manufactured them themselves. It wasn't as if it was a new trick. "I also count seventeen gunners on the roof, firing into the complex."

"Roger," the dispatcher said. Silently, she activated her helmet's systems and started sending data back to the command centre, as well as drawing a live feed from one of the drones. The enemy positions were good, but they didn't seem to have a reserve waiting for the Marines when they came out to fight, although that didn't surprise her. After what the Marines had done to the bandits, the Crackers would have to be fools to fight them in open battle. Keeping them pinned down was hard enough. They weren't even making any serious attempt to breach the gate. "You are cleared to engage at will."

Blake would have tested the dispatcher's patience by demanding to know which of the enemy was actually called Will, but Jasmine was more focused on the mission. If she was cut off from the rest of the platoon, the least she could do was concentrate on clearing the way for them. She readied her MAG, activated the sniper settings, and peered towards the mortar team's position. The standard-issue MAG wasn't exactly a dedicated sniper weapon – the Marines had been known to note that it was a jack of all trades and master of none – but it would suffice, in a pinch. She might not have had a buddy backing her up, yet she could still shoot.

She peered through the rifle's scope, carefully taking aim at the mortar team's leader – or at least she thought he was the leader. He was a tall fair-skinned man, with signs of a life spent working hard for a living, but it hardly mattered to her. She concentrated, studied his face for a long moment and carefully squeezed the trigger. The MAG launched a single bullet towards him and sent him reeling over backwards, shot through the head. Jasmine moved to the second target, and then the third, picking them both off quickly and efficiently. The remaining targets jumped out of the way and dived for cover.

Jasmine understood their confusion. Unlike a normal weapon, the MAG produced no flash when it was fired, leaving them without a way of locating her easily. It wouldn't take them long to realise that there had to be a sniper in the tower, but by then she would have accounted for a few other enemy fighters. It did help that her weapon was capable of telling the difference between friend and foe and helping her to avoid targeting the wrong side. A friendly fire incident would be disastrous.

"I am engaging the enemy," she said, as she moved her scope over a younger man carrying a small submachine gun, firing quick precise bursts of fire towards the defenders. Jasmine's bullet slammed into his throat and sent him flying backwards, blood spraying everywhere. He might have survived if he'd been rushed into a stasis tube and transported to a first-class medical centre, but no such centre existed on Avalon. "One mortar team has been neutralised."

A series of explosions warned that the other mortar teams hadn't been deterred. Jasmine's audio-discrimination programs reported that their rate of fire had slowed, suggesting that they were either shifting position rapidly or were running out of ammunition and trying to make it last as long as possible. Jasmine would have bet on the former, if only to assume the worst. It was a shame that they hadn't had time to set up a proper counter-battery system in the town, but the Captain would probably have balked at the thought of unleashing heavy weapons within the town, where civilians could be hurt. Jasmine swept her gaze over the nearby buildings and concluded, ruefully, that there didn't seem to be any civilians in the area. They had either fled or joined the insurgents. She would bet on the latter.

She watched carefully as a young face appeared on one of the rooftops, glanced from side to side, and then ran towards the fallen men. Jasmine tracked him, waited until he picked up the weapon, and shot him neatly through the head. He couldn't have been out of his teens, yet the Crackers had been prepared to use him as a soldier, not unlike many other planets locked in endless insurgencies. Avalon, at least, had only a mild case of civil war. If they could break the Crackers, and the Council, perhaps the planet would have a chance to survive and develop its own potential.

"The new bugs are pinned down," someone said, over the general channel. "They're calling for fire support and relief!"

"We don't have much to send," someone else said. "Hang on; dispatch is trying to muster more reinforcements now."

Jasmine swore inwardly, biting her lip. If there were few forces that could be dispatched to aid them, it suggested that the attacks had been far more widespread than she thought. It didn't bode well for the future if the Crackers could not just tie up the Army of Avalon, but also the Marines and the Civil Guard. So far, she didn't think that there had been many casualties, but with barely-trained and inexperienced troops out there, it was quite likely that they'd run out of ammunition. When that happened, she knew, they would be slaughtered.

She caught sight of a team of men running to the abandoned mortar and trying to move it out of her sight. She opened fire at once, picking off one of the men and blowing a second man's leg off with a misplaced shot. The others dived for cover; a second later, bullets started rattling the slats, causing her to duck back with a curse. Someone on the other side had finally figured out where she had to be and was intent on killing her, even if it meant taking the pressure off the rest of the base. A pair of mortar shells screamed down and exploded far too close for comfort, distressingly accurate shooting from untrained men – or were they untrained? It wasn't as if the Crackers were short of places where they could train their fighters, areas where the Civil Guard never penetrated. The hunting near the Mystic Mountains was supposed to be good…and a hunter of animals could become a hunter of men quite easily.

Another shell landed far too close to the observation tower and Jasmine reluctantly conceded that it was untenable. She grabbed her MAG and shimmed down the ladder, knowing that the moment they saw her they'd open fire. Snipers were rarely shown mercy in wars, even though they were nothing more than just another kind of soldier. There was something about a sniper that just marked them out for death. Something hit her in the back, just before she got under cover, and she fell to the ground, cursing. Her armour had locked up and taken the brunt of the shot, but she still felt as if she'd gone three rounds with the Marine Corps Boxing Champion, back at the Slaughterhouse.

He'd been one of her trainers back during Basic Training and had offered to graduate any of the trainees instantly if they beat him in the ring. Many had tried; none had succeeded. Red icons flashed up in her helmet, warning of all kinds of possible damage, before they faded away. She was intact, if sore. Absurdly, an image of Mandy doing a post-spanking dance popped into her mind and she giggled, ignoring the pain. She was definitely alive.

"I'm intact, sir," she said, when the dispatcher realised that she had fallen from the tower. Not a moment too soon, for a mortar shell landed dead on top of it and blew the observation position to flaming debris. She somehow managed to pull herself to her feet and run for cover as the shooting started to intensify again. "I've been through worse."

The ground shook violently as something exploded in the distance. "Good," the dispatcher said. "Get to the forward position and meet up with Second Platoon there."

There were seven Marines there, waiting for her. Blake was MIA, of course, but two others had been given a brief transfer to the Army of Avalon and were out of reach for the foreseeable future. Jasmine briefly linked into the general network and was shocked to realise that one of them had been badly wounded, despite everything his soldiers could do to help him. His suit was flashing urgent warnings, having injected him with sedatives and painkillers, but there was no way of evacuating him quickly. Joe Buckley was still living his charmed life, yet Jasmine couldn't see how even he intended to get out of the trap before his platoon ran out of ammunition. It wouldn't be long now.

A roar of engines announced that the first AFV was being moved towards the gate. The enemy might not have seen it coming, for they weren't even trying to knock it out before it could be moved outside the base. Upon an order from the dispatcher, Jasmine and the rest of her platoon ran forward to provide cover as the gate hissed open, revealing a deserted street. It had been buzzing with life when they'd arrived in town. Now, the civilians had all deserted their homes for safety…or had joined the insurgents. She had to remind herself, again, that this enemy didn't play by the Empire's rules.

She scowled as bullets started to ping off the AFV. The Empire divided insurgents into two categories; those that did their best to avoid civilian casualties and those that gloried in killing as many innocent people in the crossfire as possible, if not actually preying on the people they claimed to be fighting for. The Crackers, at least, seemed to have taken steps to get the civilians out of the way, unless they actually *were* the civilians and intended to simply drop their weapons when they were tired of fighting, melting back into the population. The AFV advanced slowly, its guns swivelling to engage the gunners that presented themselves as targets, blowing them away with high-velocity rounds. The Crackers fell back into the town, slipping into buildings and hiding from the advancing machine.

"Get the next three AFVs deployed to corners and into position to block any egress," the dispatcher ordered. Jasmine sighed inwardly, but waited as the remaining AFVs were moved out of the base. In her experience, armoured vehicles weren't as useful as they looked in street-fighting, but perhaps the dispatcher merely wanted to make a show of force. The Crackers seemed to have melted away into the buildings, perhaps even slipping into basements and underground tunnels. How long had they been planning their war? It all seemed too elaborate to have been put together on the fly.

"Drone reports enemy forces in buildings," the dispatcher added. A map flashed up in Jasmine's helmet, showing her the suspected location of the enemy fighters. Perhaps they were hiding, in hopes that the Marines would pass them by, although that wasn't going to happen. Even if the buildings had been marked as unoccupied, the Marines would have searched them anyway, just in case. It wouldn't be the first time that someone with bad intentions had managed to spoof a drone. "Clear them out; take them alive if possible."

Second Platoon divided itself into two fire teams and advanced on the first building, with an AFV moving up behind to provide heavy firepower if required. Jasmine looked at the building, made a silent calculation about the likelihood of someone inserting an IED in the doorway, and used hand signals to warn the others that they were going to go through a wall. Doing damage to civilian property was discouraged, but she knew that Captain Stalker would back her up on this one…and, besides, the Marines would pay for it. It would be far better than having a mortar shell plunge through the roof to wreck the entire building.

"Now," she muttered, as they placed the shaped explosive charges on the stone wall. Someone had been mining stone from a nearby quarry, she guessed, taking a second to admire the strange patterns running through the white stone. "Hit it!"

The charges detonated, blasting the wall inwards and allowing the Marines to charge inside, weapons raised and at the ready. A handful of Crackers had clearly been caught by the blast and stunned, but the Marines took no chances and played stunners over them, before searching them roughly and leaving them for the follow-up units to handle. Jasmine found a set of stairs and ran up them, watching for enemy contact. A single

Cracker holding an odd pistol swung around to point it at her and she shot him neatly through the chest. He staggered over, one hand pressed to the wound, and collapsed to the floor. Jasmine kicked the weapon out of reach and kept moving.

"Clear," one of the Marines called, as he checked out a bedroom. It showed the signs of having been abandoned in a hurry, suggesting that the Crackers had warned the owners to evacuate. Jasmine was grateful for that, at least. She didn't want to slaughter civilians. "Room two; clear!"

"Get up on the roof," Jasmine ordered, as she checked out a storage room. A handful of cardboard boxes had been abandoned there, without any labels or explanations. She glanced at the contents and winced, realising that they were homemade children's toys. "What have you found up there?"

"A dead body and an enemy sniper on the next rooftop," Mark reported. "I shot him down before he could react."

"Mark this building as clear and let's move on to the next one," Jasmine ordered. The sound of shooting was fading, although she could still make out gunshots echoing across the city. A quick status check revealed that the platoons trapped on the outside were still under heavy fire. "The sooner we get the bastards away from our base, the sooner we can recover our friends."

Another noise intruded on her awareness and she glanced up sharply. "We have incoming helicopters," the dispatcher warned. "Stand by for orders."

Jasmine braced herself. If the Crackers had any antiaircraft weapons, they'd use them now. "Understood," she said. A single HVM could blow a helicopter out of the sky before it could escape. "We're ready."

CHAPTER FORTY-SIX

Who wins any given battle? He who gets there first, with the most; troops, weapons, firepower and so on. Of course, in an insurgency, defining victory can be a little complex. History is replete with examples of counter-insurgency forces that have won battles – indeed, have won every battle – and yet lost the war.

-Major-General Thomas Kratman (Ret), *A Marine's Guide to Insurgency.*

"Get down!"

Michael hit the deck as the helicopters swooped down, launching salvos of rockets towards their targets. The ground shook as the missiles impacted, sending brilliant fireballs billowing up into the air. Darkness fell, just for a second, as the helicopters roared overhead, seemingly so close that he could have reached up and touched them. Silence fell as they receded into the distance, just before it was broken by the sound of the Crackers opening fire again. There was noticeably less shooting now than there had been before the helicopters had made their pass.

"We got them good," one of the soldiers shouted. He sounded delighted and tired at the same time. "Look at it!"

Michael looked. Across the street, there had once been a row of shops, all clearly closed up for the ambush. Now, three of them were little more than smouldering ruins and several more were on fire. The Marines had hammered one phrase into his mind back on Castle Rock and he heard Barr speaking in his mind, as clearly as if he'd been standing right next to him. *We had to destroy the village in order to save it.* The devastation, as if an angry god had decided to knock down half of the town, shocked him. He had known, intellectually, just how powerful and destructive modern weapons were, but it was a far cry from seeing them in action. The Crackers would have hundreds of new recruits, not least the ones who had just lost their livelihoods in the fighting.

"Yeah," he said, feeling a great weight settling across his shoulders. If the Crackers hadn't kept up the firing, he would have sat down and closed his eyes. The tiredness was almost a physical force, tearing away at his concentration. "I guess we got them."

His radio buzzed. "Report," the dispatcher said, as the helicopters started to circle back over the town. This time, they didn't have it all their own way and lines of tracer reached up towards them. The heavily-armoured helicopters could probably shrug it off unless the machine guns hit something vital, but if the enemy had any antiaircraft missiles the pilots would be dead before they realised what had hit them. "Do you require additional support?"

The helicopters started firing back towards the hidden machine guns, swatting their crews like bugs. Michael had to admire their bravery, even though he knew it was futile; they stood at their posts and kept firing until the helicopters blew them out of existence. The helicopter missiles were far too powerful for whatever firing positions the Crackers had set up. One by one, the bursts of tracer terminated and vanished.

"We need cover to get back to base," he snapped, pushing the tiredness aside. There were stimulants in his combat netting, ones that would have him buzzing for hours, but he didn't dare take one. If even hardened Marines could become addicted to them, Michael didn't dare take the risk for himself. "What is the status of our relief?"

"The base itself has been attacked," the dispatcher said. "We're driving them back from the walls now, but it may be some time before we can get reinforcements through to you. You're actually in the best position of all four platoons; one has lost over half its strength and is pinned down, burning through their ammunition too quickly to survive."

Michael swore. If they were in the best position, he definitely didn't want to see the worst. "I understand," he said, as the sound of shooting grew louder. Something exploded in a billowing fireball towards the west, sending shockwaves running through the ground. Had that been the result of the Crackers, or of the helicopter bombardment? There was no way to know. "Do you want us to remain here or attempt to assist the other patrols?"

There was a long pause. Michael used it to survey the situation. The Crackers were still firing, but the rate of fire had diminished, suggesting that they had been badly scattered by the helicopter attack. Or, perhaps, that they were trying to lure the soldiers out to where they could be slaughtered in the open. Michael was uncomfortably aware that the Crackers often came from people with a hunting background, rather than people who had grown up in a city that didn't allow the private possession of weapons. They might have a military potential that was vastly greater than anything the cities could produce.

"You probably couldn't get to the other patrols," the dispatcher said. "If you feel that you can get back to base, you may make the attempt."

Michael felt another weight falling down on his shoulders. He hadn't grasped, not really, what independent command meant! Barr had explained that Marine commanders issued general orders and trusted their subordinates to handle the situation as they saw fit, but he hadn't realised what it really meant. If he made the wrong call, the remaining members of his platoon – and two little girls – would be caught in the open and killed. If they stayed, they would eventually run out of ammunition and be slaughtered, unless the Crackers would accept surrender. If they moved, they might have a chance.

He looked up at his men and saw the same concerns reflected in their eyes. "I understand," he said. He could have asked for opinions, but the responsibility went with the Corporal's stripes he'd been so proud of when they'd been placed on his uniform. It was his call. He understood, suddenly, why the Council was so nervous about the Marines. They were trained to take independent action when the Civil Guard required orders in triplicate before they did anything at all. "We'll make our way back to base."

There was no dispute, he was relieved to see. "Understood," the dispatcher said. "Be aware; Death One and Death Two will be on standby to provide whatever firepower you need. Keep us informed of your progress and we may be able to slip reinforcements to you."

"Thank you," Michael said, dryly. "We're on our way."

He broke the connection and looked up at his men. "We're going through the walls," he said. Breaking out into the street would be suicide. "Get shaped charges set up and prepare to move."

He smiled to himself and headed up the stairs to the two girls, who were cowering on the floor. "Listen to me," he said. They might have been safe if he'd left them behind, but he couldn't take the risk. "You have to come with us and keep your heads down, understand?"

One of the girls looked up at him. "But who will look after the shop?"

Her plaintive voice sent an oddly protective feeling rushing down Michael's spine, followed by a flash of pure rage, directed not at the girls, but at the Council. It just didn't seem fair, somehow, that they should have a chance at a better life while Michael and his counterparts remained stuck in the slums, weighed down by debts they'd never assumed. If he got through the war alive, he vowed, there would be a reckoning. The Marines had taught him that uncomfortable realities could be changed with a little effort. The Council was more isolated than it knew.

"We'll come back," he promised, and beckoned to them. Slowly, they followed him down the stairs. "Come on."

The two soldiers at the bottom had already rigged the wall to blow. At Michael's command, they triggered the blast, sending the wall tumbling down. The next-door shop was deserted, thankfully, but Michael took no chances. As soon as they were through, they were already blowing their way into the next one and the next. There was no sign of anyone until they hit the sixth store, where they ran into a group of Crackers who had clearly been waiting for them to come walking down the road, somehow missing the sounds of their transit through the walls. The soldiers opened fire at point-blank range and killed them before they had a chance to react.

Michael heard a scream behind him and remembered the girls. They hadn't even had the casual exposure to violence that marked someone growing up in Camelot's slums; they'd grown up somewhere safe, where everyone could be trusted. The lucky bitches…he bit off that thought and silently prayed that they wouldn't be too traumatised by what they saw. He checked the bodies quickly, confirmed that they were dead, and then led his men into the final shop. They'd have to move quickly now. It wouldn't be long before the Crackers realised what was happening, if they didn't already know.

"Outside, now," he snapped, and led two men out into the open. The air, which had been fresh and clear only thirty minutes ago – it felt like years, somehow – now stank of burning flesh and smoke. The towering pillars of smoke hadn't abated at all, although the sound of shooting seemed to have faded. He saw a pair of armed men swinging around to cover them and fired twice, knocking one of them down and sending the other diving for cover. There had been no time to wait and see if they were hostile, but they'd been in the middle of a war zone. "Come on!"

The sound of shooting grew louder as they double-timed it back towards the base. The whole environment was taking on an increasingly surreal appearance; in places, it was blackened by gunfire and helicopter missiles and in other places it was normal, just as it had been before all hell had broken loose. He caught sight of a smaller and broken body lying by the side of the road and had to swallow hard to prevent himself from vomiting. The child – male or female; it was impossible to tell – had been shot in the head by a heavy weapon and had been left headless, completely beyond hope of salvation. His heart almost broke when he saw the doll on the ground, a few steps beyond its former owner. He wanted to study the body, to work out who had killed her and seek justice, but the truth was that it could have been either side. The child had simply been caught in the middle of the fighting and cut down in passing. No one could have mistaken her for a threat.

They rounded the corner and he swore under his breath. The enemy had established a barricade across the road, trying to prevent anyone from coming out of the base. He grinned suddenly, realising that the Crackers hadn't realised that his force was coming right up their rear end, and issued orders to his men using hand signals. The *crump-crump-crump* of a mortar started up as one of the enemy fighters started to open fire, tossing shells towards the base. Michael motioned the girls into cover, cursing himself for bringing them right into the heart of danger, and opened fire. The enemy were taken completely by surprise.

He keyed his radio as they blew through the defenders, sending the survivors scurrying for cover. "Dispatch; enemy position under attack," he snapped, knowing that the dispatcher would have located him the moment he started transmitting. "We need support as quickly as possible; I say again, we need support as quickly as possible!"

"Understood," the dispatcher said. "Help is on the way."

Jasmine threw a grenade into a room, waited for it to detonate and jumped inside, rifle at the ready. The final house had been a nightmarish combination of traps and enemy fighters, suggesting that they'd either intended to confuse the Marines or had been caught before they'd managed to withdraw from the area. A dead enemy leered at her before falling to the floor, allowing her to step back and survey the entire room. It was empty. It was also going to need a heavy repair job before someone could use it again. With soldiers and even a Marine down, no one was interested in taking chances.

"Clear," she reported, as she slipped back outside into the hallway. It was blackened, the remains of an IED that had thrown ball bearings towards the Marines when they'd detonated it. Only long experience had kept them back far enough to avoid another casualty. "Dispatch; house is clear. I say again; house is clear."

"Copy that," the dispatcher said. New orders blinked up in front of her eyes, displayed by her helmet. "Some of the locals need your help."

Jasmine surveyed the orders quickly and then fired off a stream of her own orders to her fire squad, ordering them outside to meet up with the rest of the platoon. As soon as they were out, they started to run up the street, disregarding the increasingly accurate shots from Cracker snipers. The armour could handle most of it and the remainder had their own problems. With helicopters overhead and AFVs advancing behind the Marines, the Cracker resistance was slowly starting to melt away. The battle had lasted barely an hour. It wouldn't even have been that long if there had been a Regiment of Marines in the town.

This was a nice town once, she thought sourly, as they turned the corner and ran right towards the Crackers, firing on automatic. They might not have been able to believe their eyes, she knew; they'd only faced the Civil Guard before and the Guard wouldn't do something as insane as charging an enemy position. Jasmine's thoughts were moving slower than her body and the reflexes she'd learned from the harshest training course in the Empire. The Crackers wouldn't be able to *see* her as anything other than a blur. They slashed into them as if they were made of paper…

And then, suddenly, it was all over. The Crackers broke contact and faded away, leaving the Marines and the new soldiers to mourn their dead. Jasmine found her body shaking as she slowed down from combat reflexes, trying to relax. It wasn't easy. The bandits had been easy prey. If the Crackers had had equal training and weapons…she wasn't sure how the battle would have turned out.

"All units, return to base," the dispatcher ordered. "I say again…"

"I heard," Jasmine grunted. "We're on our way."

Michael wanted to take off his helmet and pour cold water onto his head, but he didn't quite dare, not until they were safely back in the base. The AFVs and armoured Marines had formed a guard of honour for the new soldiers, covering their backs as they limped towards the base, but Michael had no illusions. They didn't look like real soldiers, not now. They looked like sweaty tramps and probably smelled bad as well. The thought couldn't even make him smile, for he felt as if he had aged a hundred years overnight. The combat had finished, but the scars it had left on his soul would never fade.

"Thank you," he said, as one of the base's small complement of staff took care of the girls. The new soldiers were pointed towards their barracks and bunks, but Michael was too exhausted to even *try* to get into the shower. He pulled off his helmet and body armour as soon as they were safely inside the barracks and then sat down hard on the ground, unable to remain upright any longer. He had never dreamed, he had never realised, he had never understood...not until it was too late. He felt the shaking welling up from somewhere deep inside and he was no longer able to resist it. The shakes swept through his entire body, leaving him shivering on the ground. He'd been in battle; he'd survived...somehow. Not all of the men under his command had been so lucky.

He knew that he should be seeing to them, that he should be carrying out his duties, but he couldn't muster the energy. If the Crackers had launched another attack, he would have been unable to resist and he didn't think that any of his platoon would have been in any better condition. He couldn't believe just how quickly the entire situation had simply collapsed into hell, or just how much damage both sides had done to the town. What would it be like, he asked himself, if they ever had to fight such a battle in Camelot itself?

"Hey," a voice said. He looked up to see the female Marine; Jasmine, her name was. "Are you all right?"

"No," Michael growled. All the frustrations boiled up inside him. "I got some of my men killed. I might as well have killed them myself."

"Don't think like that," Jasmine advised, dryly. "It doesn't make it any easier."

Michael looked up at her. She didn't look tired, yet he knew she had to be tired, even though she'd been at the base rather than trapped in an isolated shop. "They knew that this was a populated town and they decided to fight in it," he protested. "What sort of monsters are we fighting?"

"The weapons of the weak," Jasmine said, coldly. "Even Kappa Company could have beaten them in the open before they were disbanded. What did you expect from them? Did you expect that they would line up and be slaughtered?"

"I expected...I don't know what I expected," Michael admitted. "I thought that training was bad."

"It's bad for a reason," Jasmine said. "But you're right. Open warfare is worse."

She patted him on the shoulder. "You did all right, for your first engagement," she added. "I did far worse on mine, despite going through the Slaughterhouse. You did fine."

"Thanks," Michael said, sourly. "It's no consolation."

"No," Jasmine agreed. "It never is. On the other hand, you can only lose your virginity once."

CHAPTER FORTY-SEVEN

> The core goal of an insurgency is to erode the government's control and eventually cause it to collapse. The government, often having more resources on hand than the insurgents, cannot easily be toppled, unless its will can be broken. As so much else, it is mainly a matter of perception. To consider two pre-spaceflight examples, both the United States of America and France fought counter-insurgency campaigns in Vietnam and Algeria respectively. Both sides secured a military victory, but by the time they won the war the political will to win no longer existed and the wars were declared 'lost'.
> -Major-General Thomas Kratman (Ret), *A Marine's Guide to Insurgency.*

"Is it ever going to end?"

Edward looked up sharply at the Governor. The war had barely touched Camelot yet, but they both knew that it was just a matter of time. The Crackers had proven tougher than he'd realised and the fighting was rapidly spreading out of control. The Marines, the Army of Avalon and the Civil Guard were badly overstretched, even though they possessed vastly superior firepower to their enemies.

"It's been five days," the Governor continued, blankly. "Is it ever going to stop?"

Edward shrugged. After the first battles, when the Crackers had concentrated on hitting as many bases and patrols as possible, the fighting had dulled down to a steady series of attacks and counter-attacks. The bases were regularly attacked, while patrols in the towns and countryside found themselves under open and covert attack. Five Marines had been killed, along with over forty new soldiers and Civil Guardsmen. The Crackers, by the most optimistic count, had lost around seventy fighters, a low total considering the intensity of the fighting. It was hard to know for sure. They had a habit of removing their bodies from the battlefield if possible. Edward would have admired that under other circumstances.

A new contact report flashed up on the main terminal and he scowled down at it. A convoy of supply trucks had come under fire briefly; the attackers had broken contact and vanished when the convoy's escorts had returned fire. It was just another harassing raid designed to keep his men and women tired and exhausted and he had to admit that it was working. Raids into Cracker-held territory, locating bases fingered by captured prisoners, had yielded little. The Crackers had taken the art of operational security to a whole new level. If Edward hadn't known better, he would have wondered if the Crackers had been studying Marine textbooks on insurgent warfare. Their targets were carefully picked and targeted, while civilians were kept out of the crossfire as much as possible. Even so, there were over seventy confirmed civilian dead in the fighting.

"It will stop when we beat them," Edward said, projecting an image of calm he didn't feel. It was important to reassure the Governor, for he looked as if he were on the verge of coming apart. He'd had enough problems grasping the fact that the Council had tried to diminish his authority, let alone the fundamentals of insurgent warfare. The important thing was that they didn't lose their nerve. "They are not gods, Governor."

"It's easy for you to say," the Governor protested. "What's to stop them from trying to cut Camelot off from our food supplies?"

Edward knew that that was a problem, although they had handled it by amassing stores since the Marines had landed, preparing for a siege. The insurgents probably couldn't impose a physical blockade of Camelot – not unless they had enough heavy weapons to take the city in one fell swoop – but they could intimidate or harass farmers into refusing to send their produce to the city. They might not even need to be unpleasant about it. Half the farmers – if not more – were either Crackers themselves or shared their goals. Edward had, very quietly, deployed a pair of his medics to keep a careful eye on the incoming food. Poison would probably wipe out a third of the city if it was used properly.

"That would also threaten their own interests," Edward reminded him. "The farmers need the industrial produce from the city."

He scowled inwardly. That wasn't quite true, even though in the long run a mutual blockade would probably harm both sides. The farmers, some careful investigation had proven, had been stockpiling supplies for quite some time, aided by particularly inane Council policies that had been simply ignored. They would need re-supplying eventually, but they could go on long enough for the Crackers to win their war. In trying to preserve their monopoly, the Council had lost a chance to wean some of the farmers away from their deadly enemies, practically forcing them into enemy hands. The idiots could have cost the Empire the war.

The thought was galling, but it had to be faced. If the Council had been willing to make compromises, they might have been able to put off the war, perhaps even avert it altogether…but no, any hint of a change in policy was denounced in the Council Chamber as appeasement. The Council would quite happily fight the war to the last Civil Guardsman or common soldier, while they skulked in their mansions and made a profit off the war. The Governor's emergency powers didn't go far enough to prevent the Council from skimming off enough money to make themselves even more powerful.

He stared down at the map, barely seeing the notes he'd scrawled across it. The proof of High Treason they needed to find hadn't been found, not yet, leaving him wondering if the Council had realised just how badly it had been compromised. Not all of the Council were part of Carola Wilhelm's secret cabal, but those that weren't part of her group were isolated, abandoned without even a word of support from their Governor. As long as Carola and her allies controlled an absolute majority in the Council, they could effectively run it to suit themselves.

The Governor coughed behind him and Edward nodded. "It's a question of keeping our nerve and holding on to what we have," Edward said, patiently. "By taking up positions in the townships, we force them to come out and fight, giving us a chance to reduce their numbers and prove that they can be beaten."

"At a high cost," the Governor reminded him. He'd faced a Cracker insurgency before, but that had been a small thing, hardly a serious problem compared to the one they now faced. Avalon hadn't seen such high levels of violence since Peter Cracker had died and, this time, there was no Imperial Navy destroyer waiting high overhead to deal out death and destruction on command. Even if there had been such a ship, it would have been useless; the Crackers were far too close to the civilian population to risk a bombardment. Edward knew that there were Imperial Army and Navy commanders who wouldn't have flinched at the thought, but he had no intention of joining their ranks. It would have been mass slaughter. "Are we sure that it is worth it?"

"Unless you intend to disband the Council and seek terms with the Crackers, yes," Edward said, tightly. A hot flash of anger was buried in his mind before it could show itself on his face. The Governor didn't need a scare. "How badly do you want to have a safe, secure and prosperous Avalon by the time you leave your post?"

"That isn't fair," the Governor snapped back. "It isn't the task of the military to set policy objectives. They just do the fighting."

"And the dying," Edward said, tightly. There were too many inexperienced young men out there, armed and terrified. They'd all had a baptism of fire over the last few days. Truthfully, he was surprised – and relieved – that it hadn't been a great deal worse. Inexperienced soldiers tended to panic and make dreadful mistakes. "If you want a policy objective secured, you do have to tell us what it is."

The Governor took a series of deep breaths, calming himself. "That was unworthy of me," he said. He sounded surprisingly contrite. "I apologise."

"As do I," Edward agreed, seriously. They exchanged a long glance. "Has the Council bothered to make its views known on the war?"

"Oh, the majority have proclaimed their loud support for the war and their confidence that the Army of Avalon will bring us total victory," the Governor said. "A couple are suggesting that we should seek terms with the Crackers, but they're…effectively the Cracker-elected representatives."

Edward nodded sourly. The majority of the Councillors had been elected by the cities, because the cities had the greatest population concentrations, but a handful had been elected by the countryside, mainly by men and women who had managed to free themselves and their families of debt by the time the Council started manipulating the economy to keep the majority of the population in bondage. They might not have been actual insurgent leaders – the Crackers would have to be fools to risk their leaders in Camelot, for the Governor had vast powers if he declared martial law – but Edward would have been very surprised if they didn't have links with the Cracker leadership. He'd seriously considered making a covert approach to them, yet the Governor had refused to even consider the possibility. Besides, what could he actually offer the Crackers? The Council would block even the tiniest concession.

"In other words, nothing," Edward said, grimly. "Don't worry, Governor. We will win this war."

He strode out of Government House and headed across the street to his private car. Gwen had insisted on him keeping at least three bodyguards around him at all times – she took the fourth position herself – before she'd consented to allow him to leave Castle Rock. Camelot itself was being heavily patrolled by the Civil Guard, but she'd expressed no confidence in their ability to handle matters if push came to shove. Now that quite a few of their corrupt and self-serving officers had been removed, the Civil Guard should have been able to give a good account of itself, yet Gwen remained unconvinced. Edward couldn't really blame her.

The drive back to the spaceport was uneventful, surprisingly. Patrols had discovered a handful of IEDs scattered along the road and several cars had been shot at by hidden snipers, who had melted away before they could be caught. Edward had worn his armour, expecting trouble, but nothing had materialised apart from a pair of Bloodsuckers, who had eyed his armour with disdainful eyes. They probably considered him the equivalent of tinned meat.

He nodded approvingly as the guards at the spaceport took nothing for granted, checking his ID and that of everyone in the car before allowing them to proceed. The spaceport had been attacked by a handful of mortar teams in the first couple of days, but unlike the various deployment bases the spaceport was protected by a laser counter-battery system. The shells had all been destroyed before they could detonate and patrols had forced the mortar teams to seek safer targets elsewhere. It was lucky that the Crackers didn't resort to suicide attacks, he knew; a truck loaded with explosives could have made a real mess of the main gate and its defenders.

"Welcome back, sir," Lieutenant Howell said. He'd been moved to the spaceport to handle logistics now that the Company and the new units had been deployed. "I have a report on the financial situation that you need to read…"

Edward shook his head. "Not now," he said, firmly. As important as finances were, they didn't compete with the war. "I don't have the time. I'll read it tonight."

"Yes, sir," Howell said. "I should also add that Kitty Stevenson has arrived and is demanding to speak to you personally."

"That's *Colonel* Stevenson to you," Edward said, reprovingly. The various intelligence services were not well liked by those who had to do the fighting – and the dying – but he had to admit that Kitty had done a good job. "Where is she now?"

"Room 19, wearing the floor out by pacing," Howell explained. "I think that if you'd been with anyone but the Governor, she would have demanded that you forget him and come back at once."

"I'll see what she wants," Edward said. He looked up at Gwen. "Coming?"

Kitty Stevenson hadn't worn out the floor, but she looked excited and dead tired. "Captain," she said, as Edward entered the barren room. "There's been a very important break in the case."

Edward smiled at her obvious enthusiasm. "Is it one that we can use against the Council?"

"Oh yes, and more," Kitty said. She pulled a small flat terminal out of her bag and placed it on the metal table. "We've been running an investigation into the various brothels and suchlike in the city after we realised that many of the kidnapped women and girls from near the badlands had been transported to Camelot and put to work as whores. Most of them were teenagers or in their early twenties, but a handful of them were younger – much younger. It turned out that most of the preteen children were sent to a single place hidden within the warehouse district, one known only to a handful of people."

Edward felt sick. He saw nothing wrong in visiting a prostitute, provided that she'd entered the game willingly, but including children was the greatest perversion he could imagine. The Empire shared his feelings to the degree that anything to do with child abuse and molestation automatically became the concern of Imperial Intelligence, rather than any local police force or Civil Guard. The punishments for those who abused children were harsh; if they were lucky, they were dumped on a hellish prison planet and abandoned. If they were unlucky…well, they might have a little accident while in custody. Even their fellow criminals loathed paedophiles.

"We wanted to find out who used the place, so we slipped bugs into the buildings and started to build up a picture of who visited," Kitty continued, blithely unaware of Edward's growing rage. She'd known of a building that catered to paedophiliac shitheads and hadn't done anything about it? The kids should have been rescued and their pimps should have been taken into custody, perhaps with excessive levels of violence. Every Marine in the Company would have volunteered to carry *that* mission out. "A few hours ago, we struck gold."

She tapped the terminal and an image appeared in front of Edward's eyes. There was a man, with a very familiar face, and a young girl… Edward's gorge rose and he pushed the terminal away, unwilling to face what he was doing to her. The girl was clearly not a teenager. If she was over ten, Edward would have been astonished.

"The bastard," he hissed. His knuckles itched with the desire to find the man and beat him into a bloody pulp. It would have been so easy. The sight of his fat bloated body heaving away…he concentrated, remembering the disciplines, and focused on Kitty's face. The urge to hurt her was almost overwhelming, for she'd watched and done nothing as a little girl was raped. "We've got him."

"He's one of the ones who make up Mrs Wilhelm's little cabal," Kitty agreed, calmly. She was unaware of his thoughts, luckily for her own control. "We have clear proof here of an act that doesn't go under the Governor's purview at all. We can pick him up, sweat him and get him to testify against his fellows."

Edward scowled. "Are you sure he will talk?"

Kitty lifted a single elegant eyebrow. "You *do* know what the punishment is for what he's doing in that image?"

"You want to bargain with him," Edward said, in disgust. "You know just what public opinion will do to us if we let him live, once this gets out."

"I have no intention of allowing him to go free," Kitty said, tartly. "I intend to get him to testify against the others, and then we can deal with him. He won't last long on an indenture gang anyway."

"How true," Edward said. "Gwen?"

"Yes, sir," Gwen said. "What can I do for you?"

"Take two Marines and pick this fat bloated bastard up," Edward ordered. "Use all the force you need and then some." He looked up at Kitty. "Once we have him in custody, I want this fucking place shut down, the kids taken somewhere safe and a team to go through the building and identify every sad fucker who has used it ever since it was opened. Do you understand me?"

Kitty hesitated. "Sir, with all due respect, if we shut it down now the Council may realise what we've stumbled upon…"

"Fuck that," Edward snapped. Profanity was unlike him, but he was *angry*. "We're here to protect the citizens of the Empire." He tapped the terminal with one angry hand. "Does that look like we're doing that girl any good?"

"No, sir," Gwen said. She shared his anger. It occurred to Edward that she might not be the best person to send on the mission, but there was no one else at hand. "We'll bring him in alive and cooperative."

"Good," Edward said. He looked down at the map for a long moment, trying to scrub the image from his mind. It refused to fade. His memory had been excellent even before he'd gone through the weirder training exercises on the Slaughterhouse and he had been cursed with the gift of instant recall. "Kitty…good work, but remember…we're here to protect people."

"Yes," Kitty said. "And we can best do that by shutting down the Council."

Edward didn't bother to argue.

CHAPTER FORTY-EIGHT

> If insurgency is a war of perceptions rather than brute force, it must be accepted that each side will misjudge the other's strengths and weaknesses. They will see their own weaknesses and the enemy's strengths, rather than the enemy's weaknesses and their own strength. Deception and deceit play a vital role in such warfare; the appearance of being strong is often actually being strong, assuming that the enemy is unable or unwilling to call the bluff.
> -Major-General Thomas Kratman (Ret), *A Marine's Guide to Insurgency.*

"Your forces have been wiped out," Gaby said, as she breezed into the prison cell. "You're the last Marine on the planet."

"Bullshit," Blake Coleman said. He'd been fed a combination of drugs that should have helped keep him docile, but his implants seemed to be counteracting them somehow. Doctor White hadn't been able to explain how they were working, to the point where he'd wondered if Coleman had somehow been enhanced to be resistant to more than just truth drugs. Gaby would have believed him if it hadn't been for how Blake Coleman had been captured in the first place. "I know you're lying."

Gaby dropped the pretence as Blake's dark eyes turned to fix on her, mask and all. "So I am," she said, with mock surprise. "Whatever gave me away?"

Blake smiled. "You're not a very good liar," he said with calm amusement. Gaby felt her face flushing and couldn't keep the scowl under control. "Your voice betrayed a certain lack of truthfulness. You simply lack the ability to serve up a shit sandwich while calling it roast beef and horseradish sauce."

Gaby chuckled. "Your people are fighting well," she admitted as she took a seat. "How does that make you feel?"

"Pride in my friends and comrades," Blake said, dryly. "Regret and shame that I am not with them. Or did you expect me to somehow escape from this cell and return to the land of the living?"

"I have read hundreds of stories about the Terran Marine Corps from the Imperial Library," Gaby said seriously. If half of the stories were true, the Crackers were in serious trouble. "I would not have been too surprised to discover that you had chewed your way through the iron chains and vanished through the walls."

"I think that you have done too good a job on these chains," Blake said. "I couldn't get out of here if my name was Adam One."

Gaby snorted. Adam One was the Empire's favourite comic book character – or so all of his press releases said. By day, he was a loyal and conscientious bureaucrat in the Department of Colonial Representation; by night, he was the Silver Swordsman, hunting down the enemies of the Empire while cracking one-liners that never failed to get giggles from impressionable children. The comics had even reached Avalon, but by then Gaby had been seventeen and able to recognise them for the cheap propaganda they were. Even so, Adam One had had muscles on his muscles, just the sort of character to appeal to teenage boys and girls.

"I'd prefer not to take chances," she said, inspecting his bonds. "Is there anything we can do to make your stay more comfortable?"

Blake pretended to consider it. "Well, I'd like my hands unbound, some food that doesn't go into me through an IV line, a lift to the surface and a map pointing the way back to Camelot," he said, dryly. "This hotel has really poor service, you know. I think I'm going to lodge a complaint."

Gaby smiled. "I see that Adam One rubbed off on you too," she said. "I'd like to comply, but…you're our prisoner. Sorry."

"Yeah," Blake said. He looked up at her and she had the sudden, disconcerting feeling that he could see right through her mask. "I take it that you're getting worried, right? The grand attack plan not going according to plan?"

"Early days yet," Gaby said. She refused to allow him to get to her. She was merely interrogating him, or so she told herself. Everything he said would grant her insights into how his mind worked. "Your people are tough. I'll give them that."

"The toughest you'll ever face," Blake assured her. She had the nasty feeling that he was right. "You do realise that you're just digging your own graves?"

Gaby rounded on him. "Do you think that we have a choice?" She demanded. "Our choice seems to be between trying to take our freedom and bowing before the Council, one that has exploited us ever since the ADC sold off our contracts to raise some quick cash. Why the hell should we not fight?"

"Things are changing out there," Blake said, lifting his head slightly to indicate the sky. "There's a very distant possibility that Avalon might simply be abandoned. If that happens, the Captain will have far broader latitude to come to an agreement with you…but not if you kill his men. He won't be able to let that pass."

Gaby gathered herself. "There's an old story my father told me," she said, flatly. "Once upon a time in a mythical land named China…"

"It wasn't a myth," Blake said, flatly. "They were on the losing side in the Third World War and came late to the party when the Phase Drive was discovered, but they settled a couple of dozen worlds before the Federation collapsed and was replaced by the Empire. Some of their worlds are pretty nice, if sometimes a little weird; a handful of them are just hellish. They're pretty much par for the course, really."

Gaby frowned. "There was once a leader who decided that all crime had to be punished with death," she continued, refusing to allow him to distract her. "Everything from stealing a chicken to rape and murder earned the death penalty. Death spread rapidly, for who can be perfect all the time? One day, a group of labourers were walking to work when suddenly the leader turns to his men and asks them what is the punishment for being late? Death, they reply. And what is the punishment for rebellion? Death, they say again."

She snorted. "And what does he tell them?" She asked. "They're already late!"

"I know the story," Blake said. "And so they decide to go off and start a rebellion."

"That's the position we're in," Gaby said. "Quick death at the hands of your fellows or slow death at the hands of the Council. Why should we not fight? We might win."

Blake somehow managed a shrug, despite the chains. "Maybe you're right," he said. "But you should try contacting the Captain first and seeing what he might offer you."

"You don't understand," Gaby said. "I told you; I read as much as I could about the Marines. You're great soldiers; loyal, honourable, and brave to a fault…and I bet you're really kind to dumb animals. Except you're here, and you're fighting to keep the Council in power, because we know that you know just what kind of shit the Council has been pulling over the last few years. And what exactly have you done about it? Nothing! How can you claim to be a third force when you are so closely linked to the corrupt bastards who have been draining this planet dry?"

"You might be surprised by how much authority the Captain has, if you approached him," Blake said. "Until then…I'll just wait here, shall I?"

Gaby glared at him. "We could always start trying to extract information by force," she reminded him. "What would you say to that?"

Blake yawned. "Why, nothing," he said. "I *really* doubt that you can put me through anything worse than what I have already endured."

Gaby looked at him for a long moment and then stormed out of the cell.

"You really shouldn't go speak to him alone," Julian said, when she entered the meeting room. "It's not safe…"

The condescending tone in his voice almost made Gaby explode. "And nothing we've been doing since you and I were knee-high has been *safe*," she snapped. The last thing she needed was Julian pulling the overprotective big brother or boyfriend act. She'd known that he admired her from afar, but she didn't have any romantic feelings about him. Julian… was just another male friend, almost a brother. "The Marines could hit this place at any time and we'd be scooped up and arrested. This is not safe! We are not in a safe business!"

If he had smiled, she would have knocked it off his face. "You elected me the commander of this local cell," she said, knowing that it had been her name rather than anything else that had won her the position. The Cracker Family had an unbroken heritage of defeat, yet people still had faith. "Are you going to start challenging my authority at every turn?"

Julian wilted under her gaze. "I meant no offence," he said, shocked at her fury. "I merely wanted to make sure that you were safe."

Gaby looked him up and down, remembering the times they'd played together. Where had those moments gone? They'd been stolen by the demands of their war. Julian had grown up and become a fighter, just as she had…just as the eighty-odd dead Crackers had become. They had died because of her commands, shot down by the Marines or their new army.

"Good," she said, forcing a gentler tone into her voice. "I was perfectly safe."

"But he's an inhuman killing machine," Julian protested. "There's no such thing as safe…"

"Julian, behave," Rufus said, firmly. The older man had entered the room and took a seat by the table. "I don't have time to take my belt to you today."

Julian scowled, but fell quiet. "The fighting isn't going as well as we had planned," Gaby said. Julian started, as if he wanted to dispute that claim, and then thought better of it. "Although we have inflicted damage, they have inflicted damage on us and both sides are hurting."

The memory of seeing some of the wounded rose up unbidden in front of her eyes. She'd gone to see them, despite the risk, and had ended up horrified by the sight. The Crackers had taken a beating…and for what? None of the deployment bases had been overrun. The Marines and their puppets had fought back savagely and the Devil himself seemed to be helping them. She wasn't even sure how many of their people had been killed or wounded.

"And let's not forget the civilians," Rufus added, casting a sharp glance towards his son. Julian had been the least caring about civilian casualties. "We have at least a hundred civilians injured and more made homeless by the fighting. It would have been worse if we hadn't run the risk of warning people to run at the first sign of fighting. Even so, it was quite bad enough."

"The evacuation plans are working," Julian protested. "They'd be safe if they followed them."

"But they can't," Gaby reminded him. "We're talking about them walking away from everything they own, for what? Just to allow us and the Marines to wreak havoc on their property."

She stared down at her hands. Unlike Camelot and the other four cities, the countryside was decentralised to extremes; the townships didn't really have a natural existence. Once the fighting had begun in earnest, most of the uncommitted citizens had moved out of the towns and into the countryside, following an evacuation plan that had been drawn up years ago. Julian had proposed only helping those who helped the Crackers, but Gaby and Rufus had overruled him, insisting that all of their people be helped equally. Good press was worth a thousand bullets and, besides, she'd settle for just keeping people out of the firing line.

And that brought her all the way back to the true reason for calling the meeting.

"Operation Headshot," she said. "Are we ready to go?"

"Give us four days," Rufus advised. "We'll have to get all of our assets in place and prepared to move…and we'll have to rely on our source in the Governor's office to help hide the preparations. You do realise that this is a hideous risk?"

"It's worth it, father," Julian said. "If we can win the war in one fell swoop, we won't have to worry about anything else ever again. The Imperial Navy will be helpless to intervene; the Marines will either be wiped out or isolated on Castle Rock and the Council will be destroyed. The war will end."

"Assuming that we pull it all off," Rufus warned. "The problem with any kind of battle plan is that it never survives first contact with the enemy. If I was in their place, I'd be taking a good hard look at *anything* coming into the city and if they find just one of the transports, the entire plan will become exposed. Their sweep through the Civil Guard may have removed most of the Council's placemen, but it also wiped out most of our sources. We may no longer be able to bribe our way out of trouble."

"Fancy that," Julian said. His voice was faintly mocking. "A Civil Guardsman who didn't take a bribe."

"Give them a few more weeks of hard training and they'll be able to add an extra three thousand men to the enemy ranks," Rufus snapped. "Give them a few months and they'll probably be able to deploy upwards of twenty *thousand* men. There are plenty of unemployed young men in Camelot they could bring into the Civil Guard or the Army of Avalon, if they started to pay them in cash."

"Or perhaps they'll just start conscripting people," Gaby added. Rufus was right; Operation Headshot was a risk, but it was one they had to take. Given a few months, the odds would swing badly against the Crackers and the war would be on the verge of being lost. She glanced down at her timepiece and scowled. "Operation Headshot will be launched six days from now."

"And God help us all," Julian said. "With your permission, then, I will start making my way to Camelot. You're going to need our support."

Gaby nodded tiredly. Operation Headshot had one major weakness; it required her to be in the city, rather than lurking somewhere on the outskirts while others did the hard work. Rufus had urged her to let someone else take the risks, but the legend demanded that a descendent of Peter Cracker stood up to claim the reins of government. The irony was almost overwhelming. Peter Cracker had never sought power for himself either.

"Of course," she said, tiredly. There was no point in explaining that she would rather not have had Julian's support, or rather his protection. "Start diversifying our assets. If everything goes wrong, we don't want to give the Marines a chance to dismantle the entire cell."

"I'll see to it," Rufus said. "You go get some sleep. You're going to need it."

"We got him, sir," Gwen said. "He was feeling very cooperative."

"Oh he was, was he?" Edward asked. "How much did you have to beat him to get him to talk?"

"We showed him the videos and told him that if he refused to cooperate, we'd dump him in the main jail after showing the inmates the video and promising to pardon the man who brought us his head," Gwen said, darkly. "It worked. He couldn't wait to tell us everything he knew."

"It was worse than we thought," Kitty added. "It turns out that the Wilhelm Family has several allies we didn't know about."

"If we know about them now," Edward warned. "Are you sure that he was telling the truth?"

"We hooked him up to a lie detector once we had finished scaring the shit out of the fat bastard," Gwen said. "He was telling the truth as he knew it. It wasn't very reassuring."

Edward skimmed the transcript, shaking his head. Lucas Trent hadn't known the half of it. He hadn't known about the private army Carola Wilhelm had been building up, or about the plan to replace the Governor and Major Grosskopf through assassination, or about the plan to start firebombing Cracker villages to exterminate the threat once and for all, or about the indentured servitude…

"A thoroughly sick woman," he concluded, finally. He looked up at Kitty. "We have the proof we need to move and move now, before she can launch any of these crazy plans."

"It looks that way," Kitty agreed. "I suggest striking now, without bothering to consult with anyone else. Your Marines can take her mansion and…"

"No," Edward said. A single platoon of Marines, all that he had on hand without recalling one of the units from the outlying villages, wouldn't be enough. Besides, it wasn't the Marines who had the strongest reason to go after the Council. "I want you to take this directly to Major Grosskopf and tell him to move, now, before they realise that something has gone badly wrong. The Civil Guard's Alpha Company can take the lead on this one."

"Yes, sir," Kitty said. If she was surprised at his decision, she didn't show it. "I'll tell him personally."

"Gwen" – he was on the verge of saying that he would go in person, but she would never have allowed it – "take the QRF and hold them" – he glanced over the street map of Camelot – "here. If the Civil Guard runs into trouble, you are cleared to use any means necessary to assist them, but remember we want as many of them alive as possible."

"Sir," Kitty said, slowly, "do we really want to take them alive?"

"Yes," Edward said, flatly. An idea had started to flicker into existence at the back of his mind. "We have a Council problem and a Cracker problem. With luck, solving one problem will help us to solve the other."

CHAPTER FORTY-NINE

> The Empire's laws were originally intended to be blind, to serve all without fear or favour. It didn't last. The rich and powerful could manipulate the law to their own ends, destroying the faith in the law that the law needed – must have – to survive.
> - Professor Leo Caesius, *The Waning Years of Empire* (banned).

Tam Howard checked the guest's ID card, confirmed it against the list of people Carola Wilhelm had invited to her latest party and waved her in. The young lady gave him a wink that would have gotten a less well-connected woman arrested and headed through the gates, leaving Tam shaking his head. Most of the population of Camelot was remaining inside, fearing that the Crackers would soon bring the war to Camelot itself, but Carola Wilhelm had decided to throw a party instead. Everyone who was anyone in society was going to be there.

"Nice piece of ass," one of the other guards observed. He was new, having quit the Civil Guard only a week ago following an unexplained discrepancy in the regimental accounts. He'd been luckier than he deserved and Tam had made a mental note to keep an eye on him. A thief couldn't be trusted too much. "Do they sometimes come on to you?"

"Our job is keeping the mansion safe," Tam reminded him, sharply. "Playing with the guests is not allowed, particularly not when we're on duty. Concentrate on your job and visit a whore later if you feel blue-balled."

"Jesus, mate," the other guard said. "I was only kidding."

Tam shrugged. Carola Wilhelm had hired over a hundred guards to protect her family home, ensuring that they were armed to the teeth with barely-legal weapons. Tam, himself a former member of the Civil Guard, rather enjoyed some of the perks of the job, even though he wished that his mistress was less sociable. Her parties provided too many opportunities for someone to get inside and hurt her, or one of the guests. It didn't help that her guests were generally wealthy and well-connected and – of course – objected strongly to the suggestion that they might be under suspicion of anything. He wasn't allowed to search their bags, or even run them through a basic security scanner, which meant that they could bring anything inside the building. One of them could easily be carrying a bomb.

It wasn't the same for the servants, thankfully, even though it made the guards unpopular. Tam had ordered regular searches of their property and strip-searched any servant who left the mansion, if only for a few hours. Sometimes the searches yielded drugs or other surprises; more often, they revealed nothing but an irate servant. Tam knew, better than the others, that they had to remain in their mistress' favour. Without her, they would be on the streets and starving. The others who might hire bodyguards wouldn't want them.

A Civil Guard van drove past as another guest arrived, the newcomer from Earth. She was a horse-faced woman without connections to Avalon's aristocracy, but Carola Wilhelm had ordered that Fiona Caesius be given all the courtesies that she offered to her friends and family. Tam felt a moment of pity for the woman's husband as he checked her ID, and then waved her through. Another Civil Guard van drove past and he frowned, puzzled. Was there something happening in their area? He was tempted to call his mistress and ask, but she would be busy and wouldn't like the interruption…

He blinked as a third van appeared and parked in front of the walls. A moment later, armed soldiers began jumping out, fanning into a protective wall and lifting live weapons. Tam reached for the emergency button and held his finger over it, hearing alarm bells sounding off in his head. Something was very badly wrong. A final figure jumped out of the truck, protected by a cordon of armed soldiers, and he felt his insides turn to ice.

It hadn't been that long since Major George Grosskopf had dismissed him from the service.

"Sir," he said, as the Major strode up to him. Bluster was the only option. The guards were outnumbered and badly outgunned. "I'm afraid that I cannot let you into the building. You're not on the guest list."

Grosskopf's face stretched into something that even a charitable man would have found hard to call a smile. "I'm afraid that you're under the wrong impression," he said, mockingly. "We are here with a warrant for the arrest of Carola Wilhelm, Markus Wilhelm and over fifty other people, all of whom are attending this party. I strongly advise you to offer no resistance."

Tam stared at him. He wasn't bluffing, he knew. "This building is protected by Council authority," he blustered. Carola wouldn't thank him for just letting them in without a fight, yet there was no way to stop them, or even to slow them down. "You cannot come in without direct permission from the Governor."

"Which we have," Grosskopf assured him pleasantly. He looked over at the other four guards, who were standing there unsure of what to do. Their hands were on their weapons, but they hadn't lifted them, thankfully. Grosskopf's men would wipe them out before they could fire a single shot. "Put down your weapons and place your hands on your head."

"Yes, sir," Tam said, bitterly. If nothing else, he could prevent a slaughter. "We surrender."

Two burly soldiers grabbed him, secured his hands with a plastic tie and left him on the ground, waiting to be picked up. "Stay there," Grosskopf ordered dryly. Tam would have sworn at him if he dared. "We'll be back for you soon."

George took one last look at the ex-Guardsman and led the way into the mansion's grounds. Alpha Company might still be understrength, but he'd drawn reliable men from two lesser units and led almost a full company upwards towards the house. He'd only seen it twice before, back when Carola Wilhelm had tried to bribe him into supporting her ambitions, and it never failed to impress him. The Council had been able to get almost anything they wanted and Carola had wanted a mansion that didn't leave anyone in doubt about her importance. The massive stone building was testament enough to her wealth and power, built on the bones of men and women who had died indebted to her. George had seriously considered simply attacking the complex with helicopters and blowing the building into burning debris, but that wouldn't have been as satisfying as taking her into custody permanently.

He checked his radio as other teams swarmed through the other two gates. The guards had offered no resistance, thankfully, for he would have had them killed if necessary. Most of them were little more than traitors to the Civil Guard; men who had joined, accepted training and then left for richer fields elsewhere. They were effectively compliant in her crimes. A handful of guests, roaming on the lawn, stared up at the advancing Guardsmen, but before they could react they were grabbed, tied and left there for later. A happy couple necking on the grass had no idea that they were in trouble until it was far too late. George snorted when he saw them and carried on.

The noise of men and women having fun could be heard as they rounded the mansion and headed down towards the pool. At least a hundred men and women were there, swimming in the water or chatting endlessly about nothing as they watched the younger ones frolicking in the pool. George felt sick when he realised that all of the wealth and luxury on display had been extracted from people who hadn't been able to resist, rather than something the wealthy had earned for themselves. There were young girls in skimpy bathing costumes and boys already tending to fat and arrogance. They had no idea just how fragile their power actually was.

George lifted his gun and fired a single shot into the air. Silence fell, a silence that deepened when the guests looked around and saw the soldiers standing there. A handful of women fainted in shock and several others started to inch back, like sheep suddenly terrified of the wolves in their midst. The party had suddenly come to an end. The music, performed by live musicians, had come to a halt. The musicians were as scared as anyone else.

"This building is now under the control of the Civil Guard," George said, into the silence. "Until we can sort out the guilty from the innocent, we are going to place everyone in the building under arrest. Any attempt to resist will be met with as much force as necessary to terminate the resistance. Stand up, get out of the pool and put your hands on your head – and wait. We will deal with you all in a moment."

"You cannot do this," one of the young men burst out. George recognised him from the reports he'd seen, a young scion of a wealthy family with a taste for rape and sexual humiliation. He should have been spending twenty years at hard labour; he would have been spending them if his family hadn't intervened and forced his release. He hadn't learned anything from the experience. "This place is…"

"Under my control," George said, unable to keep a hint of amusement from his voice. They'd all once been the Lords of Creation. Now they were terrified sheep. "I won't warn you again, Sean. Put your hands on your head and surrender peacefully."

Sean leapt at him, hands outstretched as if he intended to strangle George personally. One of the soldiers stepped forward, but George waved him back, stepping out of Sean's way and pistol-whipping him right across the mouth. Blood and teeth went flying as the young man collapsed to the ground, whimpering. No one had ever taught him discipline; no one had ever taught him the difference between right and wrong. George watched him gasping on the ground and felt nothing, not even pity or disgust as blood pooled on the ground. Sean's life had been ruined a long time before George had come to Avalon.

He looked up and swept his gaze across the crowd. "Is there anyone else who feels like having a go at us?"

There was no one. The soldiers moved from person to person, tying their hands and leaving them sitting on the ground, after carefully separating the women from the men. George watched as they patted down their captives, removing anything that could be used as a weapon, wondering where the real prize was. Carola Wilhelm was not among the prisoners. If she had escaped…but even if she did, where could she go?

"Detail four men to watch the prisoners," he ordered, tartly. They hadn't searched the house yet. "The rest of you, get into that mansion and search it from end to end."

Carola had been lucky. She'd been wrapped up in a meeting with one of her fellow Councillors – discussing the relief package the Council would be offering to farmers caught up in the midst of the fighting – when the raid began. An alert had been flashed to her at once, but by then it was already too late to escape. The surveillance bugs she'd scattered around the walls confirmed that the Civil Guard had blocked all of the exits.

Part of her wanted to scream at the sheer *unfairness* of the universe – allowing it to happen when she was so close to success – but she knew from long experience that that wouldn't change anything. The soldiers were already cuffing her guests – she smiled inwardly when Sean was knocked to the ground, for she'd never liked the young pup – and it wouldn't be long before they started to search her house. She keyed her personal terminal and brought up an option she'd never dreamed she would need, ordering the house mainframe – years in advance of anything like it on the planet – to wipe all of the sensitive files and then self-destruct. Whatever they'd found that had emboldened them to raid the house of a Councillor, they wouldn't find the evidence they needed to have her interrogated under truth drugs. They wouldn't be able to prove anything.

Quickly, she turned to a bust on the wall and pulled its nose in a certain manner, opening the secret passageway she'd had built into the walls. The builders had thought that she was crazy, but they'd done as she'd ordered, giving her a house that had plenty of secret ways to move unseen. They'd all died afterwards for knowing too much, their celebration in a bar Carola owned marred by a rogue gunman who had mown them all down and then turned the weapon on himself. It wouldn't be long before the passages were discovered, assuming that the Civil Guard thought to look, but she'd have a chance to get out of the firing line before they caught her. Alive and free, she could link up with her contacts; in prison, her freedom of action would be circumscribed. How long would it be before the Governor worked up the nerve to actually charge her with something they could legally interrogate her for, with or without evidence?

The interior of the passageway was dark and cramped, but it allowed her to move between the walls. She'd had it designed so that sounds from outside – such as the sound of crashing boots – could be heard, allowing her a chance to deduce what was going on outside. She hoped that Markus was all right, but there was no way to know for sure. He'd been entertaining a younger woman at the time and might have been distracted. It wasn't as if she really cared about his frequent affairs – they'd married because of a mutual lust for power, not love – but losing Markus would be hard, particularly if they interrogated him. He knew everything she knew about the overall plan.

Damn it, she thought, as she found the ladder and climbed down two floors. It was harder than she remembered and she found herself panting at the bottom. *What did you find out that brought you here?*

The question seemed beyond her ability to answer. The Civil Guard had been showing a distressing independence as of late, ever since they'd walked into a trap she'd organised. Major Grosskopf's purge had wiped out most of her sources…could it be that he'd browbeaten the Governor into approving the raid? The Marines didn't seem to be in evidence, but she saw their shadow over the whole failure. They just didn't behave in a predictable manner. Or had someone talked? There was no way to know. Silently, she ran through a list of possible suspects, but found nothing. Anyone who had known the full truth would have had as much to lose as she had.

She found the hatch and checked it carefully, before keying the switch that allowed her into the basement. It was supposed to be secure, but after the raid she had given up assuming that anywhere was actually safe from intruders. It was a shame that there was no underground way out of the mansion, yet she hadn't been able to risk anyone coming in. There were too many experienced thieves in Camelot as it was. She pulled on the chameleon suit, keyed it for invisibility, and headed up the stairs. A pair of Civil Guardsmen was standing at the main door, watching for anyone coming in or out, but they didn't seem to see her at all. She held her breath as she slipped past them and out into the open, trusting in the suit to keep her invisible. They shouldn't even have suspected its existence. It had cost far more than even she cared to think about just to bring two of them to Avalon.

Her lawn, the grassy lawn she'd had made because she could, was no longer pristine. Hundreds of men and women lay on it, taken prisoner by the Civil Guard. A handful had clearly complained loudly and had been stunned by the guards. A number of preteen children sat at one end of the lawn, their hands unbound. She guessed that they'd been told to stay where they were and not cause trouble. Seeing them sent a nasty thought trickling into the back of her mind, leaving her to wonder if she knew how they'd been betrayed after all. The irony was troubling; if she was right, she'd intended to publicly hang the betrayer once she'd secured her power.

The main gate was guarded by three Marines in their combat armour, but it was open, offering her the chance to slip right past them and out into the city. Once she was outside, she could find her allies and start fighting back, perhaps even bringing down the Governor without the rest of the Council. She walked forward, reminding herself that they couldn't see her, and reached the gate…and a Marine stepped into her path. Before she could react, an armoured fist slammed into her stomach, knocking her to the ground. The Marine wrenched her hands behind her back and tied them firmly together, before ripping holes in the suit and rendering it visible. Too late, she realised her mistake. The Marine helmets could see right through a chameleon suit. They'd probably thought her walking towards them hilarious.

A hand rolled her over and she found herself looking into Major Grosskopf's eyes. "Carola Wilhelm," he said, "I arrest you on the charge of high treason. You do not have the right to remain silent; I am obliged to warn you that any lies or untruths you tell that are discovered by the lie detectors will be held against you at your trial. You have been warned."

He pulled her to her feet and pushed her roughly towards the rest of the prisoners.

CHAPTER FIFTY

There is always someone who doesn't get the word. In war, communications can be disrupted – either accidentally or as a result of enemy action. The more complex a battle plan is, therefore, the greater the chance of a random 'X Factor' affecting the outcome.
-Major-General Thomas Kratman (Ret), *A Marine's Guide to Insurgency.*

"We have to cancel the operation," Gaby said. She picked up one of the newspapers and held it out to Julian. "Read it for yourself."

Julian read the story rapidly. "The Council has been arrested and charged with high treason," he said. His voice became mocking. "Shocking developments at Wilhelm Mansion. Hundreds arrested. Civil Guard forces in control of the Councillors and their houses. The rump Council will be meeting later today to debate what it means for the future of Avalon." He scowled. "I see no reason to change our plans."

Gaby counted to ten under her breath. "Julian," she said, wondering where the young boy she'd known had gone, "this is something that changes everything! What would happen if we gave them time to realise just how badly the Council had served them?"

"It's hardly enough," Julian countered, slowly. "Even if the entire Council was placed under arrest, they'd just be replaced by others with the same interest in maintaining the *status quo*. If anything, this is a chance to go ahead with Operation Headshot and terminate the government, once and for all."

Gaby stood up, angrily. Living in a flophouse for two days with Julian had been unbearable, even though it was safe. The messy apartment had been abandoned to squatters long ago and the Cracker agents within the city had found it convenient as a hidden base. They'd even taken the time to touch it up a little, cleaning out the messes the previous tenants had left behind. It was hardly a palace, but it would do.

"We're not going to get very far if we launch the operation and fail," Gaby said. "Should we not try, at least, to take advantage of this before it's too late?"

"It is already too late," Julian said. "We have two hundred people within Camelot and the other…designated targets. We cannot cancel the operation now, for someone wouldn't get the order in time and would launch their part of the operation, unaware that there isn't going to be any support. And, Gaby, they would be slaughtered for sure. The timing is out of our hands."

Gaby stared at him, hating him, but she had to admit that he was right. Operation Headshot was easily the most complex operation the Crackers had ever planned, even back when they'd started it as an exercise in wishful thinking. Everything had to fit together reasonably well, if not perfectly, and he was right. One of the teams wouldn't get the message in time and would launch their attack. If they were wiped out, it would be bad enough, but if they survived long enough to be interrogated…the Governor and the Marines would learn exactly what had been planned. There would no longer be any hope for peace.

"God damn you," she said, angrily. It had been Julian who had drawn up the final version of the plan. Had he done it on purpose? She couldn't see how, but Julian was smarter than he seemed. "How many people are going to die?"

"This isn't the time for a political debate," Julian snapped back. Without Rufus, the tension between them was rapidly coming to the fore. "We stand on the brink of winning the war in one fell swoop or losing… only a handful of our own men. The Governor's confidence in his security measures will not survive what we're planning to do. We cannot pull back now and wait for another opportunity. There might not *be* another opportunity. What happens when they get their act together and tighten up security here?"

He made an effort to sit back on his bed. "Gaby…I know you care about our people, and I know you want to end this peacefully if possible, but we're well past the stage when we could call the operation off," he said. "We have no choice."

"I know," Gaby snarled. "I understand that. I also understand that our timing has been incredibly poor!"

She shook her head, pacing over to the window and staring out at the apartment blocks that some unimaginative engineer had designed and some equally unimaginative city-planner had ordered built. She had never seen Earth, but if half the stories were true, the designers had clearly based their plans on Earth's massive mega-cities. The community had no shops, no entertainment and no life. No one would want to live in such buildings if they had a choice. They were infested with the debris of the Council; the permanently unemployed, the drug addicts and the thousands of single-parent families. It wasn't the worst that Camelot had to offer, but it was pretty damned close.

And all of it could be removed, with a little effort. If the Council had even bothered to care, they could have done much to improve the lot of the people trapped in walls that might as well have been made of cardboard. The homeless children could have been farmed out to the farming communities, where children were valued and loved and taught how to behave. The older men and women could have been taught new skills; their debts could have been forgiven, giving them the chance to build a new life for themselves. But the Council didn't care. They would sooner see the entire planet decay into rubble than give up one iota of their power.

"Pass the final word," she ordered, feeling cold rage overwhelming her. Rage at the Council and at herself, one for creating the nightmare that she lived in, the other for pressing ahead with the war. "Tell all the teams that we move, soon."

"Of course," Julian said. He made a manful attempt to hide his delight and relief, but Gaby saw it anyway. "I'll see to it at once."

"Would you mind explaining, just for the benefit of an old and tired man, just what you thought you were doing?"

Brent Roeder had never been so scared in his life, yet somehow he managed to cover it up with bluster. No one – not the Marines, not the Civil Guard, not even the media – had informed him that the raids were going ahead until they were already over. Armed Civil Guardsmen had raided the houses belonging to fifteen Councillors, taking them and their guests into custody…all without a warrant from his office. Over five hundred people, including a cross-section of the wealthy and powerful, had been taken into custody. They'd all been shipped out to a new detention camp near the spaceport…

And no one, absolutely no one, had told him what was going on.

"Damn it, George," he thundered, ignoring Captain Stalker's blank face. It was inscrutable, yet he thought that he detected a hint of amusement. "Purging the Civil Guard was bad enough, but this…are you *trying* to start a civil war?"

"We already *have* a civil war," Grosskopf observed, calmly. "We're actually trying to prevent it from getting worse…"

"Well, you failed," Brent snapped. "I know we've had our differences, but really…why didn't you bring this to me?" The suspicion that had flowered in his mind earlier returned with a vengeance. "Or are you planning to unseat me and take the post of Governor for yourself?"

Grosskopf winced at the suggestion. "No, sir," he said, tightly. "I believed – we believed – that it would be better to act fast, leaving you with the option of disowning us if everything went completely to shit. I might add that I have broad authority to operate under certain circumstances."

Brent switched his glare to Captain Stalker, who appeared unruffled. "And what, exactly, do you have to do with this?"

"Several days ago, we discovered evidence that a prominent member of the Council was visiting a brothel, one that used small children as…sexual toys," Captain Stalker said. There was an undeniable twitch in his jaw, leaving Brent wondering just what had happened. If that was the complete story, he would eat his hat. "We picked him up – as we are authorised to do under Imperial Law – and sweated him. He confessed to involvement in the Council's plan to unseat you and replace Imperial Government with their rule. Using this new evidence, we moved rapidly to capture the traitors before they could escape or put their plans into operation."

"You should have cleared it with me," Brent said, coldly. It was hard to keep a grip on his temper with the ground sliding away under him, but somehow he managed to keep his voice reasonably even. "Was that too much to ask?"

Captain Stalker met his gaze evenly, but when he spoke, his voice was very gentle. "We know that they had spies within Government House," he said. "If we had discussed the issue with you, it might have warned them and forced them to strike first, launching their coup while we were unprepared. We had to move fast to pre-empt them."

"My aides are completely trustworthy and above suspicion," Brent said, angrily. "Or do you have reason to believe otherwise?"

"A spy who was not above suspicion would not be much good to his real master," Captain Stalker pointed out. "We'll run all of the prisoners through interrogation and find out who here is reporting to them, at which point we can remove them from their post and deal with them as seems appropriate."

"But you don't understand," Brent protested. "The people you arrested practically run the planet! They certainly run the industries, the orbital station and God alone knows what else. We can't do without them!"

"Funny, that," Grosskopf said. "I spoke to their foremen at the factories…and, well let's just say that they're not too fond of their masters. They agreed to keep working for us, at least until we can get the final disposition of the factories sorted out. Let's face it, sir. None of the people we arrested actually *ran* anything. They merely owned it. The real work was done by others."

Brent snorted. "So what do you suggest we do, then?"

"Deal with the traitors publicly," Captain Stalker said. "We have the evidence, so we hold a trial. You can do that in your role as the Emperor's Viceroy out here. We can confiscate everything they own now and put them somewhere out of the way, at least until we can report their arrest and trial to the sector capital. Once their property is confiscated, you cancel all of the debts."

Brent blinked. "All of them?"

"All of them," Captain Stalker agreed. His face darkened. "Let's face it. None of the original money is ever going to be repaid, is it? All the debts are really good for is keeping people down and that just throws people into the arms of the Crackers. If we cancel the debt, all of the debt, this instantly becomes the most popular government Avalon has ever had."

"That may not be legal," Brent pointed out. "Can we…?"

"Of course we can," Captain Stalker insisted. "Think about it; the property of a convicted traitor is forfeited to the Empire, which effectively means you out here. And you can dispose of your property any way you like."

Brent considered it. "I suppose it's workable," he said. "I'll have to give it some thought…"

"There isn't time," Captain Stalker said, flatly. He waved a hand in the direction of the Mystic Mountains, barely visible in the distance. "Out there, the war is still raging on. The Crackers are pushing us as hard as they can. If we cut the ground from under their feet, perhaps we can end the war before the entire planet goes up in flames."

He leaned closer. "Governor, the Crackers see you as being part of a corrupt administration that holds the people in bondage," he added. "The longer you sit on this, the harder it will be to separate yourself from the remains of the Council. You have to act now, because the Crackers are just as capable of making that argument as I am. How long will it be before they start pointing out that you could free the people…and have not done so?"

Rifleman Polly Stewart was silently grateful for her armour as the sun rose ever higher into the sky. The heat was already overpowering, even for someone who had spent weeks in a desert combat environment on the Slaughterhouse; the noise was even more so. The protesters outside consisted of people who had seen their relatives arrested in the purge and wanted them freed, whatever the cost. Some of them, Polly knew, were probably innocent. They still had to be held until the innocent could be separated from the guilty.

She glanced from side to side – the movement invisible behind her helmet – as the crowd seemed to grow larger. Counter-protesters had been marching on the other side of the barricades the Civil Guard had thrown up, threatening to attack the original protesters with naked force. They carried primitive weapons – everything from broken bottles to clubs – but she didn't care for the thought of what would happen if they tore into the protesters. The Imperial Charter guaranteed the right to protest peacefully, but both sides were already pushing the limits of 'peaceful'. A handful of bricks and stones had already been exchanged and worse was probably coming.

"The Old Man shouldn't have held the meeting here," Rifleman Chung muttered, through the dedicated channel. The four Marines who were serving as the Captain's close-protection detail had been horrified to discover that Government House was under siege. The two AFVs that the Civil Guard had parked in the street hadn't deterred them at all. "They should have held it at the spaceport."

Polly could only agree. The spaceport was secure; Camelot, without any real attempt to secure the borders, was not. The Governor should have moved operations into a bunker, just to make it harder for any prospective attacker. The Civil Guardsmen defending Government House might have been the best of the best, but *she* wasn't impressed. None of them would have lasted long on the Slaughterhouse.

"The Old Man's call," Corporal Feingold reminded them. He was the current fire team leader, commanding the other three…his ears still ringing with dire warnings from Sergeant Patterson about what would happen if Captain Stalker got so much as a scratch. "The Governor wishes to try to show everyone that everything is normal, so as long as the Captain is prepared to tolerate it…we tolerate it as well."

He looked over towards a pair of particularly odd protesters, women wearing tight shirts and nothing below the waist. Polly rolled her eyes inwardly. She'd grown up in a socially liberal society and even that would have been remarkable if done in public. They had to come from the upper class. No one who was not utterly convinced of their own superiority would have taken the risk.

"Man, I got to get me one of them," Chung said, dryly. Polly rolled her eyes. Chung wasn't quite up to Blake Coleman's standards as a ladies' man, but he spent most of his off-duty time chasing orgasmic relief. "Just look at them."

"Keep your eyes on the crowd," Feingold reminded him. The whole atmosphere was growing nastier. Polly didn't envy the Civil Guardsmen, who weren't wearing armour at all. A handful of rocks were thrown from one side at the other, which retaliated in kind. "There'll be time enough to chase girls after the fighting is over."

Polly scowled at the reminder. Most of the Marines were out in the countryside, backing up the Civil Guard and the Army of Avalon. Her friends – her family, in every way that mattered – were out there, fighting to hold the line against a series of increasingly complex and dangerous attacks. She, in the meantime, was stuck in a city that was run by corrupt lunatics. Even though the Council had been arrested, she had no confidence that anyone would make it better. Perhaps the Marines should just take over directly, she thought. They could hardly do a worse job.

"Contact," Chung said, suddenly. A massive truck had just turned the corner and was coming straight at the protestors, who scattered to get out of its way. No one – of course – had bothered to close the road. If they'd been in a city on any one of the Core Worlds, there would have been a hundred accidents by now. "It's coming right at us."

Polly swore as she brought her MAG up to firing position. The driver was gunning the engine, racing right towards the gates. He had to be insane, or intended to ram right into them. Feingold was barking orders, but there was no longer any time to hesitate. They squeezed their triggers as one, pouring fire into the truck…too late. The truck exploded and the entire world vanished in a blinding flash of white light.

The entire building shook violently. Edward heard crashing noises as items fell off walls and desks, while the windows blew in and a fine mist of plaster fell from the ceiling. Government House had been very well-built, unlike most of the other buildings in the city, but that hadn't been a tiny explosion. Part of his mind whispered that it had been a massive bomb, far too close for comfort. His ears were still ringing, but he was sure that he could hear more explosions sounding out in the distance.

The Governor was pulling himself up from the floor, staring at the wreckage of his office. "What…what's happening?"

Edward already knew the answer. "The Crackers," he said. There were no other suspects. No one else, now the Council had been neutralised, could have launched such an attack. "I think we left our reforms too late."

The Battle for Camelot had begun.

CHAPTER FIFTY-ONE

> The two most deadly weapons in the entire history of man are surprise and intelligence. A military force that neglects either or both of them is doomed to eventual defeat when it faces an opponent who studies both of them intensely, even if the unprepared are – on paper – the stronger force.
> -Major-General Thomas Kratman (Ret), *A Marine's Guide to Insurgency.*

Armstrong Base was the largest Civil Guard base on Avalon, situated on the outskirts of Camelot itself. It played host to Alpha and Beta Companies, the primary Civil Guard units, as well as a handful of supporting units and various military vehicles. It was also currently playing host to the First Avalon Infantry – as the new unit had been designated – which had been pulled back from the war to give its soldiers a chance to catch their breath and pass on their lessons to the newcomers and retrained Civil Guardsmen. The war was far away, but its impact was not.

Colonel Watanabe stood in the Command Room and surveyed the map with grim disapproval. It said something about the Council's – the *former* Council's – priorities that Armstrong Base possessed a reasonably modern command and control system, which was barely usable outside Camelot because the Council had been unwilling to invest in sophisticated communications systems that would keep it in secure contact with the outlying settlements. As the purge of officers and men continued, it was becoming increasingly clear that one reason the Civil Guard had failed to destroy the Crackers was because the Crackers had the Civil

Guard quite effectively penetrated. Their spies had operated in low-key posts, but they'd been more effective than an entire brigade of armed troops.

Still, the Colonel allowed himself to feel hopeful for the first time in years. His command of Beta Company might have been brought to a halt by the bandits, who had managed to shoot him in the leg and cripple him for a few months, but he'd rapidly been ordered to take command of Armstrong Base, where a busted leg wasn't so much of an impediment. The former commander was currently stuck in the stockade, awaiting trial for gross corruption and theft of government funds. It offered him a chance to learn to command on a strategic level and make sure that his former Company – and the other fighting units out in the field – received what they needed from the men in the rear.

He'd had to relieve several REMFs in his first week – two of whom would be joining the former commander at his trial – but since then, the base had started to shape up into an effective fighting unit. Hell, he'd even been promised that new Civil Guard units – who would be paid in cash, rather than electronic transfer, as would the old units – would be raised and trained at Armstrong Base. He was looking forward to the chance to place his stamp on a whole new generation of Avalon's martial history.

He was still looking forward to his chance when the main board lit up like a Christmas tree.

"Report," he barked, unwilling to panic. He might not be in direct command of anything outside the base, but he had faith in the new generation of leaders. "What's happening?"

"Multiple reports coming in from all over the city," an operator said. "We're picking up reports of bombings and shootings, concentrated around the government and military sector of town. The fusion plant reported armed men inside the control centre and then went off the air. Sir, we're under attack!"

"You don't say," Watanabe said, dryly. The problem with promoting newcomers in to replace the men he'd relieved or sent to less sensitive duties was that the newcomers were inexperienced and he hadn't had the time to run emergency drills. "Get me a direct link to the Major and inform…"

He broke off as the entire building shook. A moment later, the lights flickered and dimmed. "We just lost main power, sir," the operator said. "They cut the link to the fusion plant. Backup systems are coming online now, but they're not capable of handling the entire load."

"That might be the least of our worries," Watanabe said. He hit the emergency key, knowing that the base itself was under attack, but the emergency alarms failed to sound. "What are we getting from outside?"

The building shook again. "I'm not sure, sir," the operator said. "Security cameras are reporting armed men within the perimeter, attacking the base, while hostile forces are moving in from all directions. Half of the security systems have been knocked out!"

Watanabe saw it, too late. As the purge moved closer and closer to wiping out the Cracker penetration altogether, they had moved from spying to active sabotage, operating as a fifth column within the base to assist their allies on the outside to penetrate the defences. The explosions had been close enough to suggest that they'd somehow managed to obtain weapons from the armoury, which meant that his military police and infantrymen were likely to find themselves outgunned.

"Arm yourselves," he ordered, as another group of cameras failed. The bastards had to be shooting them out as they attacked their former comrades, slaughtering unarmed soldiers before they could arm and defend themselves. By law, the Civil Guardsmen were expected to hand in their weapons and ammunition once they returned to base, a security procedure that no one had managed to change, even in the midst of an insurgency. "Get me a line outside the complex!"

"All direct links are down, sir," the operator reported. Watanabe realised, with a curse, that he had effectively lost control of his base. He'd condemned incompetent officers before, yet history would record him as just another incompetent, one who had allowed his base to be penetrated and subverted from within. "I can't link into the Marine network without the right codes."

"Declare a state of emergency," Watanabe ordered, tightly. The main board had looked as if the Crackers were attacking everywhere, just before it had failed along with most of the power. The Marines presumably had their hands full as well. "Warn them that men in Civil Guard uniforms are engaging loyal troops within the complex and…"

Another explosion, this one far too close for comfort, knocked him to the ground. "Sir, we just received word from the internal security guardhouse," the operator said. "They're under heavy attack and…"

The guards there couldn't stop a determined assault, Watanabe knew. "Purge the computers now," he snapped, "and then trigger the self-destruct protocols. If they are going to take this base, they are going to inherit a corpse!"

The door blew open. Watanabe swung around and raised his personal weapon, but it was already too late. A spray of automatic fire cut him in half, sending blood and gore splashing all over the room. A moment later, the remainder of the operations staff were captured or shot down like dogs.

Michael and his platoon had been enjoying a moment of downtime in the R&R barracks when the attack began. They'd been called back for a few days to train with the new trainees – it seemed absurd, somehow, to think that a mere month ago he'd been even less competent than the wide-eyed kids he'd been training – and the Drill Sergeant had finally given them a chance to catch a break. Barr seemed somehow less of a monstrous tyrant now that Michael had seen combat and understood the value – and quality – of their training. He was just mildly surprised that they'd been pulled out of the line of battle.

"What the…"

The second explosion, followed rapidly by heavy shooting, put paid to any illusions that it might have been an accident. Michael grabbed for his duty weapon at once – a week on duty in Sangria had taught him to have his personal weapon nearby at all times, even in the shower – and stood up, bracing himself for a fight. The Crackers had tried to infiltrate bases out in the countryside before, but had largely failed. The two explosions, definitely within the base's perimeter, suggested that they had succeeded in the urban areas. The irony of the situation didn't escape him.

"Grab weapons and armour," he ordered, tersely. The exact legal status of the Army of Avalon's weapons was in some doubt. Marines got to keep their weapons with them at all times; Civil Guardsmen handed them in after duty. Barr had poured scorn on that concept, claiming that it only created more paperwork for the duty sergeant as well as rendering the soldier helpless, and ordered that the Army of Avalon was to keep their weapons with them at all times. The one concession they'd made to the more timorous nature of the Civil Guard was to keep the weapons unloaded. It had satisfied the bean counters, even though it took only a few seconds to reload and prepare for combat. "Secure that door and…"

One of the soldiers had scrambled up to the window. "Sir," he said, "the bastards are wearing Civil Guard uniforms."

Michael saw the problem at once. An enemy force wearing friendly uniforms would have a chance to get a shot in while the friendly force was trying to sort out friend from foe. The Army of Avalon wore different uniforms, but what if the Crackers were wearing the same uniforms as well? He considered the issue for the moment and then dismissed it with a shrug. There would be time enough to deal with it when it came up.

He keyed his communicator and swore at the burst of static. The First Avalon Infantry consisted – at present – of a single Company, although they had been promised that it would be raised to a full regiment once the men and commanders were ready. The entire Company would be needed to fend off the enemy attack, but if he couldn't communicate with the others, how could anyone coordinate a counterattack? The Cracker plan was smart, smart enough to cripple one of the advantages the Marines had painstakingly hammered into their trainees. Communications were the key to any successful offensive, along with surprise, and the enemy had already taken both.

A quick touch set the communicator to scanning for a rotating frequency, hunting for any other Marine-issue communicators in the area. A moment later, one result popped up; Sergeant Hammersmith, one of the few locals who had been promoted as a result of his service in the countryside. Michael didn't know him that well – they'd been in different training units – but he had a good reputation.

"Sergeant, report," he ordered. "What is the current situation?"

"Our barracks have been attacked after having been infiltrated by groups of armed men," the Sergeant reported. "We have barricaded the building and are trying to hold on as best as possible, but we're short of ammunition and other supplies. The bastards can't get in, but they can keep us from getting out for resupply or escape."

Michael summoned up a mental map of the complex and nodded. The Civil Guard had never anticipated fighting within its own bases and hadn't exactly designed them to withstand an assault. As long as the Crackers held the Army of Avalon trapped within their barracks, they could starve them out or destroy them with high explosives or mortar fire. Relieving the remainder of the Company would be the first priority, a task that would be complicated by an unknown amount of enemy fighters roaming the base. If they got their hands on the armoured vehicles, they'd practically control the entire complex.

"We're moving out," he ordered, glancing from face to face. There were no doubts or hesitations on their faces, just a grim determination to live up to the trust placed in them – and their own self-image. "Grab your weapons and follow me."

The enemy seemed to have missed the R&R barracks in their initial attacks, although doubtless they would have attended to them in due time. Outside, Michael could hear shots being fired in an endless wave of sound rolling across the base, broken only by screams and the sound of explosions echoing up in the distance. The command building seemed to be on fire, with smoke billowing up towards the sky. Dead bodies lay everywhere, many clearly showing signs of shock and disbelief from just before they had died. They hadn't expected an attack from within.

"If we come across any of the Civil Guard, one warning and then shoot to kill," he ordered. There was no way of separating out the genuine soldiers from the fakes, an issue complicated by the fact that some of the enemy would be traitors, rather than just fighters wearing an enemy uniform. Someone had either smuggled explosives into the base or raided the armoury - and either one proved the existence of at least one traitor, perhaps more. "Don't let them get the drop on us."

The sound of shooting grew louder as they crept towards the barracks, watching carefully for signs of an ambush. A group of armed men – wearing a mixture of Civil Guard uniforms and civilian clothes – were gathered at one side of the building, firing slow precise bursts towards the doors.

The answering fire was weak and patchy, suggesting that the defenders were running out of ammunition or had been wounded. Michael glanced at the traitors quickly and realised that they all had one thing in common, a black armband wrapped around their right arm. It brought back a memory of the funeral he'd attended on Castle Rock and he felt a surge of anger. How *dare* they pervert an ancient tradition like that?

"One warning," he muttered, even though he wanted to just squeeze the trigger and hold it down until the traitors were all chunks of bloody gore on the ground. He raised his voice to a parade ground bark. "Throw down your weapons and surrender!"

The Crackers reacted with astonishing speed, swinging around to bring their weapons to bear, but it was already too late. Michael shot the first one in the head as he was still turning and the rest of the platoon followed suit a moment later. The enemy barely managed to get a shot off before they were all dead on the ground, suddenly clearing one side of the barracks of enemy soldiers. Michael ran forward, trusting in speed and his armour to protect him, and peeked around the corner. The Crackers were completely surprised to see the newcomers and were scattered before they could react. A handful ducked back, only to be shot down by quick precise bursts from inside the barracks. The defenders were still on their toes.

Michael split the platoon into two sections and advanced rapidly towards the final Cracker position. The man who seemed to be in charge was screaming into a radio, warning his high command that everything was going to hell, but it was too late. He was shot down before he could escape, or even try to surrender. The troops who had been trapped in the barracks emerged and added their own firepower to the mix, wiping out the remaining Crackers quickly and brutally.

A sheet of fire roared into the air from the landing pads, over on the other side of the base. Michael swore under his breath, realising that the Crackers had probably destroyed the helicopters and other aircraft that the Civil Guard had based at Armstrong Base. His training wondered if it might be a good thing – at least his men wouldn't have to face the helicopters in battle – but it was also worrying. The enemy was clearly intent on wrecking as much of the base as they could.

"Sergeant," he said. Hammersmith looked far too young to be a Sergeant – Barr was old enough to be his father and had forty years of experience besides – but he'd held up well. "Who's in command here?"

"The Captain was off at a briefing at the spaceport," Hammersmith said. The Marine Lieutenant who had taken on the dual role of Avalon Captain until a local could be promoted into the post was absent. "I think you're in command."

Michael stared at him. He was just a lowly Corporal...but there was no one else. The burning wreckage of the command building suggested that all of the senior officers might have been killed. Cold logic suggested otherwise, yet he *was* the senior NCO. A chill ran down the back of his neck, despite the heat of the fires and sun burning down from high overhead. He knew how to command a platoon. Eighty-three men were too much. And yet, who else was there?

"We're going to take our base back," he said, grimly. One of Barr's favourite sayings came to mind and he smiled. "Come on, you apes. Do you want to live forever?"

"Scramble, scramble!"

The Raptor lurched alarmingly as it made a combat launch, right into the air. Flying Officer Jessica Barrymore winced as the first bursts of tracer rose up to harass her craft, before her co-pilot gave the bastards a taste of the Raptor's heavy machine gun. The tracer stopped long enough for her to climb high above the spaceport, looking down at a scene from hell. A Civil Guard convoy had arrived...and the next thing the defenders had known was that they were under attack. The Crackers had launched a massive offensive.

"This is Charlie-Four, looking at a right Charlie Foxtrot," she said, as they settled into orbit around the spaceport. They weren't carrying a full weapons load. They'd only just flown back from the front. "My sensors count at least seven truckloads of armed men...I think the Civil Guard is revolting!"

"They don't smell very good either," her co-pilot quipped. "What do they want us to do about them?"

"Remain in orbit and await orders," the controller said, from the ground. Jessica scowled. It was easy for her to say. "Sergeant Patterson is taking command now."

"This is Patterson," a new voice said. "You are ordered to fly over Camelot itself. The Captain may need recovery."

Jessica looked at the towering pillars of smoke rising up from the city. The entire city seemed to be on fire.

"Understood," she said. This wasn't going to be easy. "We're on our way."

CHAPTER FIFTY-TWO

You are better off trusting a man who is openly selfish – i.e. places his interest in how he can benefit – than a man who believes in a Cause. That Cause can be used to justify anything.
　　　　　　-Sergeant Howard Ropes, *Wisdom of the Terran Marine Corps.*

"Stay down," Edward snapped. He could hear shooting in the distance, growing closer all the time. It sounded as if an entire regiment of Crackers were advancing on the remains of Government House. "Don't even think about moving."

"Get under the table," Major Grosskopf advised. The Governor was looking pale and wan, terrified of the sudden outburst of violence. Edward didn't blame him. For all that the Governor had been in his position during an insurgency, Camelot had never been hit so hard by the Crackers. The Council had weakened the Civil Guard immeasurably and none of the Crackers would have wanted to convince the Council that perhaps neutering their bodyguards wasn't the smartest idea in the world. "The roof doesn't sound stable."

"It should be stable," the Governor insisted. Edward recognised the sound of a man trying to avoid falling into shock and scowled inwardly. Chances were that they were about to be attacked and probably killed; the Governor, at least, would be kept alive long enough to broadcast a surrender order and *then* killed. "We spent enough money on it."

Edward shrugged. "Whatever," he said. There was nothing he could do about it if the Governor was wrong. The roof might fall on their heads and crush them all, yet if it happened...it happened. There was no point in wasting energy worrying about something he couldn't help, not when everything had gone so badly wrong. The first blast, if he was any judge, had detonated far too close to the building. There was a good chance that his close-protection detail was dead, along with most of the Civil Guardsmen. The seventy-odd civilians who worked in Government House were suddenly exposed and very vulnerable. "Just stay under the table and keep your mouth shut."

The Governor, for a wonder, obeyed, leaving Edward to peer out the window gingerly, looking down towards the main gates...or where the main gates had been. There was now a massive crater and no sign of the gates, just a pile of rubble. Bodies were scattered everywhere, some seemingly undamaged, others barely recognisable as human at all. Edward had seen worse, back on Han, but the Governor wouldn't have seen anything like it in his entire career. The Imperial Civil Service dealt in numbers and abstracts. The concept of real death and destruction was alien to them.

A shot cracked through the window, missing Edward's head by bare millimetres and he swore. The Crackers had not only used a truck full of explosives to blow the main gates and most of the guard force to hell, but they'd also positioned snipers in locations where they could hit anyone still alive within the building. It was a tactic Edward recognised, suggesting that someone had been reading standard Imperial Army combat manuals, although both the Imperial Army and the Marines frowned on suicide attacks. Perhaps the Crackers had decided that, this time, the goal was worth sacrificing one of their men.

"But what do they want?" The Governor demanded, his previous silence forgotten. "What are they doing?"

"Killing us, if we don't get lucky," Grosskopf growled. He looked shocked and angry, a better combination than shock and fear. His military career hadn't actually been an undistinguished one and the Imperial Army had been sorry to see him go. "We need to get out of here."

"No argument," Edward said, wishing that he knew just what weapon the sniper was using. If it was a standard hunting rifle, they could probably crawl out of the room and into the corridor without being shot, but if it was a military-grade sniper rifle, it would have all kinds of sensors to track targets as they moved. The fact that the sniper hadn't tried to shoot through the wall suggested that he didn't have an advanced weapon, but perhaps he hadn't felt like wasting bullets on the stone walls. Taken at face value, Government House was the single toughest building on Avalon – and the most costly. It had very definitely survived a formidable explosive blast. "Major, you go first and check that the corridor is clear."

"Yes, sir," Grosskopf said, and started to crawl forward. Edward tensed as he entered the danger zone, but the sniper didn't take the shot. Grosskopf might not be first on his target list, but Edward would have been very surprised if he wasn't in the top three. "I seem to have made it."

"Check the corridor," Edward said, tersely. "Make sure it's clear."

The thought he didn't want to say aloud – for fear of panicking the Governor still further – was that the Crackers were already within the building. The plans for Government House were a matter of public record. The only proof that they weren't within the building was that they hadn't come storming up and killed the Governor…and that proved nothing, not to someone who had been trained to be careful. The only people he could rely on at the moment were the Governor and Major Grosskopf. He had a nasty suspicion that the remainder of his force had its own problems.

"It's clear," Grosskopf said. He was holding a heavy-duty custom pistol in one hand, glancing up and down the corridor rapidly. "There's no sign of any movement."

"Good," Edward said. "Governor…you're moving next."

"I can't," the Governor protested. Edward heard the fear in his voice before the smell touched his nostrils. The Governor had wet himself. "You can't make me."

Edward leaned forward until his nose was almost touching the Governor's nose. "If you don't move, I'll pick you up and throw you across the room and out the door," he said, and waited for the Governor to realise that that would mean being visible to the sniper. "Your choice; move under your own power or be thrown out."

The Governor stared at him and started to crawl, shaking as he moved. Edward winced inwardly, even though he wasn't entirely unsympathetic. There were men out there, good and true, who weren't cut out for combat. It was men like that that the Terran Marine Corps existed to defend. The

Marines studied war so that the rest of the Empire wouldn't have to, yet… was that truly wise? The Empire had been turning away from the military for years and now the wolf was at the door.

"He's out," Grosskopf said. If he harboured any doubts about how Edward had forced the Governor out of the room, he didn't show them. "Are you coming yourself?"

"One moment," Edward said, and keyed his communicator. "Gwen? Gwen; come in."

"Oh, thank God," Gwen said. She sounded relieved, although only someone who had known her for years would have been able to tell. "Captain; report your status."

Edward ran through a brief explanation. "We're safe for now," he concluded, although the sound of shooting suggested otherwise. "What's going on outside Government House?"

"An all-out attack," Gwen said. "The spaceport, the Civil Guard bases, and even the individual platoon houses…they're all coming under heavy attack. The Civil Guard bases took the worst of it – according to the reports we got, the attacks started *inside* the bases and were joined by forces from outside – and several have gone completely silent. I've dispatched drones to send back live footage from the bases and they report heavy and confused fighting. The spaceport is currently secure, but that will change when they get their hands on heavy weapons."

Edward bit down a curse. The only thing, he had come to realise, that had prevented the Crackers from just strolling into Camelot and disposing the Governor was their fear of the Imperial Navy. If they'd overcome that fear…no, they hadn't; they'd just realised that if the Marines were allowed to continue with their program, the war would be on the verge of being lost. The thought made him swear aloud. They hadn't known it, but the Governor had been on the verge of agreeing to give them most of what they claimed to want. If they'd held off the operation for a few more days, they would have won anyway…without fighting.

He shook his head. There was no point in worrying about what might have been.

"I'm dispatching support to your position," Gwen added. "It is imperative that the Governor remains alive. The Council Chamber has been destroyed and the command and control network is in tatters. They even tried to knock down our network and would have succeeded without our command protocols."

"Understood," Edward said. The sound of shooting was growing louder. "We'll try to hold out here."

He broke the connection and crawled rapidly out of the room, where he discovered that the Governor had been sick against a wall and was sitting down, shaking mindlessly. "There's help on the way," he said, to Grosskopf. "I think we'd better get down to a safer floor and wait for them to arrive."

"We might be safer up here," Grosskopf pointed out. "The bastards will certainly search the lower floors first."

"We don't want to be high up when the shooting starts again," Edward countered. He reached for the Governor and helped him to his feet. The man needed a shower and at least seven hours in bed, but there was no other choice. "If they're investing this building, they'll move in as soon as they realise that we have help on the way."

He calculated it as they both half-carried the Governor towards the rear stairs. Gwen hadn't given a specific ETA, but flight time from Castle Rock was seven minutes, assuming that the Raptors loaded up with Marines on the island. He knew better. They'd have to pick up the QRF from the spaceport – Gwen wouldn't authorise stripping the island of its final defenders, even for him – and then fly over the city to reach them. That meant at least ten minutes, perhaps longer if the spaceport was under heavy attack.

"I should have brought my armour," he muttered, as they reached the stairwell. "A direct link into the live feed from the drones would be very useful right about now."

Grosskopf nodded as they stumbled down the stairs, hearing noises echoing up and down the shaft. It sounded as if someone was searching the building, perhaps a Cracker assault force. They shared a look and stopped at the first floor, helping the Governor into the suite of private offices used by the higher-ranking bureaucrats who helped run the planet. The power had failed, casting the offices into an eerie darkness, but they were still able to open one of the private offices…and came face-to-face with a pair of bureaucrats, tied to a chair with duct tape.

"Hellfire," Edward swore, as he moved forward. Someone had been very determined that the two bureaucrats – one male, one female – would be unable to get loose on their own, wrapping them back to back with enough duct tape to hold a dozen prisoners. He pulled out his knife and started to saw through the gag, allowing the woman to speak. "What happened?"

She stared up at him, her eyes wide with terror. "They just came inside after the blast and…"

Edward pushed the two prisoners to the ground as someone started shooting behind him, throwing himself to the ground a moment later. There was at least one armed hostile on the floor, one with a submachine gun, judging by the sound. He also seemed to have plenty of ammunition, Edward realised, as he kept firing, without any concern for conserving his supplies. His lips twitched in disdain. Ammunition was not something to waste, at least outside training exercises. The Crackers should have known that.

He held up a hand, signalling to Grosskopf in the code the Imperial Army had developed years ago. It had been a long time since either of them had had to use it, but he nodded in understanding, slipping back into the shadows as the gunman finally exposed himself in the gloom. Edward put a neat shot through his head and followed up by throwing a grenade in his general direction, which detonated two seconds later. Grosskopf covered him as he moved forward, checking the four bodies quickly and efficiently. Three of them were dead. The fourth looked as if he would be wishing he was very soon. A grenade at close range left scars for life.

"Ouch," Grosskopf muttered. None of them were wearing civilian outfits. They were all dressed in Civil Guard uniforms, with a black armband around their right arms. "Their clothes fit too."

Edward followed his logic. The Civil Guard issued untailored uniforms to its men and expected them to make them fit properly themselves, for reasons that were lost in the mists of time. Someone who had just donned a new uniform would be unlikely to get one that fitted, suggesting that the four men who had ambushed him had been genuine members of the Civil Guard. Edward had no doubts about any of the Marines under his command, but Grosskopf did not – could not – say the same about his own people. The Civil Guard had been compromised by two different groups.

He keyed his communicator. "Gwen, the enemy definitely include some members of the Civil Guard," he said. The equipment they'd been using was Civil Guard issue as well. "They were also wearing a black armband on their right arms. It may be their recognition signal."

"Understood," Gwen said. "I'll pass the word on…"

The wall suddenly disintegrated as someone fired a heavy machine gun, tearing through the plaster as if it was nothing more substantial than air. Edward dived for cover as the bullets chewed up the furniture, swearing aloud as the air was knocked out of him as he landed badly. Grosskopf gasped in pain as a bullet cracked into his chest and out the other side, marring his uniform with blood. Edward rolled over, trying to get closer to the wounded soldier, but the enemy was still firing. The noise was deafening.

"Put your hands on it," he shouted. If the bullet hadn't gone through anything vital, Grosskopf would have an excellent chance of survival, assuming they could get him to a hospital in time. "Push down as hard as you can…"

The enemy stopped shooting and charged forward, clearly assuming that they had killed or demoralised the opposition. Edward leaned up and opened fire, shooting down three men before they had time to realise that he was still alive. A fourth threw himself right at Edward and he shot him through the head, just before the body crashed into him, knocking him back to the ground. His pistol went flying as he hit the deck, leaving him kicking free of the dead body. A fifth man – no, a woman – was standing there, keeping a pistol trained on his skull.

"I see," Edward said, as he realised who the woman was. "All of a sudden, quite a few things make sense."

Linda smiled at him, but the smile didn't touch her eyes. "I want you to tell the rest of your people to surrender," she said. She was struggling to keep her voice dispassionate, yet Edward could hear the stress, no matter how she tried to hide it. No wonder she'd been reluctant to suggest mass lie detector tests. They would have uncovered her and her role, the spy right at the heart of the administration. "If you order them to surrender, no more people have to die."

Edward studied her, carefully. She clearly knew how to use the weapon she held, rendering jumping her a dangerous idea. If he'd been wearing armour, he would have dared her to fire, but without armour…a bullet through the skull would kill even a Marine. He decided to watch her and wait for an opening. One would come soon enough. It always did.

"I can't do that," he said, as regretfully as he could. "There are standing orders that any senior officer in enemy hands loses all of his authority and his orders may be disregarded at will. My second will take over and the fighting will carry on."

He smiled. "How did a nice girl like you end up working for the Crackers anyway?"

Linda didn't smile at the weak joke. "I had to take a job to pay for my mother's hospital care," she said, flatly. "It turned out that most of what I earned had to go to pay my grandfather's debt or the interest on his debt. My mother died in hospital because I didn't have the funds to get her the medical care she needed to keep her alive. A while later I was approached by one of the recruiting agents in the city and offered a chance to extract revenge. You can probably guess the rest."

"You climbed up to Deputy Governor and aided the Crackers as best as you could," Edward said. "You do realise that you won't get away with this?"

"I saw the reports on the state of the Empire," Linda said. "There is a very good chance that we will get away with this. Now…"

Grosskopf coughed, loudly. Just for a second, Linda's attention was diverted and Edward lifted his hand, triggering the nerve-burst implant that had been built into his finger. She screamed in pain, her face twisted with unspeakable agony, before collapsing onto the ground. Edward slowly pulled himself to his feet and recovered his weapon. There was no need to hurry. A nerve-burst strike against an unprotected human was almost always fatal.

"Her all along," Grosskopf said. He sounded as if it was hard to speak a single word. "Brent dies; she takes over, at least until a new Governor is appointed. Without the Council…"

"I know," Edward said. It took seconds to locate a medical pack and seal Grosskopf's wounds. He'd survive. "Lie back and relax. I'll take care of it from here."

CHAPTER FIFTY-THREE

> In war, it is always the civilian population that suffers worst. The core goal of the Marines, therefore, is to keep war as far from the civilians as possible. Unfortunately, that is not always possible.
> -Sergeant Howard Ropes, *Wisdom of the Terran Marine Corps.*

"This is an emergency broadcast," the radio said. "There is a combined military and civil emergency in progress. Remain in your homes. Do not attempt to go onto the streets. There is a combined military and civil..."

Leo hit the switch angrily. The radio had been broadcasting the same message for what felt like hours, but he hadn't needed it to know that something was badly wrong. They had heard the explosions from the direction of Government House and seen pillars of smoke rising up into the air. The sound of shooting, heavy shooting, could be heard in the distance; closer, he was sure he could hear the roar of an angry or terrified crowd.

"Dad," Mindy said, from where she was lying on the sofa. "What's going on?"

Leo winced at the terror in her voice. "I don't know, baby," he said. Admitting that cost pride and he thought of the Marine communicator Captain Stalker had given him, but the last thing the Captain would want was a distraction. Whatever was going on, the Marines had to be in the midst of it. "I just don't know."

"They're attacking the Marines," Fiona said. Her voice was harsh and broken. She'd been arrested when Carola Wilhelm's mansion had been raided and even though she'd been released within a day, the experience had still told on her. She'd spent weeks trying to get close to the local power structure, only to see the rising star she'd hitched herself to crash and burn. "The whole city is coming alive and attacking the Marines."

"I doubt it, mom," Mandy said. Leo's oldest daughter was staring out the window with a fascinated expression. Leo wanted to tell her to get under cover, but somehow he couldn't find the words. He'd connected with his daughter again over the last week and he didn't want to lose that now. "It sounds more like a Cracker attack."

Fiona glared at her daughter. "And you would know what a Cracker attack sounds like?"

The noise of two fast-moving helicopters echoed overhead and Leo made up his mind. "We're going down to the basement," he said, picking up the radio. It would inform them when it was safe to come out. "We can't do anything to help, so we're going to stay out of the way."

He left his other thought unspoken. If the city was descending into chaos, how long would it be before the lower classes – the ones the Council had held down for their entire lives – started to realise that there was nothing stopping them from attacking the remainder of the upper class? Leo knew that his family weren't really upper class, not by any reasonable definition of the term, but would that really matter to angry men out for a little revenge while the Civil Guard was distracted? Mandy had almost been raped and murdered once. He didn't want to see the rest of his family face the same peril.

"Come on," he ordered, firmly. Mandy hesitated, but followed his lead. They'd spent hours planning the new University of Avalon that he intended to open one day, just chatting as they hadn't since she'd hit puberty, and he had no intention of wasting that time. "We'll be back to the surface soon enough."

Another explosion, closer, underscored his words.

Jasmine watched as the first VTOL Raptor came in to land, after spraying rockets down into a few locations surrounding the spaceport. The

Crackers had gotten far closer than any of the defenders had expected, but they hadn't broken the perimeter and the defenders – a motley combination of Marines, Marine Auxiliaries and Civil Guardsmen – had counterattacked vigorously. The Crackers had counted on their mortar fire to inflict significant damage on the spaceport, but the laser counter-battery system had detonated the shells before they could strike their targets. The entire battle seemed to have stalemated, although the intervention of the Raptors had turned the tide in favour of the defenders.

"We just got a new uplink from Sergeant Barr," a voice said, in her ear. "He was at Armstrong Base when the shit hit the fan. He's alive and met up with other loyalist forces and they're moving to retake the base."

"Understood," Jasmine said. With the local command arrangements in disarray, she'd been breveted to Corporal and given command of a platoon that really consisted of elements of Second and Third Platoons jammed together. Another military organisation might have had problems fitting two units together, but the Marines drilled for such an eventuality. Besides, her oversized platoon was all that Sergeant Patterson had to send into the city. "Do you wish us to head to Armstrong Base instead?"

"Negative," Sergeant Patterson ordered. "You are to proceed to Government House and clear the area of enemy fighters, before rescuing the Governor and Captain Stalker."

"Understood," Jasmine said, as the Raptor touched down. "We're on our way."

The pilot didn't bother to shut down the engines or still the rotor blades. He just opened the hatch and waved for the Marines to board rapidly. Jasmine had already made her arrangements; seven Marines would board one Raptor and seven would board the other, ensuring that if they lost a Raptor, help would still be on the way. So far, the Crackers had shown no sign of possessing advanced antiaircraft weapons, but it was so obvious a chink in their procurement that she would have been astonished if they hadn't tried to fill it. If they had support from within the Civil Guard – and the uniforms and weapons they'd used proved that – there was no reason why they couldn't have got their hands on HVMs.

She pulled herself into the Raptor and waited impatiently as the pilot spun up the engines again and hurled them into the sky, linking in to the aircraft's onboard sensor suite to look down at the city. Camelot was burning, with some areas clearly badly attacked and other areas left completely alone. Judging from the fires, attacks had been concentrated against government and military targets, with a handful of exceptions. One of them made no sense to her at all until she compared it against the street map of Camelot she'd been given and realised that the Crackers had hit the Bank of Avalon, the most hated building on the planet. If the main records had been destroyed, they'd also taken out all the debts. She had to smile at the concept. The Council – or whatever replaced it – could no longer prove that anyone owed money.

Assuming that they got all the records, she reminded herself. New reports were flashing up in her helmet display as bases and units reported in, although a number of Civil Guard bases remained silent. If they'd lost their commanders, the Crackers would have managed to isolate them from the rest of the network, even if they hadn't taken the entire base. The opening moves of any battle were always confusing, but in this case confusion helped the enemy and not the defenders. Jasmine had never seen anything like it, even on Han. She just hoped that the locals were keeping their heads down and out of the line of fire.

"The emergency broadcast system has been activated," someone informed her when she checked. "The civilians have been ordered to stay in their homes."

Jasmine scowled. She had no idea how effective that would be, but she wouldn't have placed money on it. For the young, the chaos and anarchy would draw them like a magnet, pulling them onto the streets as if it were a wild street party. It wouldn't be long before looters started to loot openly, while the Civil Guard was unable to stop them. The streets of Camelot would soon descend into absolute chaos. An image of Mandy popped into her mind and she found herself hoping that the girl was safe. It wouldn't be fair, somehow, if she died after she had decided to make something of her life.

"Alert," the pilot snapped suddenly. "We have incoming!"

Clinton Remus braced himself as the first Raptors from the spaceport started to head over the city and towards Government House. His team had been warned, specifically, that they were not to do anything until the Marines started to launch their aircraft, even if they saw other targets of opportunity. Reinforcing from the air was a core part of Marine combat doctrine and if they succeeded, Operation Headshot might be derailed, badly. The fighters hitting Government House were unprepared for armoured Marines joining the fun.

"All right," he said to the other four, as they lifted their weapons. "Lock on to your targets and take aim."

The HVM was a very simple weapon, one that could be fired and then forgotten, even when used by a complete incompetent. A handful of Civil Guard deserters had drilled Clinton and his men on the weapons until they could launch them in their sleep, warning them that they wouldn't have a second chance. Fire the weapons and then run, getting the hell out of the area before any survivors hosed their position down with machine gun fire or rockets. If the Marines survived the attack, they would be in a murderous mood. They would *know* that their attackers had wanted to kill them.

He peered through the scope at the lead Raptor. Unlike Civil Guard helicopters, it had stealth systems built in to make it harder to target, but at such close range it hardly mattered. It only took a moment to uncover the firing key and push down on it hard, launching the missile right towards its target. An instant later, the other missile was fired, arcing right towards the second Raptor. The others held their fire and waited.

"Don't stand there," Clinton bellowed. "Run!"

Jasmine braced herself as the missiles raced towards their targets, right towards *her*. "No dice," the pilot said, grimly. "Emergency escape systems online...now!"

Something *grabbed* at her and she found herself plummeting towards the hatch and out of the aircraft, falling down towards the buildings below. A second later, she heard a thunderous explosion behind her as the missile struck home, sending one of the Raptors up in a massive fireball. Her helmet was reporting that all seven of the Marines had been thrown out of the aircraft just before it was hit, followed rapidly by the other aircraft. Jasmine cursed under her breath as the suit automatically deployed a parachute, slowing her fall before she could hit the ground. She'd practiced HAVLO parachuting before graduating from the Slaughterhouse, but she'd never had to dive out of a crippled Raptor before. They'd been taught how to do it, yet the odds of actually surviving a direct hit were so low that they'd never had to try…

She hit the top of the building hard enough to hurt, even through the suit, but there was no time to relax. An enemy sniper had rolled over and was desperately trying to bring his weapon to bear on her. She shot him down instinctively and linked in with the other Marines. If they'd been trying it as an exercise in the Slaughterhouse, they would all have been failed, for they'd come down over a wide area. Scattered, they were vulnerable. She designated a place for them all to meet up and sprinted for the stairs. If there was an enemy force in the building, they knew that she was there…

A hail of fire greeted her two floors down, including bright sparks of light that marked the presence of at least one plasma cannon, one capable of burning a hole through her suit. God damn it, but someone on the other side was quick! They'd realised what she was and where she was going and had moved to stop her. Escape was going to be a bitch…or maybe not. She stepped over to the elevator shaft, used the enhanced servos in her armour to prise the heavy metal doors apart, and then started to climb down the shaft before she could think better of the idea. The power was out and the elevator wouldn't be running, she hoped; the last report had warned that the Crackers held the main fusion plant and had cut off all power to the city.

The climb was harder than she had expected – perversely, she found herself wondering if the fall had injured her, even if her implants insisted that she was intact – but she finally reached the bottom and started to work on the doors. By her calculations, she should be in the basement. It was easy to climb out, find the stairs and come out all weapons blazing. They'd completely lost track of her until she exploded into their rear.

She took a moment to disable their weapons, knowing that there were probably more Crackers on the upper floors wondering what had happened to their comrades on the ground, before heading out to meet up with the others. Twelve Marines greeted her; two were missing, somewhere within the chaos. Their suits weren't responding to her pings either.

"Come on," she ordered. They'd mourn the dead later. "We have to move fast."

Government House had been one of the most impressive buildings in Camelot, although it hadn't had quite the same grandeur as Carola Wilhelm's mansion. Even now, it was still intact, even though a heavy bomb had detonated right outside the building, showing a sickening lack of concern for civilian casualties. Dead bodies were scattered everywhere, some even barely recognisable as human. Jasmine swallowed hard as she caught sight of a young boy, his body shattered by the blast, and then led the Marines forward. The Crackers attacking the building barely had a moment to see them coming before they opened fire and ripped into them. They never stood a chance.

Mortar shells ripped down from prepared positions, but armoured Marines moved faster than anyone could grasp, even people who had thought they'd studied the Marines. Jasmine split her force and sent two fire teams to deal with the mortar gunners, while she led the rest of her force into the building. A pair of bodies greeted her as they burst through the remains of the door, surprising her, for they had clearly been shot in the back of the head. It spelt treachery to her and she noted, absently, that they weren't wearing black armbands. Loyalist forces, then, shot down before they ever knew that they were under attack.

She keyed her communicator quickly. "Captain Stalker," she called. "Please come in…"

"Here," Captain Stalker said. A location glyph appeared in her helmet. "Be careful. There are quite a few dead bodies up here."

Jasmine climbed the stairs, keeping her MAG at the ready, until they reached the first floor. There was a small pile of bodies there, including a blonde girl she barely recognised, and a barricade that had been thrown together in a hurry. Captain Stalker rose to greet them and she saw him smile, tiredly. The attackers had hit the barricade hard, but they'd clearly failed to break him.

"It's good to see you, sir," she said, and meant it. "Is the rest of the building secure?"

"Unknown," Captain Stalker said. "The Major needs medical treatment ASAP. The remainder of the people in this room need to be escorted to somewhere safe…and then we have to track down the people responsible for this."

"Yes, sir," Jasmine said. "The local area is *not* secure. I suggest preparing to hold Government House."

Captain Stalker smiled. "Good idea," he said. Jasmine realised with a flush of embarrassment that he would have been in contact with his Command Sergeant and probably knew the situation better than she did. "We'll see to it at once."

The fighting had raged over Armstrong Base for what felt like hours – Michael's timepiece swore that it had only been forty minutes, but it had to be lying – before they could reasonably declare the base secure. The scratch group of soldiers, trainees and Civil Guardsmen – and a pair of Marine training officers – had found other loyalists and hunted down the traitors savagely. Only a couple had survived to be taken prisoner and neither of them seemed to be particularly important.

Michael saluted Jared Barr as he entered the makeshift command post. He'd passed command to the Marine as soon as they had met up with his group because nothing in his training had prepared him to command a whole base. Barr hadn't even mocked him for calling him 'Sir,' he'd just nodded and assumed command. Besides, Michael wanted a piece of the bastards who had attacked the base and turned the Civil Guard against itself and he couldn't do that if he was stuck in the rear.

"We have seventeen AFVs and two tanks ready for deployment," he reported. Most of Armstrong Base had been badly damaged and would require weeks of repair work before the base was usable again, although the Crackers hadn't managed to completely destroy the base. "We can move on your command."

"Good," Barr growled. He didn't look happy, but somehow Michael was no longer scared of him. The Sergeant had prepared them well for combat, even though they had loathed him at the time. "Then mount up. We've got work to do."

"Understood," Michael said. He knew he shouldn't ask, but he couldn't help himself. "What's the word from inside the city?"

"The city, *Corporal*, is on a knife-edge right now," Barr informed him. "It is our task to prevent it from falling to chaos and anarchy. Get your men mounted up and get ready to move."

Michael saluted, again. "Understood, Sergeant," he said. He met the Sergeant's eyes openly. "And thank you."

CHAPTER FIFTY-FOUR

Victory goes to those who work for it, for they deserve it. Defeat goes to those who forget the fundamental nature of war and do not work for victory.
-Sergeant Howard Ropes, *Wisdom of the Terran Marine Corps.*

"So what the hell is going on?"

The first reports had suggested that Operation Headshot had been a complete success, but afterwards things had started to go wrong. Deputy Governor Linda MacDonald hadn't broadcast from Government House, declaring an end to the fighting. Some bases had fallen, but others had held out, including the spaceport…and Castle Rock, of course, had been beyond their reach. The one attempt to land troops on the island had ended badly when a patrolling Raptor had fired a missile into the boat and sunk it.

"I don't know," Julian admitted, grimly. Gaby swallowed several words she wanted to say and waited for him to finish. "The force that hit Government House has dropped out of communication."

"Dropped out of communication," Gaby repeated. "You do know what that means, don't you? They haven't just lost communication; they've lost their lives!"

"We still hold parts of the city," Julian protested. "Even though the Marines did manage to get some relief into Government House, they're still on the ropes. One final push could see us through to victory."

"Or cost us everything," Gaby said. She shook her head. "Operation Headshot has failed, Julian. Send the disengagement signal and then cut all communications."

Julian swung around to face her. "But we are on the verge of victory," he protested. "We can overwhelm them and destroy them."

"We have failed," Gaby repeated, harshly. "We have not knocked out their communications, or destroyed enough of their bases to win the battle. We have missed our chance and all we can do now is get the hell out of here before they catch us on the hoof and destroy us."

She leaned forward, silently cursing the younger generation under her breath. After this, there would be no way they could forge a peace with the Government. Free of the interference of the Council, the Army of Avalon and the Civil Guard would press their advantage savagely, aided by the stories of atrocities within the heart of Camelot itself. She'd been reluctant to risk civilian lives so badly and only the fact that they desperately needed to hit Government House had convinced her to authorise the attack. Now that particular chicken had come home to roost and others would be flocking out to join it.

"I cannot leave," Julian said. "I promised the fighters that I would stay until the end."

"You cannot fall into enemy hands," Gaby said, thinking of the suicide pill she'd concealed in her pocket. She knew too much to risk capture. "Whatever you do, you cannot risk being captured."

"I'm staying here," Julian said. "You can go if you must."

"Idiot," Gaby snapped. Was he really so adamant that Operation Headshot could still be made to work…or was he afraid to face his father, after having thrown away the chances of a genuine peace for nothing? "Good luck, then."

The suit of armour felt oddly uncomfortable as Edward pulled it on, but Gwen had given strict orders to the relief force that they were to make sure that their Captain put on his armour at once and there was no point in protesting. Besides, after everything else that had happened, he doubted that anyone would feel safe in Camelot for a long – long – time.

"We have the Civil Guard units blocking the roads, as you ordered, and the Army of Avalon is moving up to support the Marines," the dispatcher announced. There was one good thing about wearing his armour again; he could coordinate operations from his suit, without a proper command room. "Oh, and we found one of the lost Marines. It turned out that he fell into a dumpster and got stuck."

Edward chuckled, although he knew that the Marine wouldn't be allowed to forget it for a long time. "Good," he said, relieved. Too many Marines had already died this day, along with Civil Guardsmen and soldiers from the Army of Avalon. "What about the current progress on the hunt?"

"We're working on the prisoners now," Gwen's voice said. Only a handful of Crackers had been taken alive, including a pair who had been too badly injured to be interrogated and weren't expected to survive the day. Unlike the bandits, the Crackers had fought with a hellish bravery that would have made its mark anywhere. "So far, we don't seem to have stumbled across a senior commander, but they all agree that they have a commander within the city, one Gaby Cracker. Apparently she's a descendent of Peter Cracker."

Edward smiled at that. The Marine Corps tried to discourage it, but there were some great Marine dynasties, families with a long history of joining the Corps and serving out their time, before marrying and bringing up the next generation of Marines. Edward was privately grateful that he wasn't from one of them, even though it could have its advantages; the few he'd known had always felt that they had a lot to live up to. Besides, the families also tended to marry within the ranks of retired Marines and the thought of bedding another Marine felt weird, even though they would be retired and no longer barred from fraternisation.

"Poor girl," he said, humourlessly. "I take it that there has been no lead on her location?"

"None as yet," Gwen said. "The ones we captured did seem to believe that she was hiding in the poorer area of the city and I have redirected some soldiers just in case, but they could have been lied to and the lie detector wouldn't even twitch."

"True," Edward agreed. He looked over towards the fire engine which had finally arrived now that the shooting had finished. The Camelot Fire Department had enough equipment to get on with putting out the fires, although he'd detailed civilian volunteers and a pair of Raptors to assist them. The Raptors could scoop up water from the sea and spray it over the worst fires. The entire city wouldn't be lost. "Keep me informed."

He closed the connection and walked towards the Governor, who had changed into cleaner clothes. "Sir," he said. "Are you ready to speak to your people?"

The Governor's eyes twitched nervously. He'd been through the most traumatic experience of his life…and he was no longer a young man. Edward had no time to care, even though he did understand. Reports were coming in of a city on the brink and what the Crackers had failed to achieve might be accomplished by rioting youths. He didn't have the manpower to deploy to put down the riots when they started, even though the city was slowly coming back under control.

"Sir," he repeated. "You have to address the city."

The Governor nodded and waited until Edward held a mike under his mouth. "What should I say?"

"Tell them that the Crackers tried to attack the city, but that they've been beaten off and that you're firmly in control," Edward said. "You have to warn them not to riot or encourage rioting. Everything will be dealt with as quickly as possible."

The Governor considered it, and then took the mike. "Citizens of Camelot," he said. "We have been attacked by the Crackers, but we have survived. The enemy forces have been pushed back and are now on the run, hunted by our soldiers and harried until they have no place of rest. There is no need to panic. Please remain indoors and wait for further instructions. The Government has remained in control and will assist you as soon as possible."

Edward smiled. It was a fairly routine phrasing, but it would work. "Thank you, sir," he said. "I'll have it broadcast at once."

He transmitted the recording to the spaceport, where it would be broadcast on the emergency frequency, and then turned back to the military situation. A handful of Crackers had holed up in a building and were using precise bursts of fire to hold back the soldiers, but a Raptor put a missile into the building and brought it down on their heads. Another group of Crackers had realised that they were surrounded and outgunned, finally seeing sense as a tank ground its way towards them and lifted their hands in surrender. Other groups were being chased down, or forced to withdraw from the city. A couple of Crackers had even been lynched by outraged citizens.

The ones who had been captured would soon wish they hadn't, Edward knew. They'd be transported to the nearest safe location for a field interrogation, which they wouldn't enjoy at all. They'd be hooked up to a lie detector and forced to talk, whatever it took. With so many dead – the death toll was currently estimated at around nine hundred and was probably higher, once the attacks outside the city had been factored in – Edward wasn't in the mood to order any of the interrogators to hold back.

A Raptor flew overhead, heading towards one of the fires. A moment later, it dropped water on the blaze from high above, giving the firemen a chance to get in and put the rest of the fire out. It had been caused, according to the updates, by one of the Raptors that had been shot down, just after the pilot had expelled the Marines and saved their lives. Marine Auxiliaries could only be nominated for Marine awards under special circumstances, but Edward intended to ensure that the pilots would get the Golden Lion, if posthumously. A second later and fourteen Marines would have been added to the death toll.

"We got her," Gwen said, in his ear. "We stumbled across one of their commanders before he could kill himself and made him talk! We know where she is!"

"Dispatch a platoon of Marines to catch her," Edward ordered. This was too important to risk leaving to the newly-trained soldiers. "I want her alive, whatever the risk."

The new orders had come in as the reinforced Company had made its way into the city, picking its way through fortunately empty streets. They were to take up positions around a city block and allow no one in or out. Anyone who tried was to be arrested at once and held for interrogation, even though most of them would probably be innocent. Michael frowned as he checked the orders, and then repeated them to his men. The Army of Avalon was largely drawn from the poorer areas of Camelot. If the Crackers were hiding out in the area, it was something they would take as a personal insult.

"Deploy here, here and here," he said, ordering the AFVs into position to block any escape. Deploying along the roads would ensure that no one would be able to get out without being seen, even though it meant that they had encircled a larger area than their orders had specified. It would have to do. "We'll hold the line until relieved."

The massive apartment blocks cast a baleful shadow over the area. He had grown up in similar buildings, after his mother had been forced to move out of her first home, and had hated it. There was nothing to do, for anyone, and the street gangs had proven the only source of diversion. Now…now he was a soldier and had prospects, but the apartments still cast a shadow over his soul. The fires up north should have been started in the poorer areas, burning down the foul buildings and forcing the Government to build newer ones…

It would have burned them all out of their homes, he thought dully, as the first group of prisoners were taken. *We couldn't have done that.*

"Shit," Gaby breathed. She had been on the verge of leaving the building when she'd seen the army convoy race past. She'd hoped that they were just heading back to the centre of town and Government House, but instead the soldiers started to dismount and took up positions around the block. It didn't take much imagination to realise that they'd located her and intended to take her alive, if possible. She remembered her inspection of the area and realised that they were trapped. There was no way out.

She turned and ran back up the stairs. Julian was still trying to rally resistance, even though it was increasingly clear, even to him, that they'd lost. The soldiers were hunting those few Crackers who hadn't realised that the battle was over and broken contact on their own authority. He was raging into the microphone when she burst into the room, one hand holding an old pistol that had belonged to his father.

"We're surrounded," Gaby snapped, thinking of the suicide pill in her pocket. It would be so easy to take it and put her and her knowledge out of enemy reach forever, but something held her hand. "They've tracked us down!"

"Impossible," Julian said. "I was assured that this communicator was untraceable."

Gaby slapped him, hard. "Look out the window," she snapped. "There are armed soldiers out there, preventing anyone from leaving. They've found us!"

Julian recoiled from her blow, an ugly red mark forming on his cheek, and turned to look out of the window. "My God," he breathed. "We have to get out of here!"

"And how do you propose that we do that?" Gaby asked, dryly. "There's no way we can jump from this block to another outside their perimeter. I think we might have to prepare to sell our lives dearly."

Julian was still staring at her. "Sell my life dearly, you mean," he said, opening the large box. "You get into here and keep quiet. It should protect you from their scans."

Gaby blinked. "They'll check, won't they?"

"Not if I give them something else to think about," Julian said. "Get in there, now!"

"Good luck," Gaby said, and stepped into the box. It was tight and uncomfortable, rather like climbing into her coffin. The thought made her shiver as Julian pushed down the lid.

"Stay quiet," he whispered, and was gone.

There was no time to board the Raptor properly, so Jasmine and five other Marines hung from straps and allowed themselves to swing below the aircraft as it raced over the city towards the apartment block. It came to a brief hover just above the roof, allowing Jasmine to drop down onto the hard surface and open the door to the interior. The inhabitants were nowhere in evidence, but she didn't know if that meant they were hiding, or if the Crackers had convinced them to move out when they'd moved in. The city's records weren't clear on who actually lived in any of the apartment blocks. There was an entire undocumented underclass just waiting for someone to come along and organise them.

"Stunners only," she said, as they advanced down the stairs, kicking down doors and spraying the apartments with stun bolts. "We want the bitch alive! She has to know where Blake is."

"Understood," Joe Buckley said. He hefted his stunner as she kicked open another door. "We'll find him even if we have to tear the entire countryside apart."

Jasmine said nothing as they encountered a family, who stared at the monsters invading their home before they were stunned and sent falling to the ground like ninepins. A shiver of guilt ran through her heart, before she pushed it aside and kept moving. There was no time to worry about the welfare of civilians, not now. If they found the person responsible for the attacks, they could stop them for good. She kicked down another door... and a shot pinged off her armour. A young man was standing there, half in the shadow, firing precise shots towards them. The pistol he carried was harmless to a person in armour.

"Give it up," Joe snapped, lifting his stunner and stunning the young man. The grenade he was carrying detonated a moment later, shredding his body and catching Joe in the blast. Jasmine checked him quickly. He was alive, but badly shocked.

"Hell of a time to forget my shirt," he growled, as Jasmine checked the rest of the room. If someone had tried to defend it, it stood to reason that there was something in the room worth defending. She looked around and finally saw a chest positioned against one wall, one made of metal, just right for deflecting light scans. On impulse, she walked over and pulled it open, revealing a young girl lying inside. A moment later, before she could put a pill in her mouth, Jasmine stunned her.

"I think we got her," she said, as she pulled the body out of the chest. It would have helped if they had a description or a DNA pattern, but Gaby Cracker had apparently never been entered onto the system. It wasn't entirely surprising. Even a primitive system like Avalon's could have traced her descent and then the Civil Guard would have started asking pointed questions about her family. "What do you want us to do with her?"

"Get her to the spaceport, alive," Captain Stalker ordered. "And then, perhaps, we can put an end to this."

It took nearly an hour to get Gaby Cracker to the spaceport and then run a DNA test, but in the end the result was certain; she was the direct descendent of Peter Cracker himself. Or at least one of them, Edward reminded himself. It had been a surprise to discover that quite a few people claimed descent from the great rebel, enough to make him wonder how Peter Cracker had ever found the time to actually rebel. Most of the claims were spurious, but Gaby's was not. Her capture meant the end of the battle, but not of the war.

Edward gazed down at the limp body and smiled inwardly. It was time to put an end to the war altogether. Too many had died already.

CHAPTER FIFTY-FIVE

> Our goal is an acceptable peace; not peace at any price, but an acceptable peace, one that allows us to live with ourselves afterwards.
> -Sergeant Howard Ropes, *Wisdom of the Terran Marine Corps.*

The farmhouse was indistinguishable from a thousand others, miles from any large township or homestead. It looked as if it were owned and operated by a small family and only had the bare minimum of animals and fields. Jasmine wondered if it would be a good place to live, when she finally retired from the Marines, as they deployed across the field and advanced on the house. She didn't speak that thought aloud. Joe would have joked about buying the farm.

"All drones report no sign of movement," Joe said, as if her thought had summoned him to speak. "No enemy contact at all."

"Good," Jasmine said. Under their chameleon suits, the Marines slipped closer to the farmhouse wall. Up close, it was clear that someone had placed a great deal of care and attention into the building, investing it with love. She wondered what had happened to the original owners as the Marines encircled the house. Were they Crackers, perhaps, or had they been forced away from their home by the debt sharks and the Council? There was no way to know. "Go!"

Disdaining the doors, the Marines went in through the windows, ready to respond to any enemy contact with lethal force. There was nothing; Jasmine crashed to the ground in a shower of broken glass, landing in the middle of a small dining room. A single note lay on the table. She picked it up and read it. DOWNSTARES. She chuckled at the spelling mistake and finished sweeping through the farmhouse before they opened the hatch leading down to the basement, carefully checking for IEDs and other unpleasant surprises. Nothing rose up to greet them, or exploded in their face, and so she headed down. Her heat-sensors revealed one life form within the basement, lying on a table. She activated her helmet light and smiled in relief as Blake's face came into view.

"Good God, Blake," Joe said, as he pressed in after her. "I didn't know that you were into bondage."

"Ha fucking ha," Blake said. Jasmine suppressed a giggle with an effort. Blake was not only tied down, he was chained down, with a heavy metal glove over his right hand. Someone had clearly realised that he had a nerve-burst implant – or another kind of implanted weapon – and taken steps to neutralise it. "Come and get me out of this thing."

"In a moment, in a moment," Jasmine said, inspecting the chains. The life support system was clever, in a diabolical kind of way. Blake could probably have survived for months, even though he was chained up and unable to move. "I'm just making sure that freeing you won't kill you."

"I think that you should take a vow of chastity," Joe put in, as he checked the other side of the table. "Chasing women only got you tied down and kept you out of the fight."

"Damn it," Blake said, as Jasmine started to work on the chains. Without the keys, she had to break the padlocks with her armoured fists. "Did you miss me?"

"Well, yes," Jasmine said, "but we'll take another shot tomorrow."

Blake laughed humourlessly as she finished freeing him, allowing him to stand up for the first time in weeks. "I'm glad to know that I have such loyal comrades," he said, as he tried to stretch. A cramp almost knocked him back to the table. "And the Crackers?"

"Beaten, for the moment," Jasmine said. "We caught one of their leaders and she pointed us in your general direction."

"You missed out on a really great battle," Joe said mischievously. "You won't believe…"

"That's enough of that," Jasmine said, firmly. She helped Blake to his feet and started to assist him towards the stairs. "We have to get Blake back to the Raptor and get him to the spaceport, where he can be checked out thoroughly before he returns to duty. You can pick a fight with him later."

"Yes, Corporal," Joe said.

"Corporal?" Blake repeated. "Did the Old Man lose his mind and promote you?"

"It was me or you, and you were...absent," Jasmine said, with an evil grin. "You can bow down in front of me later."

Blake sighed. "Easy come, easy go," he said mockingly. "I'll catch up with you soon, I promise."

"Not until you've been checked and cleared by the medical staff," Joe reminded him. "Who knows what kind of foul torture they might have put you through?"

"There's nothing wrong with me that a few days of heavy exercise won't cure," Blake protested. "I hate spending time in the hospital."

Jasmine shook her head at his protests. It was easy to imagine the Crackers conditioning Blake, turning him into a spy or an assassin aimed at Captain Stalker, or even outfitting him with an implant that turned him into an unwitting spy. It didn't seem likely that they had that kind of tech, but the Marines had been surprised before and they would not be fooled again. Blake would have to be checked extensively before he could be allowed to return to duty, although – knowing Blake – he would try to get out sooner rather than later. Whatever else could be said about him, he wasn't lazy or a coward. A man who was either wouldn't have made it through Boot Camp.

"Come on," she said, allowing her voice to soften. "I'm glad to see you're alive."

"You won't be when I convince the Old Man to give me your stripes," Blake said, with a wink. "He was clearly short of decent candidates."

Jasmine laughed at him. "Get moving," she said. "Once we're out of here, we're going to burn this farmhouse to the ground."

She took a moment to check the underground construction and winced. Someone had built it with malice aforethought, lining the basement with metal to jam any emergency signals from Blake's communicator. If the Crackers had taken him outside, just once...but they hadn't, almost as if they'd known the danger. Or, perhaps, they were just being paranoid. Either way, if the captured Crackers hadn't known where Blake was, they could have hidden him at the farmhouse for years, or just left him to starve to death. It wasn't a pleasant thought.

"Come on," she said, as they headed outside into the bright sunlight. "Let's go home."

Lucas Trent opened his eyes, feeling his head aching as if a group of thugs had systematically lined up in front of him and kicked it several times each. Everything was blurred and it took him moments to focus his eyes, realising that the bright light overhead was the sun. He sat up in surprise and looked around in disbelief. He was lying on a grassy field, surrounded by hundreds of other men and women who were struggling awake, as if some angry god had just abandoned them there. A small pile of boxes lay at one end of the field.

Memory returned and he winced. He'd been imprisoned by the Marines, who'd drugged him incessantly and questioned him, questioned him so many times that he couldn't remember what he'd been asked…or what he'd told them. The drugs had confused him so badly he wasn't even sure how long he'd been in the cell, until one day they'd simply pumped gas into his cell and knocked him out. He remembered panicking as he breathed in the first whiff of gas, convinced that they intended to kill him, but instead…he'd woken up here. Wherever he actually was, they'd just left him there.

He pulled himself to his feet, looking around. Some of the men were recognisable as his fellow Knives; others were strangers, men he didn't know at all. The women, likewise, were strangers apart from one; Carola Wilhelm. His ally had been dumped with him, wherever he was.

"Good morning," a voice said. Lucas glanced around to see a holographic image hovering in the air, just above the pile of boxes. It took him a moment to recognise the Marine Captain standing there, the liar who'd promised that Lucas and his men would be indentured if they told everything. He had…and now he'd been abandoned, instead of returning to slavery. He silently vowed revenge. He could have escaped from slavery. "This is a somewhat melodramatic gesture on my part to explain just what has happened to all of you."

Lucas stared as the message – a recording, he saw now – continued. "For some of you, we agreed to indenture you rather than simply executing you; for others, you had friends and family who intervened on your behalf. Accordingly, we have transported you to this island, rather than letting you form a conventional indent chain gang." The image winked. "After all, we know that you intended to escape once we sent you out into the countryside and I could hardly afford to spare the men and equipment necessary to search for you. The truth drugs and interrogations made that clear."

The image's gaze sharpened. "And so we have indentured you with a single task; make this island habitable," Captain Stalker continued. "For your information, this island is one of a small chain, over four hundred miles from the nearest continent…and literally thousands of miles from any other settlement. You might want to escape, you might try to escape, but believe me…you will be eaten by sharks or drowned by storms a long time before you get near to land. You have the choice between turning the islands into a settlement or dying when you run out of food and supplies.

"We have not been completely unmerciful. The boxes of supplies here have enough to get you started on farms and growing your own food, should you choose to take advantage of it. We have provided you with medical supplies and manuals we can hardly spare; ones that should teach you how to survive and prosper. Thousands of homestead families have managed to turn unpromising land into a prosperous settlement, so you all should know that it is possible. You've certainly raided enough of them in your time. The one thing we have not given you is weapons. You cannot be trusted with them, even isolated from the rest of the world.

"Understand; this is a life sentence. You have proved that you cannot be trusted in a civilised world. What you make of your life now is up to you. Form a community or kill each other, as you please. We will not interfere. Good luck."

The image vanished. Lucas stared at where it had been, and then looked down at the supplies. Were there really enough of them to create a prosperous settlement? Or would they kill each other instead? Perhaps they'd end up fighting over the women. There were at least three men to each woman. And how long would the Knives accept his authority, now he'd led them to ruin?

He shook his head and opened the first box. Who knew? Perhaps there was a way off the island after all.

"That's them all dumped on Hell Island," Gwen reported. "The Raptors are on their way home now."

"Good," Edward said. He looked over at Leo. "It's time to see just how clever we were."

Gwen frowned. "Sir," she said. "Are you sure that this is wise?"

"I think it's our best hope for peace," Edward said. "The Crackers took a blow, but they're an insurgency based around the cell system and we didn't identify them all. The rest of them will regroup and in a few years, we'll just be back at square one. We have a window of opportunity and I don't intend to waste it. The Grand Senate may scream, if they can be bothered to care about a poor world six months from Earth, but…the punishment for that will only land on my head."

Gwen didn't look convinced, but she nodded reluctantly. "Bring in the prisoner," Edward ordered. "It's time to see how well she lives up to her own words."

Gaby sat on a bench in her prison cell, waiting. The Marines had been surprisingly civilised about holding her prisoner, but they had been very firm. She'd been taken to a different room, drugged and interrogated, and then returned to her cell, several times. The effects of the drugs had taken their toll, including making her lose track of time. She had no idea how long she'd been in the cell, yet she was convinced that it hadn't been very long. They'd certainly treated her better than she'd treated Blake Coleman.

The door opened and a pair of Marines arrived, wearing the same featureless black armour that they always wore. One of them beckoned her to her feet and they escorted her out of the cell. They didn't bother to cuff or shackle her, a gesture of contempt; there was no way she could escape from even a single armoured Marine. There wasn't even any dignified way she could offer resistance. They led her through a series of featureless corridors and finally pushed her into a room. It wasn't the standard interrogation chamber; it had a table, three glasses of water and two men sitting, waiting for her. One of them stood up and held out a hand. She recognised him.

"Captain Stalker," she said, taking his hand out of habit. She wasn't sure what she had expected, but the Marine Captain was impressive, even if he didn't have quite the same striking appearance as Blake Coleman had had. She reminded herself, as she was waved into a chair, that he commanded the respect of some very dangerous men and women and warned herself not to underestimate him. She had no idea why he had called her, but she doubted that it was good news. "What can I do for you?"

"You will be pleased to know that we recovered Rifleman Coleman from the farmhouse you had converted into a prison," Captain Stalker said. His voice held traces of an Earth-accent, but they were fading into the melange of Avalon's dialect. "Thank you for not abusing him."

Gaby felt oddly relieved. She'd come to respect Blake Coleman, even if they had been enemies. "We tried to treat him decently," she said, with a flash of guilt. They'd treated him as they had to prevent him from escaping…and few reasonable men would have called that decent. "I'm glad to hear that he is alive."

Captain Stalker leaned forward. "You were interrogated quite heavily, as you know," he said. "We know that you were reluctant to move ahead with Operation Headshot and that you didn't intend to cause so many civilian casualties. We also know that you wanted to try to seek a peace deal before continuing the war. Do you still want to try to create a peace?"

Gaby snorted. "I'm in prison," she said. "What do you think I can do to create peace?"

Captain Stalker smiled. It was a genuine smile, one that touched his eyes. "We have an offer for you," he said. "The Council has been disbanded… and its corrupt members have been dealt with. Their possessions, including the debts they owned, have been claimed by the Government. It is our intention to simply forgive those debts. There is no way that they could ever be repaid and they just kept the planet down, preventing the development of a proper industry. Keeping them serves no useful purpose."

"I see," Gaby said. Desperate hope warred with fear in her breast. "You do realise that that will give the right to vote to the entire adult population? Avalon will become an autonomous world."

"I do," Captain Stalker said. His smile grew wider. "I understand that that was what you were fighting for all along?"

"…Yes," Gaby said.

"So we have an offer for you," Captain Stalker said. "You get what you want; we get, in exchange, the end of the war. There will no longer be any reason for the Crackers to exist and fighting the Government…"

"We will be part of the government, if the elections are fair," Gaby pointed out. "Doesn't that bother you at all?"

"I read the transcripts of your interrogation," Captain Stalker said. "I know that you meant every word. I suspect that not all Crackers share your…idealism, but it's a start. Anyone who wants to carry on the fight after winning the war can be…dealt with."

Gaby frowned. "It sounds wonderful," she said. Captain Stalker chuckled. "And what happens when the sector capital says that you've overstepped your authority?"

"The blame will fall on my shoulders," Captain Stalker said, firmly. He met her eyes squarely. "I don't know how all of this is going to work out. There's a lot of hatred on both sides, a lot of relatives wanting revenge for the dead. The peace may be broken within the year. We may not even be able to create a new Council by the time war breaks out again. But if we don't try, we'll never know."

He held out a hand. "So," he said. "Are you going to join us?"

Gaby took his hand. "We can, but try," she agreed. She felt an odd flicker of…attraction deep inside, something she hadn't allowed herself to feel since she'd been pushed into a leadership position. "Welcome to Avalon, Captain."

Afterwards, Edward watched as the three Raptors lifted off from Castle Rock, transporting the remaining Cracker prisoners back to the mainland, where they would be dropped off outside Camelot itself. Gaby would be going with them to pass on the message that the war could end and that the Crackers had won. Or, at least, they'd been offered what they'd claimed to be fighting for. Who knew how it would all end up?

"You took a risk," Leo observed. "Is it really worth it?"

Edward shrugged. "This is the fourth rebellion I've been involved in," he admitted. "They always get worse the longer they are allowed to drag on. Both sides decide to commit atrocities at will. If we can end this one now…it's worth taking the chance. If not, the Crackers will be facing a united population and little support at home."

He smiled. "And who knows?" He added. "It may all work out."

EPILOGUE

Two months after the elections, an Imperial Navy destroyer appeared in the Avalon System. It waited long enough to confirm IFF signals with the orbital station, and then transmitted a long and encrypted message into the planetary communications network, before turning and heading back out towards the Phase Limit. It ignored all attempts to hail it and left the system before the message could be decrypted. It wasn't encrypted according to any of the Empire's standard codes.

On Castle Rock, Edward downloaded the message into his private terminal and, after disconnecting the terminal from the main network, inserted the golden cross that Major General Jeremy Damiani had given him, through Leo. His hunch paid off and the message unscrambled itself, revealing hundreds of terabytes worth of data…and a single recorded message. Puzzled, Edward tapped the key and opened the record. A moment later, Damiani's face appeared in front of him.

"Captain Stalker," Damiani said. There was a flat tone to his voice that was curiously unlike him. It was odd to realise that the message had been created and transmitted during the fighting against the bandits. Earth didn't know, yet, that he'd concluded peace with the Crackers, or that he'd created a new government. "I'm afraid I have bad news.

"As we talked about the last time we met, the Empire has finally made some hard decisions about funding," he continued. "I'm afraid that they're pulling the Imperial Navy out of both the Trafalgar and Midway Fleet Bases; Midway, in particular, which should supply Avalon with Imperial Navy support, should it be required. The assistance of some of my friends" – he held up a golden cross identical to the one he'd given Edward – "has proved insufficient to convince the Imperial Navy to swing a ship through the Avalon System to recover you, or other units scattered along the Rim.

By the time you receive this message, Captain, the Imperial Navy will be shutting down Midway and placing the base's components into long-term storage. Certain Admirals believe that they will be back within the next decade, but I would be astonished if that were true. I think that these cuts are only the beginning.

"I don't have to spell the consequences out for you. This message includes the final Marine Intelligence report on the sectors near Avalon, with what units we believe to have been abandoned and cut off by the Grand Senate. I suspect that the Secessionists will move in rapidly and try to pick up the pieces; the systems are already facing a colossal rise in piracy and related activities. We're not sure if the Grand Senate has bothered to inform local governments about the funding cuts and the closed bases – I had to call in a lot of favours to get this message to you – but I think that as the realisation sinks in that they've been abandoned, the results are unlikely to be pleasant. Just how much you tell the Avalon Government about this is up to you. I'm sorry to dump all this on your shoulders, but I have been left with no choice.

"I've also included your promotion to Colonel," he concluded. Edward winced at the shame in the Major General's voice. "I'll try and get other support out to you, but it's not going to be easy. All I can do is wish you luck."

An hour later, Edward convened a meeting of the new Planetary Council.

"I decrypted the message," he said, grimly. "I'm afraid it's bad news."

His gaze moved from face to face. "The Grand Senate has spoken," he continued. "They're pulling out of this sector. We're on our own."

The End

A SHORT HISTORY OF AVALON

Avalon was discovered by a scoutship in 2795 and formally claimed by the Williamson Combine, one of the Empire's most powerful corporations. The ship's captain, an admitted fan of King Arthur and the Knights of the Round Table, asserted his authority and named many of the world's continents after that era. Avalon's one moon was named Merlin, the three main continents were named Arthur, Lancelot and Galahad and the system's sole gas giant was named Genevieve. The planet was rated as a 97% – i.e. extremely suitable for human habitation – with only a handful of dangerous creatures. The Gnasher, a dog-like creature, was discovered to be the planet's highest life form.

The Combine created the Avalon Development Corporation the following year and began the process of settling the planet, along with the construction of First Landing (later renamed Camelot). Stock in the ADC was purchased by several other corporations, a religious faction (the Reformed Church of Jesus Christ) and a number of private individuals. Once the landing zones were set up, the first settlers were shipped in and assigned to their homesteads.

Following standard procedure, settlers who paid their own way were granted considerable territory on the planet, while those who signed settlement contracts with the ADC – and had their shipping costs met by the corporation – were given much smaller land grants or simply assigned to work for the first settlers. In addition, several thousand convicts were transported in from Earth and set to work as slave labour, doing the hard labour that early settlement required. The convicts were supervised by a handful of mercenaries hired by the ADC.

Everything proceeded smoothly until the ADC overextended itself heavily in 2825. Believing that the Empire intended to invest heavily in settlement and development within the Penelope Sector, the ADC had invested in a cloudscoop for Genevieve and an asteroid settlement in the asteroid belt. Unfortunately for the Corporation's Board of Directors, the Empire's ongoing political crisis – the aftermath of the struggle between the Grand Senate and the New Men was still sending shockwaves throughout the Empire – intervened and the promised investment failed to materialise. A cloudscoop was simply an untenable expense without a guaranteed market and the ADC realised, grimly, that it had purchased a white elephant. Funding intended to bring in further colonists had to be diverted to maintaining the scoop, which served no useful purpose other than building up a reserve of starship fuel that might be useful one day.

Unluckily for Avalon, the ADC made a second mistake when it appointed Tom Cromwell as Governor in 2830. Cromwell was a financial analyst from Earth and lacked any experience of life along the frontier. His position was intended as a reward for service to the corporation, but the ADC would soon have due cause to regret its decision. Cromwell spent the first week of his governorship studying the situation on the ground, before beginning massive and painful budget cuts. This provoked immediate protest.

A wiser man might have listened to the colonist protest groups – led by Peter Cracker – but Cromwell dismissed them. He added insult to injury when he invoked a rarely-used clause in the settlement contracts and unilaterally altered the contracts, effectively making it impossible for any of the indentured settlers to work themselves out of debt. Finally, he brought in thousands of additional convicts and treated them as slaves. Avalon's political situation deteriorated until 2832, when all hell broke loose.

Cromwell had, perhaps wisely, decided to concentrate on building roads leading deep into the interior of Arthur, the settled continent. The methods he used for this, however, were deeply flawed. Not only were thousands of convicts used to build the roads, but indentured settlers were requisitioned and told to spend some of their work-week on the roads, rather than working towards paying off their debt. The result was inevitable. A number of convicts, exiled from Earth, escaped their supervisors and ran into a newly-settled town. The menfolk of the town were away working on the roads and the convicts didn't hesitate to take advantage of the opportunity before them. They looted, raped and burned their way through the town. By the time the men returned and slaughtered the convicts, it was too late for their women and children, including those of Peter Cracker.

Cracker had been one of the leaders of the colonist protest groups, as well as a union organiser. He sent messengers to other towns and rapidly found himself leader of a rebellion against the ADC. The settlers took up arms and turned on the convict camps and their supervisors. The chaos spread across the continent to the point where Cromwell, far from ruling the entire system, could barely keep Camelot under control. A year after the rebellion broke out, the ADC's carefully-planned system was in ruins and the rebels were marching on Camelot. It looked as if nothing could prevent them from hanging Cromwell and ending corporate rule once and for all.

Sadly for them, Cromwell's increasingly hysterical pleas to the Imperial Navy had finally brought a response. The destroyer *Marigold Crook* entered orbit and deployed KEW strikes against the rebel army, shattering it from far out of their reach. (Peter Cracker was believed killed, although his body was never found and some people think that he merely went underground.) The ADC landed a small army of mercenaries and destroyed what remained of the rebel force, although an underground insurgency movement continues to this day. The victory was, however, too late for the ADC, which formally declared bankruptcy in 2839. Its mandate over Avalon was terminated by the Empire and an Imperial Governor was appointed.

Governor Montgomery found himself faced with an impossible task. The rebellion might have been broken, but the discontent that had sparked the rebellion hadn't faded and wouldn't fade until the causes of the discontent were addressed. The ADC had left the planet's interstellar credit at an all-time low and somehow the planet's debt had to be paid off before real development could begin. He attempted to tackle the issue through a number of political channels, including capping the debt of indentured settlers (preventing their debt from increasing at their supervisor's whim) and abolishing the hated family indentures that had ensured that children would grow up, weighed down by the burden of their parents' debt. He also created the planetary council, allowing a limited degree of democratic representation, and the Avalon Civil Guard. The remaining mercenaries were shipped off-world as quickly as possible.

However, most of his reforms were blocked by the newly-created council. The elected councilmen saw their own interests as threatened and banded together to prevent the reforms from going into operation. Unsurprisingly, discontent continued to bubble as new colonists were settled on the planet. The Cracker Rebellion might have been broken – for the moment – but other threats were rising up in the distance.

It was not going to be a peaceful future.

AFTERWORD

It has been six years, more or less, since I wrote *The Empire's Corps*; it has been four years, give or take a few months, since I uploaded the first version of the manuscript to Amazon Kindle. Since then, I have written eleven other books in the series and have developed plans for at least five more. It is no exaggeration to say that *The Empire's Corps* was the first of my books to make a genuine impact, selling enough copies that - for the first time - I could devote myself to writing. It changed my life.

What you hold in your hand, assuming you bought the paperback edition, is probably the last version of the novel. There have been no major changes - if you bought an earlier version - save for a handful of spelling and grammar mistakes. I hope you enjoyed it as much as I enjoyed writing it. And I hope you will look up the other books as they are reissued, one by one.

I wish I could say, in the time between writing this book and *now*, that things have gotten better. But they have not. If anything, they have gotten worse.

In each of the successive *The Empire's Corps* books, I have included an afterword drawing lines between the problems discussed in the books and the real world. *The Empire's Corps* was, at the time, the sole book that *didn't* have an afterword. And now that I am writing one, I feel unsure what to say. I have addressed too many subjects already.

But there is an issue I have not yet addressed in any of my afterwords, one that is closely linked to the themes of this book in particular - free speech.

This is a short essay - but, I feel, an important one. Let's start with a simple exercise.

Take the single most racist/sexist/homophobic/etc argument you can think of. Think it through, piece by piece. Consider all the implications of each and every word.

And then dismantle it. Prove to yourself, if no one else, that the argument is false.

Ok, you may ask, what was the point of that?

There are people who believe the most stupid and absurd things about their fellow men and women. You don't have to go prowling around in the darkest depths of the internet to hear people cheerfully sprouting off shocking, indeed horrific pieces of crap about [insert racial, ethnic, sexual, etc group here]. The internet confers anonymity on most people and the absence of any form of social control allows our darkest impulses to take flight. Things people would never dream of saying in public are said online, things that many people (and not just those on the Left) would consider Hate Speech.

But Hate Speech is, in itself, a slippery concept. What is Hate Speech? Answer - it's whatever the listener wants it to be. You can outline a whole series of facts - not opinions, facts - and someone will probably accuse you of committing the dread sin of Hate Speech. It is starting to reach the point where people are censoring themselves because they are scared of being accused of Hate Speech, Wrong Think, etc. A decent idea - you shouldn't call people racial slurs to their faces - has become a tool for restricting free speech.

In my blog, I talked about the free marketplace of ideas. Free speech is a key part of that market place, if only because it allows each and every idea to be tested, retested and then kept or discarded as necessary. Most racist/sexist/homophobic/etc arguments simply do not hold water when actually tested. However, classing all such arguments as Hate Speech and sealing them away, without actually debating the matter, really doesn't help. Indeed, it lends credence to ideas that are often stupid, if not downright malicious.

The human mind does not like being dictated to, even when the dictators are correct. Telling someone 'BAD THINK, BAD THINK, BAD

THINK' doesn't really help; proving, using common sense if nothing else, that the arguments are actually poor ones works to disarm them. Nor does the human mind appreciate the double-standard of 'hate speech for me, but not for thee' put forward (openly or not) by far too many so-called liberals. Hypocrisy is easy to spot and always hated.

Yes, you may find yourself dismantling the argument time and time again. It's much better than burying a festering sore by declaring all open discussions of the matter *verboten*.

And it will teach people to *think*. Believe me, there is nothing more important in this day and age.

And this leads to another point - the importance of plain-speaking.

My paternal grandmother, may she rest in peace, was a Lancashire Lass. Born and raised in Bolton, Lancashire, she was taught to be plain-spoken, in the manner of those times. The folk of Lancashire and Greater Manchester didn't see any value in tip-toeing around the truth - my grandmother certainly never did. She was always calm and polite - she rarely raised her voice and I never saw her cry - but she always told the truth, as she saw it.

To Grandma, it was always *better* to tell the truth. It was better, she thought, that a bride should be told she looked bad in her chosen dress *before* the wedding, even though the bride's feelings might be hurt by the remark. Better a cut, she would have said, than a broken arm. She would have made both the best and most terrifying of editors, I think; she had the right attitude and the willingness to tear something apart, just to make it better.

She was, in many ways, an immensely strong woman. My grandfather died when her son was very young and she brought my father up alone, in an age where single mothers were far rarer than they are today. She remained in the same house in Bolton as my father married and moved to Edinburgh, where he had me and my siblings. She would come up to Edinburgh to play with me when I was a child and, even after she grew too old to play with us she still did her best to keep in touch with the family. And yet, she tried hard to maintain her independence. She refused to move in with us until barely two months before her death.

I cannot help but think Grandma would have looked upon the current feminist movement (and many other PC movements) with scorn.

I'm sure there were more than a few assholes who used 'plain-speaking' as a cover for…well, being assholes. (They were, of course, the forerunners of internet trolls.) Certainly, the folk of that time would have thought nothing of peppering their speech with racial slurs, considering them nothing more than mere figures of speech. But the rise of political correctness has done so much harm to plain-speaking that we may be paying the bill for years to come. There are times when no amount of tip-toeing about the truth will help.

Just as there is a fundamental disconnect between *hard* science and *soft* science, between the objective and the subjective, there is a fundamental disconnect between political correctness and reality. Reality doesn't change just because the terms of the debate have been altered.

You see, the original idea behind political correctness was that people shouldn't set out to cause offence. And that isn't actually a bad idea, as far as these things go. But the nebulous concept of 'offence' has been allowed to overwrite reality. The fear of offending someone - anyone - leads to self-censorship, that most damned of censorship, rather than facing up to the simple fact that certain unpleasant truths must be spoken, that certain unpleasant facts must be faced squarely.

The problem lies in the simple fact that PC demands a reversal of the standard accuser-accused dynamic. In a civilised world, the accuser must prove the guilt of the accused; the accused does not have to prove his innocence. But when PC is involved, the accuser is allowed to claim that he or she is offended, regardless of the objective truth of the words. The mere act of saying 'I am offended,' perhaps followed by charges of racism, sexism, Islamophobia, etc, seems to be enough to put the speaker on the defensive. But *any* fool can claim to be offended by *anything*.

This whole concept has been undermining the modern world for decades.

It isn't hard for anyone who doesn't have their head in the sand to realise that Radical Islam poses a threat to the entire world, up to and including every last Muslim. But politicians, rather than coming to grips with this unpleasant truth, seem unwilling to say it out loud. Watching the reaction to the Paris Attacks from many political quarters has been downright sickening. Donald Trump's poll numbers jumped, I suspect, because Trump came right out and pointed his finger at the threat.

But one doesn't have to look at that to see just how badly PC has eroded the fabric of our world. The current epidemic of 'cry-bullies' on American campuses comes, at least in part, from the simple failure of academic authorities to stand up and tell increasingly pathetic student protesters that their behaviour was unacceptable. But PC makes it impossible for administrators to do anything of the sort. (Expelling the entire football team at Missouri would have been an excellent step to restore sanity to the campus.) There are times when you just have to say NO - like you would to a child - rather than indulge adults in childish tantrums.

It is not easy - and I say this as a writer - to face up to critical remarks. There is a tendency to be angry with the person who points out the plot hole in chapter 10, or that you killed the hero's love interest (chapter 13) back in chapter 5. And yes, writers encounter more than their fair share of critical remarks. Nor is it easy to respond with careful thought when one faces criticism from the outside. But failing to grasp that, at worst, the jerkass has a point can only lead to contempt.

Trying to put lipstick on a pig doesn't magically turn the pig into a beautiful girl. It just makes you look stupid. Anyone who doesn't have a strong reason to convince themselves that the pig is a girl can see that. And telling them that the pig is a girl merely convinces them that you're a deluded idiot.

Because, you see, reality doesn't change. And trying to put lipstick on a pig doesn't magically turn the pig into a woman. And, most importantly of all, having the safety and security to allow yourself delusions about the world surrounding you doesn't mean that others won't suffer for your mistakes.

Printed in Great Britain
by Amazon